At Dawn,
Two Nightingales

Alan Bilton

Best wishs

Alan

Bilton.

Watermark
Press

Not an inhabitant of the earth,
And not a phantom from the dead,
Not one and not the other …

ALEXANDER PUSHKIN

I complain to the wind, our life's but a minute,
Horses, turn back,
If only horses could turn back:
turn back our time once more to begin it.

JAROSLAV SEIFERT

I do declare, the Emperor's balls get bigger
every year!

TRADITIONAL PANTOMIME JOKE

Published in UK by Watermark Press 2024

A CIP catalogue record for this book is available from the British Library

ISBN 978-1-8380043-4-7

Published with the financial support of the Books Council of Wales.

Typeset in Book Antigua

Cover design by nb-design.com

Printed by Imprint Digital

Watermark Press
www.watermarkpress.co.uk

Contents

ACT I

1

Marta poked out her head just as Count Mitrovsky rolled back from The Five Small Carp, singing 'O look from thy window, dearest treasure' while covered from head to foot in dust.

"Marta!" cried the Count, the powder falling from his beard like breadcrumbs, "Marta, my darling, where are you?"

With that, the old servant's mug appeared at the gate, her face as round and flat as if stretched out by a rolling pin.

"Who's that out there, gadding about like a chicken?"

"Marta, Marta, the most amazing thing!"

"Amazing? Amazing what?" The old woman peered at the Count, suspiciously. "What, stupid man? You find lung in the lung soup?"

"Marta, my darling, open the gate and let me in!"

When the old servant opened the door, the Count strode inside in a state of great agitation, wig askew, britches torn, powder pouring out of his jacket like sawdust.

Marta sniffed at his ruffles and reached for her broom.

"Feh, what happened to you – over dusted your wig?"

"O Marta, angel of my heart – if I told you but half of what I've been through you would call me a madman."

"With you, I try a fifth."

The Count was a bearskin over which many feet had travelled, some parts bald, others balled up with stuffing. What few hairs remained stuck up like a dried-out brush, but his black eyes were

1

kind and soulful, melancholy as yesterday's dreams. While Marta was brown and wizened as a nut, the Count was wide and tall, about the size of a wardrobe.

"Sit, sit," said the old woman, "has the magistrate come in?"

"What a tale, Marta, what a tale! Fetch me a stool and I'll tell you all about it. But where to begin? You see, there I was in The Five Small Carp..."

"That dump?" At the mention of the Carp, Marta snorted loudly. "You want poison, I got poison..."

"Dump? No, no, my pet, 'tis a most respectable establishment. I mean, there may be some bones in the soup, but ... anyhow, there I was, minding my own business, when I had the strangest feeling..."

"Feeling?"

"Like something welling up inside of me."

"In The Five Small Carp? This part I believe."

"No, no, nothing like that. More a kind of tingling between my ears ... Anyhow, I looked up to see a crooked shadow walk up to my table, followed by a long skinny fellow in a cloak."

Marta sniffed.

"And who was shadow? Golowsky the bailiff?"

"Skinnier."

"Hofler the candle-stick maker?"

"Taller."

"Slodoba the jugman?"

"No, no – a fine fellow, a man of great learning."

"In the Five Small Carp? What was he, a health inspector?"

"Marta, my pearl, you'll never guess! It turned out that the fellow was a purveyor of printed matter – encyclopaedias, calendars, learned matter and the like. O Marta, why do you look at me like that? 'Tis true! First, he showed me an eight-volume study of Saint John of Nopomuk, then *An Outline of Universal*

Knowledge, and finally a dog-eared copy of *The Labyrinth of the World and The Paradise of the Heart*. 'O, my friend', I said, pushing back my stool. 'We have little need of such erudition in these parts. But if you could lay your hands on a little Cheb sausage, say, or perhaps a side of Ostrava ham…'"

"'My dear fellow,' says the book-seller – I'm doing the voice now – 'have you ever heard of the poet Nosek?' 'Pish posh,' I say. 'What kind of an idiot, do you take me for? I've never heard of this Nosek in my life.' At this the bookseller smiled and I saw his mouth was full of sharp, wooden teeth. 'Why, Frantisek Nosek is the greatest poet in all of Bohemia,' he whispered, 'nay, the greatest in all of Europe, his genius unsurpassed in the modern age. Born in Tichý in 1709, he…' 'Stop, stop', I say. 'I am not a big reader. Menus, maybe, a court summons from time to time…' At this the salesman leapt out of his seat as if about to milk me. 'Have you heard of 'At Dawn, Two Nightingales'?' he says. 'I'm not a complete idiot,' I say, 'of course I have not heard of it.' 'Tis the most beautiful, most tender, most enchanting poem in all the world,' he whispers. 'Whoever hears it spoken aloud will immediately fall in love with the speaker, hanging on their every word…' 'Hang?' 'Why, yes,' says the fellow, his wooden teeth, all a-chatter. 'And women, as the more sensitive sex, are particularly susceptible to its charms. 'Tis said that if a loved one should hear the words of this most beautiful of compositions, she will give the speaker her undying devotion.'"

At this Mitrovsky paused for dramatic effect while Marta checked his ears for webs.

"Marta, Marta, do you see? A poem that makes the hearer fall head over heels in love!"

"Are we talking about Mařenka, stupid man? Here, I would not get any hopes, I think."

"You're not listening, Marta. This poem, it…"

3

Marta strode up with her clothes brush and tapped the Count smartly on the bonce.

"Fool! Clod! Mařenka is going to need more than two nightingales to plump up your pillows. What else was this rascal selling? Eternal youth and a bottle of hair restorer? Listen Mitrovsky – this is some honey that will not spread. "

"But you haven't heard the whole of my tale…"

"I need more? If I had wheels, then I'd be a cart."

The Count pulled on his night shirt and shook his head. "Marta, my angel, you simply do not understand the way of men – and gentlemen at that! We shook hands respectfully and the fellow went off to get his books. His carriage was just across the road – an old-fashioned tarantass, harnessed to an ancient grey nag. But oh, Marta, my dove, you'll never guess – the back of the coach was empty! 'I must have left my books back at the inn,' says the fellow, teeth clacking up and down like a door latch. 'Tis dark and cold out here. Why not climb into the carriage and make yourself at home? I'll be gone but a moment and then we can conclude our business. There now – in you go! I'll be as quick as a fox and then the book will be yours'. Only five ducats for 'Two Nightingales' can you imagine?"

"With you, I imagine everything," said the old servant, handing the Count his Turkish slippers.

The Count grinned foolishly and slipped on his dressing gown, his ensemble held together by the string of a violin.

"I climbed into the carriage and was just starting to make myself comfortable when, all of a sudden, I heard some kind of commotion over by The Five Small Carp, a kerfuffle or some such thing. O my darling, I could hardly believe my eyes! Two policemen, as alike as a pair of playing cards, appeared from nowhere, leaping on my book-seller and grabbing him by the apothecary."

"By the what?"

"By the apothecary, searching his person in a most uncomfortable manner."

"This was who – the library police?"

Mitrovsky shrugged. "Ho, my queen – who knows, who knows? When I saw the *fizl* appear, I drew the curtains and hid beneath a rug."

"You're a prince, Mitrovsky."

"Of course, my darling, of course! There I lay, like Noah in the whale, until all of sudden there was a jerk, and the carriage began to rock and sway."

"The police?

"The horse! 'Tis true, O queen of my heart! The little mare was trotting down the street and pulling my carriage behind it, the tarantass rattling away like a pot on the stove…"

"The horse, hm? And what about your nightingales?"

"Who knows, my angel, who knows? All I could think about was getting as far away from the constables as possible. What's that saying? Sometimes a mouse is wiser than a lion. Or is it the other way round? Anyway, the horse had a kindly face and a large head, and I decided that she must know best after all. 'Swiftly Mistress Horse', I whispered, ''fore the officers catch sight of our heels…' But it was strange, my angel, strange. 'Twas as if some invisible coachman had hold of her reins. First the old gal clip-clopped down Ponurý, and then clattered across Strašidelný, her bell tolling like a festive promise…"

Marta poured the dust from her master's boots but said nothing. Even by the Count's standards, this story had a long tail.

"Clip clop, clip clop – I'm doing the hooves now – and Strašidelný was far behind us. Clip, clop, clip, clop – and before you could hold your nose, we were trotting between Wheel-Well Street and the Flour Gate, not coming to a halt until we reached

The Green Frog, where all the horses stop for a piss and the cabbies smell of salted beans and ale."

Mitrovsky's eyes were wide and black, as if he'd just seen a ghost, or been caught spying at a lady's keyhole.

"'What, my lad!' I cried out. 'Ho, over here!' But, O Marta, my sweetheart, not one of the coachmen gave us so much as a look. 'Ahoy, my darling,' I yelled, 'a little assistance, if you please,' but 'twas no use. I rattled the door and the catch seemed locked. I leaned out of the window, but the hole was too tight. I thumped on the roof, but nothing doing. O my dove, what a world we live in! A driverless cart, an imprisoned nobleman, the promise of a five groschen tip – and not one of the cabbies would so much as look my way! The only thing which sauntered over was a fat, black cat, tail as straight as the town clock at midnight. 'What do you want, you scoundrel?' I yelled. 'See a mouse in my beard, do you? You cheeky devil!' And with that the cat was gone, taking his little nose with him."

Mitrovsky paused in his storytelling to inspect his dressing gown, poking his finger through a particularly large hole. When he began again his voice was low and tender, like the sound of a double bass.

"Time slipped by, and by now the street was almost empty. I looked at the horse and the horse looked at me. 'For whom are you waiting, my angel?' I lamented. 'Why have you brought me here, and not some better place? For instance, The Golden Crayfish, where Dumb Pohorsky knows me and will lend me a groschen on credit…'"

Marta removed a hunk of black bread from her apron and chewed on it thoughtfully.

"Mm, mm," she said. "And what did this horse of yours have to say?"

"Mistress Horse? Very little. A drunk rolled out from the Frog, the church bell tolled, the night wrapped itself inside its scarf. Bored, I rapped angrily on the window: little horse, little horse, why do you tarry? And – what do you know? – with that the carriage really did start to move, the horse trotting along Prázdný Ulice as if we had all the time in the world."

"First, we mooched along Okouzlení, passing under the sign of a razor – the barber and his wife snoring soundly in their beds – and then under the sign of an hourglass, the sand going nowhere, the picture hanging on by a nail. From Okouzlení we clip-clopped past Půlnoc, rounding the fountain and the gallows, then rattling along by the Church of St Bartholomew, patron saint of bad debts. But O, it was a beautiful night Marta, the moon pinned to the sky like a general's medal. And the air – so warm, so sweet! From The Green Frog we took Půlnoc all the way along the Needle's Eye to The White Turnip, where the little grey horse shuffled to a halt, batting her eyelashes like an actress. The Turnip was all closed up for the night, but Mistress Horse came to a stop anyway, as still as that statue in Nočni Můra square, you know, the one with the fat fella, the rascal in the hat."

"'I fear you are mistaken Mistress Horse,' says I, 'the Turnip is closed, and even the mice are abed.' 'Twas no use though; like an elegant Countess, the horse turned her head from me, till all I could see was her bony behind, her tail long and black as a chimney sweep's stick. O Marta! What we doing here? What did this little horse want? And such a beautiful night – soft, gentle, warm as a mother's embrace – and here I was, trapped inside a wooden box while outside the stars winked like frogs… O, what a trick, what a snare! … Finally, after a spider's blink, the horse flicked her ears and took off again, heading through the Nun's Gate and off along Nudný, her harness bell tolling like the last sound on earth. The streets were empty, shutters bolted shut, no more customers to be had for love or money – so for whom was she waiting? Why this strange journey? But the horse had no answers. Instead, the carriage rattled this way and that, first along White Bread Street and out then toward the crooked wall…"

"The Six of Hearts, The Golden Mitre, The Cunning Beast – at each pub the carriage stopped and waited, though we saw no one, neither traveller nor soldier nor drunk. By The Old Lady we spotted an old lady, and by The Two Lambs, a pool of blood. From there, we took a tour of The Ploughman, and The Three Little Stars the little horse stopping at each establishment as if waiting for some traveller who would never come … or maybe a whole carriage-load of passengers, who knows? And all the time, that bell of hers rang out like a sign, the signs swinging too and fro, a jug, two shoes, a hunk of meat."

"O Marta, 'twas strange, strange! From there we moved to The Two Golden Bears and thence Under The Cow-Shed, but there were no stragglers, no tramps – not even that old hunchback who goes round begging for alms from door to door. Instead, the little horse flicked her shiny black tail as we circled the crumbling shanties round The Devil's Arm, not a single lamp burning, the filthy hovels drowned in silence like kittens in a pail.

From there we passed the Owl Mill and Papoušek's orchard, the night smelling of mud and lilac. Pretty soon the gardens turned to fields, the fields to woodland, the woodland to forest, and still the little bell kept ringing, like some village idiot at a fair."

Mitrovsky rocked from side to side, his nose twitching with the dust.

"The curtains were blue with little white stars, and when I pulled them back, the outside was just the same – blue trees with blue leaves, blue sky, blue grass, and, I swear Marta, the sound of the horse's bell was blue too! I called out to the little horse, but the old girl merely shook her head, following the trail as if her hoof-prints lay before her, not behind."

The Count turned toward the window as if, even now, the horse might be waiting just outside.

"I don't know…it was dark both inside and outside the carriage, as if the coach was made of glass. Or perhaps made of nothing, which is even worse."

The Count sneezed and a puff of dust rose up like a thought.

"Ah, me! Was I in or was I out? Eyes open or eyes closed? When the coach hit a bump, we seemed to lurch upwards, and that's when I realised we were flying through the sky, the darkness falling away to reveal a blue forest with a little blue lake below, the sand all blue too. 'Steady now my beauty' I cried, 'keep to the well-worn path!' But the grey horse kept on climbing, stepping on each cloud as if it were some kind of staircase, a staircase leading up to the heavens above...

A pair of geese passed me, looking awful surprised, and I have to admit, I felt a little light-headed too, as if my head had floated free from my body. Out of one window I could see stars strung up on a washing line, and through the other, the moon hanging from a stick, newly painted and left out to dry… O Marta, it was too much to take in, too much for my head! I pulled shut the curtain and began to pray, but no sooner had I pressed my hands together than the cab began to rattle, the rug flew up in the air, the coach-door opened and – O my darling – I felt myself tumbling from the carriage, falling and falling, though whether up or down I could not tell, till I landed in a bed of dust and ash, dust everywhere – dust up my nose, dust in my eyes, dust in my ears – and the worst of it was, I'd just had my britches cleaned by Andulka, you know, the red-head who works behind the Two Golden Bears."

The Count paused and looked down at his toes as if he'd never seen them before His beard was that of an old man, his hair white, as if dusted with plaster.

"I tell you not to take strange cabs," said Marta, handing the

Count his night-cap. "Did you tip?"

"No, no. After that I had to walk all the way home, dust pouring out of me like a torn sack of flour. And I thought – all I have to do is get hold of a copy of this Nosek's poem, read her Two Nightingales and poof – the prize is in the purse!"

Marta picked up a candle and placed it by the Count's bed, "Yes, yes, you whistle that tune, stupid boy…"

"'At Dawn, Two Nightingales' – write that down, Marta, in case I go to sleep and forget. Two Nightingales – or was it finches? Birds, at any rate. O my dear Marta – who knew that this writing had a purpose after all?"

Marta patted the blankets and gently tucked him in.

"Smart boys leave those birds alone. You want to pay rent on a grave? Driverless carriages, shadowy strangers, policemen… Where will this end – a tinker's pot?"

The Count pulled on his night-cap but didn't seem to be listening.

"The bookseller, yes, yes, you're right … he'll know where we can find this secret book. We'll get him to tell us even if means springing him from jail – or from The Five Small Carp. Well, no matter! The main thing is that this Nosek he, well, Mařenka…"

The Count looked as if he were about to jump out of bed again, but Marta shoved him back in.

"Get some rest, Mitrovsky. Tomorrow's a long day, and you have to read a whole poem."

"O Mařenka, my darling!" Mitrovsky whispered. "What dreams but sketch, the coming day will ink…"

To soothe him, Marta began to sing a soft-hearted lullaby, her voice surprisingly gentle and clear. After just a few bars, the Count rolled himself in a ball and fell into a deep and innocent slumber.

"Stupid man," she whispered, tapping him tenderly on the head and slipping one of the Count's goblets into her apron. What a story, what rot! How did the Count dream all this stuff up? Nosek and his Nightingales? Pure fancy. Apart from the cleaning bill, everything would be forgotten in the morning.

With that a warm breeze blew in through the window, the night smelling of clover and dogberries and wormwood, sweet as a stolen kiss. A mosquito buzzed past, a fox yowled, and if you strained your ears, cocking your head like a hound, you could just about hear a little harness bell, some horse clip-clopping as it dragged its box along the lanes. But was it drawing closer or moving farther away? Who knows? Every day is a just little breath between nights. And with that Marta blew out the candle, and poof! – the whole world was gone.

2

The next day, the Count rose early – just before eleven – declaring in a loud voice that he had to go and see Mařenka right there and then.

"Marta, my heart, go and prepare my carriage."

"Carriage, what carriage? We chopped it up for firewood, remember?"

"We did?"

"It was cold. Your stockings had holes. You said 'Where is there to go?'"

"Okay, okay. Then saddle my horse."

The old woman spat.

"No horse?"

"The bailiff took it away. We have rooster – you want I should saddle him?"

"Is he busy?"

"Not since we sold the hens."

The Count nodded and kissed the old woman on her cheek. "Marta, my pearl, I'll walk. Bring me my boots – unless they've gone too?"

"Feh – even the ragman has standards."

It was another beautiful day, the Count's lemon-coloured stockings glowing in the fine spring light. The yard was full of life: chickens, sparrows, mice. In one corner two magpies discussed the price of rye, while in another, two pigeons talked over the price of corn. True, Mitrovsky's place wasn't looking at its best: the barn sagged, weeds covered the lawn, and the hen house was little more than a pile of sticks. But what of it? What we own will one day bury us. In the meantime, the rabbits still ate the grass, and the owl still ate the mice.

Old Count Mitrovsky had sold first the mill, then the woods, and finally the orchard too. What else should he do? There were taxes, debts, expenses. The tailor needed paying, the ironmonger too. Servants swiped the silver and peasants hid the rent – or was it the other way around? Either way, the Estate had seen better days. The Old Count's son, Matej, had gone off soldiering and never came back. The milk from the cows turned grey. The nut trees started to wither. As the saying goes, bad luck gathers flies. On Monday Old Zofie caught a fever and turned green. On Tuesday, the cook ran off with the groundsman. On Wednesday, Ondrej ran off with the bull, and before the week was over, the whole estate was filled with nettles and dog-berries, the pond the colour of spoilt pears.

Was this when the new Count snuck in? Of course, by this point the old man's noggin was somewhat addled; moreover, he was blind in one eye and couldn't see out of the other. And nor did Marta care: one saddle was much the same as the next.

On the day the old man died, two storks were seen taking off from the manor roofs. "'Tis The Master and the Mistress reunited' said Marta with tears in her eyes, though that didn't stop her shinnying up to the roof to look for eggs.

The way to the Drtikols was by the old post road, flanked by lilac bushes and the occasional dusty tree. It was very hot. Swallows flew high in the sky, while a council of midges held some kind of meeting just above Mitrovsky's hat. Everything green was turning

13

to brown, everything brown turning to yellow. A film of golden dust rose up from the track, the mud baked the colour of biscuit. Even the cowpats looked dry as a wafer. According to Father Smiřicky, the practice of spreading manure on the ground was a crime against God, an attempt to improve the perfect – was this true? Of course, Father Smiřicky's nature could do with a little improving too; last week Mitrovsky had seen him emptying his pipe on an alter boy. The Count plucked a bunch of cow parsley from the hedgerow and placed it under his nose. Yes, 'twas all a mystery … so, why not call in at the Drtikols for a bite to eat? No one ever fathomed the riddles of the world on an empty stomach.

The air was filled with a bittersweet fragrance, the path wavering in the heat of the day. The Count squinted into the sun, and in the distance a horse and cart came and went, as if a pebble had been dropped into time.

'Ah', thought Mitrovsky, 'perhaps this fellow can take me all the way to Mařenka's – and mayhap has a jug to sip from too'.

The cart emerged from the haze as if the scene had just put on its spectacles. It was an old, spring-less droshky, driven by an ancient peasant, his beard turning green at the tip.

"Honoured sir!" yelled the man. "Fancy a lift? That's it, jump in – no need to stand on ceremony, the straw is lovely and soft. Where are you going, my lord? The next estate? Just so. A hot one, eh? Hot enough to make the Devil sweat…"

Mitrovksy hauled his frockcoat onto the back of the cart and clapped the peasant on his back. "You're very kind, my good fellow. God will reward you…"

"That He will," said the peasant, "that He will."

Jugs and bottles were packed in amongst the dirty straw and the Count picked up a jar inquiringly. "And what do we have here?"

The peasant beamed. "Worms, sir!"

14

"Worms?"

"Silkworms for spinning, fat worms for fishing, skinny worms for the compost heap, glow worms for the night…"

The Count peered more closely at the dirty glass, the creature curling itself up as if to say 'the jug's empty and I'm not here'.

"This one looks a lively lad. What a beauty!"

"That one will hook you a perch sir: those perchies, they can't resist a juicy red-belly."

"Who can, my fellow, who can? And this one?"

"Why, he'll snare you a catfish, my lord. A cat-fish swims past, spots one of these here wormies and thinks it's his lucky day. Stick one of these on your hook and before you know it, you'll have a cat-fish in your sack."

"And what should one do then?"

"A cat-fish is best boiled, sir. The meat slips off like a coat…"

"O, you saucy fellow! I wasn't hungry, but I am now! And what of this fine chap, a prince among worms?"

The peasant squirmed in his seat, almost sending the cart off the road.

"O my lord – what an eye for the worms you have! Slip that fine fellow into your drink – vodka, slivovitz, turpentine, it doesn't matter – and you are guaranteed a long life and a healthy glow."

"Really?"

"I uses them myself, sir! Why now, look at me? How old would you say I am?"

"Ah…"

"Nearly forty, sir! And all on account of that there worm!"

The Count nodded, tapped the side of the glass and then placed the jug back under the filthy straw. "Remarkable, quite remarkable."

"There's a lot of good things in a worm, sir."

"I don't doubt it. What a romantic life you must lead, you and

15

your worms! A wooden cart, a keg of ale, the promise of boiled catfish for your supper…"

The old man grinned, revealing a line of yellowed stumps. "'Tis like a beautiful dream, sir! The only thing is: digging 'em up is a bastard sir, if you don't mind me saying so. These wormies they just want to stay in the ground, and I have to dig and dig till I think I'm half-way to Hell."

"Mm."

"'Tis not like the old days, sir. No, back in the day we'd hold what was called 'Wormie balls'. A learned man like you, you'll have heard of them, of course…"

"Um…"

"One worm man brings a fiddle, two more dance, and those wormies race straight to the surface like princesses at a ball. S'no magic, sir: they think it's raining, on account of these wormies having very little knowledge of the world. Up they come and there's another worm-man waiting there, and he shovels 'em up into a big sack. There's no more wonderful sight in the world sir! All the fiddling and the dancing, and the worms dancing too…"

"What a scene! Oh, if only I had a brush to paint it!"

The old man grinned but then suddenly looked downcast, an oily film welling up in his eyes. "But these days – where can I find another worm man? Dying out, we are, sir, a thing of the past. Do you know, sir, I don't believe I've danced with another worm-man for a good ten years?"

"Oh my good man!" All of a sudden Mitrovsky felt like crying himself. "Yes, yes, life is hard – like winter ground to the gravedigger."

"Aye, those days are gone. Now it's just dig, dig, dig – and no handle on my shovel, either."

Mitrovsky nodded, searching in his pocket for a coin to give the old man.

"And, um do you have something for sale, my good man. Ah, for the ladies, perhaps…?"

The old man looked back at him and scowled. "What's that, Spanish Fly? That's beetles, sir, beetles. I do worms – don't touch them things. You should be ashamed of yourself sir, and you at your age…"

"No, no – I mean, something romantic, something that the lady of the house might find *trés charmant.*"

Immediately the old peasant relented. "Oh, romance is it, sir? Why a jar of glow worms, sir – the ladies, they love 'em. Creates a lovely atmosphere, see. Do you know what us worm-men call 'em? Lamps of love."

The worm-man grinned and passed Mitrovsky a jar of fat, red insects with ugly stubby wings and a poisonous looking tip.

"O my lands – what a brute!"

"What's that, sir? My ear-trumpet is full of soil."

"But isn't this a beetle?"

The peasant's gums beamed. "Those are glow worms, sir – I would show you the receipt, but alas I cannot read."

"No need, no need – 'tis all marvellous," said Mitrovsky, handing over a groschen. "Shouldn't he be lit up?"

"Not in the daytime sir – but at night – like a vision!"

The cart rolled on past dusty bushes and tall nettles, grasshoppers serenading the travellers with their dry, monotonous song. The air was hot and translucent, as if magnified by a shard of glass. The peasant began to sing some timeless tragic song and the Count joined in with his rich baritone, making up the words as he went.

Half an hour later, as the cart passed an old fishpond filled with slimy, reddish water, Mitrovsky jumped up and clapped the peasant on the back.

"Stop, stop, my good fellow – here will do nicely. God will

17

reward you for your good deed."

The peasant dropped his reins and nodded soberly. "Thank you, kind sir. The Lord go with you."

"God speed and fare thee well. If ever I am without a hornet, I'll be sure to call. Farewell, farewell!"

As the cart slowly trundled away, the Count held the jug up to the light and squinted. Ah, what lady wouldn't be thrilled with a jug full of beetles? Yes, yes: 'twas important to approach a lady with a gift, no matter how little thought has gone into the purchase. And with that thought, the Count followed a line of neatly trimmed firs toward the house, the bushes carefully manicured, the path aristocratically pale. By the time he reached the end, the Count was as red as an egg at Easter time. How hot it was! The air felt motionless, infused with prickly heat. The Count sought the shade of the trees, soft gold dust sticking to his sweaty cheeks. 'Neath the pines, the needles formed a soft, brown carpet, slippery underfoot. A single white chair nestled among the trees, supporting a delicate porcelain teacup filled with dew.

"What a peaceful spot," said the Count, mopping his brow. "Like an enchanted world… "

Up ahead, the house was mustard coloured with a new green roof and tall, white pillars, topped by the family coat of arms. Everything was clean, fresh, newly washed in colour: even the honeysuckle grew where it was told.

Mitrovsky threw back his head and puffed out his chest. The glue securing his wig was starting to melt, and he felt the resin drip down past his eyes.

"Mařenka," he whispered, shaking his ruffles, "Mařenka, your swain awaits…"

And with that, the Count marched energetically toward the house, whistling 'Blow Hard Ye Bellows of Love' while flapping his hands at a wasp.

3

Mitrovsky had fallen into the habit of calling in on the Drtikols almost by accident, led there as if by his nose, or some other organ. They had become his neighbours only recently, Baron Drtikol having amassed great wealth and retired to the country. Alas, they had never known the Old Count or his son, Matej, and by the time they came upon Karel, the Mitrovsky Estate had already fallen into a sorry state, blight afflicting the potatoes and dogweed choking the beans.

Mitrovsky's account book told a sad but familiar tale. A quarter of the land had been sold to the crown, a second quarter to Lame Patočka, a local businessman, the third quarter slipped through various fingers while playing 'Fool', and the fourth quarter had been impounded by the magistrate to pay off his debts. What remained – the fifth quarter, as they say – was the Count's.

Whenever Marta chased him from his chaise with a broom, the new Count fell into the habit of slipping on his jacket and dropping in on the Drtikols every day, almost like an extra chair at the table. Well, he was their neighbour after all, how could they refuse him? And it was there that he had met Mařenka, Drtikol's enchanting wife, who with one flick of her fan had stolen the Count's tender heart. Never mind that the Drtikols were a rich, happily married couple of handsome middle age, or that they had two young daughters and doted upon them. 'Tis true what they say – the heart looks not at the thorns but the rose…

As the Count approached the house, a huge grey wolfhound appeared from behind a pillar, barking energetically as if about to devour Mitrovsky whole. The Count, paused, bowed, then threw open his arms.

"Betka!" cried the Count, "Betka, my darling, how are you?"

At the sound of his voice the hound flung herself into his arms, straining to lick his beard while wagging her tail deliriously.

"O Betka, my sweetheart!"

Yes, the dog adored the Count. In a frenzy of excitement, she pushed herself against him, thick strands of drool pouring from her huge black lips.

"Betka, my angel, please..."

But the dog could not be pacified: instead, she knocked the Count to the ground and proceeded to climb on top.

"My darling, my darling, stop!"

At that moment a liveried footman appeared from inside the house, his frock coat stamped onto the garden as if with a rubber seal.

"Ah, Žloudek!" said the Count, the dog's long tongue seeking out his lips. "Would you be good enough as to inform the master and mistress of the house that Count Mitrovsky has come to call?"

Žloudek watched the Count wrestle with the dog impassively. Betka was now straddling his chest with her behind very near his face.

"Whenever your lordship is ready," said the footman in a dignified voice.

"What? Yes, yes, Betka – desist!"

Žloudek nodded and bowed discreetly, ushering man and dog into a pleasant anteroom, filled with a long couch with gold tassels, two armchairs covered in Genoese velvet, an unlit fireplace, and an enormous oil painting of some jerk on a horse.

"If you would be so kind," said the footman, "I will inform the mistress of your presence."

"Marvellous, marvellous!" said Mitrovsky. "Good fellow!"

The Count seated himself on the couch, Betka beside him. The couch was upholstered in fabulously expensive damask, the cushions a delicate duck-egg blue. Across from it a bowl of oranges glowed with good health, while in the ante-chamber nymphs and shepherds played peek-a-boo among the alcoves, frozen in time, their heads full of nothing.

"Betka, Betka … stop!"

The Count's britches had barely sat down before two blonde girls flew in through a doorway, swooping 'pon Mitrovsky as if stepping down from a canvas.

"Uncle Karel, Uncle Karel!" they chanted in unison, their voices bright as trumpets.

"Ah, my angels," said Mitrovsky smiling. "How kind of Heaven to let you visit."

"Uncle Karel, come, come quick, we need you! We're putting on a play."

"A play?"

"Yes, a play! You can be the bear."

The girls were twins, but not identical: one was much plumper than the other, the plump one – Lida – having the most amazingly bright green eyes.

"I'll be the hunter, you be the bird-catcher," said Lida.

"I don't want to be the bird-catcher!" cried her sister, Lena. "Why can't I be the hunter?"

Lida pouted. "'Cause I'm the one with the Magic Bullets."

"I want the bullets!"

"Well, you can't have them."

"Why don't I be the bird-catcher?" said Mitrovsky, smiling.

"You're the bear."

"Why not make Betka be the bear?"

21

"I can't shoot Betka," said Lida. "She has a sweet nose."

"Yet you can shoot me?"

"Of course I can, silly! You're the Bear."

The girls scooped the Count up and dragged him into a second drawing room, transformed by means of an old, dusty curtain, into a kind of makeshift stage. The only audience was an extremely thin old lady, narrow as an eye-lash. When she saw Mitrovsky, she threw up her hands and gasped.

"Good gracious!" she exclaimed. "Girls, girls, who is this?"

"It's me, Count Mitrovsky, Nanny," said the Count. "I come here most every day."

"Really? Extraordinary, extraordinary!" The girls' governess, Fräulein Friedrich, stared at Mitrovsky as if she had never seen him before in her life. "And is that your frock coat? Are these your boots?"

"Well, the heel may have come loose, but…"

At that moment Betka bounded up to the old woman causing the respectable lady to scream. "What, what…"

"It's Betka, Nanny, She lives here."

"A dog in the house? How amazing! I don't know, my dear Count, sometimes this world seems quite incredible to me…"

In truth, Nanny Friedrich was astonished by pretty much everything: the weather, a passing wasp, the state of the Count's wig. 'Twas as if she lived her life in a state of eternal anxiety, her gloved hands pressed to her cheeks as if to prevent her bonnet taking off.

Mitrovsky bowed. "The girls wish me to perform in some kind of *theatre d'occasion*…"

"Goodness gracious, I really can't imagine…"

"Uncle Karel, Uncle Karel," chorused the girls, "we need you to be the bear!"

Mitrovsky picked up a rug and draped it over his wig.

"Grr!" he said, "Grr, I'm the bear!"

Nanny screamed, Betka barked, and the girls giggled, the two of them dancing round and round him in a circle.

"Roar, I'm coming to eat you," snarled the Count, swaying from side to side. When he made a grab for Lena, she screamed, unseating a jug of flowers by the window seat.

"Grr, grr, I'm a hungry bear," roared the Count, unable to see anything beneath his powdered wig and heavy rug. Instead, he crashed this way and that, producing a deep tremolo from the bottom of his throat.

"I'll stop you, you filthy beast," said Lida, bravely.

"Grr, grr," said the Count, rug low upon his brow.

The girls screamed, while the Count roared, lunged, and upended Nanny Friedrich's sewing table.

"Oh my goodness!" the old lady exclaimed, her lips as tight as Lame Patočka's purse.

"Grr, grr, I'll eat you all!"

Lena squealed.

"Howl, howl!"

"I'll stop you, you dirty bear." The girls, the dog and the Count all circled the old lady until from behind the armoire, Lida produced a heavy musket, struggling a little with the weight.

"Grr, grr," growled the Count.

Lida fumbled with the catch, aiming the weapon directly at the rug.

"Yes, yes, here I come," growled Mitrovsky.

"You're a naughty bear," said Lida but before she had a chance to fire, the gun was gently but firmly, plucked from her grasp.

"That's enough now," said a gentle, kindly voice. "Girls, please, don't shoot our guest "

Mitrovksy pushed back the bearskin and looked out. There was Drtikol, smiling genially and proffering his hand in welcome.

"I'm terribly sorry," said the Count removing the rug from his head. "It seems that I'm a bear."

The two men shook hands, and the Count flourished his handkerchief, causing dust to fly everywhere and Betka to sneeze.

"Ah…"

"O, don't worry dear fellow, no trouble at all," said Drtikol, righting the table and retrieving the fallen jug. "Žloudek will take care of any stains. How lovely to see you again old friend … and so soon too!"

"I fear I may have damaged poor Nanny's crotcheting…"

"Think nothing of it. Fräulein Friedrich, are you discommoded?"

"Well, I…"

"There now, no harm done."

Drtikol wore stiff coat tails, yellow knee breeches, white stockings, and an open jacket 'in the military fashion'. Instead of a wig, he sported a *zopfzeit* or pig tails, his thinning blonde hair carefully combed. His voice was lively and agreeable, his eyes warm and only gently sardonic.

"Have you come to see Mařenka?" he said, brightly. "She'll be with us presently and I'm sure she'll be delighted."

Mitrovsky beamed. "O my friend, I always feel so happy here – 'tis like a little bit of paradise here on earth! And how are you my dear Anton – still well?"

Drtikol bowed. "Since yesterday, you mean? Yes, yes, still well. And how are you, my good man? How fares your pleasant estate?"

"Marvellous, marvellous! Of course, the porch collapsed yesterday." At this the Count paused, laughed and pinched his nose. "Between you and me, I blame the woodpeckers."

"Well, yes, indeed."

"But they are such bright and cheerful birds, who can begrudge their jests? Besides, the garden is now much closer."

"And your cucumbers?"

"Oh, there are some that the green-fly have yet to nibble. A little yellowish, 'tis true, but, when served with cream of kidneys – delicious!"

Drtikol, who had seen the depressed state of Mitrovsky's backyard close up, nodded discreetly. In truth the Count's estate was gently vanishing from this world. In the garden, straggly gooseberry bushes overran the line of withered sticks where peas had once grown, the pumpkins flat and the onion leaves covered in a fine dust. The roof of the byre had fallen in and the yard was overgrown with a strange wispy grass, as pale as whiskers. Everything was crooked, aslant, broken. Yet here was Mitrovsky every day, in his ridiculous wig and ancient waistcoat with its suspicious stain and bright copper buttons.

Before Drtikol could say another word, Žloudek threw open a second set of doors, and the Lady of the House appeared, Mitrovksy snapping to attention as if his fingers had been caught in a trap.

"Why, Count Mitrovsky," said Mařenka, offering her hand. "How kind of you to visit."

"I've been counting the minutes," said Mitrovsky, kissing Mařenka's glove.

"Well, that won't take long," said Mařenka, smiling. "I've barely had a chance to change."

"And change into something even more delightful if I may say so…"

Baroness Drtikol wore a loose-fitting *Adrienne* with an ornamented hoop skirt and enormous white train. Her *coiffure* was as high as the chandeliers would allow, besprinkled with powder like a mountain peak dusted with snow. A butterfly pin glittered near the summit.

"So what have you been up to, my dear Count? I swear, they could hear the banging in Vienna…"

The Count produced a modest face. "Ah, it's not easy being a bear. But look, my sweet, I've brought you a gift."

"My, how kind! And what a lovely jug…"

"There's a worm in it."

"Of course there is."

"No, no – a glow worm! To bring a gentle bloom to your cheek."

Mařenka shook the jug from side to side and inspected it suspiciously. "The perfumery was shut, I take it?"

"Shall we take lunch in the garden?" said Drtikol, looking at the broken vase and where Betka had trampled mud all over the carpet. "The Count can tell us all about his worm…"

"It came from a most remarkable peasant…"

"But of course," said Mařenka, brightly. "Let's go and wash our hands."

4

As any connoisseur of fine dining will tell you, when it comes to *slivovitz*, good is better, but bad is no disaster. *Slivovitz* gives warmth twice: once on the way down and once in the memory. Moreover, it accompanies any dish like a faithful hound. Whether hoof or horn, the drink 'twill never leave its side, a loyal companion to the end.

As the Count ate and drank, the last few specks of yesterday's dust seemed to finally fall from his shoulders. Little grey horses, see-through carriages, an eerie tolling bell – all that now seemed no more than a dream. Besides, what did any of this witchcraft have to do with him, Count Mitrovsky, a man of simple pleasures? Was he so old he should be measured for a winding sheet? True, his knees creaked like the kitchen floor and his hips locked like a barn gate – but for all that he felt in his heart of hearts like a babe who'd just hopped from a comforting bath, soft of skin and rosy of cheek.

Yes, yes, it was all nonsense. Why dream of death when the world was so full of life? The air on the Drtikol Estate was warm and drowsy, a gentle green light filtering down between the trees, the colour of a dragonfly's wings. Above the Count, swifts swooped with astonishing agility, their whistles shrill and unearthly, flitting from building to building like notes on a page. Yes, thought Mitrovsky, everything is beautiful when you think about it, from the daisies to the bird droppings. Why was there so much worry in the world? Lose a coin in a pond and a carp will throw it back. Industry, toil, the multitudinous activities of nature – what a joy it was to contemplate these things, especially in a beautiful garden, with a glass of *slivovitz* in your hand.

"I heard about your deal with Lame Patočka," said Drtikol, passing Mitrovsky more palačinky. "That swine's as slippery as an eel."

Mitrovsky pulled a face. "O, I wouldn't worry about him. Flies do not bother the horse."

"Of course, of course." Drtikol paused. "But have you sold all your late father's timber?"

"Yes, yes … all gone now. What can one do? You wouldn't believe the price of ribbon these days."

"And for a mere two hundred gulden…?"

"Drtikol, my dear fellow," said Mitrovsky tapping his friend's hand, "such are the mysteries of commerce. A kopeck to the prince, a kopeck for the army, a kopeck to the Priest at Easter time: it all adds up, old chum! You know what they say – even the woodlark cannot live on song alone."

"And what of your brother, Matej? Has he…"

"Anton, it's far too beautiful a day to talk about ducats and gulden," Mařenka said, removing a spool of golden thread from her bag. "Here Count: help me with my *parfilage* and you can tell me all about your enchanting worm…"

The Baroness's eyes glowed with great warmth and as Mařenka wrapped the thread around Mitrovsky's threadbare gloves, the Count began to spin a long story about worm-hunting with a wise old peasant with a green beard, a tale which grew steadily more fantastical in the telling.

"Of course, glow worms can only be seen by night," said Mitrovsky, burping loudly. "During the day they are as transparent as a drop of water…"

"Really, my dear Count?"

"Yes, yes … 'tis on account of their Latin name. They belong to the invisible class of creatures, along with jelly fish, certain kinds of moths, and tax inspectors."

Mitrovsky was an inveterate taleteller, although, under the influence of strong liquor, his stories could easily become confused. As the story went on, he was no longer pursuing a humble worm but rather a wild and enormous boar, its tusk the size of table lags.

"It reared up at me and 'twas all I could do to climb on its back…"

"The worm or the boar?"

"Oh the boar, my dear – I used the worm to dazzle him and thereby draw my sword. Marta, I cried, Marta! The beast is dead – fetch me a pot of mustard and a broom."

"Mmm. And this worm is all the treasure I get?" said Mařenka, righting the Count's glass. "Or do you have a ham in your knapsack too?"

"Oh, I gave that to the peasant," said the Count magnanimously. "The fellow was so thin he could've slipped between two sheets of paper."

After that came Brno cutlets in wine sauce, followed by sour lentils. At some point another bottle of *slivovitz* was opened, as well as a jug of delicate, rose-coloured wine, which the Count promptly proceeded to spill, a mosquito landing on the stain, looking up at him accusingly.

"'Tis these ruffles," murmured the Count in a low voice. "I once lost a whole ham in there…"

"Oh, don't worry," said Drtikol, his smile as warm as the food. "Here, try the bread dumplings – they're very good…"

Ah, what a marvellous couple the Drtikols were! In this light, Mařenka's face looked enticingly green, as fresh and inviting as a pear. "And a most beautiful pear at that," he whispered, his words stumbling from the cart. Wasn't there something he wanted to ask Mařenka about – something about two birds in a sack? Oh, well: the words would scratch at his door soon enough. To be honest, the exact hour – and indeed, the exact number of courses – seemed a little hazy now. Was it lunch or was it dinner? As in Heaven, time seemed to move somewhat differently on the Drtikol Estate, accompanied by the burr of crickets and a waterfall of green light.

"Count? Karel? My dear sir, are you alright?"

Mitrovsky nodded and tried to collect his thoughts. How empty the sky was! It was as if all the clouds had been ironed, folded and neatly put away: even the swallows seemed to have knocked off work. The Count squinted at the surrounding buildings and tried to work out where the little birds had gone. The little holes of their nests were far too small for their bodies, a mystery not even the wisest of philosophers could solve.

"Count Mitrovsky? Another cutlet, perhaps?"

The Count burped, glanced across at his hosts and saw – almost like a wish! – that he and Mařenka were now all alone, her husband mysteriously, inexplicably, nowhere to be seen. But what had happened to everyone? Had Drtikol been called away, Nanny Friedrich devoured by a bear? Mitrovsky's thoughts scattered like sparrows. Was it early or late? Morning or afternoon? It was all very strange. Once there had been a Drtikol here and now there was one Drtikol less: beyond that, he felt all at sea.

Well, no matter. Betka lay panting at Mitrovsky's feet, while the two girls were off by the carp-pond, playing Mummy and Daddy with sticks. When the Count looked back at Mařenka her décolletage seemed very low, breasts dusted with sugar like *vdolky*. What a beauty, what a dish! As Mitrovsky batted his long, mulish eyelashes, her lips floated up to Heaven like a leaf heading in the wrong direction.

'Yes,' he thought, 'I'm a very lucky man …'

And in that moment, it seemed that all this was really his: the garden, the estate, the two girls, Betka. It was as if he had already found Nosek's poem and was living inside it now, his life with Mařenka made of ink and paper, squeezed in between two covers.

"Yes, I'm a very lucky man," the Count repeated, this time speaking out loud. Mařenka looked at him curiously.

"I mean," he said shyly, "to be married to you…"

"Hm, I think that's enough to drink," said Mařenka, taking away his glass. "I don't believe you have the slightest idea what you're saying…"

"There's the truth we dream about, and the truth that happens."

"What rubbish! The truth's gone to talk with the game-keeper." At this, Mařenka gave the Count a significant wink. "Let's go for a walk my dear Count. It might help clear your mind."

"O my angel – it's you that intoxicates me."

"Count, what nonsense you talk! Now, have you seen my hat?"

"I think that's it, perched atop your wig."

"Mm? Well, just so."

The soft, sandy path zigzagged between laurels, oleanders and sweet-smelling orange trees, the perfumed air both warm and close. Mařenka whisked him past a trellised summerhouse, and on toward a secluded arbour, the trees so close, they seemed to be holding hands. All at once, Mitrovsky's heart began to flutter, and a delicate blush stole across his cheek. Was this why Mařenka had brought him to this place? To declare her love, or better still, to demonstrate it, preferably using actions?

"O Mařenka," said the Count, with deep feeling. "I, I…" He placed his handkerchief to his nose, so agitated that he could not think of a single thing to say. "My sparrow, it, er…"

Damn it, where was Nosek and those blasted birds of his? Curse those poets! They might not have two pfennigs to rub together but they could hang out fine words like washing. "My sparrow, it, ah, beats inside my pocket…" Locket, docket – what the hell rhymed with pocket? Fortunately, Mařenka wasn't listening. Instead, she stared slightly to one side, her eyes hidden by her parasol, her *coiffure* blocking out the sun.

"Count, as you well know, my family and I all think of you with the greatest possible affection."

"O, my darling."

"Betka, for example, why, she absolutely worships you…"

"'Tis because I always hide a meaty-patty in my cuff…"

"And the girls! They always have so much fun. When you're not here they count the minutes like buttons. What would they do without you and all your games and sport? And Anton, he, ah, he too admires you enormously. Why, he admires your, um…" At this, the Baroness paused. "Count – Karel – may I speak seriously with you for a moment?"

The Count looked deep into her eyes and his whole frame began to shake. Yes, yes, this was it: the moment he'd longed for was now at hand, and not a nightingale in sight! Mitrovsky's beard trembled and Mařenka's lips quivered. How red they were! Like the seal on a vellum scroll.

"He … ah, that is to say, I…"

Her eyes were so near they merged into one enchanted orb, like a beautiful robin's egg.

"Count, I … I … this isn't easy for me."

"No, no…"

"I love my husband dearly."

"Why, me too! His snuff box, his salmon-coloured tights…"

"He deserves only happiness."

"My angel, your husband is the most charming of men, a pearl, a prince…"

The Count paused, unsure where all this was going. Pale

beneath all that make-up, Mařenka was trembling too. And why not? The Count was wearing his special cologne, *Lillas de Perse*.

"Count … Karel … you must tell no one of what I'm about to tell you…"

"My lady, your honour is, ah…"

"Soon, very soon, I'm going to have to go away from here. To a place far away. A realm where others cannot follow."

"To Pilsen?"

"No, my darling, not to Pilsen."

Mitrovsky stared at her lips and struggled to focus. "My angel, I have no carriage but…"

"When I go away, I, I need you to promise to help Anton and the girls. Do you understand me, Karel? I cannot stay, but neither can they follow."

"Follow? Well, no…"

"Will you promise, then? Promise that you will do all in your power to assist them when … when I am gone…"

The Count bowed gravely, and when he struggled back up, it was as if Mařenka were much, much older: indeed, it was as if many years had passed between her first words and her last.

"Karel? Karel, are you listening?"

"Of course, my angel. Just say the word and I, um…"

Mařenka sighed and put a gloved finger to his lips. "You must tell no one of this, Count Mitrovsky. No one, do you understand?"

"My darling, who would I tell? I've no more servants and we let the last horse go."

"You're an angel," Mařenka said smiling, "an angel sent from Heaven above."

It was a romantic scene, right enough – but who was the old dame and what had she done with Mařenka? It was as if another actress were playing the part, one entirely wrong for the role. Or perhaps Mařenka's older sister had turned up – or her mother, maybe?

"My dearest Count, are you alright?"

The Count blinked and mopped his brow. Above him, the rooks chattered in a foreign language, the sun burning through the clouds like a bald spot. Had the heat broiled his brain? Or was it that his precious slivovitz had unaccountably turned on him, the dog! Still, what did all this matter? The important thing was that Mařenka had looked deep into his big black eyes, pressed her gloved hand to his lips. Compared to this, everything else was just an aside.

"Your obedient servant, Madame," he said, bowing once more.

Mařenka nodded and returned to the house, her tiny shoes moving invisibly beneath her gown. Going away, thought the Count? No, not when he produced his nightingale! And with that the Baroness exited stage left, leaving only the shadow of her wig behind her.

5

That evening, the Baroness was as lively and charming as always, the very embodiment of feminine grace. She smiled graciously at the Count, exchanged pleasantries with her husband, and kissed the children an affectionate goodnight. No tears, no sighs, no furtive looks. 'Twas almost as if the mysterious scene in the garden had never happened.

After dinner, the men played cards while Mařenka sat at a table with her golden thread. It was late by now, the clouds stained red like a dentist's handkerchief.

"What a wonderful pad," said the Count, smacking his chops like a dog. "Yes, yes, you are truly blessed…"

Outside in the garden the sun was sinking low beneath the horizon, the trees merging to form one black mass, the pink sky darkening to a deep blue, like a lady swapping her underclothes.

"Well," said Mitrovsky, "the hour falls late, and the day falls into the grave."

If he was to get his hands on Nosek's birds, then he must tarry at the Drtikols no longer. The best thing to do was to walk from here into town – seek out that mysterious bookseller and slip the nightingales into his pocket.

"My dearest Anton – I fear that I have intruded upon your indulgence too long. Let me gather my things and bid both you and your lovely wife a fond *adieu*."

"So soon, my dear Karel?"

"Oh, I wouldn't want to overstay my welcome!" The Count leaned back and broke wind softly. "Besides, what is it that they say? Visitors give pleasure twice – once upon arrival, and then upon departure."

"Ha, ha," said the Baron. "Look, here's your hat."

There followed a long drawn-out scene where the Count searched for first his cloak, then his jacket, then his shoes. Then he needed his stick, his handkerchief, and his pomade brush. When all had been secured about his person, he rose up on his toes and tottered over to Mařenka.

"My angel, I …"

The Count leaned in for a kiss but was presented with only a decorous glove.

"Good night, my dear Count," she said, almost tonelessly. "May the Lord keep you safe on your journey."

"Journey?"

"Journey home, I mean."

"Ah, yes, yes, of course! Till we meet again, m'lady."

Did she pause? Did she tremble? No – their parting was accompanied only by a soft plop inside Mařenka's belly, like an apple falling from a tree.

"'Till we meet again, my Count."

Executing a series of extravagant bows and flourishes, Mitrovsky backed out of the room as if attempting to park a cart. No sooner had he got to the door, then Betka came barrelling straight toward him, whining and yapping and throwing herself against the Count as if she might never see him again.

"Betka, my sweet, please," said Mitrovsky, struggling to stay on his feet. "Betka, my darling, what's wrong?"

But the dog would not let Mitrovsky go. She whined, yipped, and pushed herself against him as if a thing possessed.

"Betka, Betka, I'll be back," said the Count in a soft voice. "And

I'll bring you some of those kidneys you like so much, maybe a little sausage…"

With sad eyes, Betka was forced to lie down, her tail bent and nose turned toward the ground.

"Betka, please, don't be so sad. We'll play another day, when your paws are not so painful and your joints are not so stiff…"

Betka whined and pleaded with the Count with her big, brown eyes.

"Shh, shh! There'll always be another rabbit left to chase…"

Eventually Žloudek appeared and hauled the heartbroken dog away, her paws struggling to find purchase on the carpet.

"Goodbye Betka, goodbye sweet dog. In Spring, it is easy to say goodbye…"

At this, the Count pulled himself to his feet, raised his arms in a dramatic gesture and called out "And farewell my friends, goodnight, adieu!" as Žloudek slammed the door in his face.

'Yes, thought the Count, 'the night buries the day as a dog buries its bone.' Time slips so swiftly through our fingers. And then he remembered: it was only just gone eight, and he still had much to do.

The evening air was warm and fragrant, perfumed with the sweet scent of oranges and clover. The Count sniffed and breathed in hungrily. Ah, how he loved this time of day! A promissory note for the night ahead. An orchestra of insects started to tune up, and a single star appeared enchantingly above the lime trees, the first letter of the night.

The Count stole across the lawn and drifted crab-like toward the violet shadows. Light was fading from the day and the woods grew uncertain and dim; in a few minutes night's curtain would fall and all this – the villa, the lawn, the ornamental garden – would be gone.

Pausing for breath, the Count took one last look at the villa, and as he did so, happy tears spilled across his cheeks.

"O, my darling!" he exclaimed.

There, upstairs, in what may very well have been a boudoir window, sat his jug of worms, the creature glowing with a kindly, friendly light.

"So, she loves me after all," murmured the Count through his tears. "And that gentle lamp shall burn until the hour we meet again."

And with that the Count waved his hat and slowly took his leave.

6

It was a tender night, the moon shining like a five-pfennig piece, right down to the Emperor's nose. The Count's own nostrils quivered with delight: how wonderful to be caressed by the night, blessed with a full stomach and an over-flowing heart! The air was soft, gentle, perfumed with hyacinth and honeysuckle, like an actress' boudoir. Yes, Mitrovsky thought, the main thing was to get hold of Nosek's nightingales before Mařenka packed her bags or the birds flew away. Where she was going was of no consequence – what counted was to head her off at the pass.

Just then the Emperor's mug rolled behind a pile of clouds and the scene fell into a deep and impenetrable darkness. A bird shrieked, a bat swooped, and the Count heard a strange snuffling nearby, as if some kind of creature was trying to find its seat. 'If only I had bought two glow worms,' thought Mitrovsky. 'One for Mařenka, and one to light my way'.

And with that some cursed creature, fleet of foot and long of tail, leapt from the branches of a nut tree, taking hold of the Count's wig with its nimble, pointy claws.

"Scoundrel, knave!" cried the Count. "Paws off my peruke!"

He felt something bushy brush across his face, heard an infernal chirruping.

"You devil, you swine…"

The imp turned full circle, bared its teeth, and then pulled the wig from Mitrovsky's head – twenty groschen, and that wholesale too.

At this the moon re-emerged, the Emperor's face looked down, and the wig scurried off into the forest like a rabbit.

"Demon, foul fiend," cried the stricken Count, "come back with my hair-piece this instant!"

It was no use, though: the wig squeezed between two currant bushes and disappeared, an ominous squeaking emanating from the darkness.

What should he do? Should he pursue it? After all, the curls were heavy, and the wig couldn't get far on foot. Or should he just buy a new one? Vrata the dog man opened at six and maybe he could rustle something up from his bins.

'As long as it's not collie,' reflected the Count with dignity. "Their hair gets up my nose."

After that, the Count proceeded more cautiously. Every once in a while, he thought he saw his wig sitting on a branch observing him ironically, but more likely it was just an owl or just some odd shaped stump, placed there by some joker to fool him.

The night was deep, and the moon came and went, like gout, or taxes. The stars though seemed to glow with a peculiar intensity and when the Count reached Blindman's Bridge, he heard the welcome sound of a horse and cart clattering along the post-road, its lantern giving off a merry and welcoming light.

On closer inspection it turned out to be an old spring-less cart, driven by an ancient looking peasant with a filthy grey cap, his beard turning yellow at the tips. Round his neck he had a kind of scarf carrying four eggs, along with a dirty length of string and an ear trumpet.

"Ho there, fancy a lift my fine lad? Just jump onboard, no need to book. Now where might a gentleman like yourself be going at this time of night? Out carousing, or some such naughtiness, I expect! Right O. That's it, climb in, the straw is lovely and soft."

Mitrovsky stared at the peasant suspiciously. "Do I know you, sir?"

"Me?" The peasant placed the trumpet to his ear. "I don't know sir, on account of the dark."

His face was as innocent as a babe's, pockmarked and brown, with bright, lively eyes and a blunt, turned-up nose.

"You aren't selling worms, by any chance?"

"Worms? Feh – a dirty business is wormsies. No, no, fine sirs – I sell historical oddities, by which I mean ancient artefacts of great educational significance…"

"Artefacts?" said Mitrovsky, climbing up onto the cart. "You mean rags and bones and the like?"

"No, no, sir, not at all," said the peasant, handing Mitrovsky some kind of dirty tool. "Why that's a piece of Přemysl's plough share, the bit that fell off when he happened to hit a bull."

"Really?" Mitrovsky pulled on his beard. "It's in very good condition for something fictional…"

"And in this jar I have hairs shaved from the chin of Saint Wilgefortis, daughter to the king of Portugal … you know the story?"

"What kind of a simpleton do you take me for?" Mitrovsky roared. "I have never heard of this Wilgerfortis in my life!"

"Or perhaps you would like to take a look at Jan of Nepomuck's tongue?"

"Tongue?"

The tongue had been carefully pickled although in truth it looked much more like a cow's: long and black with sharp spiky hairs at the end. Still, the peasant had other treasures to offer if the gentlemen might be so inclined: a set-square used by Master Hanuš the clock-maker, Empress Marie Therese's milk teeth, and, right at the back, a plaster-cast model of Saint Agnes of Rome carrying her breasts on a painted platter.

"Quite a haul," said Mitrovsky, eying up St Agnes. "But tell me, my dear fellow, do you have any, ah … books?"

"Books, sir? Foo – there's little call for books, out here sir – though I do have a print showing how the earth rests 'pon three fishes."

The Count rubbed up against the peasant like a cat. "Tell me, my lad – have you ever heard of the poet Nosek and his two nightingales?"

At Nosek's name, the purveyor of ancient artefacts turned pale. His cheeks began to shake, his eyes lost their colour, and even the tip of his beard seemed to blanch.

"Nosek, sir?"

"Yes, yes, born in 1709 he…"

"Never heard of him, sir. There 'aint no call for books round these parts, on account of the general lack of learning and reading glasses and the like. Nosek, you say? No sir, don't believe I've ever heard of him…"

With that the normally convivial peasant grew quiet and thoughtful. He made no mention of his used *skřipke*, once owned by Prince Dalibor in the famous play, or the box containing his Turkish turban, or his bag hiding the Golem's big toe. Instead, the peasant contented himself with watching the stars go by, whistling 'I remember days, long departed' under his breath.

"So you haven't heard of this fellow's nightingales?"

"I'm sorry sir, my trumpet is full of dust…"

"But…"

The peasant looked away, studiously picking his nose.

'Curious, very curious,' reflected Mitrovsky. 'And we were getting on so well! Well, no matter – we'll be in town soon enough…"

And with that the horse and cart went on its way, one wheel too big and one wheel too small, as if going uphill and downhill all at the same time.

After a while, the Count fell into a sentimental *reverie*, dreaming of Mařenka, birds and Jan of Nepomuck's long and hairy tongue. Suddenly the cart came to a violent halt, crude voices echoing in the darkness.

"What ho, what's this?" Mitrovsky murmured, still dreaming about Mařenka and only half in this world.

"Police," hissed the peasant. "Lie low."

"Hide? But…"

"Shh, shh – they're coming."

The wagon had ground to a halt just outside the main gate. Police were searching all the carts going in and all the carts going out, the guards as alike as lead figures in a box. One strode over and inspected the peasant suspiciously.

"What do we have here, Uncle? Scraps from the midden pit?"

"These are antiquities of great value," said the old peasant, proudly. "Items of great worth and historical interest. I also have a bottle of *schnapps* if you gentlemen might be interested…"

"Old?"

"Old enough."

The first fellow hesitated but the other shoved him out of the way.

"Go take a look in the back, see if he's hiding anything in there. Historical objects, you say, Uncle? And what kind of objects are these? Not books by any chance?"

The peasant's lips twitched, and he played guiltily with his eggs.

"Books, good sir? No, no, I fear I cannot read. 'Tis on account of the letters, sir, which refuse to stand still and scamper about like kittens."

"Constable, take a look."

"Oh, there's nothing."

"Nothing eh? Well then, what's this?"

It was fair to say that the Count did not look at his best: no wig, a bright red coat with patched pockets, a short cloth vest, somewhat stained, woollen stockings, knee britches adorned with ribbons, burrs and leaves. The policeman waved his lantern and Mitrovsky's eyes shone back.

"I am Count Mitrovsky, owner of the Mitrovsky estate…"

"Is that right? And what are you doing on the back of this peasant's cart?"

"I was, ah, taking a look at the kind fellow's wares."

"In the dark?"

"Such treasures are easily damaged by the light…"

Alas, the officer was having none of it. If this tramp was a count, then he was the pope – either the German, or the other one.

"Right you two, down you come. Constable, search the cart."

As the police went about their business, a small boy appeared from behind the House of the Golden Horseshoe, a ragged little brat in bare feet, sauntering toward the scene with the air of a connoisseur.

"Kid, hey kid," whispered Mitrovsky. "The *fizl* – what are they looking for?"

The boy shrugged and inspected the Count indifferently. Although the boy's feet were bare, he was wearing a green felt hat and had cat-skin gloves: both filched, no doubt.

"You, you my lad," repeated Mitrovsky. "I said, the police –

what is it they want?"

The boy grinned revealing a mouth full of broken teeth.

"Bok," he said.

"Bok?"

"Bok."

"What kind of Bok?"

"Ritting Bok."

At that one of the policemen gave a sudden cry. "Found something, sir! Look here…"

Several hardbound volumes were tied together with a piece of faded pink ribbon. The two officers gathered under their lantern to take a look: *The Pleasures of Conjugal Love Explained, A Physician's Guide to Feminine Anatomy*, and *The Orgies of Ancient Rome*.

They passed the *Physician's Guide* to the peasant, but he merely shrugged. "I would like to be able to help you sir, but alas I cannot read."

He then passed the book to Mitrovsky. "Yes, yes," he said, thumbing the pages. "'Tis a bad business – and badly printed too. Why the ink here is so smudged, it's impossible to work out who's coming or going."

"Give me that here, you dog," snapped the officer. Grabbing the book, he gazed intently at page seventeen, soundlessly moving his lips.

"Are these on the list, sir?"

"Mm?"

"The list, sir. Are these on the list?"

"The list, yes…"

The officer continued to peruse the pages when his companion suddenly spotted someone moving about atop the peasant's cart.

"You there – what do you think you're doing?"

Unbeknown to the others, the young lad had skipped up onto the top of the cart, swiping Jan of Nepomuck's tongue and

45

concealing it 'neath his jerkin.

"Stop thief!" yelled the peasant.

The guards stared at the boy dumbly.

"That dog's got my tongue!"

The two guards drew their swords, and with that the lad took off down an alleyway between the Golden Horseshoe and the Red Eagle, pursued by the two policemen, one of them tooting a whistle.

The peasant looked at Mitrovsky, and Mitrovsky looked at the peasant. Yes, the old saying was true: better to scatter like birds, than stay in the hunter's net. And with that the gentlemen took to their heels, Mitrovsky grabbing his cloak, the peasant holding his eggs, and a passing leatherworker clutching a copy of *The Pleasures of Conjugal Love Explained*, making off into the shadows like a ghost.

8

Despite the lop-sided sign, carp – whether small, large, or in numbers greater than four – rarely made their way to patrons' plates in this rather shabby-looking establishment. Instead, the chalk-board was rather less specific: Granny's patties, Hunters' kebabs, Pleasant soup, and so on. The sprinklings of hair, lumps of fat, and occasional sighting of tail suggested that some kind of animal had ended up in the pot, though whether blessed with hoof or claw remained a mystery; either way it was unwise to scrape away too diligently at the bottom of one's pan.

Fortunately, all dishes were served with a kind of sticky, orange-coloured sauce which hid the crime as a cat disguises his leavings. This sauce was unique to The Five Small Carp and one could identify its patrons by the strange orange tinge of their whiskers and chins. No, no carp had ever swum in this particular pond – even the flies were wary.

The proprietor, Nyergesujfalusi, sat slumped by the counter, his beard as long as his name. He owned a pair of fierce, spiky eyebrows, a large, bulbous nose, and a fore-head criss-crossed with wrinkles and scars. He listened to Mitrovsky's story and belched.

"A bookseller," repeated the Count, sucking on a piece of rye and lard, "skinny fellow, crooked as an Auntie's finger."

"We had a tanner in here once," said Nyergesujfalusi in his thick, Hungarian accent. "Paid for his drinks from a purse made entirely from a cow's ear."

"Well, yes, but…"

"Sold leather to the cobblers in O, as well as a funny kind of glue mixed with hair."

"Ah…"

"Did you ever meet him, Count Mivtovessky? His boots squeaked as he walked – one louder than the other."

"No, no, I can't say I…"

"Well, this tanner, I once saw him with a book … a Farmer's Almanac, bound in pig hide. He swore that this almanac could predict when your hens were likely to lay."

"A book?"

Nyergesujfalusi nodded and picked something edible out from his beard.

"And this book – did he purchase this from a tall thin man with wooden teeth?"

Nyergesujfalusi smiled, his tiny eyes like dimples. "O Count Mistrovoshee – I should say not! That Almanac had been in his family since the time of the Papal Bull. His father had sworn that it would bring great prosperity – although he himself fell into the pot they boiled the skin in, a great metal cauldron the size of a bath. When they pulled him out he was wearing no more than his bones, his eyes like two poached eggs."

Mitrovsky shook his head and went back to his bread. "Ah, I fear you misunderstand me, my good man. This fellow I'm looking for – this book seller – why, he was here in the Carp, just last night."

"In the Carp?"

"Yes."

"Just last night?"

"Indeed."

"O Count Muzzorgsky, I'll tell you just who I saw last night:

48

Havránek the peddler. Going from table to table, he was, trying to sell a broken cup which he used to catch spiders…"

"Not books?"

"Had a samovar that had once belonged to the Russian Tsar – swore that one could capture rats with it, using only a hunk of bacon fat and a piece of string."

"Mm," said Mitrovsky thoughtfully. "This doesn't sound like my fellow."

"Yes, but still…" Nyergesujfalusi picked his crimson, pock-marked nose and shrugged. "Rats and spiders – such a cup is worth thinking about…"

"Did you buy one?"

"What am I, an idiot?"

Mitrovsky nodded and surveyed the room. Unsavoury citizens, clad in rags sewn together with cobwebs, lay slumped at rough wooden tables, the tables marked with a series of chalk lines like the wall of a prison.

"So: you have no memory of any such book seller?"

Nyergesujfalusi grinned, his gums red and puffy. "In the Carp? O my Count, here you are fishing in the wrong pool."

"But…"

"Once a young fellow came in here, a student or a novice by the look of him, nose in a book, like a pig in a trough. Didn't even know where he was – just sat down at a table, held up a finger and kept on reading. Pink cheeks he had, and very small, soft hands. When his pig knuckles arrived he didn't even look down – munch, munch, munch – quietly turning the page. Even the jugged hare couldn't rouse him. Like a sleepwalker he was. This book, it had him under its spell…"

Mitrovksy stroked one chin, then the other. "Yes, yes, this sounds like the kind of thing I'm looking for. So what happened to this bookish fellow? Did he…"

49

"Urbanec the pickpocket took his purse, Vohnout swiped his hare, and Tiny Katz managed to snitch his belt. When the fellow left, his britches were practically down by his ankles … and still he kept on reading. I tell you Mizziggy, these books, they're no good for honest folk. You should stay away from 'em, Count – use one to prop up a table if you must, but open one up and – snap! Like a trap, they are, Count, like a trap…"

Mitrovksy nodded, wiping his mouth with a rag. No, there were no clues here. It was as if the bookseller had never existed at all.

"Many thanks, good man. You have been most helpful, but I fear I must search for this Nosek elsewhere…"

At this an old lady looked up from her plate of tripe and spat angrily to one side. "Nosek? He can go to the devil for all I care."

Mitrovsky paused and glanced in the old crone's direction.

"Um, Madam?"

"That Nosek is a dog and a swindler. Love poems? There's no such thing. It's all just a pack of lies."

"Nosek? You know him?"

The old woman resembled a sack from which the potatoes had been hastily removed. Her coat had a long gash on one shoulder and her bonnet was turning yellow.

"Madam? Madam, this Nosek – you know him?"

"Once," she croaked, "many years ago…"

"Ah! And this Nosek, did he…"

"Left me, he did – for another girl, of course. Always running round with his muzzle up a skirt … but what did I expect? Just because something rhymes, don't make it true! Quite the opposite, in fact. O, the things he said to me … just to make me sweet. And sweet I was, good to him … and all the time he was dipping his quill elsewhere…"

Beneath the woman's thin, dry skin, her skull shuddered and

clacked. She might have been eighty or she might have been forty – old as the world's sorrow, timeless as a woman's lament.

"And this Nosek … is he still alive?"

The dame's lips twisted bitterly. "How the hell should I know? Ran away to P he did – with some floozy with red knees and a red scarf… It's all lies, you know. Lies and poison. Men say it, but they don't mean a thing."

"Yes, yes," said the Count, looking shifty, "a scoundrel, and a knave. P, you say. And did he mention any other letters?"

The woman scowled.

"Or a poem, perhaps, a ditty, some lines of dashed off verse?" Mitrovsky paused. "At Dawn, Two Nightingales? Have you, mayhap, ever heard it?"

All at once the woman's hands stopped trembling and her whole body became deathly still.

"Yes," she said, her voice as bitter as the grave. "Yes, I know it."

"Yes, so…"

"He wrote that poem for me." When the old woman's skull turned to look at Mitrovsky, it was if her skin were but a veil. "For me, I tell you! For me!"

At this the Count took two steps backwards, colliding with a dry-goods merchant behind him.

"Hey you, you clod! What do you think you're doing?"

Mitrovsky bowed and fluttered his handkerchief in response. "I do beg your pardon," he said graciously, "I was just conversing with this lady."

"Clumsy oaf!"

The merchant looked down at his spilled pewter bowl and the pool of dark liquid by his boots.

"I'm most terribly sorry…"

"I'll give you sorry, you drunken fool."

Mitrovsky bowed a second time, playing with the buttons on

his waistcoat.

"Come, come, there's no need for that! Here, let me buy you another bowl of beer soup – You'll find the seasoning most mysterious…"

Mitrovsky led the angry merchant over to Nyergesujfalusi and then skipped out of the door. What: he should waste his groschen on such a dog? Besides, the old woman had rattled him – her and her bowl of tripe. Had she really been this Nosek's lover? If so, all this had happened a long time ago – back when Princess Libuše was a little girl. Still, what did her tears add up to? All women cry – 'tis because they're made from salt water, rather than flesh and blood. At least it proved that this Nosek was real, not merely some signature in a book. And if this scribbler had written his poem once, why shouldn't he write it out again? Mařenka, Mařenka – what the hell rhymed with Mařenka? Well, let the poets figure it out: they were the ones with their noses still wet from the ink.

9

As he left The Five Small Carp, the bells of St Tomaš rang out eleven. Yes, thought Mitrovsky, just like the miller's wheel, Time keeps on turning, no matter what tune we play on our drum…

The first thing, then, was to find that mysterious bookseller: but where should one seek such a pearl? The Count slunk past the town jail, head down and cloak up. Should he enquire within? Or would that make the authorities believe he was some kind of accomplice? 'No,' thought the brave Count, 'maybe not.' Besides, what were these mysterious 'books' that the *fizl* were looking for? Not Nosek's robins, surely – how could a few scribbled lines of verse do anybody any harm? Most likely 'twas a case of mistaken identity, or perhaps mis-shelving – these damned scribbles had a life of their own. Either way, it seemed unwise to bother the authorities – sleep with dogs and you wake up with fleas.

Nodding to the guard, Mitrovsky re-traced his steps from Ponurý to Strašidelný, cutting down between The Street of Cloaks and Long Leg Street, the signs lined up like petitioners. From there the Count took Wheel-Well Street toward the Flour Gate and the Green Frog – the very route he had taken when a prisoner inside the little horse's carriage.

But – O – how different things felt tonight! Rather then the streets being eerily deserted, a steady stream of merry peasants rambled up and down the cobbled alleys, singing 'I walked in the Meadows of Green' like the chorus in an opera. There were drovers and panhandlers everywhere, a regular circus. A rough-looking fellow in a rabbit-skin hat offered Mitrovsky a speckled hen, her legs tied together with twine, while an ancient beggar cursed him from the steps of a church. No haunted carriages, no black cats, no diabolical booksellers. Instead, the streets smelt of horse dung and tanner's fat, the aroma of pork shoulder and barley porridge drifting out from an open window.

Glancing over his shoulder, Mitrovsky made his way to the row of cabbies loitering in the square by the Green Frog, the air thick with the smell of garlic and tobacco. A heavy fellow with a square head and high cheekbones was feeding grain to his horse, man and beast dressed in the same course grey material.

"Good evening my fine fellow," said Mitrovsky, mopping his head with a rag. "What a beautiful night – fresh and fragrant as a peach."

The droshky-driver stared balefully at the Count through heavily lidded eyes. "Cab, sir?"

"A cab? Oh no, no, no. Why, the very thought!" The Count gave a little laugh and tapped the horse's muzzle most affectionately. "No, my good man, all I want is a little chat. To ask you some questions, if you don't mind…"

At this the fellow's expression darkened still further, his lips as thin as a knife.

"Chat?"

"Were you on duty last night, sweet prince? I mean here, at The Green Frog? Say around midnight?"

"Who wants to …?"

"And did you perchance see anything that night? A driverless tarantass pulled by a little grey horse?"

The driver and his horse exchanged glances. What kind of an idiot was this?

"A driverless cab, you say? No, sir, I did not."

The Count giggled. "Ha, ha, of course not! Why the very thing!" At this he paused, looking behind his back distrustfully. "And did you, perhaps, see a thin, crooked fellow carrying a sack-full of books, dressed all in black with a set of wooden teeth?"

The cabdriver stared as if the Count were speaking in tongues. "Books?"

"Yes, yes," said the Count. "Perhaps, I don't know, a slim volume of posey…"

"I don't know anything about any books, sir," said the cabdriver swiftly, "nor any horseless carriages either…"

The Count smiled and wagged his finger. "No, my good friend, driverless … there was indeed a little grey horse, a most unusual creature."

"I don't know nothing … now if you'll excuse me, there's a customer right behind you…"

"Ah, yes, of course," said the Count, though in truth, there was no one there at all. "You carry on, my good man, well done…"

The Count stood there awkwardly while the cabbie drifted over to his fellow droshky-drivers, the men glaring suspiciously at the shabby-looking lunatic out front. Fearful as to where all this might be going, the Count pulled down his waistcoat and stepped smartly inside the Frog, leaving the cabbies behind.

There the Count treated himself to a tankard of ale and a slice of greasy sausage, seating himself at a table of morose looking shepherds, their rags redolent of sheep pens and clover. Alas, none of the elderly herdsmen had any interest in books or supernatural carriages, and why should they? They were simple, God-fearing folk whose chief concern was ticks.

After a second cup, the Count bade *adieu* to the Frog and slipped unnoticed out onto Strašidelný and thence through the Needle's Eye, the alley dark and narrow, smelling, for some reason, of sour bird-cheese served with a rich plum wine. In the slim space between the rooftops the stars burned merrily, and the air was warm and sweet-tempered.

'Something will turn up,' reflected Mitrovsky. 'All I have to do is to re-trace the path I took last night: surely I'll see that little horse again, her little bell a-tinkling…'

From The White Turnip, Mitrovsky passed through the Nun's Gate – crossing himself, as was the custom, and saying Saint Markéta's name three times – before following the Crooked Wall down to The Six of Hearts. The Hearts – or 'The Welcome' as it was known by the locals – was just about closing, but the Count still managed to down a flagon of Bavarian beer and snaffle a side order of dumplings from a passing plate. By now he didn't even bother to ask about the bookseller or any small, pale horse. His plan was simply to follow the same route the carriage had taken and wait and see what might turn up, whether bookseller, dybbuk or demon.

In truth though, the Count was having some difficulty piecing together his route. Had he taken Nudný or The Street of Mirrors? Under the influence of the strong Bavarian beer, and still pleasantly lit from his dinner at the Drtikols, Mitrovsky felt a little unsteady on his pins. At the Golden Mitre he had a snifter of vodka, followed by a cup of beer. At the Two Golden Bears he had a *myslivec*, accompanied by a particularly horrible type of pie. He didn't know what he had at The Old Lady, but by the time he left his throat felt on fire and his guts churned like the waters beneath the Devil's Arm. At The Three Little Stars, he met a hairy Moravian and together the pair sang ''Little Bird, Where Have You Been?' – after that, everything was a blur. He was refused entry at The Two Lambs and The Cunning Beast was closed.

O, why had the bookseller's carriage stopped at all these dives – was it collecting lost souls, or had the groom mixed brandy with the oats? Ah, it was all a mystery, a maze without any end.

By now Mitrovsky's boots were aching, his belly as heavy as if a cannonball was lodged inside. Sore of foot and weary of heart, the fat, sozzled Count laid himself down by a statue of Saint Václav, waiting to recover his strength. In his mind's eye he could see Mařenka's face painted on a shop sign, her hair dappled a fetching shade of green.

"O Mařenka!" he cried out, "Mařenka, my heart yearns for love. Also, I seem to have mis-laid my wig – have you seen it my dove, my name is on the label?"

The night was warm and downy, brushing against him like a cat. How close the stars were! Like a candelabra, set out on a plain black cloth. But who would clean it or shake out the crumbs? Yes, the night sang its own tune. Mitrovsky felt like singing, or maybe crying, but instead he fell into a shallow and restless sleep, his legs twitching from time to time, like a dog snoozing by the fire.

When he came too, the Count's nose was wet and the air felt noticeably chillier. How much time had passed? It was impossible to say.

Still, for all that, 'twas a pretty spot – kindly linden trees, sweet-natured birds, the softest of sandy paths. Ah, if only he could make his nest right here! But alas no, no, it was already time to go. Dawn was approaching and he could stay milling the wind no longer.

Mitrovsky bade farewell to the statue of Saint Václav and headed for home, his head heavy and his legs bending under the weight.

It was still before dawn, but already the night seemed thinned by a drop of turpentine, the edge of the sky curling up like an old bill of sale. Mitrovsky felt a little tired and defeated. What was he doing? His quest had led nowhere. No bookseller, no nightingale, no little grey horse: all he had to show for his peregrination was an empty purse and two buttons missing from his coat. Aye, it was time to head home. From the park, a little cobbled lane led to the Flour Gate and thence to the countryside beyond…

Look! There was the Owl Mill, and there was Papoušek's orchard, the trees already looking a little grey in the pre-dawn light. The Count blinked and pulled on his beard. Why, was this where the tarantass had taken him last night – unless, of course, the whole thing had been no more than a dream. Mitrovsky shook his head like a horse stung by gadflies. Then he stretched, clapped his hands, and tramped off along the dusty road, the first finches already chattering away inside his skull.

Yes, it would be a long walk back – and little prospect of a cart at this half-forgotten hour. Were even peasants up and about at such a time? Mitrovsky doubted it. Why, even the baker had yet to pull on his socks. And yet for all that, night rolled inexorably into day. Hedges appeared, followed by fields and meadows. A tree formed itself from the gloom, arms aloft as if threatened by a bandit.

'Aye, 'tis a lonely spot,' reflected the Count, rubbing his red-rimmed eyes. And with that the last few stars blinked shut, the sky the colour of a wine glass when the final dregs are gone.

After a while the post road rounded a corner and began to descend down a steep, dark hill. At the bottom, a lean brown hare ran out from the opposite field, leaving little brushstrokes on the path.

"Hello, my lad," said the Count, "what a fine fellow you are."

The hare stared at him for a moment and then bolted into the hedgerow, a series of tiny paw prints in the dust behind him.

Paw prints? Mitrovsky bent down and ran his fingers through the dust. What was it his poor old brain was trying to say? Something about dust, age, time? Among the powder, Mitrovsky could see the faint remnants of hoof prints and coach wheels, perhaps a horse and cart, or a carriage of some description. All of a sudden, his heart seemed to beat a little faster. What strange omen was this? Was this close to the point where he'd fallen, like a comet from the sky? True, many other carriages must have come this way since that fateful night, but still ... something about this place spoke to him, in a voice familiar yet strange.

His eyes trained on the carriage tracks, Mitrovsky followed the markings along the road. Were these prints some kind of sign or clue? Or was it simply that Wohlmut the dairy man had been this way, carrying a load of sour cream? Mitrovsky couldn't say – to be honest, he couldn't even see. All around him were grey fields striped with shadowy trees and the occasional hayrick, the picture vague and indistinct, like a watercolour painted by the blind.

Mitrovsky was still pondering these things when he came to an abrupt halt. Near a small copse of aspen, the tracks passed over the edge of the road and headed toward a low ditch, the line zigzagging crazily as if the driver had suddenly lost control.

Feeling a nagging sickness in his heart, the Count walked over to the edge of the road, where the grass was flattened, and the earth seemed somewhat disturbed. Licking his lips, Mitrovsky took two steps forward, right to the very edge of the ditch. Then he stopped. How could he not? There, abandoned like last night's clothes, lay his body.

The Count stopped and regarded himself objectively: overweight, bald on top, patches on his britches. His brown topcoat was torn, his wig was lying to one side, now home to a small mouse. No, the Count did not look well. His skin was the colour of porridge and he had a bullet-hole in his jacket. Well, this can't be good, thought the Count, looking at two dull, brown birds pecking at his eyes.

Expressionless, the Count scared away the birds and, slowly, methodically, covered his body with bracken and dead branches, leaving a small stone marker there as a sign of respect. He thought for a moment of retrieving his wig but decided against it: finding your own dead body seemed an ill omen, and besides – the mouse had left behind its droppings. Instead, he backed away from his corpse, slowly retreating to the hill. As to what happened in the following hours, the Count could not recall; he walked back home in a daze, his gait that of a sleepwalker, or perhaps the risen dead.

Eventually he heard the sound of a horse and wagon trundling along behind him, clunk-clank, clunk-clank, as if one wheel were larger than the other. When he turned around, he saw it was an old spring-less cart, driven by an ancient looking peasant, with a white beard turning ginger at the tips. The fellow had a pair of lively brown eyes and a kindly expression, an embroidered leather pouch hanging from his straggly neck.

"What ho, my lad! 'Tis awful early to be out walking – care for a lift, good sir? You don't look so well, if you don't mind me saying so – like you've seen a ghost, or some such thing."

Mitrovksy, hauled his frockcoat onto the back of the cart and clapped the peasant on the back. "You're very kind, my good fellow. God will reward you…"

The peasant grinned, revealing a soft, brownish mouth, his teeth the colour of a bog.

"Aye, in this world or the next." The old man inspected the Count's badly patched coat as if sizing up what kind of fish he had caught in his net. "So, what's a gentleman like you doing out and about at this peasant's hour? Not hunting, by the looks of you, nor looking for mushrooms. So, what is it my lad – just back from the Pope's wedding?"

The Count smiled a melancholy smile, looking back at the

peasant with his big, sad eyes, currants in a gingerbread face.

"Ha ha, ha – oh, no, nothing like that…"

"Ah! Out carousing were we? An assignation with some lovely lady, I expect…"

"A lady? Well…"

"Aha, I thought so! The fox smiles on his way back from the hen house."

"O, my friend, if only it was so simple! But this lady is going away and I know not where. Besides I may have to go on a journey of my own soon … a most unexpected business … Ah, 'tis impossible to explain…"

The peasant turned around to look at Mitrovsky with a kind and thoughtful expression.

"Downheartedness, is it, sir? Lucky for you, I've got just the thing. Crushed willow bark, bitter vetch, and the bones of a small vole – caught in a trap at midnight."

"Sorrow? No, no, I …"

"I'm a physick, sir: proven remedies for all afflictions. Have a look in the bags behind you – something for every ailment, sir, if I do say so myself."

"O Uncle, I'm in no need of …"

The peasant shook his head and assumed the expression of a preacher in a pulpit. "We're all in need, sir – in one way or another. What is it that ails you sir? Sleeplessness? Disquiet? For restless legs, I recommend a tea made from prunella, musk, and the hair of a strong young man."

"Legs? I…"

"'Tis something else then, sir? Something that worries and appals? For fear of policemen, I serve a spoonful of turnip water and an adder's tongue."

"No, no…"

"Toads? Dogs? Death?"

"Death?

The peasant cocked his ear like a dog.

"What?"

"Death?"

"Breath? Sorry sir, I can't quite hear you – my trumpet is blocked up with silt. But if 'tis pestilence of the maw that ails you then you're in luck. Foulness of breath can be cured by ground liverwort, a pinch of pepper, and the milk of a cheeky goat. Makes your mouth fragrant and fresh ... that'll bring your lady back, my lord! You'll be beating the ladies off from Brno to Vienna. That's it, sir, open wide." The peasant inspected the Count's mouth as a hunter might his trap. "And for the whitening of teeth I have a paste made from white lead and plaster. Takes years off you, sir. The lady won't believe her eyes..."

The cart gave a sudden jerk and a large sack of moss fell in Mitrovsky's lap. "Have we met before, Uncle? It seems that..."

"I'm sorry, sir. My hearing is not so good and my ears are full of wax."

"Why, you saucy fellow! I'm surprised you have no cure for that..."

"What?"

"No cure!"

"O, but there's a cure for everything, sir." The peasant raised one finger and then pushed it up his nostril. "I knew this fella once, Svoboda by name – got his hand stuck in the sawmill at Chulm. Sliced his mitt clean off! But they rubbed on some ash sap and the crushed bone from a leg of a deer, and it grew back within the week – even stronger too! This Svoboda, he could fell trees without an axe, just a well-placed slap on the trunk..."

"Remarkable, quite amazing..."

"And of course you must have heard of that peasant from Tabor."

"What kind of a fool ... I mean, go on, go on."

"Well, it seemed that this fellow was fond of smoking oak leaves, because as everyone knows, smoking oak leaves is good for your constitution, but one day, on account of some passing girl, he swallowed his roll-up in one gulp, and this ember, why it started up a fire inside him, down in his belly it was, and pretty soon all of his innards were alight, and there were sparks coming from his cap and his rear."

The peasant shrugged sagely.

"Now you might think that water would put out those embers, but nothing of the sort – all that happened was that smoke poured out of him like a blocked chimney. The only cure was to add a tincture of fish oil to his jug, mixed with aniseed, camphor and those pondweeds known around here as a goose's arse. Dowsed those flames right quick, they did! The fella's insides calmed down and he was able to eat a little Hungarian salami, with some pickle on the side"

"Miraculous, quite incredible..."

"Yes, yes ... you can cure all things if you put your mind to it. One fellow, Brandejs his name was, he got sick after eating a green chicken, sick like there's no tomorrow, and his nails turned to claws and feathers started sprouting from his cheeks. O, a terrible state he was! The cure was half a cup of trotter-oil, a large swig of lemon, and a good plucking ... after that he was right as rain. 'Tis all in nature's larder, sir ... all you have to know is what to weed."

Mitrovsky nodded sagely, weighing up what few coins remained in his purse.

"My fellow, you are a marvel!"

The old man smiled modestly.

By the time the wagon reached the edge of the Count's estate – or at least what remained of it – Mitrovsky had purchased a pouch of colewart for indigestion, a tincture of nightshade for headaches, and a handful of Blessed Thistle to bolster a gentleman's performance.

"Well, fare thee well," said the old man, surveying the sorry state of Mitrovsky's house and garden. "Be of good health and may the Lord protect your body and soul."

"Goodbye, goodbye. If ever I have need of ragwort or butter bur, I'll be sure to yell…"

The peasant waved a merry goodbye, and with that the old fellow, his horse and his cures, rolled along the waggoneers' road, past a copse of alder trees, and was gone.

10

Marta poked out her head just as Count Mitrovsky staggered across the yard, singing 'The Devil with his fiddle/The Angel with his harp', and smelling of fox-glove and kelp.

"Marta!" cried the Count, stretching out his arms. "Marta, my darling, where are you?"

The old woman regarded the Count suspiciously. "What happened to you, stupid man – squirrel took your wig?"

"O Marta, Marta, the strangest thing…"

"Foo, foo … that tale is so long, it has fur on it … come inside little goose – good luck goes out with a draught…"

Marta led him from the hall to a small anteroom, pursing her tiny black lips. Still singing softly, the Count seated himself at a rickety round table while the old servant bent down to remove his boots.

"O Marta, angel of my heart – if I told you but half of what I've been through you would call me a madman."

"Ja, ja, this is a tune I've heard before…"

"It all started when I left The Five Small Carp…"

"That dump?" Marta placed one hand over her heart and put the other to her lips. "You want poison, I cook you here at home."

"No, no, no, all I was doing was looking for that bookseller, you know, the one with the wooden teeth and the blackbirds…"

"Stupid boy…"

"But this fellow, Marta, he's vanished like a mouse down a

hole, the devil take him. And now my Mařenka is going away too, the Good Lord knows where … and she wants me to watch over Lida and Lena, and take care of her husband – Betka, too, I would imagine … but Marta, my angel, who will take care of me? Who, Marta, who?"

"Who?" said Marta, removing the final boot and passing the Count his slippers. "Who, indeed?"

Marta wiped her hands on her apron and went off to fetch Mitrovsky a slice of black bread and a little pot of fat, muttering to herself under her breath. Where did she find this treasure of a master? He had a room full of brains, but the key was lost.

Meanwhile the Count leant back in his chair, pondering all the strange and fantastical things that had befallen him. The crooked bookseller, the flying carriage, the little grey horse: such wonders! But even as he contemplated these marvels, a picture of his body on the old post-road popped into Mitrovsky's head, and the Count began to shiver uncontrollably. What was it that dead rascal wanted – a coin, a prayer, a kick up the arse? True the fellow had looked just like him – but then, wasn't the Count sitting at his table right now, as real as that jug on a stool? How could he manage to be in two places at once? Not even the Pope could manage that, and there were two of him…

No, no … such thoughts would lead to the briar patch: wiser to dream of Nosek's pigeons, to plan how he might clap hands on such a pair…

Ho, if he could find this book before Mařenka took flight … if he could win her heart, convince her to take him with her, wherever she might go … with a carriage behind for Leda and Lena and maybe a little cart for Betka, with straw and her little red bowl. Mitrovsky looked at his boots as if they'd just walked in through the door. The important thing was finding this book – or if not the book, then why not Nosek himself? What did that old crone in The Five Small Carp say? He'd run away to P, taking with him his quill and pot of ink. Yes, this Nosek was bound to have a copy of his own book – or the rascal could scribble something new, why not? One nightingale, two nightingales – why not a third?

The coach to P passed along the road once a week, the post house not so very far away. Pish, squirreled away somewhere he must still have something of the Old Count's he could swap for a ticket: a candlestick or spoon or orchard of some type. P was five days there, and six days back: the important thing was to get back before Mařenka vanished, stop her flying up the chimney and out of his grasp...

And still dreaming of Mařenka, the Count fell into a long and troubled sleep.

ACT II

1

For such an important journey, the Count had donned his most distinguished travelling apparel: red silk breeches and stockings, black shoes with gold buckles, ruffles the size of cauliflowers, and one of the old Count's wigs, though in truth the old peruke was more of a cobweb than a hairpiece, a foul smelling nest for mice.

By way of luggage, Mitrovsky had with him a small chest of drawers, lined with French newspapers and filled with scraps of satin, curls of ribbon, old ladies' handkerchiefs, and brightly coloured off-cuts, the tailor's trifles soaked in camphor to deter hungry moths. Of course, such a box was hardly intended for long journeys – the edges dug into Mitrovsky's shoulders, its bulk was awkward to carry, and the drawers had a tendency to open without warning – but nevertheless a member of the nobility cannot be expected to travel without his accoutrements, and besides, a bright spool of ribbon is both a balm and a joy, as all true gentlemen know.

But O, how hot it was, how hot! The Count could feel the shadows lengthening, the grains of time ground together like pepper in a pot. Mitrovsky rested his drawers and slowly mopped his brow. The sky was enormous, cloudless, purple at the edges. The sun seemed to melt everything it touched into coloured water, rays spilling everywhere.

Sweating profusely, the Count spread out his handkerchief like a tablecloth, feasting on a slice of bread and two peppered eggs.

Aye, it was a pretty spot, right enough, the grass dry and sandy, ringed by goosefoot and little yellow flowers, the ones that peasants call angels' pee. After a few minutes the Count was joined by a glossy jackdaw, the bird cocking his head in a comically inquisitively manner. Mm, what a character! When Mitrovsky whistled 'Awake her not/'Till dawn has broken', the bird answered with a series of odd squawks and cries, singing along in unison before hunching his scrawny shoulders and giving a couple of jumps to one side.

Mitrovsky watched it cavort about gleefully and then clapped his hands, the bird taking flight, turning to a shadow, then a speck, then the merest breath. Minutes later the carriage – a handsome copper-yellow coach driven by four piebald horses – appeared around the corner, Mitrovsky heaving up his bureau and holding out one arm. Unlike the bookseller's cart, the carriage was a thing of real beauty, its lacquered doors painted with floral bouquets and the cab trimmed with red leather drapes. The Count fluttered his handkerchief and the drivers pulled on their reins, the vehicle coming to a halt in a great film of dust.

The Count's face broke through the clouds like a big hairy sun.

"One for P, my good man."

"P?"

"Or O or Q: I can walk from there."

The drivers looked at the Count's lopsided bureau, the drawer sticking out like a tongue, and scowled: what kind of goose was this? Still, a fare was a fare, the devil's coin as good as Saint Peter's. Straining under the weight, they installed Mitrovsky's tallboy on the roof and Mitrovsky's fat belly inside the cab.

"Much obliged," said the Count. "A window seat please, with a fine view of the world."

Alas, the cab was already pretty full. On one side sat a wide, matronly woman in a shawl of Flemish lace, accompanied by a young girl in a modest grey dress and rabbit-fur trim, while on the other side sat a stern looking gentleman in a long, wide-sleeved *justacorps*, worn over a vest, knee breeches and grey stockings. Next to him was a bare-headed youth with a winter scarf round his neck, and some little guy in an enormous black hat.

Betwixt the span of the ladies' hooped skirts and the height of the gentlemen's headwear, there seemed little space for a Count.

"Greetings, greetings," said Mitrovsky affably. "How wonderful to be blessed with so many charming companions on such a pleasant day!"

The fellow in grey stared at Mitrovsky as he might a louse found crawling on his collar. Then the guy in the hat tapped the door.

"What ya waitin' for – an invite from the Pope? Sit, sit – I've cleaned my teeth."

The fellow's name was Bilek, travelling to P for 'a theatrical engagement', though the exact nature of his business had to be kept secret, 'cause I got rivals everywhere.'

In particular Bilek was most concerned that his battered-old case – a small wooden box, about the size of a jeweller's casket, or a good set of knives – should stay with him at all times.

"What? You want I should tie it to the roof like a hat? What am I, an idiot? Listen, there's a crock of gold in there, a whole keg of gunpowder. The suckers in P have never seen anything like it. S'true! They'll have to change their drawers when they get a whiff of this beauty."

Mitrovsky stared at the fellow's case and licked his lips.

"Right there in that box? But – 'tis a very tiny treasure, is it not?"

Bilek had a sunken double-chin, rosy cheeks, and a generous paunch. Despite his lack of stature, his hat reached all the way up to the roof, as long and black as a chimney.

"Tiny? I tell you, kid – this box of tricks is going to blow that burg right open."

The Count nodded. Could he open it up and take a peek? No, no, not a chance: the miser held it tight, as a mother does a child, or a drunk coddles his pot. The Count bowed his head.

"Count Mitrovsky, sir. Travelling to P on literary business."

"Really? Don't take this the wrong way Mitrovsky, but you don't look the scribbling kind."

"Well…"

Mitrovsky suddenly realised that the fellow in grey was staring at him most intently, his filthy yellow eyes focused on the Count's wig and ribbons.

"Books, you say?" said the fellow, leaning in a little closer. "And these 'books' – are they, ah, volumes of a special kind?"

"Special? Well…"

At this the Count bit his tongue: I mean, who was this stiff anyway? His eyes were those of a demon, even if his clothes were as drab as a Moravian Sunday.

"Oh no, nothing special," said Mitrovsky, quickly, "just something to block out the draught. Or perhaps a thick volume to allow me to reach the shelf in my pantry."

At this he gave a little chuckle to prove that all of this talk of books was really of no great importance at all.

"And what about you, sir?" inquired the Count agreeably, "are you too interested in letters and words?"

"I travel to Hrůza on business."

"Business?"

"Business."

"And what sort of …"

"Important business."

"Yes yes, the very best kind!"

The fellow's smile was thin as a paper cut.

"Count … Mitrovsky, is it?"

"Mitrovsky, yes, yes…"

At this the stern-faced gentleman picked up a quill and scroll.

"M … I … T … R…"

The gentleman wrote in a great black ledger, its pages smelling of tobacco and mould.

Watching him, the Count gave an awkward little laugh and fluttered his handkerchief distractedly. Something about the fellow's horrible filmy eyes unnerved him – it was as if there was something terrible inside him, just peering out.

Smacking his chops, the Count turned to the fellow sitting opposite, addressing him in the most cheerful of tones

"And you my good lad – where are you bound, and for what purpose?"

The young fella gave a shy smile, his eyes as gentle as a cow's.

"The kid 'aint got no voice," said Bilek, butting in. "It's why he's wearing that muffler. Look, here's his card."

Mitrovsky took the small square from Bilek and read it swiftly: 'My Name is Janos Halas. My throat is enflamed. Can you please direct me to Doctor Pustrpolk, 5 Temný Street, P? I do not know the way.'

"Ah," said Mitrovsky. He handed the card back to the young man, who smiled back like a saint. "Hello, hello," boomed the Count. "Can you really not say a word?"

The boy nodded sadly and produced another card: 'Is Temný Street far? I have nowhere to spend the night.'

"O, you poor, poor lad," bawled the Count, his handkerchief reeking of *Lillas de Perse*. "Don't you worry, my lad, we'll take care of you, won't we, eh?"

The lady sitting across the way nodded with her beautiful double chin. "O my dear Count – I tried to feed him a pancake and the lad just shook his head. What's a boy to live on – fresh air and dreams? O, my Count, 'tis not right, a young man drinking his dinner through a straw…"

Madame Jedličová was travelling with her daughter to P where the young lady was to join the Nuns of the Order of the Visitation at Žádost. The convent? Yes, a strict order, but very pure. The girl, Eliška, gazed sullenly out of the window, brows pulled shut, but Madame Jedličová was a lively old soul, bubbling away like a pot on a stove.

"Here, try some honey cakes – look, some of 'em have poppy seeds as well…"

"O-o-o-o," said the Count, spraying crumbs all over the carriage. "What happy bees to make such sweetness!"

At this, Madame Jedličová made space for the Count to sit beside her, plopping her enormous straw bag on her lap.

"You're too kind, my dear Count … here try some of the shredded pancake … look, there's sugar in the bag…"

The Count rolled his eyes in ecstasy. "Beautiful, beautiful!"

The Count swept a whole mess of sugary dough from his britches.

"So your charming daughter is to become a, whatjamacallit, novice. You must be very proud."

The girl squirmed, pressing herself flat against the door like a painting.

"O yes," said Mrs Jedličová. "'Tis a great honour."

"The Convent at Žádost, you say?"

"Yes, yes … it's all been arranged by the girl's uncle. For I am a poor widow, as you see."

Mitrovsky nodded, though in truth there was nothing about Madame Jedličová to suggest mourning in any way. "O my darling! What a calamitous misfortune to afflict one so young."

Mrs Jedličová's beautiful eyes shone with a strange light.

"Here, have a *vdolky*… they're delicious."

Mitrovsky nodded and shifted his belt to a more commodious notch.

"Ah, my dove! Were they baked by an angel?"

"O my darling Count! Why, you'll make a poor widow blush …"

And with that he felt Mrs Jedličová's hand land on his arm, her palm light as a crumb.

2

Yes, it was another beautiful summer's day. Outside, the countryside glittered with a cheerful light, the fields flat and hard-edged, as if etched in stained glass. Great clouds of golden dust rose up from the track, sticking to the horses, the drivers, everything. It was as if the entire kingdom of Bohemia had been stretched out by some great celestial rolling pin, the land as hot and flat as a biscuit.

Despite the crush, the carriage was comfortable and well-sprung, and soon the Count felt very much at home, crunching on sunflower seeds and telling tales to make Mrs Jedličová laugh.

"… and when I came back in the morning, the whole out-house was gone! Fat Slánsky had tied it to his cart and led it away like a cow. O, what a thief! But he said he needed the wood to build a bathhouse, so what was I to do? Besides, should Slánsky and his wife go around caked in mud? And with seven children to feed …"

"O Count," said Mrs Jedličová touching his arm, "you are far too tender-hearted, I fear. And look at you, practically wasting away…"

"Me? Oh…"

"It's true – like the crows have stripped your bones. Here, have some more pancake – you'll blow away on a strong wind! Eliška move up and give the Count some room."

The girl shuffled along, still retaining her sullen silence. Pff, why did she have to sit next to this fat slob? The world was full of idiots, as a pomegranate is full of seeds.

Oblivious, Mitrovsky smiled and took a bow. Behind the curtain, the landscape opened outwards, as flat and distinct as a picturebook. First, they crossed an old wooden bridge, then they skirted a tumbledown mill, and eventually they trundled alongside a wild and bedraggled orchard, wasp-filled plums littering the yellow grass. Fortunately, the road was good and the carriage's heavy iron wheels rolled smoothly and cheerfully, the world unfurling like a scroll painted by children, or a brush tied to a stick.

For lunch, they stopped at 'The Pike's Tail', where they ate cooked chicken hearts and floury dumplings outside on long wooden tables. The inn was lively and busy. Near the back stairs, a troupe of soldiers in bright, child-like costumes sang patriotic songs, while over by the trees a party of lumber merchants broke bread together noisily, their pointy beards dipping in the soup. The landlord – a coarse, knobbly turnip of a fellow, with ears like flowery growths – carried trays of beer hither and thither, tripping up and down the steps without ever spilling a drop. Inside the kitchen his wife could be heard singing 'Hurry Home My Darling', and from time to time even their old arthritic mutt staggered to his feet, tottering from his resting place to go and look for scraps.

"What a marvellous spot," sighed the Count, wiping the sweat from his eyes. "I'm sure I've seen it in a painting somewhere, eh, Master Bilek, eh?"

Bilek shrugged and sniffed his chicken heart suspiciously. "You think these hearts are cooked? I…"

Mrs Jedličová eyed up his plate. "'Tish – they just need a little more pepper is all. Here, help yourself to my dumplings – you travelling gentlemen, you never get a proper cooked meal, wasting away you are… Eliška! Eliška! Don't you dare nod off!"

Mrs Jedličová's daughter had her head resting in the crook of her arm, her hair spilling out over her plate.

"Eliška! Are you listening?"

The girl stirred and pushed her plate aside with a sigh.

"I can't get her to eat a thing," said Mrs Jedličová in a loud whisper. "Eats like a bird. I only hope the Sisters can get something hot into her … heaven knows, I've tried…"

"These hearts don't taste like no bird," said Bilek, resting his knife and fork by his side. "These chicks never clucked in their life."

"Foo, these hearts are delicious," said the Count, spearing one with his fork. "Here, my dear Master Halas, why don't you try one?"

The mild young man looked at the heart, blinked twice, and pointed at his scarf.

"O, you poor pup!" boomed the Count. "Here, let me clear your plate!"

Drenched in golden sunshine, the garden teemed with life. Grasshoppers clicked, mosquitoes buzzed, and swallows darted left and right as if the very air were made of soup.

"You can never tell with these country places," complained the sour-faced fellow, licking his quill. "Any filthy peasant thinks he can put out a table, but does he wash his hands after milking?"

"Oh, hush," said the Count. "Everyone likes a little shit with their cheese! Ah, beg my pardon, ladies…"

Mrs Jedličová tittered and placed a cloth to her brow.

"I mean, in the countryside, one does not stand on convention. A cow pat here, a cow pat there…"

At this point the Count seemed to lose his thread and lapsed into a satisfied silence, a smear of sauce on his cheek.

"These hearts are definitely screwy," said Bilek, sweating. "You ask me, they didn't come from no egg."

"The Emperor's laws on cleanliness are very strict," expounded the fellow with the book. "Livestock should be removed from all sites of food preparation. Rodents are not permitted in pots or cooking vessels. Aprons must be washed in lime and doused in vinegar…"

"Isn't that the dead?"

"It's all written down, right here in this book."

"I don't feel so good…"

"Master Bilek?"

"S'not right…"

"Master Bilek, are you quite well?"

"Quick, quick, outta my way!"

And with that the impresario leapt to his feet, holding onto his innards as if they might come undone at any minute.

Mrs Jedličová blinked. "Master Bilek, can we help?"

Alas, the *impresario* did not answer; instead, he took off to the privy with some alacrity, holding onto his middle as he ran. The Count watched him go, smacking his lips contentedly.

"He moves awful quick for such a tiny fellow."

For a moment the party lapsed into an uncertain silence.

"These hearts do smell a bit funny," said Mrs Jedličová, bending down to sniff his plate. "Maybe we should…"

"Oh, 'tis just the heat," said the Count, his head hot and red like a griddle. "The fellow will be right as rain in a moment."

Mitrovsky felt a wet nose pressing against his lap and looked down to where the landlord's ancient hound was staring up at him adoringly.

"Ah, you're an old fellow aren't you?"

The Count reached down to pat the elderly mutt and spied Master Bilek's case all alone on the bare ground, the box looking lost and forlorn, like an abandoned child.

'Why, what's this?' reflected the count, giving the bag a crafty kick. 'The little fellow's prize if I'm not very much mistaken.'

Nothing about the case seemed special, though the clasp was sealed with a large copper lock. What was it that the little fellow was hiding? Something screwy, for sure. If he cocked his head to one side, Mitrovsky could hear a vague buzzing inside the box, like a small, muffled voice, or some kind of bee practicing its scales.

"Eliška!" boomed Mrs Jedličová, banging the table, "Eliška, you goose, wake up!"

The Count gave a jump, banging his head on the table.

"Eliška, what did I tell you? Don't you dare nod off…"

The girl looked back at her mother with an expression of infinite weariness, black lines painted 'neath her eyes.

"M'tired," mouthed the girl.

"My girl, you know as well as I…"

"Leave me alone. Wanna sleep…"

"Later, Eliška, later, when all is safe…"

Mrs Jedličová was interrupted by the sight of the landlord carrying a tray of enormous mugs, the beer glowing like buttercups in the sun.

Mitrovsky smacked his full, meaty lips. "O-o-o… soft and honeyed as a bear's paw…"

Halas grinned foolishly and burped. Then he shuffled around in his pockets and produced a card reading 'Excuse me'.

"What a lovely meal," said Mrs Jedličová, downing her pot with a satisfied gasp. "What a shame that Master Bilek is missing it. Should I go and check on him, do you think? He seems to have been gone for an awfully long time…"

"Oh, he'll be fine," said Mitrovsky grinning. "Who could die on a day like this?"

As he spoke, the soldiers' singing at the next table became ever more raucous and unruly, the strains of 'By the Stream/Young Anna was sitting' drifting up from their steins.

"A jolly company, no?" said the Count with a wink, only then remembering Mrs Jedličová's daughter and her tender ears.

"Disgraceful," muttered the pinch-faced fellow gripping his pen. "Those lyrics are unbefitting decent company. Why, the swine! I'm going to write them down in my book, you see if I don't."

The Count waved his arms dismissively. "Tsk – no need for clouds on a sunny day! You sit here and I'll go and talk to them. I've had some dealing in military matters, um, soldiers and muskets and the like…"

With that the Count waddled over to the ensemble, the soldiers decked out as if for a pantomime, singing lustily and perfectly in tune.

"What ho, lads!" announced the Count cheerily. "A quick break from the hundred years war, is it?"

The troupe seemed a merry bunch, readily accepting the Count's offer of a mug of black beer and a plate of rye bread smeared with grease. There was a drummer in a broad, gold-trimmed cap, a laconic pike-man with a big black sash, a scrawny powder-monkey, and a long bearded infantryman with a canary-yellow beard.

"Much obliged m'lord," said the drummer, removing his cap, "kind of you to think of us."

"Off on manoeuvres, are we? Not off to war, I hope!" said the Count with a wink, holding onto his belly and roaring loudly.

"No, sir, nothin' like that. We're off to O, sir – catch up with our battalion."

"But not too fast, eh, eh? Yes, yes … 'tis a good life in the army…"

"Sir?"

"And such beautiful costumes! Just look at the braiding on that sleeve…"

In truth, the uniforms seemed a little ill-fitting, as if the duty manager had supplied the wrong size, or there'd been some kind of mix up in camp. The sleeves seemed too long, the hats too big, the large, heavy cloaks swamping the tiny men and their comical weapons. The belts were loose, the colours over bright. Rather than soldiers, they looked like children who had discovered the dressing-up box, or members of the chorus-line, dressed in a hurry.

"Thank you kindly, sir. Josef here, he did the sewing himself."

Josef the powder-monkey, blushed timidly, showing off the fine filigree on his cuffs.

"'Tis thread from Dresden, m'lord."

"Beautiful, beautiful – you're a credit to your corps."

Aye, a fine bunch of lads – all of a sudden the Count felt the need to curry favour, or impress.

"My brother, Matej – he serves in the army. The forty-third I believe – or maybe seven sixes…"

"We're the thirty-sixth sir – we don't know no forty-third…"

"Ah…"

"The thirty-fifth yes – we'd even break bread with the thirty-seven. But not the forty-third, sir … we don't know 'em at all…"

Mitrovsky patted the powder-monkey on his head. "Well, well fear not – what is a few numbers between friends? But my brother, eh, Matej … perhaps if you see him you could give him this ribbon, let him know that I'm thinking about him – his brother, Karel, can you say? 'Tis a most beautiful ribbon, the colour of a robin's egg…"

Josef looked at the ribbon and nodded. "Tis a beautiful bit of bobbin, sir…"

"Yes, yes – it most certainly is! I'm sure that Matej will be able to use it – tell him that his brother sends a kiss! Thank you gentlemen, thank you most heartily…"

The men raised their cups and the Count slowly backed away, whistling the tune to 'Hearts that love/at dusk are riven' while fluffing up his sleeves. When he looked back, the cast of soldiers seemed more like children than ever, their britches too big, hats over-hanging, tiny hands lost inside voluminous sleeves. O what games are played!

Marching back to his table in what he imagined to be strict military fashion, Mitrovsky was accosted by Mrs Jedličová, her beautiful hands all a flutter.

"Count Mitrovsky! So that's where you've got to, you naughty man."

"Madame?"

"I went to check on Master Bilek and now my Eliška has disappeared – wandered from the path."

"Path?"

Mrs Jedličová's beautiful cheeks were flushed.

"Yes, yes … she's gone, drifted away, my little bird! Count Mitrovsky, my darling man – might you go and check on Mister Bilek – make sure he's still in the land of the living? I need to look for Eliška – she's really a very special girl, you've no idea…"

"Hm, Bilek, well … of course my dear, of course, you can count on me! Worry not, my sweet princess, I'm sure no harm has befallen your beautiful daughter. What could happen on such a beautiful day? Pish posh, leave it to me. I'll fish Bilek out with a net."

"What a kind man…"

"'Tis nothing, nothing at all…"

The privy was little more than a dilapidated hut, located somewhere to the rear of the inn. A scribble of flies floated cheerfully above it, dead grass marking the threshold.

"Master Bilek? Master Bilek, are you there?"

As he approached, Mitrovsky smelt a terrible stench emanating from behind the ill-hung door. Handkerchief clutched to his mouth, the Count held his breath and crept a little closer.

"Master Bilek?"

No answer. The flies buzzed merrily, but from time to time could be heard a sound too terrible to be put into words. Undeterred, the Count pressed on.

"What ho, my fellow, are you there?"

"Get lost!"

"Sir, I come to your aid…"

"I said beat it, you ape."

By now the Count had made it all the way to the wooden plank.

"My dear fellow, fear not!" boomed Mitrovsky. "Whatever happens, I will stay with you – aye to the very end! What is it that philosophers say? Even death is bearable in good company…"

"What a minute … Mitrovsky, is that you?"

"Yes, yes, 'tis I! Madame Jedličová was concerned for your soul and…"

"Knock it off you clown. Listen, you gotta get my gravy…"

"Gravy?"

"My case. I need you to make sure it's okay."

"But of course! Why, I…"

"Make sure no crook has filched it…"

The Count wrinkled his nose, holding his handkerchief to his lips. "Worry not, sweet prince! I will ensure your case…"

At that a terrible sound issued from Master Bilek's backside, and the Count took two steps back.

"Master Bilek, Master Bilek, are you still there?"

"The bag Mitrovsky…"

"Okay, okay…"

"Go get it now."

"The case, why yes indeed."

Mitrovsky bowed like a courtier and scuttled back toward the Inn. Bilek didn't sound so good: maybe those weren't chicken hearts after all? What was it Father Smiřicky always said? 'The most awful terrors come from the darkest holes.'

When Mitrovsky got back to the table he found the yellow-eyed fellow with the pen trying to jimmy Bilek's bag with a knife.

The Count stopped and stared.

"Ah..."

The fellow pulled a sour face and put down the knife. "What? Why are you looking at me like that? Bilek's case tumbled over, and I was trying to fix the lock..."

"What kind of idiot do you take me for?" demanded the Count, pushing out his chest. "I can clearly see that! But Master Bilek is much exercised on the subject of this bag and anxious no harm should befall it."

"Of course, of course..." The fellow's smile was as thin as a spider's leg. "Why, I was thinking the very same thing."

Mitrovsky paused. "Really?"

"Why yes, I was just keeping it safe..."

"Safe, ah, yes indeed."

With great reluctance the box was handed over, a soft buzzing coming from within.

"Why thank you sir. I shall return it to, forthwith."

"Yes, yes..." And with that the fellow went back to scribbling in his book.

What a swine, thought the Count: he'd pick God's pocket, if you let him. And those eyes! Like the peepers of an owl or some such bird. Why, you felt dirty just looking at them.

The Count whistled a little tune and banged the side of the box: oh, what mystery was contained within! Perhaps he could just open one catch and take a peek… but then he felt a hand on his back and leapt up like a cat.

It was Young Halas, his genial face poking up from his scarf as if he'd just woken up.

"Hello my fine lad!" boomed the Count, hiding the case behind his back. "Why, I was just, er…"

Halas regarded the Count with an expression of great innocence, like that of an angel, or an idiot.

"Well my lad, what is it you need? Master Bilek has charged me with retrieving his gravy and, um…"

The lad took Mitrovsky by the arm and steered him across the beer garden to a secluded area, the land all dark and boggy, as if the site of a spring. There, standing all on her own, was Eliška, the girl as still as a drawing, her eyes closed as if at prayer.

Mitrovsky looked at Halas uncertainly.

"The girl! But…"

Halas blinked and pointed toward where the maiden was standing. What a peculiar pose! The girl stood stock still like a statue, one slipper suspended in mid-air, the other plopped in the mire.

Mitrovsky gasped.

"Those beautiful, beautiful slippers! But what on earth…"

The Count looked from Halas to Eliška and back again. Was she under some kind of spell, dazed asleep? The girl's face was expressionless, her eyes like the first drops of rain on dusty ground. One foot up and one foot down – like a stork.

"Is she asleep? 'Tis most strange and remarkable. Perhaps you should go and find Mrs Jedličová. I find that ladies usually know what to do."

Waiting for Halas to return, the Count inspected the girl's character most wonderingly. Should he wake her, shake her, pluck her from the mud? He was awfully worried about Eliška's slippers – and such pretty fabric too! As he inched a little closer – careful to save his own boots from the muck – he felt a strange coolness pass over the hot summer's day, though in truth there was not a cloud in the sky. Nevertheless, the Count felt a cloistered chill that seemed to emanate from another world – the convent at Žádost, perhaps. Cold walls, cold stone, a musty dampness – or was it just the scent of the old Count's wig? Before he could figure it out, Mrs Jedličová entered stage left, pursued by Master Halas, the landlord, and the landlord's dog.

"O my chick, there she is, wandered from the path!"

Mrs Jedličová's beautiful – but powerful – arms plucked Eliška from the mire, mother and daughter gratefully reunited.

"Stupid, wicked girl! What do I tell you about falling asleep? Now look what you've done – and in front of all these fine gentlemen, too."

The fine gentlemen all looked a little shifty: the landlord's dog likewise.

"Right, back to the carriage with you – and look at your slippers! Do you think such things grow at the bottom of the garden? Wayward girl!"

At the sound of her mother's voice the girl slowly opened her eyes.

"M'tired."

"Hush now, you wicked thing. Look what these gentlemen have done for you…"

Mitrovsky put up his hands. "O Madam!"

"Hush, such a kind soul you are … and look at you, barely had time for a snack, what with all the fuss and commotion…"

"No, no, I…"

"Skinny as a way-post. Naughty girl! You see what you've done."

And so it was that the party's stay at 'The Pike's Tail' came to a somewhat premature end. Master Bilek was liberated from the privy and re-united with his strong-box. Eliška was freed from her dream and re-united with her slipper. Mitrovsky was re-united with a chunk of cheese in his pocket and nibbled at it thoughtfully.

"Well, 'tis all a strange business, is it not?" he whispered to Halas, brushing the crumbs from his lap. "What do you think, my lad? Some kind of devilment or plot?"

Halas blinked and handed the Count a card.

'This isn't Temný Street', it read. 'Where are we going?'

The Count looked at the card uncomprehendingly. "No, no," he said, "Temný Street it is not."

The cabbies busied themselves preparing the horse and carriage, and then it was time to go.

3

Afterward, the mood in the coach seemed somewhat subdued: Mrs Jedličová watched her daughter, Master Bilek watched his case, and the sour-faced scoundrel watched his book. But what of it? Outside the wheat was still yellow, the grass green, the sky a deep blue – why, a child could have drawn it! And as the sun shone, the carriage rolled forth on its smooth metal wheels, the day as long as a length of rope.

Mitrovsky spent the time snoozing and dreaming of Mařenka. Whatever did she mean by her instruction for the Count to assist Anton and the girls? What kind of assistance did they require? It seemed to the Count that the Drtikols already had everything, that he was the one with holes in his boots. Well, no matter. Instead of worrying about such things he occupied his idleness by picturing Mařenka's creamy stockings, the sweet little bows on her hoop-skirt, the butterfly broach in her wig. Was she old or was she young? Was she married or was she not? The picture seemed pleasantly woozy somehow, as if made hazy by the sun.

The Count was still dreaming of Mařenka when he noticed Young Master Halas mooning over Mrs Jedličová's daughter, Eliška, with a most foolish look on his mug. Was he sweet on the poor girl? Well, how could he not be? Were not women the sun around which all men turned? The Count looked at the young lover with a fond grin – why he made him think of himself! And that in turn made him think of Mařenka and her beautiful, beautiful trim…

It was still light when they reached the village of S, the hamlet too small to warrant any other letters. S was a small, forgettable affair: houses with sagging timbers and piebald thatch, a smoky ironsmith's shack, and a run-down store, pigs bathing in the late evening sunshine. On one side of the road a woman in bare feet was chopping wood, while on the other a peasant in a greasy cap was nailing the same bits back together. In short: no Vienna,

The coaching inn, its walls the colour of coarse tobacco, was the largest building in town, looking out onto what may have been a pleasant little garden if not for the great rubbish heap dumped in the centre. As the coach and horses pulled up alongside it, a big black watchdog came rushing out, one of the cabbies jumping down and driving it back with his whip. Only when Mitrovsky descended the steps did the beast calm down, the wolf fussing around him as if the pup had known the Count all its life.

The innkeeper – an ill-looking fellow with deep smallpox scars and unpleasantly yellowish skin – welcomed the travellers and led them to the public room: a large empty space covered in dry straw, with only a single threadbare curtain to separate the sexes. Examining the veil, Mrs Jedličová immediately took fright. No, no, this would never do, her daughter required, 'special provision' and the addition of a lock and key. Shaking his head, the landlord escorted Mrs Jedličová and Eliška up a set of wooden stairs, leaving the gentlemen to find a cosy nook on their own.

"Why, this will do for our needs," said the Count, slapping Young Halas on the back. "Aye, I've slept in worse ditches, right enough."

Bilek looked at the Count's beard and nodded. "No kidding.

Hey, has anybody seen the out-house? My insides are still a bit dicky, if you know what I mean."

Supper was pork knuckles served with a jug of mustard – what Count Mitrovsky insisted on calling 'the sweet, sweet, fruit of the pig'. Bilek ate little, but Mrs Jedličová insisted that the Count should fill his face, loading up his plate whenever she could. O what a dish! Outside it seemed as if the day would go on forever, but when night came, it came suddenly, like a black cloth thrown over a cage.

Mitrovsky yawned, Master Halas nodded off at the table, and before long the ladies retired to their room. Aye, it was time to sleep. Fortunately, the public room was pretty empty. A couple of horse-dealers, with long scraggly whiskers and long scraggly cloaks, curled up together in one corner, while a dark, hairy drover, completely inebriated, lay in a heap by the door. As for the cabbies – who knows? Perhaps they slept like horses in the stables, or perhaps they hung from a barn like bats; it was late by now and no one had time for any more mysteries.

After such a long day's travel, the room seemed to sway from side to side, just like the carriage. The horse dealers soon set to snoring, and from time to time Mitrovsky could hear the gentle scritch-scratch of a family of mice, searching through the luggage for crumbs.

Sometime after midnight, the Count was awoken by the sound of a most violent eruption inside Master Bilek's innards, the poor fellow being still afflicted by the squits. With a vigour and urgency unexpected in such a tiny man, the impresario made his way to the privy with the utmost haste, a foul smell pursuing him like the Devil.

One of the Count's big black eyes opened, then the other.

Aye, there was the fellow's mysterious vessel and there was the fellow's jacket, the key to the lock tucked inside. What was in the case, anyway? The world's seven treasures or some other dish. It wasn't as if the Count had any intention of stealing anything: he simply wanted to see.

Rolling his bulk to one side, the Count stretched out a meaty paw and caressed the side of the fellow's bag.

Again, it seemed that he could hear something humming or buzzing within, like a trapped mosquito or a tiny orchestra, the musicians scooped up and placed in a bag. O, if only he could take a peek! Rolling over twice more, the Count came to a rest by Bilek's frock coat. Surely, this was where Bilek would keep the passkey, in some kind of leather sack or purse? There was little light in the room, and Bilek's things were in one of the darkest corners, but still: light enough for a peep?

Keeping his breathing low and steady, the black-eyed Count poked his fingers into Master Bilek's jacket – only to encounter another handful of fingers there before him. The two hands froze, then caressed one other rather tentatively. The foreign hand had long fingers, sharp nails, and odd calluses, as if rubbed by a stick or a quill; Mitrovsky's paw was large, hairy and soft. Immediately the digits disentangled: in what little light there was, Mitrovsky could make out two yellow eyes staring back at him malignly: the fellow with the pen. The Count attempted a crooked smile, but neither spoke. Instead, each rolled silently back to their spot, like a fox going back to its den, or the dead climbing back in their graves. Neither spoke of the incident again.

4

It was another beautiful morning, but – with the exception of the beatific Master Halas – the passengers seemed out of sorts, even the horses acting a little skittish, pulling back on the bit, biting at the drivers with their long, yellow teeth. Still, why should they tarry? There were still many leagues to go, and 'twas best to set off 'fore the sun climbed too high in the sky.

Breakfast was porridge with millet, and for the gentlemen, coffee made from chicory. Master Bilek would take neither, and the dour-faced fellow – O if only he had a name! – got some kind of seed stuck in his teeth.

"Will we get to the town of Hrůza before nightfall?" he inquired of the drivers, somewhat irritably. "I have important business and…"

"God willing, we'll be there, sir."

"Well, you make sure that we do." The fellow clicked his heels together like an Austrian. "I'm noting down your schedule, right here in black and white, don't you think I'm not…"

The drivers laboriously hauled the travellers' luggage back atop the coach, Mitrovsky's bureau at the edge, scuffed at the corners. Some strips of lavender coloured silk tumbled out from the chest of drawers, but these were soon found, and when the drawers were tied shut with string, the carriage finally got underway.

The sky was blue as a baby's eye, without a cloud to be seen. Though the road danced and quivered in the heat, everything else seemed incredibly vivid and clear, from the feathers of a blackbird to each individual head of corn. It was as if some great glass had been placed over the carriage, rendering the world, perfectly visible yet terribly, terribly hot.

The first post-house was by the river Nudný, the second at a farm on the outskirts of a hamlet too tiny to even merit a letter, never mind a name. How small was it? Smaller than the dot of the letter 'i'. There the carriage stopped to take on provisions for the day's travel – bread and millet cakes, smoked sausage and an enormous jug of something sticky and red and flavoured with damson berries.

Though its timbers bowed like an old man, the farm was a most pleasant spot, with a hutch, a henhouse, pigsty, and shed for the goats. For some reason, the apple tree in front of the farmhouse was dotted with items of underwear – pantaloons, stockings, scanties and the like – as if a washing line had snapped, or the garments had been left where carefree lovers had cast them off the night before.

The cabbie hollered and a middle-aged woman, red of face and ample of portion, and came out with a large straw basket and a generous smile, dressed in a plain white night-dress, despite the lateness of the hour.

"'Tis a hot one, sir," she said cheerfully, blowing a strand of hair from her eyes. "Barely worth getting dressed at all... here you are, sirs, ten thalers for the lot."

The cabbies looked a little flustered and struggled to meet her eyes.

"Aye, 'tis awful hot."

"Hot."

The woman beamed and playfully pulled at the first cabbie's

cap. "Ooo, and you poor lads up there in the crow's nest ... why it must be as hot as an oven, you poor scamps! Why not unbutton that jacket, eh ... take off that cap..."

"M'okay," said one.

"Kay."

The peasant woman winked, opening up her dress and blowing inside as if cooling down a cake.

"O you lads! Always so right and proper. Imagine a world where we didn't have to wear anything at all – oh, would be Heaven on a day like this..."

The cabbies blushed and hurried off with the woman's wares, looking most hot and uncomfortable.

"Thanking you kindly..."

"Kind."

The woman looked about to say something else, when a gruff peasant voice yelled "Jana, Jana, where are you?" and the woman smiled, blew back a lock of golden hair, and hurried back upstairs.

"What's wrong?" she yelled, to someone inside. "Didja miss me?"

The drivers looked at one another and pulled a face, the pair as alike as a mirror and its reflection.

"Well, she seems a merry soul," said the Count to Mrs Jedličová as the carriage set off once more.

"I've heard that peasant folk have four stomachs – just like cows," said Mrs Jedličová, wisely. "One for bread, one for beer, one for milk, and the other, ah, I forget..."

"Is that so?" said the Count, stroking his beard in wonder. "Do you know, I once knew a fella who could could eat anything – dirt, clay, nails, glass. 'Twas a wonder! Enormous head, strong brown teeth ... no, hold on I'm getting him mixed up with a horse..."

At this a white nightie suddenly flew out of an upstairs window to cheerfully join its companions.

"Aye, peasants are a merry lot," said Mrs Jedličová, punching the Count's arm. "No wonder they're always singing."

"Really?" said the Count, watching the nightie dangle from the tree. "I always thought that was the birds…"

The night-dress hung there like a white cloud caught in a net, a robin chattering angrily.

"Yes, yes, 'tis a healthy life," said Mrs Jedličová thoughtfully. "It must be lovely to eat peas straight from the pod, drink cream straight from the cow."

The Count nodded. "It's why country folk live as long as trees – all that fresh air and sunshine…"

Mrs Jedličová nodded, searching in her bag for a snack.

The third post-house was again by the River Nudný, the sight of which caused the fellow with the yellow eyes to bang the side of the carriage and complain bitterly.

"Why are we stopping again? Such delays are completely unacceptable. I have obligations in Hrůza and …"

The nearest cabbie chewed on a stalk of grass, shielding his eyes from the sun.

"'Tis a hot day, sir. Need to change horses. We'll get there soon enough."

"Soon enough," said his mate.

The fellow's eyes bulged unpleasantly. "Soon, soon? I don't think you realise the importance of my task, you rascal, you swine," but in response, the drivers pulled the self-same expression, as if they shared the same face.

"It can't be helped, my good man," said the Count. "Here, come and join us for some nutty cake and a cup of sour milk."

The fellow looked at the Count and muttered something under

his breath: idiot, clot, goose, that sort of thing.

"I'm writing it all down … right here in black and white!"

Then he took himself and his book over to the shaded side of the cab where he wrote furiously, constantly crossing out and correcting his entries, his quill racing across the page like a ragged squirrel's tail, his ink pot balanced by his side.

The party had rested by the riverbank for nearly an hour when a most peculiar personage made his way along the road, his shape so singular that at first it seemed impossible to make head or tail of it.

The figure – crookbacked, wrinkled, and lacking anything below the knees – shuffled along on two thickly bound stumps, the vagrant without sticks or carriage or feet at all. Aye, he was a wild fellow, sure enough. He wore a ragged jerkin, filthy brown britches, and had nails grown to talons and claws. His only concession to propriety was a sweet-bag of lavender worn around his neck, which did indeed bestow upon his person a most pleasant and agreeable odour, not at all in keeping with his tattered appearance. On his back was a pigskin bag, tied together with hemp.

"Greetings!" he yelled, approaching the picnickers on his stumps. "Share a bite to eat in Jesu's name?"

"And where are you going, you poor unfortunate scamp?" asked Mrs Jedličová, her voice filled with tender concern.

The fellow grinned, revealing a mouth vacant save for one rotted stump. "O, here, there, round and about. I don't like to stay still, you see Madame: 'tis in my nature. I'm born to roam."

Mrs Jedličová nodded and looked down at the parcelled butt-ends 'neath his britches. "But your legs?"

"Taken by the heathen Turks, Madame. Though what good it did 'em, that's not for knowing…"

"Turks?" The Count scanned the horizon somewhat

apprehensively. "What would the Turks be doing round here?"

The fella smiled.

"No, no … back when I was off a-warring … oh, many long years ago now … Turks took 'em clean off with a cannon ball, and though I looked and looked, I never did find 'em, curse my toes."

"A soldier?" At the mention of soldiering, Mitrovsky's black eyes seemed to shine. "Then perhaps you knew my brother? A brave lad, he too went off to war…"

"Your brother?"

The old soldier shook his head and patted the Count's knees somewhat tenderly.

"No, no – 'tis many years since I last fought, sir. Your brother would have been but a bairn…"

"O sir, sir, I would say not! His name was Matej – perhaps you know it?"

At this, the tramp-about's cloudy eyes became sober and reflective.

"Yes, yes, I knew a Matej once…"

"Yes?"

"Why, that's my name! Matej!"

"What?"

"My name, sir, – Matej they call me…"

Mitrovsky looked confused, and slowly patted the veteran on his back…

"I'm sorry, my dear fellow. I'm speaking of another Matej, I believe…"

"Yes, yes, Matej! That's me!"

"I think you are getting your Matejs mixed up, my good fellow," said the Count. "My brother, Matej, he, ah, well… let's say no more about it. He had two good legs for a start! Besides, he, um…"

With this the two drivers appeared, pulling angry faces, and shooing the beggar away like a goose.

"That's it, off you go – don't you be bothering these good ladies and gentlemen with your prattle."

The veteran, however, was not about to give up his nutty cake so easily. Instead of backing off, he stood his ground, pulling on the last few curly hairs on his head.

"Hrůza, sir?"

"Sorry?"

"Heading to Hrůza, are we, sir?" said the tramp, one eye fixed on the cabbies, the other on Mitrovsky's wig.

"What's it to you?"

"Have to turn this cart around, me laddies! Can't get through this-aways. Bridge is down – Slavik the wagon-driver drove over it with a full load of tanner's dye, and the whole lot plopped right in. S'true sir! Turned the whole river purple – the bridge's been closed ever since."

The drivers looked at the legless fellow suspiciously.

"Closed, you say? And when did this happen, if we might ask?"

"Just two days ago. Look – you can still see where the weeds were dyed the colour of periwinkles."

And indeed, the tramp was right: the water was indeed something of a plum colour, a lilac-coloured heron looking for violet fish.

The two cabbies spat simultaneously: perhaps the old fool was right.

"And there's no other way across, you say?"

"Not in these parts, sirs," said the soldier, sucking on a piece of cake with his gums. "You'd better turn back, take another route…"

At this, the fellow with the yellow eyes popped up and down like a jumping jack. "This is completely unacceptable! I'm writing all this down, don't you dare try to stop me…"

What should the cabbies do? The horses lacked wings and could not fly. Instead, they had to slowly, laboriously turn the carriage around, a manoeuvre involving unhitching the animals and manipulating the cab by hand. It was hot, difficult work, and sweat poured from the drivers' backs. Finally, though, the carriage was facing in the opposite direction.

"Much obliged to you sir," said Mitrovsky, slipping the footless vagabond a coin. "Will you join us, Uncle? We can take you as far as you wish to go."

The fellow beamed but slowly shook his head. "Thank you kindly sir, but I prefer to make my own way. 'Tis a beautiful day, and I don't have nothing to do with my time but rambling … but I will help myself to more of that nutty cake if there's any going begging…"

The fellow's black tongue picked out the last few crumbs, beaming as if it were his name day.

"Thank you sirs, thank you madam. Giving food to a beggar is like storing up treasure in Heaven. Goodbye, goodbye! I'm bound for the next hill. If I see your Matej I'll tell him."

And with that the fellow slowly took his leave, wandering across the countryside as if searching for his toes, or some other great treasure.

"Didn't he say his name was Matej?" said the Count as the carriage overtook the tramp, throwing up a great cloud of dust.

Mrs Jedličová pulled a face.

"O, I think he was somewhat addled, on account of the sun."

Watching his stumps disappear, the Count quietly nodded his head.

"Yes, yes … but to have no legs … it's a sad thing. Do you think we should have given him a bit of sausage? He looked awful hungry."

Mrs Jedličová patted the good Count's arm. "Don't you worry

about that chap, my dear count – he'll be fine. All that lovely exercise and such a pretty day – fie, he'll be as right as rain."

Mitrovsky's big black eyes blinked slowly

"Really? Well, perhaps. But I should have given him something – even if just some thread or a lovely bit of cloth. Ah, me! Alas, alas! Poor Matej."

But it was all too late. The horses hurried on and by now the soldier was a thing of the past.

Afterward, Mitrovsky settled back in his seat, his thoughts inevitably turning from the legless tramp to the ribbons of his beautiful Mařenka. Ah, how close they had sat in the garden, surrounded by the children, swifts, Betka! Like two chicks in the same nest.

Suddenly, he noticed Eliška staring at him and rolling her eyes. Could she read his mind? But then he realised he was dribbling, his mouth open in a stupid smile.

"Ah, Miss," he said, wiping his chops, "are you well, recovered?"

Eliška looked at him blankly. "What?"

"I mean from your, ah, absence…"

"What?"

"At The Pike's Tail."

Eliška turned away, staring sullenly out of the window. "M'okay."

"Are you sure my dear? I hope you don't mind me saying so, but when I saw you down by the mud, well…"

"I said m'okay."

"Um, yes, well, good."

Eliška scowled, as if pulling a curtain across her face.

Mitrovsky nodded. "So, ah, you're to become a nun, eh?"

Eliška sniffed.

"The Order of the Visitation and whatnot."

"Mm."

"Nuns are such enchanting creatures, wouldn't you say? I mean with their vestments and wimples and sparkly little eyes."

"If you say so."

"Pff, who wouldn't want to be a nun? It must be like cleaning the very windows of Heaven."

But the girl was no longer listening, preferring instead to gaze despondently at the parched earth passing by. Mitrovsky fell silent. What did he know of young girls? About as much as he knew of nuns.

Instead, the Count fell into blissful dreams of Mařenka, picturing himself sitting at her table in a perfectly green garden, the children playing, Betka snoring, the entire world filled with the most exquisite and painful joy.

5

At the next crossroad, the carriage left the post-road to take a fine, sandy track, the cab's metal wheels struggling to find purchase in the dust. Fortunately, this route seemed no less broad than the last one, flanked with the same banks of baked dirt where the mud had dried since springtime. The ground was parched, the grass dry as straw – even the birds looked a little chalky. A few minutes later however, and the track began to narrow, briars and nettles growing ever closer to the carriage windows, spoiling the woodwork and scratching the horses most terribly. From this point on, the going became even more difficult. Deep ruts appeared on the track and stones grew to the size of rabbits. O what a journey! The carriage creaked and the cab rocked from side to side like a rowing boat unmoored at sea.

"Scoundrels! Rogues! This is disgraceful, unacceptable," yelled the fellow in grey, his quill sliding across the page.

The Count poked his head out but could see nothing: the grass was as tall as the cab, with no farm buildings or way-signs at all. Rather, the lane seemed to go on forever, the dusty trail repeating itself as if tied up in a knot.

Mitrovsky yelled, and banged on the roof.

"Cabbie! Cabbie! I say, do you know where we are?"

At this the driver's voice came down from above.

"S'alright, sir. The village of Tichý isn't so very far – no more than an hour or two. There's an inn there – The Crooked Tooth –

we can spend the night there, and then get back to the post road. We'll only miss one day – not so very bad, really and Tichý is a pleasant spot."

His mate nodded, gently lowering the reins.

"Aye, aye, 'tis fine. Nice drop of stuff at the Tooth."

"Nice drop of stuff," agreed the other.

"A most pleasant spot."

"Spot."

"Well," bellowed the Count, "you lads know best."

By now the horses had slowed from a trot to an amble, the lead-pair shaking their heads and whinnying unhappily. The Count held up a glove and sniffed; amid the smell of bitter herbs, baked earth, and his own potent cologne, he could discern a trace of ash and smoke. Had somebody set a bonfire nearby? Or was somebody cooking on charcoal, flames licking the meat? O, it was awful hard to say! The smell seemed both earthy and homey, like when Old Marta cleaned out the grate, or the local sweep was visiting. Perhaps there was a smithy nearby, or peasants burning the chaff? If so, the village of Tichý must be close – 'as close as a razor and a throat', as Marta liked to say.

Breathing deeply, the portly Count pulled the curtains back and squinted out at the landscape. Dust speckled the meadow like snow at harvest time, a strange grey-white powder coating grass and weed and ditch alike. "What queer blossom," said the Count, turning to Mrs Jedličová. "Tell me my darling, do you see it too?"

Mrs Jedličová held onto her wig and peeped through the curtains.

"Yes, yes, I see! What is it – clinker?"

"Most wondrously strange," whispered the Count, tiny white specks landing on his tongue.

"'Tis like crumbs," said Mrs Jedličová. "Manna from Heaven,

like is said in the Bible."

"Do you think?" said Mitrovsky, sticking out his tongue. "They look a little sad, and the taste is most irregular."

On the other side of the meadow, a dead-straight line of beech trees shuffled off toward the horizon, all speckled with the selfsame dust. And behind these were a road or at least a country lane, this one considerably more expansive than the sandy track.

"Woa, I say, woa, that's it – Tichý!"

The horses pulled on their reins, their brown eyes open wide.

"Woa, I say! Tichý it is!!"

The passengers pulled back the curtains and stared. Ahead lay a random jumble of blackened shapes, the stumps all ruined and sooty.

"Tichý?" said Mrs Jedličová. "O, dear boys, I fear Tichý has gone…"

"Gone?" said Bilek. "Gone where?"

"Gone the way of all things," said Mrs Jedličová, "burned to the ground."

Mrs Jedličová was right: the only thing to survive the fire was the inn's sign, a crude painting of a long, canine tooth, hanging from a blackened pole. The inn itself was now no more than a great pile of begrimed timber, one low wall remaining, along with a couple of obsolete door-frames, leading, or so it seemed, to nowhere. The ashen ruins of shutters opened onto dust and filth, the floor a scorch-marked shadow. Aye, the place was in a pretty poor state, right enough. No roof, no thatch, only the skeleton of a staircase: everything else had been devoured by the flames.

And nor was the inn the only victim – no, no, far from it! The entire village had been burnt to the ground, foul stumps marking where once wooden houses had stood, timbered barns reduced to squares of dark, scorched ground. Only the occasional chimney place or well protruded from the ash heaps, everything else consumed by the flames. No beds, no furniture, no straw: instead piles of soot and slag-heaps lay everywhere, the air full of dust, the sight enough to bring tears to one's eyes.

As soon as the carriage rounded the corner, a bare-headed man dressed in a filthy apron ran out, the horses rearing up in alarm.

The fellow rubbed his hands and addressed the party cheerfully. "Greetings, ladies and gentlemen, greetings! A room for the night is it? Ah my dears, you're in luck, why, just this way, don't be shy…"

The cabbies looked at one another with identical expressions.

"Four gentleman and two ladies, is it?" said the proprietor, rubbing his dusty hands. "Right this way, ladies and gentlemen! I'll call Max to get your luggage. Max? Max!"

The passengers stared at the wreckage with some dismay.

"But your inn…" said Mrs Jedličová, surveying the scene.

"What? Oh yes – burned down last Tuesday! But no need to stand on ceremony, my friends! Special rates for special guests!"

From somewhere in the ruin a servant-boy scampered forth, hauling down the passenger's luggage with a practiced air. The lad had no shoes and his feet were the colour of coal.

"This way, this way," said the landlord, cheerfully. "Separate rooms for the men, private quarters for the ladies…"

Mrs Jedličová took a step forward and then halted. "My dear man, we cannot possibly stay here."

"No need for keys, Madam! Follow me, that's it, over the plank, mind the hole as you go."

The travellers gazed up at the wreck, trying to take it all in. There were no walls, no roof. It was not so much an inn, as the absence of one. Piles of wood had been heaped into pyres, the furnishings of the inn now no more than kindle.

The man with the quill noted it all down in his book.

"Outrageous, unacceptable…"

"You need ventilation, sir? Ah, such a close, confining night! Fortuitously, you are in luck. Enough fresh air to go around! Perfect for those averse to the stuffiness of ah, less commodious establishments…"

No one seemed to know quite what to say. The sun was low in the sky and everyone felt exhausted, from the horses to the cabbies to the guests.

The landlord found Mrs Jedličová the last remaining stool, its top all blistered and singed.

"Here, Madam – sit, sit! I'll ask Max to see if we have any more sticks to put together some kind of dressing table."

"Table?"

"'Tis no bother, my good lady. No extra cost, either!"

For once, even the voluble Mrs Jedličová was lost for words. It was hard to say whether one was inside or out. Every step produced great clouds of dust, the hems of the ladies' dresses black as the devil's hooves. In places, the ground was still warm.

Mitrovsky tried to peep through the remains of a doorframe, but the landlord moved to block his way.

"I'm sorry sir – that room is private."

The Count pointed at the empty space and stared.

"I'm sorry, sir, but we do insist that you respect the privacy of all our guests."

"Well…"

"This way, if you please…"

The landlord led his lodgers to a patch of bare, powdery earth, inviting them to 'attend their *toilette*' before dinner. Then he and Max took their leave – though they could be plainly seen just ten feet away, the landlord still rubbing his hands. The passengers looked round The Crooked Tooth as if the reception room of Gehenna.

"I'm writing all this down," muttered the fellow in grey,

"composing a harsh review, you see if I'm not…"

Bilek held onto his safe-box and scowled. "What, they want us to stay here? Even the rats are fire-damaged…"

Mrs Jedličová nodded her beautiful chin. "'Tis no space for respectable ladies – and no lock and key for Eliška…"

The cabbies swapped expressions.

"Horses need rest – and getting dark, too."

"Dark."

"We'll have to stay the night. Set out again in the morning…"

"Morning."

"'Aint no choice…"

"Choice."

The passengers inspected the slag and clinker, rather unhappily: but what else could they do?

"At least they've got vacancies," said the Count, his beard besmirched with soot.

Dinner was potatoes, baked in the earth, their innards soft and tasty, washed down with a pint of good Rhine wine.

The disaster, so the landlord told them, had started with burnt comestibles; ironically, the buns were those flavoured with cardamom and ginger spice, known locally as 'good fortune'. The flames had then spread from oven to house to barn, and before long, the whole village was alight. Still, was that any reason to close? The hamlet of Tichý had burned down before, and no doubt someday it would all burn down again. Better to sweep the old town away and start again fresh. At this the landlord grinned, showing his guests the wasteland of his gums.

After dinner, it was agreed that Mrs Jedličová and Eliška would sleep in the carriage, everyone else to bed down at the inn – or what remained of it, at least. Bilek, and the guy with his book, pissed and moaned, but all to no avail: the landlord took their money, and slipped it into a foul, goat-skin purse.

From the Crooked Tooth, one could see the inhabitants of Tichý going about their business, sweeping away the cinders, sawing wood, boiling up roots and tubers for the pot. Yes, despite everything, life went on. Among the remains of one cottage, a peasant and his wife were having a blazing row, while in another two little boys chased a little girl round and round a blackened box, a little black dog yapping happily. "Ah, 'tis not such a bad place," reflected the Count, philosophically. "A brush pan and broom and all will be well…"

After dinner, Mitrovsky took himself off for his evening constitutional, peering at the smoky peasants as an old dog might stare at rabbits. Smudgy birds pecked in the dust and a lone rooster promenaded down the street. Eventually, evening shuffled in like an old, familiar relative, heavy footed and smelling of cabbage. With no walls to screen them, Mitrovsky watched the good people of Tichý wash, undress, and get ready for bed. How resilient was Life! Farm animals huddled up next to their owners, the night heavy with the sound of snoring, grunting and farting. Insects chirruped and birds sang. No one lit a flame of any kind. Fortunately, the moon shone down as if rubbed clean on a sleeve, and the Count could pick his way through the ruins with ease. Once again, the moon reminded Mitrovsky of the Imperial Emperor, from his scowl down to his conk. Aye, the Emperor looked out over all – and why not? The world was filled with lines, shapes, and daubs. It seemed as if there was no such thing as nothing after all, despite what the free-thinkers said.

After a while, the Count turned back to the Crooked Tooth, singing 'O happy ray of moonlight' and stumbling over a blackened plank.

As he approached the ruin, the figure of the landlord emerged from the gloom, goatskin purse still jiggling.

"Sorry sir – we lock up at nightfall. Rules of the Inn, Sir."

"What? Ah…" The Count looked at the smouldering ruin in despair.

"Can't be helped sir, I'm sorry. No admittance after nightfall. Apologies, my lord, but I'm sure you understand."

The good Count stood with his travelling wig in his hands, like a bridegroom turned away from his wedding.

"Ah. I assumed that because your hostelry lacked partitions of any kind, that…"

"It's for the guests' protection, sir – bandits prowl this place at night. All guests must be locked inside…"

"But, ah, your hostelry lacks doors."

"Mm."

"Indeed walls of any kind."

"Nevertheless, sir…"

"Indeed, there look – I can see my companions all curled up on the floor…"

"Rules of the Inn, sir – I'm sure you understand." The innkeeper rubbed his hands, and then clapped Mitrovsky on the back. "You don't want to make a fuss, do you sir? Make me get Max up out of bed?"

"Bed? Ah…" Mitrovsky blinked and shook the fellow's hand. "No, no – my fault entirely! Pff, I was taking in the delights of your town and plain forgot the time. Ah, I can only apologise…"

"No harm done, sir," said the landlord, disappearing back into the gloom. "G'night, sir. Sleep well."

The Count waved. "Aye, good night sweet prince – I will find another grave to lay my bones…"

"G'night sir! And don't you worry – you can still pay up in the morning."

"Yes, yes – but, of course! Well, good night again. Worry not, kind sir – I'm sure I'll find some pillow for my head."

The Count padded over to the carriage, but 'twas no use, the door was shut and the cab's curtains firmly drawn. No, he thought: Mrs Jedličová and her daughter would not wish to receive him at such an hour.

Instead, he wandered back through the village of Tichý like a ghost. With no illumination save the moon and the stars, it was hard to work out where one ruin ended and another one began. But what else could he do? After all, all the earth is a bed, whether sooner or later.

Eventually the Count found a secluded spot and nestled down among the pillows of ash and soot. There were still sharp fragments of slag among the cinders, and the powder made him sneeze, but fortunately Counts can sleep anywhere, like cats.

He said his prayers and before long he was fast asleep, dreaming of Mařenka, dark of eye and green of skin, her butterfly broach alighting on flower after flower after flower.

Mitrovsky was awoken at dawn by an angry voice and a heavy broom.

"Out, out, get out! Rascal, burglar, thief! Get out, I tell you!"

The Count held up his arms in self-defence. It was morning. An angry woman was beating him with her bristles. His wig lay off to one side.

"Forgive me Madam! I was just looking for a little nest. I'm a stranger here and…"

"Swine! Scoundrel! You get out of here, this minute. What do you think you're doing, breaking in, in the dead of night?"

Mitrovsky got to his feet and bowed. Where was he? Dust and rubbish heaps lay everywhere. The woman was not unlike her broom: thin, prickly, with odd twigs sticking out from her dishevelled hair.

"My darling, forgive me. I was lost and must have stumbled into your delightful home by mistake. Please accept my most grateful apologies…"

The woman stared at the Count with dark, bitter eyes, her hair wild and tangled.

"The museum opens at ten on a Tuesday. You'll have to wait until then."

"Yes, yes, but of course…" At this the Count paused. "Um, museum? Ah, museum of…"

The woman's face flushed angrily from the tips of her crazy hair to the speck of soot on her nose.

"Why of the poet Nosek, of course! Tichý is his home village, as any fool well knows."

Mitrovsky nodded. Nosek, Nosek – now where had he heard that name before? And then he remembered: the birds, dawn, all that jazz!

"Nosek, you say? But…"

The woman's steely grey eyes narrowed. "Frantisek Nosek is the greatest poet in all of Bohemia, perhaps, the greatest in all of Europe, his genius unsurpassed in the modern age. Born in 1709, he…"

The woman kept on reciting dates, but the Count's thoughts were elsewhere. Nosek, the nightingales, that famous poem. His dusty beard shook and his cheeks took on a peculiar glow – 'a lover's bloom', as the poets say, not to be confused with 'the horseman's complaint'.

"Yes, yes, yes," said Mitrovsky, somewhat impatiently. "But do you have a copy of his posey? I mean, for purchase and the like?"

The woman – Miss Sukova, the chief curator – nodded, leading the Count by his beard over to a great mound of ash.

"But of course! Here we have his collected works, as printed and bound by Master Nussbaum of Dresden."

Miss Sukova pointed to the darkened corner, the ash swept up into a tiny tower.

"'Tis a very rare edition, one of a mere three hundred acknowledged by scholars."

Mitrovsky looked at the little mound of dust and felt his heart sink.

"Ah, yes, so I see…"

"'Tis the jewel of our collection…"

"Um, but of course. Ah, may I?" he said, extending a glove.

"Certainly not!" scolded the curator, whacking the Count with her broom. "Patrons may not manhandle the exhibits. Stand back behind the line!"

Mitrovsky looked down where a thin white line had been chalked on the earth.

"O, my apologies, madam, I did not see." He paused, eying up the scorched pile uncertainly. "But do you have any others of his work on display? Um, less baked perhaps?"

Miss Sukova sniffed. "But of course! This museum is dedicated to Master Nosek's life and works. We hold the most important artefacts relating to the poet's illustrious career."

"Ah," said the Count, biting one knuckle. "Perhaps I might …"

"The Museum opens at ten. If you would like to come back then, I would be more than happy to…"

At this Mitrovsky sidled over to her, winking one of his enormous black eyes. "Alas my carriage departs this very morn. Please, my darling – could you not open up your treasures and …"

"Absolutely not," replied Miss Sukova, icily. "Opening times are clearly displayed on the board outside. If you wish to take a tour of the museum then I suggest you return at ten, stupid man."

Like a broom, her voice was stiff, dull and prickly. One look at Miss Sukova's magnificently disdainful expression and the Count knew he would never breach her defences.

"Ah, but do you have a copy of Master Nosek's poetry, perchance? I mean for purchase, as a keepsake or such like…"

Miss Sukova's face resembled that of every official who has ever lived: blank as a fresh sheet of paper.

"This is a museum, not some gift shop! We have his school books, his diaries, his letters: both to his parents, and to a certain Madame J…"

"Yes…"

"Alongside a fine selection of other artefacts: his crib, his first tooth, the hoop that he played with, the stick with which he was beaten…"

"Um…"

"His first wig, his first cravat, his school trousers, cap, a pen and ink drawing of his ginger cat, Mizzy…"

The Count looked around the room with his sad, black eyes. Where once might have stood chests, cabinets and tables, now only burnt wood and filthy residue remained. Mitrovsky picked up a singed stick and nodded.

"Yes, yes, a most marvellous collection."

"Back behind the line!" Miss Sukova bellowed.

Ah, it was no use: the carriage was getting ready to depart, and the nightingales had gone up in smoke. Mitrovsky nodded, wiping the soot from the back of his hand.

"Madam, I thank you for your time but alas, I must depart. Farewell, kind lady! Here, please take this coin as a sign of my gratitude."

Miss Sukova took the coin as if rendering the Count an enormous favour. "This way, if you please," she said curtly, though in reality, there was no other place to go.

"You have a marvellous assemblage…"

"But of course."

"Quite the best in Tichý."

"Yes, indeed."

Outside – if the museum could still be said to possess an inside – the pair halted and Mitrovsky surveyed the town's scorched remains.

"A charming spot you have here – charming! A most wonderful place for a poet."

Miss Sukova clicked her tongue and pointed out at the smouldering waste as if at the seven wonders of the world.

"Yes, yes. There is the schoolhouse, where his father was a teacher. And over there is the silversmith, where he worked as an apprentice. And if you look to your left you can see the bridge by the mill, where he penned his first poem, 'O May Time Witch'."

Alas, none of these places now existed. In their stead were ruins, slag heaps, a dusty rooster wandering down the street, coughing a little and walking with a stoop.

"He was in love with a peasant girl, even made some kind of promise to her, though it didn't amount to much. As soon as he could, he was on his way. You have heard of the poem, 'The Milk and The Bucket'? It was composed just there, by Roh's dairy. And he wrote 'The World is Beautiful' while mushroom-hunting in the woods nearby."

Woods? Alas, reflected Mitrovsky, the days of woodcocks and finches were long gone. Now the sticks stuck out of the ground like burnt matches, any mushrooms long since cooked. Mitrovsky surveyed the stumps and paused.

"Tell me, my dear, have you heard of a poem called 'At Dawn, Two Nightingales'? I've heard that …"

At the sound of these birds Miss Sukova visibly paled, her lips closing up like a flower for the night.

Mitrovsky stared at her uncertainly. "I think that's the title. At least, I…"

Miss Sukova gave a gasp and slapped Mitrovsky on the chops.

"Fool! Idiot! What if somebody hears you?" The curator's eyes darted from side to side, as if the Emperor himself were listening, or customs-men were just outside the door.

Mitrovsky rubbed his cheek. "O my dear, 'tis..."

Miss Sukova's eyes flashed. Ho, was this the spark that had burned down the town?

"From whom did you hear of this? What did they tell you?"

The Count smiled, playing with his moustache coquettishly. "'Tis a most dreamy and amorous ditty, a most soulful little number. Why I've heard that no lady can..."

Miss Sukova slapped him again.

"Wherever did you hear such nonsense? Why, At Dawn, Two Nightingales is the saddest poem in the world! Whosoever hears it is afflicted with such melancholy that they immediately take their life – and thereby forfeit their immortal soul."

Life? Mitrovsky looked at the curator with some confusion: death, suicide, gloom? "No, no, my dear, you must be misinformed. Two Nightingales is a love poem! When read aloud by an ardent lover, the source of his affection immediately succumbs, entertaining feelings of the warmest and..."

Miss Sukova slapped his cheek for the third time, staring deep into Mitrovsky's big black eyes.

"Listen to me now: you must never speak of these nightingales again. That poem is cursed – its words are bitter. To read them is to sip poison."

Mitrovsky rubbed his cheek and gazed at the curator uncertainly. "O, my angel! The theme is love, not..."

"No, no, no. It's bedevilled, I say. Hear me well: such idle prattle will be the death of you. This poem ... just reading it is enough to make one lose one's life ..."

Something about the lady reminded Mitrovsky of the crazed

crone he had met in The Five Small Carp, same sour expression, same anguished eyes. 'Ah me,' thought Mitrovsky: 'Don't tell me this dame was one of his lovers too!'

"Forget those birds," she whispered. "And speak of them to no-one. Do you hear me? No one!"

"Well, yes, yes, if you say so..."

With that Miss Sukova struck him one last time, then released him. Mitrovsky rubbed his cheek and bowed.

"I thank you, Madam, for your time."

"We open at ten on a Tuesday," said Miss Sukova, coolly. "Half day closing on a Wednesday, open every alternate Saturday in school holidays."

Mitrovsky nodded and took his leave. Should he have asked for the poet's address in P? No, no: his cheek was sore enough as it was. What was it with these poets, anyway? Why did they leave so many unhappy women in their wake?

Mitrovsky wandered back through Tichý deep in thought. A woman in a head scarf scrubbed her last remaining floorboard. An uncle with a long beard loaded a dog-cart with rubble. A fat man was squatting over a hole, while a beautiful young woman endlessly brushed the dust, holding her broom as if in a dream.

Only a few precious things had survived the inferno. In one dust-heap, a large gilt mirror balanced precariously against the last standing beam, whilst in another, a large white bedspread had miraculously withstood the conflagration, even though the bed itself had succumbed: heaven alone knew how!

Most of the old stone church still stood (was this where Young Nosek had been baptised? More than likely) and in what might once have been the town square, a black and scorched statue still stood. Was this the poet himself? Alas, no. On closer inspection it turned out to be yet another Jan of Nepomok, the saint's head on a sooty platter, his tongue poking out like a naughty child.

Mitrovsky doffed his hat and moved on.

So from this poor nest, the peasant had flown? Well, why not? The best potatoes grew on good Bohemian soil. Besides, peasants had big heads, like horses: who knew what dreams went on inside? But what was all this nonsense about sorrow and suicide? Miss Sukova must be mixing up her birds: everyone knew that nightingales were symbols of love-making and smooching and such like.

By the time the Count reached The Crooked Tooth, the other travellers had already breakfasted, though fortuitously Mrs Jedličová had hidden some black bread in a basket 'just in case'. Everyone looked tired and achy, their garments smudged with soot and dirt. Young Halas' nose was as black as a berry, and the dour fellow's eyes rimmed with grime.

There were no clouds in the sky and the sun beat down mercilessly. You could imagine the whole world burning up like an old piece of paper.

"Oh, the poor people of this town," said Mrs Jedličová, dabbing her beautiful eyes. "How my heart aches…"

Mitrovsky slapped her on her back. "Oh, the good people of Tichý are an industrious lot. They'll be back on their feet in no time."

Mrs Jedličová blew her beautiful nose. "Do you think so, my dear Count?"

The Count smiled. "A few nails, a bucket of paste, and the place will be as good as new. Look: the tailor is fixing the bedclothes and the bread seller is already pushing his cart…"

Mitrovsky was right. The baker gave a little wave and with that the carriage left Tichý behind forever.

6

From Tichý, the carriage followed a pleasant country lane, the grass yellow and dusty, the bushes dry as tinder. Bees buzzed lazily and the grasshoppers played a dry and repetitive tune, as they had since the beginning of Time. Meanwhile, in the cab, the fellow with the big black book watched Mitrovsky craftily, his eyes like foul pickled eggs.

"Mitrovsky – where did you disappear to last night?"

"Me? O, 'tis not much of a tale. I went off for a wander, and our host would not let me back … a foolish misunderstanding, I'm sure…"

The Count inspected the contents of his handkerchief, as if some rare treasure might be found within.

"Hm, is that right? You sure you didn't have some kind of business in town?"

Mitrovsky shrugged. "Business? In Tichý? What sort of business would…?"

The fellow leant forward and breathed hard in Mitrovsky's face. "Literary business?"

Count Mitrovsky coloured immediately. "Literary? Whatever would give you that idea? No, no, I was looking for flowers to give to Mrs Jedličová. Here you are, my angel – a *devětsil* plucked just for you."

The Count produced a rather crumpled looking butter-burr from his pocket and passed it to Mrs Jedličová, who took it and blushed.

"O, he's a charmer, isn't he?" she said to the assembled carriage. "I'm amazed no Countess has snapped him up…"

And with that she slipped the flower through a buttonhole.

"Eh, Eliška, eh?"

The pale girl said nothing. She had her head in her hands, dreaming of whatever young girls dreamed of – ponies, maybe. Halas watched her closely, opened his mouth, and gulped.

After a while, Master Bilek produced an ancient pack of cards and the passengers started to play 'Fool', the Count soon ten thalers down. Only the youngsters declined: Halas on account of his sore throat, Eliška, because, said Mrs Jedličová, such games were unbecoming for a young lady. Strangely the fellow in grey, although dressed like a clergyman, played like a demon. "Yes, yes," he hissed, writing down his winnings in his big book, his quill scratching alarmingly.

At first the carriage made good time, but after an hour or so the hedges started to close in again, the lane narrowing just as before. In fact, it was impossible to tell if they weren't somehow back where they started.

"Listen," snapped Bilek, "I'm sure I've pissed in this hole before. You sure we 'aint going in circles?"

The other passengers started to rouse themselves, looking most alarmed.

"Circles, circles? We're driving in a straight line, you dolt," spat the dour-faced gentleman, rubbing his book. "There are no other roads – how can we be going in a circle?"

Bilek bristled, pushing forward his chest. "Who you calling a dolt?"

"There is only a single road. Here, look, I've drawn the map, right here in my book."

"Yeah? Well, you can shove your book right up…"

"Calm yourself, my dear Master Bilek," said Mrs Jedličová, handing the impresario a pickle. "Here – chew on this. Such treats are good for travel sickness and all ailments of the gut." She turned to Mitrovsky and whispered in his ear. "It's well known that theatrical types travel badly – just like sheep. 'Tis because of their nervousness and air of general agitation." And indeed, it wasn't long before Master Bilek had to put down his cards and thrust his head out of the window.

"Listen pal, we've passed that ditch once before…"

"A ditch, sir? No, no, we…"

"What is this, some kind of roundybout? I tell you, we're…!

"Not to worry, sir," said one of the drivers. "We're making good time. We'll be in Hrůza before lunchtime. You can saddle me like a horse if I'm wrong."

"Wrong," said his mate.

They were wrong. The road became increasingly rocky, the sand blistered and cracked. It wasn't long before the lane once again tapered and darkened, the weeds tightening like a noose. At every side, spiky grasses pricked the horses, clouds of flies pursuing them like indigestion, or guilt.

And then, just when it seemed that things couldn't get any worse, the carriage rounded a bend and came upon a second conveyance, a four-horse contraption, completely blocking the lane.

"What ho, whoa, stop!" cried the cab-men, the horses nose to nose.

The second carriage was also pulled by four piebald horses, though these were white and black, while the originals were black and white. Otherwise, the carriage was very much of the same type: a bronzed-yellow exterior, black lacquered doors, sky-blue curtains. The cab men looked at each other as if looking in a mirror.

"Back up, sir!" cried one of the other cabbies. "Back up, I say."

The two drivers pantomimed the act of looking up and then down, squinting their eyes most comically.

"Can't turnabout here," said one, "no room, not here."

"No room," said his mate.

The second set of cabbies stared back at them.

"'Tis too tight for us – you back up, you dog. What are you doing on this road, anyway? 'Tis our route, right enough."

"Route."

On the side of the carriage was written 'Thurn und Taxis', on the other 'Holan a Holub'. Both had smart metal wheels, although one was in black, and the other silver. The uniforms of the cabbies also differed, although it was awful hard to tell under all that dust.

"There's no moving this cab around," said the first driver. "You'll have to unhook the horses."

"You unhook your nags – this is our beat, you swine!"

"It's too narrow – you'll have to back up."

"What?"

"Turn around or you'll get a dose of the whip, you see if you don't…"

"Whip."

All four drivers scampered down from their cabs, but before things could come to blows, Count Mitrovsky opened the door and bellowed "Lads, lads, no need to crow! Here, we still have a scrap of bread. Why not stop here and make a picnic out of it all instead?"

With that, a second Count descended from the other carriage, this one dressed in a lavender frock coat with black buttons, a high white cravat, white nankeen trousers and blue worsted stockings. It must be said that the second Count cut a rather more imposing figure than Mitrovsky: his jacket was brand new, there were no patches on his elbows, and his ensemble smelt of neither moth balls nor musk, but rather something subtly masculine, with delicate undertones of leather.

"Out of our way, you wretch," jeered the second Count. "I command you to order your servants to desist."

"O, my angel," sang Mitrovsky, assuming a gentle pose, "there's no need for such harsh words. I'm sure that…"

"Dog! Swine! I demand that you move out of our way at once!"

At this the dour-faced gentleman with the yellow eyes popped out behind Mitrovsky and shook his quill at the fabulously angry nobleman.

"And who are you to issue such a command? I warn you, sir, I will write your name in this book, you see if I don't – right here in black and white, sir, in black and white, I say!"

In response, the other Count merely curled his lip in lordly disdain. "What do I care about such scribbling? You should respect your betters, sir, and …"

At this, other voices began to pipe up and it wasn't long before passengers from both cabs had disembarked, the parties lined up along the narrow lane as if queuing for the privy. Alongside the second Count was a saucy young girl and her tiny mother, a young man with bandaged eyes, some dandy in a purple coat and pea-green stockings, and a tall fellow in a tiny hat. The passengers chattered away like finches, while the drivers squared up for a fight.

"Mother?" complained the girl in a high whiny voice. "Mama, tell them to move. It's awful hot and my powder is beginning to shine."

"O darling, please don't make a fuss," said her tiny mother in a tiny voice.

"Mama, that man with yellow eyes is looking at me: tell him

to stop this minute!"

"Darling, please..."

"Your name, sir," said the dour-faced gentleman, menacingly. "For the record if you please..."

"Lout! Churl!"

"What's going on?" said the chump with bandaged eyes. "Is this Brno? I have an appointment with a Doctor Skripol. Are you he? I have obligations..."

"We all got obligations," snapped Bilek. "Now get your cart out of our way."

The tall fellow in the wee hat piped up, his voice surprisingly high. "Our cart? What about..."

"Why, what a fantastically theatrical costume," said the young peacock, eying up Mitrovsky's britches. "What are you playing? A vagabond? A tramp?"

"He be a count," yelled Mrs Jedličová, hotly. "Can you not tell? He has enormously ruffled cuffs."

"A Count," scoffed the other Count, incredulously. "Then where is your valet, sir, your sword? Why just look at his jacket – 'tis like some ruffian has died in it."

Mitrovsky inspected his cuffs. "We do have a moth problem, 'tis true..."

The colourfully attired young man was the Count's servant, accompanying his master to Brno on 'a personal matter of great delicacy': his handkerchiefs were delicately embroidered, his ruffles as exquisite as a fresh lettuce. As for the other passengers, the good Count swiftly became confused: there were so many of them! The miniature woman and her daughter were travelling to a nearby Spa 'to take the healing waters', although the Count couldn't work out which of the pair were ill. The gentleman with the bandaged eyes was a silversmith or some such fellow, who had rubbed lead into his peepers by mistake: "a hazard of the trade", as he said with a sickly smile. As for the tall fellow in the tiny hat, well, he alone kept *schtum*, hiding something large and awkward behind his back.

"Mama, can we go?" said the girl, holding onto her tiny mother. "I can't stay here much longer – I'm starting to tan…"

"Go? Yes go," snapped the drab fellow wielding his book. "Turn your carriage around and get out of our way."

"Bah, you turn your cart around," snapped the second Count, his magnificent wig rising ever higher. "We're much further along the road than you."

"Further?" The fellow with the foul yellow eyes glowered. "And how do you know, may I ask? Out of the way, you charlatan! I have important business and …"

At this the other Count became apoplectic, his face as round and red as a child's drawing of the sun.

"Charlatan? Charlatan! Why, I'll take my stick to you – Franz, Franz, whip him I say!"

The cabbies immediately started pushing and shoving each other, insulting the firms of 'Thurn und Taxis' and 'Holan a Holub' most vociferously. Caps were knocked, uniforms dishonoured. The ladies averted their eyes. The sun beat down as if through a magnifying glass.

"Okay you apes, knock it off," said Bilek in his loudest voice, waving his arms about wildly. "This crying 'aint getting us nowhere. Listen: let's toss for it. We win, you reverse. You win and we unhitch the horses. Deal?"

On one side of the coin was the Emperor and his nose, on the other a bear, trying to lick honey from its back: it was hard to say which of the two looked most foolish.

"The Emperor!" cried the second Count.

"The bear!" roared Mitrovsky.

Master Bilek nodded and tossed the coin in the air. But then, perhaps dazzled by the sun, the impresario dropped the ducat in the dust, stumbling as he did so.

"Damn and blast!" swore the fancy-pants Count. "Can't you do anything right, you cur?"

"Okay, okay, keep your wig on. Here it is – bear."

He was right: a shaggy muzzle looked up from the dust.

"This is ridiculous, unacceptable!" yelled the splenetic Count. "If that fellow's a Count, then I'm the Pope…"

"Really?" said Mitrovsky. "Which one?"

Still, a wager was a wager, and the other two cabbies had no choice but to release the horses and slowly shove the carriage back through the sand. Unfortunately, the wheels soon became stuck, and the other passengers – with the exception of the ladies, naturally – had to help.

"This is an outrage, a disgrace…" hollered the second Count, sweat dripping from beneath his wig. "I'll have the whole lot of them whipped, every last one…"

The sand was deep and the lane awful narrow. It took a long time for the carriage to reverse all the way, but eventually the party rounded the corner, the cabbies hollering to the horses and the second count still complaining loudly.

"A most disagreeable company," said Mitrovsky, waving the fellows goodbye. "I mean, except for the servant with the beautiful hat – capital fellow! I wonder how much he charges per month?"

"Ah, how fortunate you are with games of chance," said Mrs Jedličová, beaming. "O sir, the angels love you!"

"'Tis true," said the Count, modestly. "When I was born, an owl called out, which, as everyone knows, is a sign of good luck."

"Owl nothing," said Master Bilek, butting in. In one hand he held a coin with two emperors, in the other two bears. "Let those jerks back up: why should we whistle? You ask me, we've wasted enough time already."

"Aye, but they will be some time," said the Count. "What say you we tarry a while, perhaps have a bite to eat?"

Mrs Jedličová opened her seemingly endless bag and the passengers settled down on a woven, Moravian rug. Fortunately, the carriage had come to a halt beneath a walnut tree, and the lane was a pleasant spot, despite all the dust and cinders.

"Did you catch the name of that swine?" asked the fellow with yellow eyes. "I'll write it here, in bold."

"O, let him go," said Mrs Jedličová, producing a large and crusty lump of cheese. "Counts are like cockerels – they crow and crow but won't risk their feathers. No offence, my dear Karel…"

"None taken," said the Count, his beard speckled with scraps of food. "Do you know, I'm not even sure if that oaf was a Count after all. He seemed like a ham actor playing a part – what do you think?"

"Why yes," mused Mrs Jedličová. "There was something of the *singspiel* about him, you're right."

Mitrovsky nodded but it was too hot to think about such things just now. The sun blazed down and the corn crackled. How hot it was! The light seemed less a matter of illumination than a solid block of colour, weighing heavily upon the day.

When the repast was over and sparrows had consumed the last few crumbs, the party rose to their feet, climbing stiffly back inside the carriage with aching behinds.

"Ho! Walk on!" cried one of the drivers.

"Walk on!" said the other.

The lane was still narrow, with no breaks in the greenery of any kind: no gates, no fields, no farm tracks. The horses started to pick up speed, but there was still no sign of the other carriage.

"How strange!" said Mrs Jedličová. "But perhaps there was some kind of turning, and we missed it."

"Mm," said Mitrovsky. "Though 'tis odd that we haven't caught up to them by now." The Count looked down from the window. There were no tracks in the sand except those made by their own metal wheels. "Oh well," he thought, "no one sheds a tear when the wolf goes out." And with that the carriage went on its merry way, the lane stretching on as if to eternity.

ACT III

1

Ask anyone – Hrůza is famous for just three things: its beer, whose earthy smell permeates the whole town; the half-crooked church of St Rudolf, patron saint of swine-herders; and a popular almond-flavoured roll known locally as 'The Emperor's Favour'. Otherwise Hrůza is a dull provincial town much like any other; merchants, tinkers, tinsmiths, blah blah blah. Why such a place should have succumbed to an epidemic of dreaming is anybody's guess.

Mrs Blühová, the barrel-maker's wife, was the first victim, dreaming of the Emperor's nose hidden inside a loaf of bread, his sniffer baked in the dough like a mouse fallen in to the pot.

"Bohoušek, Bohoušek, wake up!"

Mr Blühovsky scowled and pulled on his beard: what were they, gypsies? A dream was a dream, nothing else. Why heap coals upon your head? Trouble flew from people's lips to the Emperor's ears.

"But Bohoušek…"

"Tell no one – I mean it. Dreams are curses in disguise."

And with that Mr Blühovsky went back to his barrel-making.

Two days later however, Mrs Blühová went to borrow a pan from her neighbour, Mrs Thalemann and – guess what? – Mrs Thalemann had been dreaming of the Emperor too. At midnight the Emperor had winked at her from a ten ducat piece, the coin rolling off down the middle of the street, singing 'Let us Enjoy the Days of Beauty', before disappearing – plop! – down a crack.

"Olina, these fancies, what do they mean?"

"Who knows?" said Mrs Blühová. "But keep it under your bonnet. Bad dreams sour the milk."

Alas though, this wasn't to be the end. While all of this was going on, the two ladies' dreams flew out of the window, down the street, and settled by a water pump, where they were overheard by Mr Kroha the wagon-man, the old crook lugging a barrel of tar over to Pelán's store. When the wagon-man heard the women's dreams, his blood ran cold – what was this witchcraft? Feh, just the other night he'd dreamt about the Emperor too, his Imperial Majesty hanging from a gibbet outside Linhart's brewery, the Royal tongue so long it seemed to lick the ground. Kroha groaned and twitched – what if the authorities were to learn of such follies? Everyone knew the rules: His Majesty's person was not to be libelled in a disgraceful or disrespectful fashion. Alas for Mr Kroha, the old fool talked in his sleep, and pretty soon all the wagon-men of Hrůnza knew of the gory details.

When Havliček mentioned it to Haar the dairyman, the old man grinned from ear to ear: "Seems like everyone's dreaming of the Emperor these days!" Hájek the butcher had seen the Emperor's head peeping out from a basket of cauliflowers, while Vobechý the rope-maker had dreamt that the Emperor used the town well for his privy, his buttocks pale and terrible in the moonlight. Not even the schoolteacher, Master Kašpařik, was immune: he'd seen the Emperor's mug hanging from every shop-sign in town, his Imperial Majesty talking in tongues, or perhaps some special language known only to bats.

2

Well, as the old saying goes, the truth goes barefoot while gossip flies on wings, and it wasn't long before the town's dreaming began to gather in tap-rooms, market stalls and post-houses, the tail of the dog growing steadily longer in the telling. To Knap the glazier, the Emperor scuttled out of the privy like a spider, while to Součova the scullery maid, His Majesty hid in the kitchen, playing the pots and pans like an orchestra. Heaven alone knows what kind of rubbish was talked! Eventually the authorities were compelled to act. Testimonies were gathered, depositions checked, and before long the police had compiled a Dossier of Official Evidence, listing the dreams in order of foulness, impertinence and degree of sedition: needless to say, Constable Povolný was careful to omit any mention of his own fancy, the Emperor thin as the thread from a tailor's needle, sewn into the lining of a pair of pantaloons.

When the dossier reached a certain weight – heavier than a carp from Trčka's pond – the papers were dispatched to the Imperial Capital by courier, both box and rider bearing the Emperor's sacred seal. There the work collected further signatures and stamps, passed from office to office by officials and administrators, gaining weight like a baby. After a week or so taking in the sights and sounds, the dossier landed on the desk of an Inspector Honzl, an Investigator of the Ministry of Cases of Extraordinary Importance, sometimes known as The Emperor's

Ear.

Honzl picked at his nose with his goose-feather quill and scowled. Treason! Dissent! Infamy! What kind of town could come up with such nonsense? Only one filled with the most foul and disreputable minds…

When he had finished annotating his manuscript, Special Investigator Honzl arranged to travel to Hrůza anonymously, purchasing a seat in a public cab in order to arrive more discreetly. To this end the Inspector adopted the most inconspicuous clothes, assuming an expression of deliberately unostentatious modesty. The only things he could not disguise were his eyes, which were cold and yellow and horrible.

3

Inspector Honzl arrived in Hrůza in the company of Master Bilek, a 'theatrical manager' from Brno, Mr Halas, a patient of some kind of throat doctor, Mrs Jedličová, and her daughter Eliška, travelling to a convent in Žádost, and some clown by the name of Mitrovsky, who claimed to be a Count, but who wore a threadbare cloak and a jacket patched with cat.

After checking into the Golden Tiger, the Special Investigator quietly made his way to the local police station, where he was greeted by Constable Povolný, a lumbering, awkward fellow, younger than Honzl's oldest pair of boots.

Yes, Povolný confirmed, the plague of dreaming continued unabated, insulting the person of our most gracious Emperor in a most slanderous and impolite manner.

Hora, the candle-maker, had been overheard relating a dream in which the Emperor was milked by a pair of dairy-maids, the maids filling up the best of two pails and a quart of a butter jug. Mrs Bertuška had written to her sister that she had witnessed the Emperor floating over the town square in the form of a baby, his face red and furious. And nor was this the worst! The cobbler Funke had confessed of a dream in which he pulled the Emperor up out of the ground whilst digging up his carrots; his Majesty had beans for eyes, a pea-shoot mouth, and a nose in the shape of a Swede. Funke had then – the Lord forgive him – boiled up the Emperor in a pot, serving him to his wife as "a most delicious soup."

Honzl nodded, noting down the depraved fantasies in his heavy, leather-bound ledger. Madness, madness, all of it! But what had brought about such unholy pictures? From whence did they come, and why?

The first crop of dreams more or less coincided with the full moon, witnesses reporting that the moon seemed unusually close and clear that night, "like a coin in your pocket". Some whispered that witches had been seen flying by the old town clock, others that goblins had been spotted lurking by the old town well – the usual nonsense, in other words. The only real clue was that a bookseller had passed through town just around the time the dreaming started: a most singular fellow, according to reports.

"A book-seller?" asked Honzl, suspiciously. "What would a bookseller be doing in Hrůza?"

Povolný shrugged. "All sorts of strangers pass through here, sir, Wagon-drivers, drovers, peddlers – 'tis on account of the Post Road."

"Hm. And this bookseller was peculiar, do you say?"

"A very thin gentleman by all accounts – a sort of stickman. With a pair of fancy wooden teeth…"

"Really?"

"Very sharp, sir. Like a rat."

"Hm." Honzl waved his quill about absent-mindedly, his nose quivering as he sniffed. "And what exactly was it that this devil was selling? Almanacs, seed catalogues, things of that type?"

"Ah, I don't…"

"Or was it something else? Poetry, for instance?"

Povolný shrugged. "Poetry, sir? I don't know anything of such…"

"No, no: of course you don't, you dog!" Honzl's eyes glittered horribly. "And this … book-seller … where is he now?"

"Left town, sir," said the Constable. "Had no reason to detain him. Books ain't illegal, though they should be. Cleared out before the first report could be filed."

Honzl sniffed. "Yes, yes – well, there it is."

The inspector's lips moved as if he were whispering to himself, his eyes greasy and foul.

"I'll return to The Tiger now. I trust you, Constable Povolný, to keep me informed of any developments."

"Yes sir," said Povolný, thinking of the Emperor stitched into his under-garments. "Of course, sir. You can count on me."

And with that the doltish Constable saluted, tapping the side of his cap.

Alone in his office, Special Investigator Honzl felt his mind stewing like a chicken in a pot: a bookseller, a common peddler – could this swine really be the source of all these dreams?

In Vienna, Honzl's office was right next door to the Ministry of Forbidden Texts: if one pushed one's ear to the door, one could hear the brush of their beards, their quills scratching away like mice. Books, poems, words: aye, such things were highly suspicious, right enough. And what was it that that idiot Count had said on the way here? Something about 'literary business', the dog! At this Honzl's nose twitched and he began to grind his teeth. The bastard was hiding something: that Count disguise couldn't fool a blind man! Well, he would cut it out of him – what's the expression? 'As the butcher removes the marrow'.

Honzl moved his mouth as if laughing. No, no, Count Mitrovsky would not be departing town by carriage tomorrow. He would leave in either a prison cart or a wooden box.

And with that the Special Investigator made his way back to the Tiger's cage.

4

"O good sir, don't go in there," wailed the landlady, Mrs Koppitz, blocking the Investigator's path. "'Tis terrible, sir, terrible…"

"Terrible? Terrible what? Out of my way Madam, I'm in no mood to…"

"It's awful! They're dead, sir, murdered in their beds."

"What? Unhand me, I say! Here, I order you, let me through …"

"Sir, you mustn't."

"Unhand me I say, or I'll write it straight down, you see if I don't…"

The landlady, Mrs Koppitz, was right: the two cabmen had been disturbed most rudely, dead from two stab wounds to the heart. As a result, the common room was in a state of great confusion, with a great many shouts, whispers and moans. It didn't help that the space was awfully dark and crowded, the room packed with peddlers and street-vendors, as well as a rowdy gang of drovers from České Budejovice and a learned party of seminary students from Ruthenia – oh, and the unfortunate cabbies' passengers, of course.

"Out of my way, you swine! Where are they? Unhand me I say…"

Under a kindly lantern, the two corpses looked surprisingly content, each wearing the same sweet, sleepy expression, as if enjoying a night off, or a nap above a warm stove. Close–up the two cabmen really did look alike, as if one were a drawing of the other, copied by hand in a mirror.

The Inspector sneered, while the tender-hearted Count looked close to tears.

"O, o, o … those poor brothers! But at least they died in each other's arms, as all cabbies wish…"

Honzl shoved Mitrovsky out of the way, taking in the scene with a glance.

"What's this – murder? Nobody moves, nobody leaves. You sir, stay where you are! Nobody goes anywhere until I've written everybody's name down. Hm? Yes, yes! Down, I say, right here in my book."

Bilek – who had been sleeping closest to the cabbies – pressed his strongbox to his chest and gave Honzl a shove.

"Yeah? Who died and made you Pope?"

"What did you say?"

"You heard me – where were you anyway? Out waltzing with Maria Theresa?"

"How dare you sir!" replied Honzl, grinding his teeth. "I'm writing it down, Bilek, right…"

"You and your stupid book. Why don't you shove it…"

'Tis hard to say where this lively discussion might have led, because at that moment the debate cut short by the appearance of Mrs Jedličová in the doorway, a fine-wool shawl pulled around her beautiful shoulders.

"Eliška, Eliška, where are you, naughty girl? O gentlemen, I'm sorry, but has anyone seen my goose of a …"

At this, Mrs Jedličová spotted the two cold cabbies and paused.

"Oo, look at that poor pair – lying there on a bare board, they'll catch their death! Quick, quick, cover 'em up! The dead need their beds, just like the rest of us. O, what a palaver! Karel, Karel, don't stand so close. Deadness is catching, as even the worms seem to know."

"Dear heart, fear not," said the Count, wiping his eyes. "I stand guard like a dog…"

Mrs Jedličová looked upon the Count most tenderly.

"Poor dear – how tired you look. Here, wait, I'll go and fetch a pillow. Are you getting enough sleep? Look at those big black eyes of yours – you'll lose your youth…"

"Hush Madam, there's no need to concern yourself. Now what's that you say about Eliška? Has she…"

But at that moment Constable Povolný appeared, the fellow popping up as if waiting in the wings for his cue.

"Inspector Honzl! What on earth happened here?" asked Povolný, reaching out to take the Inspector's hand.

Honzl curled his lip.

"Inspector? No, no, officer, you must be confusing me with somebody else … why, I'm just a travelling merchant, as any fool can see."

"I can clearly see that!" yelled the Count.

Povolný crouched down to inspect the bodies. The pair had been snipped with a very thin blade, unpicked like a cheap pair of pants.

"Yes, yes … definitely dead," said Povolný with an air of experience, stepping back onto the feet of Young Master Halas, who was standing just behind him.

"Aha!" said the Constable, turning around, Halas nervously fingering his scarf. "Your name, good fellow, if you please…"

Halas blinked, staring back at the constable benevolently.

"I said, your name, if you would be so kind."

The lad smiled, pulled an innocent face, and began to fish in his jacket for a card.

Quick as a flash, Povolný grabbed his arm and wrestled the pup to the ground.

"I've got him, sir…"

"Oh for heaven's sake…"

The Inspector ground his teeth with frustration. Amateurs! Idiots! Saboteurs! Only the cabbies lay there peacefully, side by side like cuts of meat in Klima's store.

"You stay still," yelled Povolný to Master Halas. "Don't move an inch! You're all under arrest, arrest I say!"

In time, a semblance of order was finally restored. Names were taken and statements given. Master Halas's infirmity was explained. Mrs Jedličová secured bedding for the corpses and Mitrovsky found a stool and helped himself to a large piece of cheese.

"Name?" said Povolný.

"Mitrovsky, Count Karel Mitrovsky. You may have heard of the famed Mitrovsky Estate…"

"Mitrovsky, yes, yes … I know that name. An old Count lived there right enough. His son went off soldiering and never came back…"

"Ah, you're thinking of my brother."

"Brother?" Povolný looked confused. "I don't believe I've heard of any brother. Mitrovsky with a 'v' you say?"

"Yes, yes. It's Matej you're…"

"Another Mitrovsky brother?" Povolný shook his head. "No, no, I can't say I've heard of him."

"Well, the estate is quite far from here," said Mitrovsky, fluttering his handkerchief in the policeman's face. "'Tis very easy for stories to get all muddled up."

At that moment there was a sound of footsteps outside the door, and a second policeman arrived, escorting Eliška by the arm.

"Stable boy found her wandering around outside, sir," the lad informed Povolný. "In her night gown, nothing on her feet."

All eyes turned to look at Eliška, the girl pale and swaying from side to side. her night gown stained with blood.

"What?" said the girl. "What's everybody staring at? Mama? Mama, tell them to stop. Dirty dogs! I..." All of a sudden she caught sight of the drops bespattering her night gown. "Oh."

The room fell silent. Honzl stopped scribbling in his book. Povolný walked away from the corpses. Mitrovsky stopped nibbling his chunk of cheese.

"O Eliška!" cried Mrs Jedličová, staring at her daughter's ill-stained gown. "O foolish chick, what now?"

5

The town gaol being no place for respectable murderers, Mrs Jedličová and Eliška were sequestered on the top floor of the Powder Gate, in a sealed room normally reserved for the safe provision of nuns, gunpowder and the like.

Assuming his most serious expression, Constable Povolný ordered that the two ladies must remain 'under lock and key' until the matter had been 'scrutinized by officers of the law', the other members of the party warned not to 'skip town' but stay put.

"You have my word of honour," said the Count, "We will not leave Hrůza 'til the cabbies have been returned to life."

There being no more hours of night-time, the remaining guests gathered in the dining hall for breakfast. Breakfast at The Golden Tiger was a kind of millet gruel, flavoured with honey, beer and tears. The landlady, Mrs Koppitz, was most upset: two dead bodies, and the common room to scrub! The good name of The Golden Tiger was sure to suffer – perhaps their hygiene rating too.

"Those poor lads," said the Count, sucking on his spoon, "and such merry souls, too! Why they brought light into all our lives, like opening a window…"

Master Bilek said nothing, his thoughts elsewhere – 'buzzing with the flies' as country-folk say.

Undeterred, Mitrovsky went on.

"And the good ladies arrested: awful, awful! As gentlemen, we simply cannot allow, ah…" Here he seemed to lose his train of thought. "Eh, Master Bilek, what say you? Master Bilek?"

Bilek looked up from his mush. "What you yapping about now, Mitrovsky?"

"The two ladies – we should take them a basket. Bread, fruit, ribbon – that sort of thing. I find a nicely curled ribbon cheers me up no end…"

"Ribbon? What do these gals want with your schmattes? They're under arrest for murder, not shopping."

The impresario seemed to have aged since the events of last night, greenish bags hanging beneath his eyes.

"But as gentlemen, we must, ah…"

"Listen," said Bilek, "you seen that schmuck with his book?"

"Book? Oh, you mean, um … what is his name?"

"See? He doesn't even own a name. Listen Mitrovsky, I don't trust that dog. He's the kind of guy – if you were drowning, he'd give you a glass of water."

"Do you know," said the Count, "I once caught him peering at my bureau in a most peculiar fashion."

"He's hiding something under that stupid wig of his, that's for sure. You see his eyes? There's something not right about 'em. Like they belong to – I don't know – an owl or something."

The Count nodded. "The whole world is a secret. It's what the mice talk about at night…"

"I say we get out of here for a bit," said Bilek, "clear the air, you know? What do you say?"

Mitrovsky and Halas both nodded.

"Okay. Now wait a 'sec, I gotta go get my box…"

"Hm? O, your strong box, you mean…"

"Can't let it fall into the wrong hands."

"The world is full of crooks," said the Count, straight-faced.

Minutes later the three travellers were strolling along Goat Street, Bilek trotting along on his fat little haunches, Halas and Mitrovsky following close behind.

"We gotta get ourselves a set of wheels as soon as possible," said the impresario, walking as fast as he talked. "You see a carriage-shop? Keep your peepers open – we've gotta get out of this burg…"

"But the constable…"

Bilek scowled.

"Constable? Constable, nuttin'. You want your name carved on a headstone? I don't know about you suckers, but I plan on climbing out of this crapper as soon as possible…"

"Aye but…"

"Listen pal: I got me important appointments in P. This box, it's gonna turn the city upside down. I mean it, Mitrovsky. The shmucks in P – they've never seen anything like it…"

The Count gazed at the fellow's strong-box and felt his heart begin to quicken. What was in there anyway? And how could he jimmy the lock?

But then another thought came to him. P, P, P … aye, he too had business in P: Nosek and those damn birds. O Mařenka! He pictured her stockings and her slippers, all in silver as if spun from moonlight… ah, for a moment, the Count thought he might faint! But then he remembered Mrs Jedlicová and the manner in which she bestowed her charms most teňderly – not to mention all that pastry and those little sugary cakes too. O Mrs Jedličová! How splendid her pancakes, jam patties, her beautiful eyes…

"Ah, but the ladies, no, no, no," spoke the Count, most vehemently. "Tish tosh, we cannot abandon them like a box of kittens! No, sir, we must…"

Bilek looked at the Count's sad eyes and snorted. "Quite the prince, 'aint we? Okay, okay. We take the ladies some baked goods from the market, then slip away. Hey, don't look at me that way. We've got to get out of this dump before someone snips us too. I mean, why ice those cabbies anyway? Someone sore about the soiling charge?"

The Count thought of the cabbies and felt a gentle melancholy misting at his eyes. "Yes, yes … such jolly fellows…"

"Jolly dead. You feel that Mitrovsky?" Bilek mimed a sinister clawed hand. "That's darkness tearing at our cloak."

The three men passed along Spanish Street, turned left onto The Cripple's Row, and then ducked under the sign of The Three Stags; whether they were getting close to the market was anybody's guess.

"Awful quiet, don't you think?" said the Count, shaking his handkerchief in the air. "Where is everybody? Still a'bed, and hiding from the heat?"

"Dumps like this," said Bilek, "time moves different here. It's like the hands of the clock are bust."

Rounding a corner, they came upon a wooden stall owned by a shabbily dressed Auntie in a bonnet. Spying her table, the Count gave a girlish little skip.

"Ho, aren't those the same delicious rolls that we ate just last night? Yes, yes – I do declare they are!"

The Count bustled over to the stall – a kind of roofed wheelbarrow that could be rolled from place to place – sidling up to the Auntie whilst fluttering his handkerchief. "O my darling – these delicious rolls – pray tell me, what are they?"

"They're known as The Emperor's Favours, sir," the Auntie said, offering him a taste, "on account of the fact that the Emperor's face is pressed into the dough while cooling. Round here, sir, the people of Hrůza like to joke. They say 'O, the Emperor is doing us a favour!' Or they say, 'O, we're the Emperor's favourites!' O sir, how we laugh and laugh."

143

"I bet you do, you simple country folk!"

The Count took a bite and beamed.

"Mm, mm, delicious! Look at the Emperor's nose – just like his majesty's conk! Ha ha ha … do you know, last night I had the queerest dream. The Emperor was a big black crow, chased around a yard by a gang of chimney-sweeps in rags. Hm, what's that? No need for alarm, my darling! The fellow had long black feathers and beady eyes, but I knew 'twas the Emperor on account of his enormous beak. Ha, ha, ha, quite the sight! The sweeps were chasing him with their brooms and the fella flew up high and shat on the lot of them … yes, yes, a wonderful fancy! Then I woke up and the cabbies were dead and everybody was shouting. Tell me my darling, what does it mean?"

The Auntie looked back in horror and began to slowly inch away.

"Yeah, yeah, it's a beautiful story," snapped Bilek. "You gonna eat all those cakes?"

"Ah, how divine they taste! Like honey mixed with one's mother's milk!" Mitrovsky winked and turned back to the stall. "Four more of your rolls, my good woman, and …"

But the Auntie was already pushing her cart away, muttering curses under her breath.

"Auntie?" cried Mitrovsky. "Auntie, if you please…"

'Twas was no use: the bread-seller was gone, pushing her cart as fast as her legs would carry her.

"Must have business elsewhere," said the Count, cheerfully. "Ah well, never mind. I'm sure that the market will be a treasure-trove of infinite riches…"

Bilek squinted. "Yeah, you think?"

From outside The Three Stags, they followed Blindman's Moat past the sign of a saddle, a horse shoe, and a bone, before spotting an old granny lugging a sack of coal from a half-broken stall.

"Well," said Bilek, "here's your treasure trove."

Bilek purchased a bag of sour apples, Master Halas a loaf of black rye, and Mitrovsky a spool of bright coloured ribbon. They also bought a bushel to put it in, the straw nibbled in places by mites. "Guaranteed to bring a bloom to a lady's cheek," said Mitrovsky, hooking the basket over his arm.

"Okay, okay, let's hand over the dough and blow this town," said Bilek, anxiously scanning the stalls. "Our tickets should be good for forward passage, no extra cost. Hey, was it our fault the drivers got rubbed out? I…"

With that the impresario suddenly froze on the spot, an icy chill passing through him from hat to heel.

"Master Bilek? What…"

"Shh!"

Walking on the other side of the road was another gentleman, the fellow also wearing a tall, chimney-pot hat, accompanied by two figures in black, the figures long, thin and narrow, like shadows on a sunny day.

"Moosendorf!" Bilek exhaled. "What's that snake doing here?"

"Moosendorf? Who's…?"

"Shhh…"

The gentleman – Moosendorf, if Bilek was to be believed – and his two companions seemed deep in conversation, their noses almost touching.

"Get down," hissed Bilek, crouching behind a tar barrel. "Don't you know who that is?"

"What kind of fool do you take me for?" said the Count. "I've never…"

"Moosendorf! He must have got wind of my box." The colour drained from Bilek's face, his lips dry and sticky. "We gotta get away from here. You hear me Mitrovsky? Skip town before…"

"Before?"

"Shh, shh, he's looking our way. Run, you idiot, run!"

With that the impresario took off along the main road, holding onto his strongbox as if for dear life.

"Well, that's most peculiar," said the Count, looking at the space Bilek had occupied just a short moment ago. "Ah well – I'm sure our friend will soon return – people always do, one way or the other. Now, let us find the ladies, Master Halas: I'm sure the sight of these streamers will gladden their hearts…"

Halas blinked.

"You take a leaf from my book," said the Count. "If you want to curry favour with the ladies, a piece of ribbon is like a magic key. Oh, the stories I could tell. Us Counts are like tom cats – always seeking out a warm lap…"

Halas nodded, Across the way, Moosendorf and the two spindly fellows vanished back into the crowd, like spiders disappearing down a crack. "Rhubarb, rhubarb, rhubarb!" yelled the fruit seller.

The Powder Gate was a fortified tower on the town's old wall, one of the few stone buildings in this otherwise wooden town. The guard winked as he let them in, Mrs Jedličová's beautiful lips racing down the stairs to greet them.

"You look pale, thin. Are you eating? Did you have breakfast? Come in, come in, see what the guards have left us."

The bread from the market was dry and sour, but fortunately the two ladies had been well tended to, the Count helping himself to white bread with black-current jelly followed by a slice of pie and sour cream.

"What beautiful ribbon," said Mrs Jedličová, wiping away her tears. "Why I could use that to put tassels on my travelling bag."

"'Twas very cheap from a bucket," said the Count, waving his 'kerchief rather modestly.

"Eliška, Eliška, come and see what the kind gentlemen have brought! O, such a lazy girl…"

Eliška appeared in a doorway, pulling in her shoulders to make herself as small as possible. She looked at the ribbons and pulled a face. "Ribbons? Just what we need. What are we going to do? Wrap ourselves up like a parcel?"

Mrs Jedličová glowered at the girl, clapping her beautiful hands. "Take away the gentlemen's plates, that's it, quick, quick. Now go give them a rinse in the pail."

"What, Counts don't do washing? Or is it just men?"

Mitrovsky coloured. "Oh, there's no need…"

"Such a lazy girl, you really can't imagine."

"Um…"

As Eliška carried the plates away – Halas, staring after her longingly – Mrs Jedličová turned to the Count and whispered *soto voce*. "She wanders from the path, my dear Count! Her feet carry her off…"

"Well, we all meander from time to time…"

"No, no, you don't understand. At night – she wanders off, her feet drag her away. During the day too, if she falls asleep. Closes her eyes and – poof! – she's gone!"

Mitrovsky glanced over at where Eliška was doing the dishes, shoulders slumped, neck drooping, as if her whole body were being poured from a glass.

"Really? Why, 'tis most mysterious…"

"It's worse that that Count – it's scandalous! A young girl abroad in the middle of the night in just her bed-clothes? Not to mention the colour of her feet…"

"Feet, well, yes…"

"But what should I do? Tie her to the bed like a dog? I'm a respectable widow, my dear Count…"

"Well, yes…"

"And Eliška is a virtuous young lady…"

"But of course…"

"What happened back home – with that boy, I mean … well, I don't care what the neighbours say…"

"No, no…"

"Or his la-di-da parents…"

"Mm."

Mrs Jedličová opened her beautiful eyes wide. "So you see, don't you? Why she must travel to the sisters in Žádost – the nunnery, I mean. They'll know what to do! They'll be able to look after her – stop her wandering from the path…"

"Hmm, mm, I see. Well, worry not, my angel. Nuns are good at things like that. Ah, preventing deviations and diversions and the like. Yes, yes, 'tis a good plan…"

The guard banged on the door – it was time to go.

"Do you know," said Mrs Jedličová, as the two men made their way back over to the door, "last night I had the strangest dream. I saw the Emperor being chased by a pack of mangy dogs, his nose an enormous string of sausages. O good Count, what do you think it means?"

"The Emperor, eh? Yes, yes, 'tis a mystery right enough. Those sausages probably mean something – I'll look it up in a book."

"O thank you, Count – you're such a comfort." And with that the good lady smiled, bestowing upon the Count a gesture of such sweet tenderness that the fellow almost fell down the stairs.

Afterward, Mitrovsky strode away from the gate, deep in thought.

"O, those poor ladies – it bothers my heart, young sir, it really does. The poor darlings, I could weep!"

Still thinking of Eliška, Young Halas nodded.

"I don't care what Master Bilek says: we cannot leave such angels languishing in gaol. But how do we free them, my pet, how?"

The Count waved to the cheerful turnkey and headed into town.

"Yes, yes … we must go and plan. Perhaps some kind of disguise, a ruse … what is it that players do on stage? Well, leave it to me, lad. Us Counts know all about finding secret passages … especially to an honourable lady's boudoir…"

Master Halas opened his mouth, but nothing came out, not even a peep. With a spring in their step, the pair then went forth to look for a platter of meat and a jug, the sun beating down without end.

6

After concluding their interview with Mrs Jedličová, Count Mitrovsky and young Master Halas proceeded to spend the day in the most profitable and productive manner they could think of.

First, they called in at the Four Thieves, where Mitrovsky sampled the house speciality – cows knees boiled in aspic – before moving on to The Silver Conch, the good Count partaking of a dainty dish of calves' muzzles, the lips and nostrils particularly soft and unctuous. Young Halas watched him silently, his expression placid and patient. This was all washed down with yet more strong black beer – beer that could clean hog bristles – after which the rest of the evening became something of a blur. Mitrovsky could remember the eel broth at The White Owl, and a plate of pig's feet at The Executioner's Block, but as for the rest – alas, not a single crumb remained.

Fortified by a carafe of strong Rhine wine, Mitrovsky returned to the Tiger singing 'Midnight is here, and I see no one, no one', accompanied by Master Halas in a guardsman's hat. Struggling to open the curtain while stumbling up and down the single step, they became entangled with a small woman in an enormous bonnet heading in the opposite direction.

"Hey, hey, you clowns," she snapped, "let a lady through…"

It was only when the Count fell over a stout metal box that he saw the lady was in fact, Master Bilek, the impresario attired in a bonnet and lemon-coloured frock.

"Master Bilek," breathed the Count, "but…"

"Pipe down, you big ape," whispered Bilek sourly. "Can't you see I'm in disguise?"

Mitrovsky examined the manager carefully. "Aye, those are beautiful stockings – and the trimming on your petticoat – enchanting!"

"Knock it off, you jerk." Bilek anxiously stared up and down the street, his eyes as round as tea-cups. "You wanna get me killed?"

"Oh, I'm sure it's not as bad as…"

Bilek clapped a meaty hand to Mitrovsky's lips.

"Listen – we can't talk here. Meet me at The Poisoned Elm, clippity-clop. And if anyone asks – I'm Mrs Matušková, right?"

"Um…"

"Matušková. Don't forget the hat on the 's'."

Ten minutes later, the travellers were sitting around a plate of chicken livers at The Poisoned Elm. Even under his thick, white make-up, Master Bilek looked pale and shifty, his little piggy-eyes constantly darting about the room.

"It's Moosendorf," he sneered. "He's the one who stiffed the cabbies – trying to get his hand on my gravy."

"Gravy?"

"My case, you ass. Listen, this Moosendorf – he's the second most successful theatre manager in Brno. Little squirt's been snapping at my heels for years."

"Ah."

Bilek pursed his generously painted lips and tapped his bag. "He's after this, don't you see? He must have heard about what's inside it – sniffed it on the wind, so to speak."

Mitrovsky looked thoughtful. "The wind, well, yes. And what

exactly is…"

"He hired those two goons to go and collect – the two beauties we saw at the market. Did you see 'em? They could have climbed in through the Tiger's window no problem – the cabbies clocked 'em, so they went and cut their strings."

"Strings?"

"Iced 'em, you dope. Nothing personal – those two pigeons were just in the way. Luckily someone must have heard them, otherwise" – Bilek pulled his finger across his throat – "I'd be a snack for the worms."

The Count and Young Master Halas nodded, Halas still smiling: maybe the lad was deaf as well as dumb, who knows?

"But…"

"No buts – We've got to get out of here. If Moosendorf gets his hands on this bag – well, I hate to think what might happen."

"Happen?"

"This stuff is explosive, kid – boom!"

Mitrovsky again stared longingly at Bilek's mysterious luggage. O, what was it about it that made his heart ache and his hairy paws twitch? It was all he could do not to tear it out of Bilek's grasp there and then.

"Listen Mitrovsky: I've managed to get tickets on the twelve o'clock coach to P – Holan and Holub came through. You and Young Halas need to come with me – Moosendorf doesn't care who gets in his way. Those guys we saw earlier? They ain't no choir-boys, believe me."

"Oh, I'm sure." All of a sudden, a light seemed to come on in Mitrovsky's eyes. "But if your Moosendorf is behind the killings then Little Eliška is innocent – tsk, she didn't cut up the two gentlemen after all! O, my darling, don't you see? Eliška's soul is unblemished, and the ladies can go free."

Bilek shrugged.

"Yeah, yeah, yeah. Listen, Eliška is a sweet girl and all, but it don't cut no cake. What, you want us to hang around here while the *fizl* stick their noses in? Moosendorf's goons will knock us off before the cops put on their capes."

The Count again tried to interrupt, but the manager slapped him down.

"We 'aint got no choice – we got be out of here on the twelve o'clock coach – if not, then it's first-class tickets for the undertaker's cart instead."

Mitrovsky's handkerchief fluttered up and down.

"But Master Bilek…"

"Bilek? Bilek who? The name's Matušková, remember? Listen, you want an angel, you follow the feathers. Now if you'll excuse me, I gotta use the powder-room…"

As Bilek struggled to his feet, a serving boy swept away the livers, replacing them with a plate of the Emperor's Favours. Mitrovsky seemed paralysed by indecision.

"Oh, dear sir, I fear we cannot…"

With this Mrs Matušková leaned in so close, some of his rouge rubbed off on Mitrovsky's cheek.

"Listen Mitrovsky, I 'aint playing patty-cake and neither is Moosendorf. You want to put your head in a noose, be my guest. But if there's anything under that wig, you'll get the hell out of the Tiger and be at Holub and Holan at Twelve…"

The Count nodded, but looked at Halas uncertainly: what was a gentleman to do?

"Twelve o'clock, Mitrovsky. You better be on that coach…"

7

While Mitrovsky and his fellow travellers were deep in their cups at The Poisoned Elm, Special Investigator Honzl secured modest lodgings in a humble abode on Parrot Street, a simple room, with but bed, desk and piss-pot. There, the Investigator cradled his weighty tome, ruminating on the mysterious intricacies of the case. What a mess! The strange dreams of the Emperor, the infernal bookseller, the two dead cabbies – all were somehow connected, but by what?

All of a sudden, there was a knock on the door: Povolný.

"We've brought the teacher, Kašpařik, to see you sir."

"A teacher? Why on earth…"

"We've had word, sir, that he's been dreaming – dreaming about the Emperor, I mean. And we have witnesses – the pot boy Medek, as well as Schenckel the Limp – who swear they saw Master Kašpařik talking to a bookseller in The Black Cat – a most disreputable establishment, if I may say so."

"Ah." Honzl's eyes opened and closed like those of a toad. "And have you searched this fellow's schoolroom? Do you know what volumes he purchased?"

Povolný nodded and produced two leather-bound tomes. Honzl looked at them with distaste.

"Ah yes, so I see. Well, well, show this Kašpařik in…"

Kašpařik was pale, unkempt and shaking like a mouse. Why on earth had he been dragged here? He was but a simple, provincial schoolteacher, with chalk on his britches and ink in his hair. What crime could a teacher commit – mis-mark some kid's sums?

"Master Kašpařik, sir," said Povolný gravely, "This gentleman over here, sir – he has some questions to ask, questions relating to your recent activities…"

The schoolteacher stared at the fellow's eyes with horror. "Activities?"

Honzl sneered. "Activities, yes. Activities of a – how shall I put it? – nocturnal nature. Tell me, sir – how do you sleep at night?"

"Sleep?"

"Aye, sleep. Do you sleep well, sir? Awake refreshed, ready to face the day?"

Master Kašpařik's mind raced. None of this made any sense. What did the fellow care about his sleep? And why had he been dragged to this room anyway?

"Sir, I don't quite understand…"

Honzl sniggered, mimicking the teacher's simpering little voice. "Sir, I don't quite understand…"

The Investigator picked up his quill and made a single mark on the page.

"I asked if you sleep well, sir! Or perhaps your dreams keep you awake? Your nights must be … most restless, sir, most active…"

He knows, thought the teacher, he knows! My dream, the Emperor, the signs. But who the devil could have told him? Not his wife, nor his children, nor the pupils in his class. True, he had mentioned it to his assistant, Kamma, but that was just in jest. Would Kamma inform on him? No, it was impossible, absurd! Besides, who was this fellow and how did he know these things? Could he light a candle and peer inside his head?

"I'd imagine it difficult to close your eyes at all…"

Kašpařik pushed his hands deeper into his britches, squirmed and gurned. O, why were so britches so uncomfortable, his legs so terribly long?

"I sleep very well, sir," he muttered. "My duties, they tire me out…"

"Ah, yes, your duties," said the Special Investigator. "Your … books…"

Honzl opened one of the two books and began to leaf through its pages. Sums, words, pictures: teacher's things.

Confused by the Investigator's silence, Constable Povolný butted in.

"We have received information … ah, intelligence, that is to say … that you met with a certain book-seller, a purveyor of printed matter, so to speak, with the intention of purchasing items…"

"Items?"

"Ah, periodicals and the like…"

The teacher removed his glasses and looked at the policemen blankly.

"Dear sir, I really don't…"

Honzl was on him like a shot. "This book-seller, sir – what were your dealings with him?"

"Many salesmen pass through town …"

"I speak of a most singular book-seller, sir: thin as a pencil stroke, and with teeth made entirely of wood."

"Mm…"

"What did he sell you, Kašpařik? Something illegal? Some forbidden text?"

Kašpařik squirmed uncomfortably. "Please sir – books for the children, nothing more…"

"Ah yes, schoolbooks. So I see." Honzl cast his eyes down to the open pages. "Write down the expression, 'The cow, it is grazing. The cows, they are grazing…"

"Sir, I don't understand what…"

"Enough!" The inspector closed the book with a bang. "Very poor, Master Kašpařik, very poor indeed."

Licking the top of his quill, the Investigator turned to the second tome, a slim volume in a blue cover. Again, Honzl leafed through the pages with a degree of disgust: poems of some sort, moons, lips, clouds, all the usual rubbish. The last page was torn out. Honzl pressed his fingers to the binding, tracing where the paper had come away from the glue. Only a few tattered shreds remained: most suspicious.

Sniffing, the investigator turned the book over to read the name on the binding: Nosek – now where had he heard that name before? Hm, wasn't this Nosek the author of some infamously sacrilegious and offensive poem, Two Magpies or such like? Yes, yes, there had been much talk about it at court. This poem was said to mock the Emperor, ridiculing his Holy Emperor in a most crude and offensive manner. Some said that the two birds of the poem referred to his mistress's breasts: others that they related to the size and colour of his Imperial Majesty's balls. Either way, the poem was a direct act of provocation, maligning his Majesty in a most unbecoming and illegal manner.

Aye, thought Honzl, staring straight ahead: there was more going on here than simply dreams. Was it this Nosek's scribbles which had so inflamed the thoughts and tempers of this town? But if he mentioned this Nosek, then the Ministry of Forbidden Texts would get involved – and with it that damnable Horáck, curse his pen…

When he came back to himself, he was surprised to see the school teacher still there, cowering in his seat.

"Well? What is it you want? You are dismissed, Master Kašpařik, dismissed. Constable, take this fellow back to his cell."

"Sir?"

"I said take him away! We will talk more of this, Master Kašpařik, oh yes indeed! Many a dog has been drowned in an ink well, you mark my words. Your name, Master Kašpařik, is in the book. In the book, I say!"

And with that the schoolteacher was led from the room.

Alone once more, the Investigator leapt from his chair, strode from bed to window, and then sat back down.

With a look of infinite disgust, he again picked up the slim book of posey. Aye, all the usual dross: midnight assignations, birds, deathless sighs, eternity. Honzl wanted to spit. Heaven alone knew why so-called educated folk lapped up this kind of muck.

Disappointingly, and despite his best efforts, the Investigator could find no reference to his Imperial Majesty or discern any trace of subversive material of any kind: not that this meant it wasn't there, of course.

'There is a deeper meaning in every parting/fleeting kisses, eternal love/dreams are but a moment lost...'

Did any of this mean anything? Honzl leafed through the book as if through a dog's leavings. Birds, rivers, goats, the cat of knowledge and his pretty little ditty – O what rubbish these scribblers write!

Of course, none of this was his area. No, such duties belonged to The Ministry of Forbidden Texts – or The Emperor's Eye, as it was known, and to Horáck, damn his soul...

At the thought of his rival, Special Investigator Honzl ground his teeth in frustration. The Devil take that smug bastard and his pointy head! How Horáck loved to lord it over the other Departments, claiming the search for prohibited material to be endorsed by both Popes as well as the Emperor – the conceited little shit! But if Horáck were called in then the case would be taken out of his hands – a case into which he had already poured so much black wine. No, no, no: Horáck was not about to pinch his birds – not when they were so close to hand.

Honzl's reflections were rudely interrupted by a knock at the door, followed by a serving-woman, a plate of Favours, and a pot of tea.

Honzl shooed away the wench and sniffed at the buns most suspiciously. There was something odd about these 'favours', neither cardamom nor cinnamon nor any spice he recognised. What was it? Still, he had better things to think about. He picked up his pen and shoved the buns to one side.

None of this dreadful posey referred to his majesty's person, right enough. But what of the missing page, that torn sheet indicated by the tattered paper stuck to the binding. Was this where Nosek's birds had once made their nest? Well, perhaps. Had that fool of a schoolteacher carefully removed the poem and then craftily hidden it? Or – worse still, and worse for him! – had he copied out the poem and distributed it among like-minded souls in the town, spreading his filth through the streets much as the plague is spread by rats. Was this the cause of the seditious dreaming that had taken such a hold on the town of Hrůza?

Honzl tickled the end of his nose with his quill. Of course, the simplest thing would be to have Povolný work the schoolteacher over for an hour or two – see what the learned gentlemen had to say about poetry after that. But that would mean telling Povolný all about Nosek and his damnable book – and that in turn would bring in Horáck and his filthy eyes. No, swore the Investigator, absolutely not! Honzl was not about to hand over this case to The Ministry of Forbidden Texts – register of prohibited books be damned...

With that, there was another knock on the door, Povolný appearing as if summoned by the Investigator's thoughts.

"Sir? Sir, there's a nun here to see you. A sister from the

Carmelite convent in Žádost."

"A nun? But…

"Says it's about the young girl we arrested, sir. The one who murdered those two cabbies…"

The cabbies?" Honzl's yellow eyes glittered. "Hm, well, send her in."

The sister was dressed in modest grey vestments, a rosary hanging from a silver belt slung about her gown. For some reason she was also wearing pretty pearl ear-rings, fox-coloured stockings, and a very nice pair of boots.

"Inspector," she began. "I belong to the Blessed Order of the Nuns of the Visitation – from the convent in Žádost. There we await the arrival of our sister Eliška, entrusted into our care by her most gracious uncle, an exceedingly Godly and well-deserving man."

"Mm, well, I don't see what…"

The nun put her hands together and spoke most earnestly. "It is because of our sister that I have come to speak with you today. Inspector, please, I beg of you – Eliška is innocent, as any fool can see! How could a girl overpower two fully grown men? A mere girl of seventeen without weapon or accomplices or motive of any kind?"

"I…"

"You know as well as I that the poor girl is no murderer. And yet she may be in real danger…"

"Danger?"

"Danger from the real murderer, still at large."

The nun flung her arms open as if about to launch into song. "Is she really safe in the Powder Gate?" she asked, her pearl earrings catching in the light. "Would she not be safer behind the thick walls of our convent at Žádost – at least until your investigations are completed? Please Inspector, I beg of you!"

The nun had very sweet breath – what was it, some kind of berry or liqueur? Whatever it was, the Special Investigator found it most distracting.

At that, the sister suddenly paused.

"Inspector, might you ask the constable to step outside?"

"Bah, anything you want to say to me can be said…"

The sister looked down at her rosary coquettishly. "Sir, I bring you a message from the Abbess which she told me to convey to your ears alone."

"Ears?" Honzl looked over at Polovný.

"Yes my lord, ears."

"Ears, eh? Well, well, I suppose…"

And with that Honzl dismissed Polovný with a wave.

"Sir?"

"Be gone, be gone. If we have need of your services, I will ring this bell."

"Yes sir, of course sir."

"Well," said the Special Investigator, after the constable had departed, "what is it?"

The sister moved a little closer.

"The Abbess is most anxious to receive Miss Jedličová without attracting unnecessary attention. Her uncle is a most important and, ah, generous person, and he has asked that she be admitted to the convent away from the eyes of all but God."

Honzl scowled.

"I don't see what any of this…"

With a practiced movement, the nun reached into her wimple, removing a small, velvet bag.

"This gentleman has been kind enough to advance the Order a small sum in order to facilitate her swift passage…"

"Small?" said the Investigator, "how small?"

She passed him the velvet bag and Honzl weighed it in his

hand: no, not so small, after all.

"If we understand each other, Inspector?"

"Yes, yes, I believe we do."

Honzl pocketed the bribe and rang a small silver bell. "Constable! Constable, here, I tell you!"

The Constable returned obediently.

"Povolný, please make plans with the Sister for Miss Jedličová to be transferred to Žádost as soon as possible."

"To…?"

"Do as I say, damn you! The girl is to be conveyed to the convent by noon – and you will make all the necessary arrangements, do you hear me?"

"But sir, I…"

"Oh, and take away these buns – they have a strange smell…"

"Sir?"

"Your Emperor's Favours! They are most disagreeable. Well, thank you Sister. God speed back to Žádost."

"The Lord bless you…"

"You too, my good lady."

Povolný sniffed the buns suspiciously. "These cakes, sir? What seems to be…?"

"Oh, for heaven's sake, just take them away," snapped the Investigator. "And close the door behind you. I need to think, damn your bones…"

After Povolný and the Sister had departed, Honzl opened the little velvet bag and counted out the gulden. A hundred? Well, enough to sweeten the cup. Besides, the good Sister was right: there was no way Miss Jedličová could have done away with the two cabbies without anybody seeing. No, no, the cabbies were a false lead: they had nothing to do with the real matter at hand. Better to ask what that clown Mitrovsky had meant by 'literary' business – or what that Master Bilek was hiding in his box.

Honzl began to scribble in his book, humming to himself tunelessly. Ah, let the ladies go to Žádost! He could reel them back if necessary. For now though he had other bones on his plate – starting with the cursed scribbler, Nosek.

The Investigator placed the nun's purse next to the teacher's book in a drawer in his desk. It was hot and stuffy, and he struggled to open the shutters of the window above. The evening air was warm and inviting, scented with tallow and smoke and glue. Somewhere, on the other side of town, a little bell was ringing – a carriage bell, mayhap.

8

For some reason it took Mitrovsky and Halas a long time to find their way back to The Golden Tiger, each street a black thought, the town a riddle without end. Finally though, the Tiger's filthy curtain appeared in the gloom, as if some kindly stage-hand had spotted the Count and obligingly rolled it into view.

The Count and Halas stumbled in, but in their somewhat confused state, they took a wrong turn somewhere, entering not the common-room, but some sort of pantry instead.

The space was dark, damp, worse than a beggar's pot. Halas hiccupped silently.

"That's it, Master Halas," said the Count, slapping him loudly on the back, "better out than in."

Lit by a single smoky lantern, the storeroom was piled high with mouldy sacks and sagging boxes, bags of dusty herbs hanging down from the ceiling. Mice ran everywhere, cockroaches waggling their feelers as if conducting an invisible orchestra.

From there the door opened to some sort of cold room, chops and cuts lying next to the brawn and offal, a table of victuals and meat. Had Eliška, while sleeping, wandered down here? Was that why her gown was bespattered and red? And then had she simply wandered outside, as, indeed, was her nocturnal wont?

Pish-posh, thought Mitrovsky, 'tis the perfect solution! But why hadn't anybody else thought of this?' Mitrovsky shrugged. Of course, everyone knows that Counts are tremendously cunning, especially when it comes to nocturnal adventures and mysterious perambulations and the like.

Jigging up and down as if in need of the privy, Mitrovsky turned to inform Master Halas, only to find the youngster fast asleep, splayed out like a beggar at a wedding.

Mitrovsky leant over and gave the boy a shake.

"Lad, lad, wake up, I have important news!"

Nothing doing: Halas was out like a light.

'Ah, youth!' thought the Count, though in truth he too felt awful drowsy, his eyes as heavy as coal. Mitrovsky looked around at the sacking and straw and stretched. Was there time for a quick nap? Aye, why not? The mystery would still be solved when he woke up! The Count smacked his chops like an elderly mutt. Forty winks, not one more and not one less: what harm could come of it? Then he would inform the authorities, spring Eliška from the joint, and skip town before this Moosendorf returned – Moosendorf and his lanky friends…

'Aye,' thought the Count tipsily, 'he had to get out of this place – get hold of those nightingales, read Nosek's poem, prevent Mařenka's carriage from passing through the gate…'

The Count rolled onto his side and farted. Ah, sweet Mařenka – how lovely your stockings, um, the ones with the little white tassels and the ankle bows in blue… And with that the lovelorn Count finally fell asleep.

When the Count opened his eyes, the Emperor was standing over him, His Majesty painted a beautiful shade of lilac, like the shadows behind his head.

"M'lord?" said Mitrovsky, struggling to get to his feet. "Your highness, is that you?"

The Emperor's nose stood out like a candle, his eyes black and empty, as if winnowed out by beetles. But 'twas him nonetheless: Mitrovsky recognised his mug from a pfennig. When the Count rose to face him, the Emperor's wooden teeth clacked shut like a trap.

"Your Imperial righteousness, ah, that is to say…"

Instead of replying, the Emperor put a pale finger to his lips, beckoning Mitrovsky hence.

Bowing deeply, the Count tottered after him, leaving Halas to his bed of sacks. To be visited by The Emperor was quite the honour: but where was the Imperial Beak taking him?

The night was warm, perfumed, dark: if it hadn't been for the clacking of the Emperor's teeth, Mitrovsky would have lost him in the gloom. They walked from New World Street and thence down Moth lane, the Emperor first, followed by his subject and a little black cat, its tail sticking up like a pencil. But why so quiet? 'Twas as if all the good people of the town lay snugly in their beds, the streets empty as a beggar's purse.

Somewhere between Our Lady's Well and Berger's malt-house, the Emperor suddenly came to a halt. Extending a long, white finger – the digit almost as long as his nose – the sovereign indicated a dim back-street where a dismal figure stood begging, an empty hat lying by his foul, be-stockinged feet.

Mitrovsky turned to his lord and bowed. "Your Majesty? What…?"

The Emperor's jaws clacked loudly and he moved his finger to his lips. The beggar was bent as a hook, and as bristly as a hedgehog. Mitrovsky looked at the fellow and shrugged.

"Sire, I don't…"

Teeth still clacking, His Imperial Majesty gestured toward the beggar, and then withdrew from the scene.

Squinting, Mitrovsky took his first uncertain steps toward the fellow, his handkerchief held up like some amulet of protection.

Aye, 'twas some hobo, right enough. The beggar gazed down at his hat as if it were a pot of soup: pish posh, what could he see there, the future? Whatever it was, he paid the Count no heed. The fellow wore a shaggy cloak and a dog-skin coat all covered with dirt, as if he'd just risen from the grave to go and look for work. Mitrovsky edged a little closer. For all his decrepitude, something about the figure seemed familiar. Then it came to him: Father! Aye, it was the old Count standing there, the late Count Mitrovsky, looking at his son, a shy expression on his lips.

"Son, son, is it you?"

"Father?"

"Son! My son! 'Tis you!"

"Papa!"

The two embraced, the old man smelling of soil, Mitrovsky of booze and paprika.

"Father, O Father, what happened to you? What are you doing here? Why…"

"Shh, shh – I've come back to visit, see how you're getting on, check you're keeping well…"

With this the old Count took a step back to survey his son, narrowing his eyes as an auctioneer might size up a sheep.

"Yes, yes – you've put on weight, that's good. But your clothes! And that poor wig! 'Tis awful…"

"And you father, I … ah, I did not expect to see you in such a poor man's garb."

The old man gave a sad smile and bared his dirty palms. "Yes, yes: where once a feast was spread, now stands a coffin. But it can't be helped. As the good book says, in the next world, the first will be last and the last will be first."

With this the old man patted his son on the shoulder, his breath like bitter herbs.

"'Tis the tragedy of age, my son: we all learn wisdom too late. But tell me: the timber from the Estate – are you still getting ten thousand a year? 'Tis good timber, my lad – don't listen to a word that Lame Patočka says, the old thief!"

"Yes, yes, father," he said, haltingly "'Tis good wood."

"Ah, I knew I could rely on you! And the repairs to the mill?"

"All done, Poppa."

"Good lad! You should get Ondrej to take a look at the hen house too; in a strong wind, it lists to one side…"

"Yes, of course…"

"And Marta?"

"O, the same! Still complaining 'bout the wasps in the pantry."

"Ha, Ha, yes, I can see her now!"

When he laughed, you could see the old Count's black tongue and empty gums. But he seemed much gentler now, as if a spell in the grave had done him good. What was it Marta used to say? Even an executioner's block was once a pretty tree.

"Yes, Marta misses you – and the dogs and horses too…"

The Count stared at his father with great feeling. How wonderful that even on the other side people still cared about him, wished him well, marked the very hairs on his head. And he'd come back to this world to check on him, like a kindly Daddy mumbling a lullaby under his breath.

Mitrovsky wiped his eyes.

"And Matej, Father – he's back from his soldiering and as strong and handsome as ever, a row of shiny medals on his chest…"

"Matej?"

At the mention of his name, the old man's expression seemed to darken.

Mitrovsky laughed.

"Aye, he came back with a sack of Turkish gold and stories to tell – cannons and caves and carpets and the like…"

The old man shook his head like a horse bothered by flies, his jaw all twisted and clenched.

"But… but… aren't you Matej?"

The Count smiled, trying to steady the old man. "Ha ha ha. No, Father, I'm Karel, the younger son … Karel, Poppa, don't you remember?"

The beggar stared at his son blankly.

"Not Matej?"

"No Father, Karel…"

"Karel?" The old man scowled. "Karel you say?" He spat on the ground and out of nowhere – from the Devil's pocket, as they say – produced a stick and began to beat the Count about his person.

"Matej! Matej, where are you? What's this scoundrel done with you?"

The blows were heavy and cruel, the old goat stronger than he looked.

"Father, please…"

"Matej, Matej, where are you? Impostor! Crook! Thief!"

The Count placed his elbows in the way to protect himself as best he could, the blows falling down like rain.

"Daddy, Father, please…"

"Matej, Matej, my son…"

The blows continued to fall, but now from a broom rather than a stick. Wait, a broom?

"Shoo, shoo!" shouted the cleaning-woman, "you get out of here! What are you doing here anyway? Shoo, be gone with you…"

The woman clobbered Mitrovsky on the bonce and turned to Young Halas. "Out! Out! Find another ditch to die in, you dirty pair…"

Retreating from the hail of blows, Mitrovsky and Halas fled from the cellar and outside. There, the big red sun beat down indifferently. Halas rubbed his sore head and blinked while the Count looked about him as if this too were part of a dream.

Somewhere a bell tolled dolefully: six o'clock. Six hours until the carriage to P. The Count looked back at the storeroom door but there was no sign of beggar, Emperor or Pop; no, Old Mitrovsky had disappeared with the dawn, like foxes, or money. Father, father! But it was no use, Hrůnza was waking up and the old man was gone, taking the night's blue mystery with him.

9

Fleischmann's bakery was the most famous in all of Hrůza, occupying one whole side of the square between Flour Street and Sinners' Row, the entrance 'neath a mural of some exotic beauty eating a pretzel. At this hour, the carts were just starting to line up, the bread smelling sweet and warm and good.

Constable Povolný, still carrying the Investigator's plate of favours, hailed Borchotz the wagon-man as the fellow loaded his cart with loaves. The bread was packed into large wooden baskets, Borchotz tall as a church door and wide as a country gate.

"Beautiful morning, Borchotz! What say you – sleep well?"

"Sleep?" The wagon-man climbed down from his cart and looked at the policeman's plate most suspiciously.

"Aye – an honest night's rest, no strange dreams of any kind?"

Borchotz's cheek twitched: last night the wagon man had dreamt of an enormous chicken, the Emperor hatched from a speckled egg – but how the devil did this swine know?

"You'll have to ask my missus," said Borchotz, grinning through beer-stained teeth. "If you can wake her, that is."

"Wake her? Ha Ha, I wouldn't dare!"

Povolný adjusted his cap and rested his plate on a box.

"And what about you, Vobecký? Any odd fancies?"

The wagon-man's mate jerked awake. Last night Vobecký had dreamt of the Emperor as an old dead tree, the leaves falling away to leave his Majesty naked as a babe.

"Can't say I have, Constable," he said, looking up the policeman with sleepy eyes. "Slept like a baby – up all night, crying for a bottle!"

"Ha ha, a bottle!" laughed the policeman. "Ha ha, a bottle, indeed!"

Then, seeing that the wagon men had already turned back to their business, Polovný saluted and sidled slowly toward the storehouse, carrying the favours before him like St Denis carrying his head.

Inside, Mrs Fleischmann was over-seeing the deliveries, her beautiful face red and flushed, flour covering her cheeks like freckles.

"Who's there?" she cried. "O, but you look tired Constable. A hard night? Ah, what's that saying? At noon he frolicked like a young goat, by evening he looked dead." Mrs Fleischmann blew a strand of hair from her face. "I bet you know all about frolicking, you devil…"

Povolný reddened and looked down at his boots.

"I'm here on official business, Mrs Fleischmann, police business."

"Oo, police business, is it? At this early hour? O my sweet! A young man like you – you need to get your sleep. You work too hard, all that arresting people. You need a good woman to sort you out. Give your whistle a rub once in a while, eh?"

The Constable flushed from his cap to the tips of his boots.

"Mrs Fleischmann I…"

"Oo, what lovely long lashes you have, Constable! Wasted on a boy…"

Constable Povolný swallowed. What had he come here for? Oh, yes, the favours…

"Mrs Fleischmann – have a sniff of these favours. Do they smell correct to you?"

"Correct?" Mrs Fleischmann leant over the buns and sniffed. "They seem fine to me. What is it Constable – you arresting rolls now?"

"Ah…"

"You policemen – always sniffing out criminals! O, what noses you must have!"

"Ah, is your husband here, Mrs Fleischmann? I have to ask him, ah, a number of questions."

"He's out by the ovens – if he hasn't fallen in! Come on in, take the weight off your boots."

"Mrs Fleischmann, please…"

"O hush. I knew you when your Ma was wiping your arse."

Still blushing, the Constable followed Mrs Fleischmann past the flour barn and into a little yard, white powder covering everything, sparrows pecking at the seeds and rye.

"Sit yourself down and…"

"Do you ever dream, Mrs Fleischmann?" Povolný blurted out.

"Dream?" Mrs Fleischmann's apron stopped in its tracks. "Ha ha, what a question!"

"It's just that…"

"Dream?" said Mrs Fleischmann again. "Now what would a young man like you be doing worrying about my dreams?"

"Ah…"

"A young man comes in asking a married lady about her dreams…"

"I…"

"With his beautiful eyes and all…"

Povolný felt as hot as an oven boy. "O Mrs Fleischmann, I didn't mean…"

At this the baker's wife smiled. "Foo– look at you! I'm just teasing, my lad. Of course I dream you ninny! Last night I dreamed of you…"

And with that she flounced off in a puff of flour, two little footprints left behind in the dust.

Povolný rubbed the back of his neck distractedly: ach, he wasn't cut out for this job. Making his way over to the largest of the barns, he paused for a moment where the sacks of rye and wheat were lined up under a large wooden hook, a black cat sunning himself in one corner – the ratter, Povolný supposed. Keeping one eye out for Mr Fleischmann and the other for Mr Fleischmann's wife, the Constable snuck across the barn and opened one of the sacks. The seeds were flat, brown and sour. Povolný sniffed: aye, not just yeasty, but spoiled and bitter. Something was amiss here, something…

"Constable! What can I do for you? Find a groschen in a black loaf?" Fleischmann was a squat but sinewy barrel of a man, tanned a deep mahogany from the ovens, his eyebrows burnt right off. "Here, come and take a glass of good Rhine wine with me. Not too early, is it? Ah, another beautiful day! You can hear the grain yellowing in the fields…"

The baker picked up two stools, planting them in the ground like cabbage plants.

"Now then Constable – how can I be of assistance?"

Povolný eyed up the baker uncertainly: how should he proceed? "Mister Fleischmann," he began. "Do you ever dream?"

At this the baker roared. "What a question! Ha ha! Even little ants dream of big ants, my boy…"

"Yes, but special dreams…"

"Special dreams?"

"Yes, dreams in which – ah, how shall I put it?"

All at once the baker pulled his stool a little closer. "Oh, those dreams…"

"Well, yes…"

"A gentleman's dream…"

174

"What? No, I…"

"Oh lad, we all have those dreams from time to time – 'specially in the days of your youth! Just keep a rag by the side of your bed, my lad. And change your night-gown right away."

"No Mister Fleischmann…"

"When you're married, these dreams won't come so much – 'specially not if you're married to my Julinka, ha ha! Hush, here she comes…"

Mrs Fleischmann approached carrying a bucket of wine and fresh plate of Favours. "Now what are you two boys whispering about?" she said, hand-on-hip, Povolný the colour of beetroot.

Mr Fleischmann winked at the young fella. "None of your business, eh young fellow? Now here, try one of these fresh ones … a present from the Emperor."

Was it his imagination or did these rolls too taste strange? The Constable chewed carefully, his tongue looking for clues, his head throbbing. The Favours were dry and bitter, like dust.

"Mr Fleischmann, these rolls, do…"

"And how's your mother? Still well?"

"My mother? Yes, yes, still well."

"You need to tell her to take better care of you," said the baker's wife, butting in.

"Oh…"

"Look at him Bohus, wasting away he is…"

"Julinka, please…"

"And those dark shadows under his eyes – what he needs is a good night's sleep and a chicken in the morning."

"Julinka, he's a grown man…"

"Grown? Hush now – I know what you boys need! And look at that uniform, all worn out on the cuffs…"

"Mrs Fleischmann, I…"

"Quiet woman! The Constable's a big boy now, eh? What he

needs is plenty of exercise and fresh air. You need to get out of town, my lad – breathe in the smell of pine."

Mrs Fleischmann pulled a face. "What, tramping around in all that mud? I would think not. Why, next you'd have him sleeping with the windows wide open…"

"In this heat? Why, of course I…"

"Stupid man! All sorts of things blow in through an open window. My Aunt Masha caught her death…"

"What? Foolishness blew in through a window? Your Masha was crushed by a cow."

"Yes, but…"

"Did this cow come in through a window?"

"No no, but she needed milk for her health…"

"She had a sore throat."

"Smallpox!"

"And she caught this from the cow? It sat on her."

"Because she needed the milk!"

"The milk should stick in her throat."

Constable Povolný felt his eyes closing. Aye, it had been a long night, right enough, long as a rat's tail. The combination of sun, Favours, and strong Rhine wine made his head swim: ah, if only he could close his eyes, if only for a second… He imagined one of the Favours leaping down from the plate and rolling off in the direction of the barns, the Emperor winking and singing 'Bold you were/And lighter than a bird's wing' in a strange and wonderful voice.

"Constable, Constable, wake up!"

"O hush, let the poor boy sleep…"

"Constable, are you alright? You dropped your Favour."

The Constable opened his eyes. "Favour?"

"Yes, yes, here it is. Here now, take a bite – you need to build up your strength…"

"His mother neglects him…"

"Julinka, please…"

"Look at him – withering on the branch…"

The Constable could hear voices but couldn't make any sense of what anybody was saying. Just what was going on here? When Povolný looked down at his roll, the Emperor stared back, his nose sticking out like a finger.

10

"You Mitrovsky?"

"Me? Ah…"

"Count Mitrovsky?"

"The Count? Why, yes indeed…"

The urchin boy surveyed the fellow suspiciously.

"You don't look like a Count."

"Ah…"

"Are those patches made from cat?"

Mitrovsky glanced down at his sleeves.

"What is it you want, my lad?"

The urchin reached into his filthy pocket and produced a slip of paper. "Got a message for Count Mitrovsky."

"A message, eh?"

"From a lady."

"A lady? Ha ha, well, us Counts … ah, let me have it then."

The lad looked first at the paper, and then at the Count's big eyes.

"You sure you're Mitrovsky?"

"Ha, ha, quite a character! Here's a shilling for you – ha, ha, yes indeed!"

The note was from Mrs Jedličová, written in her own beautiful hand, the 'p's and 'f's riding across the page like seahorses. Eliška had vanished yet again. Heaven alone knew how it had happened: the guard must have been drunk, or asleep, or 'answering the call of nature'. In other news, Mrs Jedličová had been baking spelt rolls and finished knitting a scarf for Young Master Halas. 'Come quick!' it said. Also 'Could you pick up some raisins on the way?'

Mitrovsky and Halas bustled over to the Powder Gate at a fair trot – 'before the dog barks', as they say. The same good-natured turnkey was outside the door, watching two dogs fight over a bone, while humming 'Above the forest dark, I saw a little star' – the turnkey, that is, not the dogs.

"Morning sirs," said the fellow cheerfully. "See the ladies, is it?"

Once up the stairs, Mrs Jedličová greeted them with her beautiful lips. "My chick," she cried, "she's gone, wandered from the path!" At this, Mrs Jedličová paused, taking the Count's hand in hers. "My dear Karel, you look awful. Where did you sleep last night? Just look at you – big black rings round your eyes. And how is your back? Do you need a cushion?"

"A cushion? No, no, 'tis fine. But what of dear Eliška?"

Mrs Jedličová's tale was shorter than a pig's snout. Eliška had vanished sometime after midnight. The turnkey hadn't noticed – when he brought their breakfast, Mrs Jedličová had said her daughter was still on the pot.

"O, what am I to do?" said Mrs Jedličová brushing the crumbs from Mitrovsky's jacket. "My girl is lost in Hrůza and up to who knows what? O Count – look, here's a handkerchief, you've got honey on your lips."

The Count looked at her, but his mind was elsewhere. The carriage to P left at twelve, so, if the bells of St Rudolf were right, there were only … um, four, five, hours to pluck the goose.

He patted her knee protectively. "Fear not my sweet! I give you my word as a gentleman that we will find…"

But before he could finish there was a knock at the door.

"Knock knock," said the guard, poking his head through. "Carriage outside – come to take the ladies to Žádost."

The occupants of the room looked at one another in alarm.

"Ah, a carriage, you say?" said Mrs Jedličová, looking rather flushed.

"Yes, a carriage."

"To Žádost?"

"Um, yes, Žádost."

Mrs Jedličová and the Count exchanged glances.

"Says you're to leave right away. Sorry to interrupt." The guard twisted his collar like a rabbit in a trap. "Well, I'll leave you to get your things…"

When he'd gone, the Count looked at Mrs Jedličová and Mrs Jedličová looked at the Count.

"The convent? But I thought we were under arrest? O my dear Count, what does it mean? Are we free to go?"

"Free? Well, yes, ah, yes indeed…"

"And what of Eliška?" Mrs Jedličová took hold of Mitrovsky's sleeve. "If they discover that she's gone then … O my dear Count … it's a catastrophe, a calamity! Whatever should we do?"

Mitrovsky strode over to the window and peeped through the shutters. Outside waited a carriage with a mustard-coloured cab and golden wheels – a most stylish contraption and not at all what might be expected of The Nuns of the Visitation. Rather than two holy sisters, a pair of burly cabbies waited alongside it, one checking the harness and tack, the other smoking a pipe.

"Aye," said the Count. "a carriage right enough."

"But Karel, what do we say? If they discover that Eliška has absconded, then – O Lord! – we'll be arrested all over again. But how can I go on to Žádost without her? Stupid, stupid, wicked girl! O, why couldn't I have been blessed with sons – big strapping boys like you…"

"Aye, 'tis a pickle," said the Count, pacing up and down the room. "Unless…"

At the rear of the chamber stood a tall Viennese wardrobe, the box made from cherry wood with two little wings on the top, as if seeking to take off. Mitrovsky rapped on the door, undid the latch, and then smartly climbed inside, the closet swallowing him entirely.

"Nuns and novices are often housed in Powder Gates," said the Count from inside the box. 'Tis on account of their sensitivity, to protect their purity from the rough fingers of the world. But I wonder… wait, wait … Aha!"

Mitrovsky emerged holding a novice's gown and wimple, the vestments covered in mouse droppings, but serviceable at a pinch.

"Quick Master Halas – put this on."

Halas stared back at the Count with his blank, innocent eyes.

"What? No, no, the size looks right enough. Be quick, Master Halas, for we have no time to lose."

The young pup nodded and began to remove his clothes. Mrs Jedličová watched him keenly.

"But Karel, whatever are you…?"

"Madame Jedličová – sweet lady – please step behind the screen and remove your womanly garments."

Mrs Jedličová's beautiful cheeks blushed deeply. "Why Karel, whatever do you mean?"

"'Tis the only solution, my darling. I will disguise myself as you, and Master Halas will pretend to be Eliška. Thence we shall ride to the Convent at Žádost. Hush, hush, hear me out. When the sisters are at mass or some such holy thing, we can escape through an open window and…"

"But Count, your beard…"

"Tish tosh, unsightly hairs can always be disguised with a

carefully applied shawl or fan..."

"O Karel!"

"Swifty, my dove – you must remove your attire before the turnkey returns."

Minutes later Mrs Jedličová had divested herself of wig, bonnet and bodice, the Count struggling to smuggle his girth within their delicate folds.

"Ah, but what ribbon to adorn the blouse?" pondered the Count, though alas there was no time to decide: the guard was already at the door.

"Ready, good ladies?"

The Count flicked Mrs Jedličová's fan coquettishly. "Yes, my good man, we're coming…"

As the guard turned, Mrs Jedličová's beautiful head appeared above the screen, the rest of her modestly hidden.

"Count … Karel … please my prince, take care! O dear Count! And make sure to cover your chest, convents can be terribly damp."

"Yes, yes! 'Till we meet again, my angel…"

With that the Count blew her a delicate kiss and descended the long, rickety stairs. Underneath his wimple, Halas's eyes blinked weakly.

"Fear not, Master Halas," whispered the Count, "us counts are good at disguises and play-acting and that sort of thing. Why, 'tis almost second nature."

When they reached the carriage, the cabbies took one look at them and spat.

"C'mon sister, we ain't got all day," said the one with the pipe, opening the carriage door for Halas. "That's it lady. You can finish putting on your blusher at the convent…"

They lifted the Count into the back, then tossed his bag in after him. "C'mon, c'mon – this thing is on a meter."

Mitrovsky put one foot on the step and his gown ripped loudly.

"Leave it," snapped the Cabbie. "I'm sure the Abbess has got a needle and thread..."

"But..."

"Leave it, I said. You dames have kept us waiting long enough..."

With that Mitrovsky and Halas settled into their seats and the carriage set off. It didn't take long to quit Hrůza. The coach passed the river and its locust trees, the House of Silver Eaves and Ježek's brewery, the carriage trotting along the Post Road at a fair old clip, the cabbies swearing loudly.

"Um, are you sure this is the way to Žádost?" asked the Count, pulling back the curtain. "It's just that..."

"We're taking a short cut."

"But..."

"The other road is closed – bandits and brigands."

"Bandits? I haven't..."

"Look, d'you wanna get to Žádost or not? Just pipe down and leave the driving to us."

"Ah..."

"You gotta problem with that?"

"No, no – God speed, my prince."

Mitrovsky pulled his head back inside. "Fear not," he said, "I'm sure these fellows know best. Cabbies are like crows – they always fly the shortest route."

Halas' eyes looked like they were about to pop out of his head.

From Hrůza, they took the Post Road south, eventually turning off onto a weed strewn track littered with rocks, dips and patches of broken earth. In the fields, the ears of grain gave off a brownish dust, the sky a deep blue doom. Shadows lengthened as if on a rack, the sun a cruel yellow.

Mitrovsky banged on the roof, calling out in a soft voice, "Lads,

O sweet lads, how long till we stop for a sup?"

"Listen lady, we'll be there soon enough…"

"Aye, but 'tis hot as an oven in here and…"

"You dames sit tight. I'm sure the nuns'll have a pot to piss in."

"But…"

"Zip it lady – we don't need your yapping."

Mitrovsky pulled his head back in. "Such jolly fellows!" he exclaimed, straightening his wig. "Must be all that fresh air, and the sweet, sweet company of horses."

Nevertheless, the journey seemed interminable, the motionless air aflame with heat. The rye glowed yellow, the buck-wheat a rusty brown. Everything green seemed to have been burned by the sun – what remained was the colour of sand.

Beneath Mrs Jedličová's wig, the Count's thoughts turned like a key in a lock. Ditches full of brushwood, a jumble of sandstone rocks and junipers, a stake leaning to one side like a dead tree: ah, he seemed to be drifting ever further from Mařenka and her birds, her beautiful white stockings and expensive-looking broach. The Count sniffed. O Mařenka, wait for me! 'Late blooms I find more pleasing/Than any bright first flower.' He imagined her lips fluttering this way and that like a moth, her lily-white skin, the row of ivory buttons on the back of her bodice… O, what a dish! But at the same time, it felt she were moving further and further away, disappearing beyond the horizon as it were, where the plains all turn to mist…

He shook his head. A signpost stretched out four arms. Gossamer threads hung from the bushes. Little purple flowers grew everywhere, even among the dust. Aye, time passed awful slowly here. Mitrovsky tried regaling Young Master Halas with tales of his standing-order at Tomášek's haberdashery – "such beautiful, beautiful lace" – when he was interrupted by a loud pop somewhere just above him .

"Ho, what the devil?"

The Count looked out of the window in time to see one of the cabbies abruptly plummet from his seat, hands gripped to his chest.

"Halas, Halas, what…"

Then there was a second shot and the other cabbie tumbled from his pew, his body landing in the dust.

"Remarkable!" said the Count, poking his head out of the window. "Halas, my lad, we seem to have lost our drivers!"

In this, the Count was right. The two cabbies were lying dead on the road while the carriage bounced along the rocky path, the horses throwing back their heads and galloping wildly.

Halas looked at them, wide-eyed.

"Worry not," said the Count, "this kind of thing happens to me all the time. In my experience…"

All of a sudden, the sound of a pistol shot – or perhaps a branch, snapped by the carriage wheels – echoed angrily. The two men held tightly onto their seats and the cab rocked wildly, one of the horses neighing most peculiarly.

"We are most fortunate," yelled Mitrovsky, his body flung from side to side, "that horses possess a keen instinct and unerring feel for the road…"

At that moment the central shaft of the coach broke in two, removing the cab from its axle and sending it down onto the road with a great crash of broken wood and screaming metal. Halas' lips were open as if he were trying to scream too.

The cab turned over once, then twice, upending itself in a ditch. There was a mighty groaning and splintering of wood, accompanied by a great and terrible crash. One wheel bounced off along the road, another landed by a poplar tree. Only Mrs Jedličová's wig made it out in time, taking flight like a magpie, a tiny speck against the dark blue sky. Afterward: silence.

11

The guys plastering the wall outside Kusý's brush-makers, the penitent begging outside Saint Jerome's, the Auntie selling finches on Podebradý Square: all of 'em looked like the Emperor. No kidding – His Majesty was everywhere! Same conk, same weak chin, same nasty eyes. Hell, even the dog sitting outside Koćab's Butchers looked just like him, the mutt growling most regally, looking down its muzzle like an aristocrat. But why so many Emperors? Two Popes were a lot – but this? It was all the fault of those damn Favours. Something was wrong with the seeds, or the yeast, or something. But Povolný didn't want to go back to the Fleischmanns right now. What he wanted was to go his bed, close his eyes, and dream of something else instead.

In his distracted state, the Constable failed to notice the little round woman hurrying for the twelve o' clock carriage, or the shadowy figures off to one side, their bodies long and thin as a shadow at evening time. Nope, what he saw was the Emperor's conk poking out of apple barrels or peeking from wool-merchants – and what a conk! Long, thin, well-bred, with two patrician nostrils and an elegantly tapered tip. It was a nose that followed you all about the room – or in this case, all the way through Hrůza, Polovný stumbling over his boots as he tried stepping over it.

Feverish, pale, and still a little drunk on the Fleischmanns' strong Rhine wine, the Constable staggered this way and that like a crazy person. Imagine the Emperor's nose looming out of the river, or lashed to the back of Milota's cart! What if the very sun had the Emperor's face? What then?

Fortunately, the Constable made it home without any incident. Unfortunately, someone had painted the Emperor's moustache upon his Ma's face, the paint still wet on her cheeks.

"What are you doing back here? Don't you have a job to go to? Naughty boy! And reeking of strong Rhine wine...

"Mum, please..."

"And don't go thinking that I'm going to launder that uniform. Look at all that dust! What a mess! Rolling in the dust at your age."

"'Tis flour."

"Flour? Out baking are we? Oh, you must think I was born yesterday, all your lies and dissembling – and you a police officer too, the shame of it..."

"Mum, I need to lie down..."

"Lie down when I've just finished making your bed? Pff, I've got better things to do than run around after you all day, young man. You think those chickens pluck themselves? They just jump in the pot?"

"Mum..."

The constable pushed his way past his mother – her mean little eyes, long snout and courtly moustache exactly those of the Emperor – and stumbled awkwardly toward the stairs, his mama's voice still following.

"I've just mopped those floors! And then you walk all over them in your policeman boots! Well, thank you very much. Ungrateful child. You think a maid comes and scrubs the dirt away? We've got servants to wipe your arse?"

Polovný looked very pale, strands of wet hair sticking to his forehead. He seemed to have shrunk inside his uniform, as if he were inside looking out.

"Mum, I've got to sleep…"

"Sleep? At this hour of the day? So, you're a fox now are you – out all night and abed all day? O, you policemen – t'aint natural, running around in a hat like that. What would your father say if he were alive today? Sluggard, lazybones, snail! And don't you go climbing into bed in those boots – I won't have that filth trailed through my bedding."

"No, Mama."

The Constable pulled shut his door, his mother clucking away on the other side of it.

"What – still growing is he? Growing lazier! I've never known such an idle boy. Busy? Busy like a cat. And don't you start muttering 'bout police business either. Playing cards and drinking strong Rhine wine is police business, is it? Chasing after skirt and tramping in dog mess – police business too? Indolent child! No wonder you aren't married. What girl would want a policeman as a husband? A policeman's the same as a crook in dim light. Why couldn't you have been a brick-maker like Mrs Novakova's son? Now there's a proper job…"

But Polovný was no longer listening. Instead – after removing his police boots like a good boy – he climbed into bed as if lowering himself in the grave, a strange yeasty smell filling his nostrils.

His limbs felt like wood, his head a chopping block on which an axe softly fell. No, no, something wasn't right here! It was the Favours – or rather those sacks in Fleischmanns' store. Aye, the smell, that was it. He needed to jump up and tell Chief Investigator Honzl – if he ever rose from his bed again, of course. O, why was everything so heavy? His body sank into the bed, the mattress enveloping him. Those feathers – so soft! Soft as, soft as … but what was this? Something long and thin was poking in his back ... a lump, a shape – the Emperor's nose.

Polovný looked down in horror. The Emperor was in his mattress! His Imperial Majesty was in his bed!

"Listen – forget the cakes," said the Emperor through the sheets. "The cakes are nothing – just a sign..."

"Sign?"

"Listen Polovný – what's happening in Hrůza, soon it'll start to happen everywhere. P, R, S, all the letters in between. It's the nightingales you've got to stop."

"Nightingales, your Majesty?"

"Nightingales – two of them. They're kept in a box. But if they make it to P – revolution, Constable, open sedition in the streets!"

Polovný looked down at the bump in terror.

"I'm sorry sir, I don't understand. These birds, these nightingales, what do ..."

"Republicanism, democracy, sedition! You must stop the birds, Polovný. What if everyone dreams of the Emperor? What if he appears naked in the street – like a baby, or a harlot? Do you want that, Constable? Open insubordination. Criticism of the nobility. Is this the kind of thing that people should be allowed to hear? That landowners are immoral? That they act outside the law? That the people are oppressed and suffering? It will end in blood, Constable Polovný. And only you can stop it."

Suddenly there was another voice at the door.

"Who are you talking to in there? Did you smuggle someone in? A girl? Eh, naughty boy?"

"No Mother, I..."

"Dirty little urchin. This ain't no bordy house, you know. You think you can bundle some tart in through the window, mess up my sheets, when it's still a week till wash day?"

"Mother, please..."

Inside the mattress, the Emperor's face resembled a death

mask.

"The nightingales must never reach the stage. They're kept in a stout metal box. You must find them, Polovný. Otherwise, the dreams of Hrůza will be but the start."

"The start, my lord? The start of what?"

"Who is that?" yelled Mrs Polovnova. "Who you talking to?"

But the Emperor had already sunk back into the feathers, his nose disappearing back below the surface.

"What you doing in there? Dirty boy! Filthy child! You better not have your boots on…"

"Police business, Mama."

"Police business? In bed at twelve o'clock?"

Polovný touched the mattress with his hand: nothing.

"On the orders of His Imperial Majesty…"

Behind the door, Mrs Polovnova snorted.

"Hmph, that old crook…"

12

From her bed, Eliška had a clear view of the churchyard, the gravedigger moving from stone to stone like a waiter tending tables, brush and pot in hand. Slowly, methodically, the gravedigger filled in the letters on the rich folk's tombs – gold for councilmen, black for everyone else. A pup followed him through the long grass, black, brown and grey, as if patched together from scraps in the furrier's pail. Eliška followed it with pale, bored eyes, the pup yapping, the man singing 'It comes again to me that moment/You passed before my eyes'.

Eliška was about to pull up the sheets when the gravedigger's wife nimbly bustled in, her apron seeming to enter the room before her.

"Awake, my dove? I've brought you a plate of Favours – and a cup of beer to warm you…"

The woman's apron was bright as a gypsy's, her eyes sparkling merrily. She too was round and short. The apron smelt of bread, her scarf of mustard, her red hands of vinegar. Just what I need, thought Eliška: another mother! The woman propped the tray by her, smiling kindly.

"O my chick! Gave us an awful scare, you did."

The girl shrugged.

"And those poor feet! Wandering around unshod after midnight – 'tis lucky the night was so close, or you'd have caught your death…"

"Yeah, right," said the girl, poking her finger in the Emperor's eye. Mothers! They were everywhere, like mice.

"Your teeny, tiny toes – goes right through me it does, thinking of you going about without shoes. All those nettles and stones – fair makes me shudder!"

"Mm."

"Whatever were you doing out there, princess? Past midnight and in your night things and all! O, makes me shiver just to think about it! Those feet wandering about without hose or stocking or sock…"

"Yeah…"

"Like two blocks of ice! You're lucky not to have lost a nail … go around barefoot, nails' liable to blacken and drop off……"

Eliška shrugged and took a slurp of beer. What did this wifey want from her? Mm, what did all mothers want? To put you back in the sack, that's what.

The grave-digger's wife blinked, dabbing at her eyes with her apron. "O you poor thing! All tired out and such dirty toes. You want to watch you don't get them infected. My sister, she got her nail infected and started to grow big talons – all yellow and long they were, curved at the end like a rooster's…"

The woman stopped: Eliška had buried her head 'neath a pillow.

"Well, maybe I should let you get some rest," said the wifey, patting the girl's lump affectionately.

Eliška moaned.

"Hark, is that husband of mine back? Well, we'll see what he has to say…"

When the door closed, Eliška poked out her head and listened. She could hear them talking in the parlour, the gravedigger and the gravedigger's wife pacing up and down the floorboards, talking in hushed tones. What had the girl been doing outside

Saint Vojtěch's, abroad in her night-things? Was she some crazy person escaped from Pithart's Hill? Or had she run away from home, her parents beside themselves with worry?

"We should tell Father Vobecký," said the gravedigger's wife. T'aint right, a girl wandering around without stockings."

The gravedigger shook his head and fussed with the puppy. "Nu, nu – no reason for that. Let her come round, tell us her story. We'll find her a cloak, I'll take her back in the undertaker's cart …"

"Poor little chit."

"She'll be right as rain. Cup of beer and all's right with the world."

Eliška sighed – why did she have to share this world with such idiots? Eliška had known it for a long time; she lived in a world of fools, daubed by an idiot with a stick. Little wonder that her feet kept carrying her off, her toes looking for the way out. But where, oh where, had they brought her now?

The night before, she'd awoken to find herself not in the Powder Gate, but rather in a dark and gloomy graveyard, surrounded by stones worn and crooked as peasant's teeth.

Shivering, Eliška had gazed up at the steep spire of Saint Vojtěch and sighed. Why had her feet carried her off *here*? She knew what these provincial towns were like, with their drunks and hooligans and beggars in dirty hats. Towns like that were full of oafs and fatheads; if they caught her in her night things, they'd paint her feet with mustard. Yes, yes, it was a universal law of nature. There were morons everywhere. Just try handing someone a piece of chalk and a slate.

As Eliška made her way across the churchyard, she heard voices close by – low, gruff, male. She slunk back into the shadows, trying to make herself as small as possible.

"'Tis a boneyard…"

"Yard…"

"But how did we get here?"

"Here?"

"Here, yes here! And where did the Tiger go? Where's our beds?"

Head down, Eliška edged closer, clinging to the darkness as best she could. Near the church wall, two slobs in uniform – cabbies? – clung drunkenly to a post. Cabbies? Aye, that was the garb of Holan und Holub. Eliška would recognise the insignia anywhere.

"I don't like this, mate…"

"Mate…"

"Something 'aint right. There now – you feel it?"

"Feel?"

"That post."

"Post."

"Can't feel a thing…"

A quiver passed through Eliška's night-things, as if both girl and nightie were hung up on a line. Weren't the cabbies dead – murdered? Eliška peered at the figures through the gloom. It must be someone else. All cabbies looked more or less the same – like sparrows. The two clots tapped the post and shook their heads in wonderment. They looked just like the dead cabbies, though – same dull eyes, flat noses, ugly chins. But what were they doing, out of their graves and flapping around Saint Vojtěch at midnight?

"We need to get back home, my lad."

"Home."

"A sup at the Tiger, and then bed."

"Bed."

"T'aint right, wandering around in this gloom. Someone'll

come and unpick us, you mark my words…"

Eliška moved sideways, stumbling on a stone. Immediately the cabbies heard her.

"What ho, who's there?"

"There!"

Eliška plucked herself from the wall and ran. Behind her, she could hear the cabbies calling out, but didn't dare look back. Stupid clods – what had they come out of their graves for? Did they think she'd murdered them too?

"Missy, please! Tell us where we are! How did we get here?"

"Here!"

"Missy, please!"

"Please!"

Outside the church wall was a dusty, cobbled lane, a horse-drawn carriage drawn up outside, some kind of ancient tarantass, pulled by a little grey nag. Eliška slowed. How strange to find a cart at this time of night – even if the carriage did look pretty dilapidated, the doors scuffed and warped, paint almost rubbed away. No driver, no groom – just an old, doddery horse, looking up and down the road as if guessing the price of rye.

Eliška threw up her arms.

"Help! Please help!"

All at once a gloved hand opened the curtains, revealing a stick-thin man with sharp, wooden teeth.

"O my dear," said the fellow, taking in Eliška's night-dress and pale, bare toes and flinging open the door. "O my dear child, whatever's wrong? What are you…?"

Eliška pointed back toward the graveyard.

"Please…"

"The churchyard? Is there someone there? Someone chasing you? Quick, my dear, jump in!"

Eliška looked first over her shoulder, then back at the carriage.

The night was dark and the cabbies right behind her. What a pair of clowns! She could hear them huffing and puffing, surprisingly out of shape for ghosts.

"Quick, quick, climb in!"

Aye, better the rabbit hole than the wolf. But as Eliška ran toward the carriage, the moon rolled out from behind the steeple like a coin, bathing the dusty little lane in a strange blue light.

The figure beckoned Ěliška closer.

"Quick, my darling, quick!"

Ěliška paused. Something wasn't right here. Horse, carriage and stick-man seemed illuminated by the same unearthly glow, the light passing right through them, as if through a window or a cloud. Ah me, 'tis true! The coach seemed as thin as chiffon, its curtains made of gauze. 'Twas as if the light emptied them out, rendering cart, passenger, and mount as transparent as glass.

"What's wrong my girl? Jump in, jump in!"

Jump? Eliška gazed at the diaphanous outline and blinked. What kind of apparition was this? The carriage seemed no more solid than a cobweb, thin as a beggar's coat, its doors a filmy screen.

"Here – let me put down the steps. That's it, jump onboard! Quick before they come…"

Shaking, Eliška turned and ran back toward the churchyard, ignoring the calls of the fella in the cart.

"My dear, where are you going? Come back, come back…"

Eliška threw open the gate and fell straight into the arms of the gravedigger.

"O Miss, what a fright!" cried the good man. "Why, I thought you a spectre or hobgoblin abroad at night…"

Only then did he realise that the girl's eyes were tight shut, focused not on this world but the next one along – pff, maybe even the one after that. Was she awake or was she asleep? It seemed impossible to tell. Taking her hand, the gravedigger led the girl toward his hut, his wife waiting with a lantern and a plate. There the girl seemed to come round, but refused to give her name, or say where she came from. Nor did she mention her mother or the convent at Žádost, never mind dead cabbies or a see-through carriage pulled by a grey horse. Instead, she laid her head on the gravedigger's pillow and closed her eyes. Where would she be when she awoke? In a graveyard, an inn, some crooked alley? Ah, who could say? Only her feet knew the truth. And they would take her there, whether she willed it or not.

13

When Mitrovsky came to, he found two small brown birds hopping up and down on his chest, as if checking out his beard for nuts.

"What? Away foul fiends!" the count growled, the birds taking flight and disappearing like gunpowder.

The Count's body had been thrown from the carriage, lying in a ditch next to a field of sun-baked stubble. Of Halas, there was no sign. Mitrovsky tried to move his arms but felt as if some tremendous weight were resting on his neck, like a sack of potatoes, or his Aunt Vanka. How painful everything felt! Was he injured, hurt, dead? The Count's ear was very warm and very wet.

"She alive?" asked a voice.

"She? Lady needs a shave, that's for sure."

The sun vanished, replaced by the shadows of two rough and unseemly gentlemen: brigands, the Count supposed.

"You search the carriage. I'll talk to our beauty here."

The fellow came closer. Under his shabby peasant jerkin, the scoundrel was surprisingly well dressed, with fashionable britches and a particularly well-made pair of boots. There was something odd about him though. His eyes were red and inflamed, his skin the colour of vellum.

"Okay Bilek," said the bandit. "Tell us where the box is and we'll let you go."

"Bilek?" murmured the Count. "My name is Madame Matuškova and…"

"Listen, what kind of an idiot you take me for? This is the worst disguise in the world, Bilek – it wouldn't fool a goose."

"Um…"

The fellow grabbed hold of the Count by his bodice and lifted him to his feet.

"So where is it, you clown?"

"It?"

"Your strong-box, you half-wit. You leave your brains in your hat?"

Suddenly there was a yell from over by the fallen carriage.

"Sir, sir, I've found another one – a nun."

"A what?"

The first fellow glowered at the Count, and then went over to join his mate. Aye, 'twas Master Halas, the poor lad alive but rendered insensible by a wound to the head – not that the lad was particularly chatty when awake, of course.

"What's a nun doing here?"

The second fellow shrugged. "Maybe she fell from Heaven." He delicately re-arranged Young Halas' skirt and made the sign of the cross. "Poor little thing. Seems to have bashed her head."

"You see a box?"

"There's a basket."

"Not a basket – a strong-box, big heavy thing."

The second, younger bandit, shrugged.

"I dunno – there's some ribbon."

"Ribbon? What the hell do we want with ribbon?"

The fellow searched the upended carriage but to no avail. The coach was empty of boxes of any kind. Spitting, the bandit with the red eyes strode back to Mitrovsky.

"Okay Bilek – where is it?"

"Bilek? My name is Mrs Matušková, a poor and innocent widow, as any fool can see."

The fellow stared at him with sore, tired eyes – the eyes of an insomniac, or a murderer.

"Okay Bilek, if that's the way you want to play it."

The bandit reached beneath his jerkin and removed a pistol, pointing the barrel not at Mitrovsky, but rather at Master Halas.

"Where is it Bilek? No jokes, no disguises. Tell me where the box is or the nun gets it."

The Count looked back at his assailant blankly. For some reason the song 'Mrs Dombrova's drawers' was playing over and over in his head.

"Well?"

Mitrovsky opened his mouth but nothing came out. Maybe it was fear, or maybe Halas' condition was catching – who knew?

The second fellow looked at his boss rather anxiously.

"Sir…"

The guy with the sore eyes ignored him.

"Well Bilek? What's it to be – nun or nothing?"

"O my darling, please, please, there's no need for all this unpleasantness. We're all God's creatures, are we not? The box is back in Hrůza – in a safe place, where neither mice nor moths can damage it. Let us go and I'll go and get it. Trust me, my darling – I wouldn't let that box out of my sight."

"That so?" The fellow's inflamed eyes stared back. "So where were you going in your fancy carriage then? A quick spin around the *Ringstrasse*?"

"Well," said the Count, "it was a lovely day and…"

The bandit glared at Mitrovsky most angrily.

"Listen Bilek, you have until midnight. You know Černý's's hill, where they dump the rubbish?"

"What kind of fool do you take me for? Of course, I don't…"

"Bring the box at midnight. In the meantime, the sister stays with us. If you don't show, you know what'll happen."

"Um…"

"Černý's hill: this is your last chance, Bilek. Don't piss it away."

Mitrovsky straightened up and pushed out his chest.

"You have my word as a gentlewoman, sir."

The bandit narrowed his eyes, then hauled Halas up onto the rear of the second fella's horse. The horse shook its head, Halas said nothing.

"You better be there, Bilek."

And with that the bandits galloped off, clipperty-clop, taking the post-road all the way back to Hrůza.

The Count crouched in the dirt in his ill-fitting gown. O, what was he to do? He looked first at the broken wheel, then at the shattered shaft from which the carriage-horses had obviously fled.

"Well that Moosendorf is a saucy fellow," he reflected, "and terribly keen on that box."

But come to think of it, *was* it Moosendorf? Neither of the two bandits looked like the spindly guys he had seen in the market. Come to think of it, neither of them looked like the second most successful theatrical manager in Brno either…

Retrieving Mrs Jedličová's wig from the ditch, the Count wiped the dirt from his jacket and plodded off down the dusty trail. It was late morning by now, the heat settling on his back like a heavy coat. How to find some shade? And how to get back to Hrůza 'fore Bilek's coach departed? Mitrovsky squinted at the sun, his brain spinning like a wheel. He imagined Bilek's strongbox making its way to P, galloping away on four swift legs, Fliška led to the gallows, Mrs Jedličová sobbing into her beautiful handkerchief. O what a mess! The road was long and dusty, the Count's stockings laddered in three places.

Alas, there was nothing to do but walk. The sun shone, fields glowed, and the heat beat down like a press. As usual it wasn't long before a gang of midges started to follow the Count, Mitrovsky singing 'A Poor Lover/Like some Pilgrim' in a rich baritone, his armpits stained with sweat. O Mařenka, he thought; it seems as if I travel further and further from your sweet gaze...

The Count had been tramping for an hour or so when he heard an old, spring-less cart approaching behind him, the cart driven by an ancient Auntie, white hairs poking out of a big brown mole on her chin.

"Miss, Miss!" yelled the old woman. "Fancy a lift? That's it, jump in – no need to stand on ceremony, the straw is lovely and soft. Where are you going, my sweet? Hrůza? Just so. A hot one, eh? Hot enough to make the Devil sweat..."

Mitrovksy hauled his tattered frock onto the back of the cart, the hem all covered in dirt. "How very kind, my dear lady. God will reward you..."

"Think nothing of it, little miss. But what's a noble woman like yourself doing out here on the road, her tights all dusty and soiled?"

Smacking his lips, Mitrovsky told the tale of how the carriage had gone off the road, leaving out the bit about the assassins, the strong-box, and the captured nun.

"O, you poor love – awful, just awful. What a terrible shame! But our hut isn't far from here. Come and take some tea with us. We'll find a needle for your hem and a bandage for your head."

"You are very kind Madam, but I fear..."

"Hush! Rich lady like you shouldn't be wandering the lanes on her own..."

"But..."

"Pish, I won't hear another word. Come and take tea with us. 'Taint right, a rich lady tramping up and down the lanes like some vagabond…"

"Well, if you insist…" The Count lay down on the straw, stretching out his aching bones. O, what a day! His shoulder throbbed, his head pounded, his knees aching in a manner most uncommon. Perhaps some refreshment would help? It certainly could do no harm.

The ladies' hut was a cheerful yellow, dusty wisteria growing up the walls and pots of pink geraniums on the sills. The vegetable garden was ringed by acacia bushes, a pretty linden tree offering some respite from the sun.

As soon as the cart pulled up, a second granny appeared, accompanied by two dogs, a cat, and a goat. The party clustered around Mitrovsky excitedly, the dogs barking and licking his knees.

"O my darling, please…"

The second woman turned out to be even more ancient than the first, peering at the Count through dim, cloudy eyes as if inspecting a tablecloth for dirt.

"Ah, who's this beauty?" she yelled, holding herself up by her stick.

"A noble-woman – found her on the road…"

"Toad?"

"Road! Found her on the road!"

"Feh, must you mumble so?" The woman turned her brown, shrivelled face to Mitrovsky. "Won't you take some tea with us, young lady? The pot's boiled and we can always wash another cup."

"O dear lady, you are too kind…"

"Tsk, look at the state of your gown – like you've been savaged by some wild beast! Ljuba, fetch my basket. O you poor chick, wandered from the road…"

The Count was led into the hut the women shared with their animals, stove, and Yetta the hen. A few of the planks had come loose, and ants queued up everywhere, but for all that, the place radiated an enormous sense of good will. Cracked cups, wonky stools, a faded rug – bliss!

Seated at the scarred kitchen table, Mitrovsky was called upon to recount the tale of the accident once more, embellishing the yarn with ever more colourful detail, the cab drivers running off, the passengers eaten by bears.

"And the men left you all on your own – what swine…"

"Aye, fled like rabbits…"

"And you surrounded by bears – awful, just awful."

From under her chair the woman produced her sewing basket – though heaven knows how she could see to thread a needle with those eyes – and as she mended the run in Mitrovsky's tights, the conversation slowly began to turn to more pleasant subjects: ribbon, petticoats, the price of silk. O, you wouldn't believe what they were charging for underwear these days!

After a while the Count felt very much at home. Ah, what wonderful ladies! And how pretty they had made their hovel, too,

"Are you two lovely ladies sisters?" asked the Count, rummaging through a box of trimmings and bows.

"Sisters? Ha ha, I should say not, young Miss! Hear that, Lottie? Sisters!"

"Blisters?"

"Sisters!"

Mitrovsky reached to the bottom of the box, pulling out a particularly moth-eaten and discoloured frill.

"And yet you live out here without a husband of any sort?"

The first old woman shrugged. "Is that such a mystery? Women need men like a broom needs a tail. All the rest of it – love songs and such like – it's just a tune played on a broken reed.

Now hold still my angel, we need to sew up this seam…"

"O, no need…"

"What hairy legs you have! How long did you say you were on the road?"

Mitrovsky ran his hands through his beard and shrugged. "Alas, I've been without the services of my maid for many days …"

"Well, no worry," said the old woman, biting the thread with her strong peasant teeth, "'tis only foolish gentlemen who worry about a stray whisker or two…"

"Yes indeed," said the other woman. "Amorous Counts, lovelorn poets, foolish suitors and the like…"

"Swine the lot of 'em…"

"Ha ha, ha," said the Count.

"It's all a lie, you know…"

"Hm?"

"Poetry, music, all those things. They burn away like kindling. And then, my dear, what's left?"

Mitrovsky opened his mouth, but then closed it again. What *was* left? He looked across at the old ladies and then at the basket of lace and frills. Answer, there was none.

"Well, you've really been most kind…"

"Foo, least we could do…"

"Poor chick, attacked by bears…"

When Mitrovsky's wardrobe had been repaired as much as possible, the ladies retired to the garden, taking tea and cake under the linden tree, scattering crumbs to the sparrows at their feet. The dogs and cats lay out in the sun, Yetta the hen clucking gently by their side. What time was it – after twelve?

Mitrovsky stroked his beard. Didn't he have to be somewhere, hand over some goods? And then he thought: yes, poor Master Halas!

Sricken with gulit, the Count thanked the ladies, but said that – alas! – he had to take his leave; he had business in Hrůza and…

"Business?"

"Yes, yes. Lady business…"

At this the two old women exchanged glances.

"My dear, would you be able to help us? We have a drawer of bees that we promised to Prolucky, the shopkeeper. From our hives, they are: the sweetest honey in all of Bohemia… tastes of dandelion, you see, as any fool can tell…"

"I can clearly…"

"Would you be able to load the box on your hump and take it to Hrůza?"

"Hump?"

"Yes, yes – it isn't far – no more than a mile, if you cut across Filla's meadow. And the bees are most peaceful. We'll give them a smoke, before you go."

"Um…"

"Calms them right down. Instead of thinking about stinging or fighting they snuggle up tight as kittens and dream sweet dreams. Besides, the bees will be in the box, along with the honey."

Mitrovsky looked across at the dilapidated hives heaped among the weeds and smacked his lips.

"Well…"

"Thirty groschen the lot – or forty, if you can stick it to 'im…"

"A mile, you say?"

"A mile or two. You're such a dear! Then hurry back with the cash, my angel – thirty groschen, make sure he counts it out, the old swindler."

"But…"

"'Tis an awful way for an old lady in this heat. But a young woman like yourself…"

"Woman, why, yes, indeed…"

In no time at all the two women had retrieved the frame, loading up Mitrovsky as if he were a donkey. The beehives were all painted blue, hidden in a little clearing in the trees.

"Now make sure you get there before they wake up."

"Um…"

"A shaken bee is an angry bee."

"Well, yes, of course…"

Mitrovsky looked at the little painted hut, the blooming acacia bushes, the sparrows bathing in the sunlight and smiled. "O ladies! What a beautiful interlude this has been…"

The old granny beamed. "Tish! 'Tis lovely to chat with such a sweet and well-spoken lady. Now remember: thirty groschen for the bees, and don't trust Prolucky, that crook…"

Mitrovsky nodded. The box on his back was warm, heavy and smelt of smoke and dandelions.

"Farewell dear ladies! I will return with your thirty groschen …"

Was that a buzzing? Well, perhaps. The Count, carrying his box, hurried across the fields, something warm and sticky dripping down his back. The hour was late, the day carried away on a bier.

14

Special Investigator Honzl watched the passengers boarding the twelve o'clock carriage: two silversmiths, a knife-grinder and his skinny wife, some round woman carrying a strongbox, and a priest in a pointy hat. No, no, nothing special. So where the devil was Mitrovsky?

The Investigator paced up and down the street, glaring at passers-by with his horrible yellow eyes. Mitrovsky, Bilek, Halas: all had vanished, like bubbles in a stream. Damn their bones! He should have got Povolný to arrest them when they had the chance – but now that fool of a constable seemed to have been swallowed up too, gone like a key down a well. Honzl sneered. Curse this town and its malicious dreaming! He'd wake it up, you just see if he didn't.

Mrs Koppitz, the landlady at the Tiger, was adamant: none of the gentlemen's fellow travellers had returned last night. And nor had their beds been slept in. No, they had not paid up. And no, he couldn't go and search Mitrovsky's bureau or Bilek's box: what was he, the police? Besides, some lady had come to collect Bilek's luggage.

"Lady?"

"A little round dame in a big hat."

Honzl moaned and ground his teeth. He would write all this down – oh yes, right there on the page, in the finest Genoese ink.

Next Honzl made his way to the police station. Constable

Povolný hadn't returned. He lived with his mother on Medvidek Street: maybe he was just having a 'little rest'.

Rest? Honzl's repulsive eyes bulged. That fellow could rest in a grave for all the use he was.

On Polovný's desk were more reports of illegal dreams. Mister Bohlado, the leather worker, had borrowed the Emperor's nose for a hat stand. Pecháchek, a local farmer, had admitted to employing the Emperor as a bull to sire six calves. Emma Barshevsky, a bar maid at The Green Fox, had seen his Majesty swimming in a puddle of beer under a table – and so on and so on, until the end of time. If anything, the number of dreams seemed to be increasing – much longer and no single book could hold them. The Special Investigator slammed his ledger shut and stalked back toward his lodgings. Curse this weather! The sun beat down without mercy, the sky too blue to bear.

Outside the Parrot was the nun who'd slipped him the hundred gulden just the other night, wearing the same pretty shoes and pearl earrings as before.

"Inspector? Can I talk to you for a moment?"

"Um, well…"

"Perhaps inside, where we can speak in private?"

Honzl led the sister up to his room, whereupon she slammed the door and pushed her cowl tight into the Investigator's face.

"Okay Honzl," she snapped, "where are they?"

"I don't…"

"You said that Jedličová and her chit would be handed over to us."

"Um."

"So where are they? We had a deal you little shit, we handed over the dough…"

Honzl stared back at the nun in confusion, his yellow eyes bulging.

"Sister, I tell you, I don't…"

"Listen Honzl, if you don't want the cops to find out all about our little deal then you better deliver the package. We're not playing games here. Saint Vojtěch's Church at midnight. Pankrác Square. You got that, *fizl*? The daughter better be there, okay – otherwise, who knows? You might wake up with your throat grinning from ear to ear."

"I…"

"Saint Vojtěch's Church, midnight. Eliška or nothing. And no funny business: we've got our eye on you, *fizl*, don't think that we don't."

And with that the nun crossed herself and strode out of the room.

Honzl dusted himself down and moved over to the window. The nun – if nun she was – crossed in front of a hay wagon, berating the driver in the foulest language imaginable. Violence, bad language, ill temper: something wasn't right here – for a start, where would a nun get earrings like that? Pulling his hat down over his wig, the Special Investigator raced down the stairs and onto the street, hugging to the shadows like a cat. But where on earth… wait, wait, there she was! Honzl's quill twitched in his hand as he set off smartly behind her, following the sister (sister?) through the streets of Hrůza, careful to stay at least three steps behind, one foot in the gloom. Eventually the earrings made their way down to where the bars clung to the river like a tidemark, a rough part of town, and no place for a Sister of the Order of the Visitation. With a glance over her shoulder – no, no, he was safe, she hadn't seen him! – the nun flounced into The Little Pig, a most disreputable looking bar if the outside was anything to go by.

Wise enough not to enter by the front door, Honzl checked out the street, then peered in through a window. Inside, the sister was speaking with a gang of colourfully tattooed thugs, many missing either teeth or fingers or hair.

The Inspector's quill quivered. Yes, yes, he was writing this all down…

Minutes later, the 'sister' – and if she was a nun then Honzl was the Emperor – took off once more, dressed in the clothes of a respectable and most well-to-do-lady.

Her earrings climbed into a carriage and took off, Honzl hailing a cab and following close behind. The trail led from the river to the townhouses on Karlüv Hora, high above town. There, the carriage stopped before a fashionable-looking dwelling, the woman speaking with a liveried doorman before disappearing smartly inside. Honzl paid the cabdriver and waited. Ten minutes later the earrings emerged once more, climbing back inside the well-appointed coach before taking off in a cloud of dust.

Honzl waited until the carriage had departed and then approached the doorman.

"Excuse me, my man," he began. "I wonder if you could help me. I am new to this town and fear I have lost my way. Could you tell me whose home this is? You see, I…"

The footman looked at Honzl and spoke most condescendingly.

"This home is occupied by Mr and Mrs Ančerl, sir."

"Ah, yes, yes, well…"

"Are you here for the wedding, sir?"

"Wedding?"

The footman stared with distaste at the Special Investigator's eyes.

"Indeed. Mr and Mrs Ančerl's son, Ernö. Are you a guest sir?"

"A guest? No, I am afraid I am not. Well, thank you my good man, but I fear I am in the wrong place entirely."

Turning on his heels, the Investigator returned to the waiting cab and took out his book. As the streets of Hrůza flew past, he wrote 'Ančerl' then 'Wedding' then 'Little Pig'. He then licked his long finger and pressed it to the page. Yes, yes, the answers all lay within: it was merely a matter of reading them correctly...

15

Count Mitrovsky greatly esteemed the work of bees, prizing their shape, sound, and surprising hairiness. And always so cheerful too! Cooking up honey, bumming around, humming a little tune. How such creatures actually went about their sticky business was, of course, a Holy Mystery – though the Count had also heard that glue was made from horses, so in this beautiful, maddening world, anything was possible.

Alas the box of bees wasn't really intended for long journeys. The sharp edges dug into the Count's shoulders, its shape was awkward to carry, and all the time Mitrovsky worried the drawer might open without warning. But what else could he do? In order to soothe his charges, and placate any temptation to flee or sting, he spent his time pointing out the local landmarks – "Look! What a beautiful tree!" – speaking in a loud, yet comforting voice, which he imagined to be most pleasing to bees and other creatures of that type.

'Twas a hot one, though. Sweat clung to the Count's back in large geographical patterns, the air dull and heavy, filled with dust and flies. And yet for all that the Count remained cheerful. What, should he simply fling the bees in a ditch and skip off on his own? No, no, no – a gentleman did not countenance such an action! He had promised those delightful ladies their thirty groschen, and Count Mitrovsky did not go back on his word. Besides, when you've opened the bottle, you might as well drink!

Not that there was anything to drink round here, of course. The ditches were dry, the ponds waterless, even the brown sludge of the river many miles away.

"Look!" said the Count. "What a magnificently yellow field!"

A low humming came from the back of the box. Were the bees waking up? Well, who could stay abed on such a marvellous summer afternoon? Or perhaps the two old dears hadn't applied enough smoke? Either way, it seemed wise to proceed to Hrůza as swiftly as possible. But was he going in the right direction? The Count had been walking for a very long time. How long did those old dears say it would take him – no more than an hour? Well, a long hour at that – crooked as a shepherd's stick.

Mitrovsky shook his head, trying to calculate the time by the passage of the sun. Had he missed the twelve o'clock carriage? Most definitely. But how would he get to Černý's's hill before those bandits filled Halas full of lead? Not to mention the small matter of the bees: their humming had taken on a somewhat capricious tone, and the Count was most concerned should they elect to flee.

Hrůza, Hrůza, where the hell was Hrůza? Time here seemed to move in fits and starts, the hours shuffled like a gambler's pack of cards. For an eternity the fiery orb refused to budge, glued into place in the sky; then the threads suddenly gave way, and – ah, me! – 'twas as if the whole day flashed by in the twinkling of an eye, one hour chasing the next, like a reader idly thumbing through the pages of an endless book.

Ah, thought Mitrovsky, how wonderful it would be to be back in Mařenka's arbour, Lena and Lida playing, Betka panting at their feet, Mařenka's sweet lips settling on her face like a delicate and graceful butterfly. O Mařenka, swooned the Count, where does your carriage take you? Whence do you go without me? Still, eventually he would find some kind of cart track or post-road, would he not? Everything could be found if you looked hard enough. There's no such place as nowhere on a map.

As the Count descended a low, chalky hill, he came upon two peasant boys staring into a dried-up hole, the little lads hopping this way and that while poking the desiccated ground with a stick.

"What ho, you scamps!" bellowed the Count, delighted to be among human company once more. "What are you fine fellows doing out and about? Searching for gold and adventure, I'll be bound."

The two lads looked at the Count as if he were some kind of vision, or a lunatic, mayhap.

"It's the spring, sir. It's all bunged up."

The Count jabbed his own stick at the clay. The ground was an ugly brown. So was the stick.

"Mmm. Aye, you're right, completely parched. But look, we can still draw in the clay. There now – a bear! Grrr!"

One of the boys looked about nine, the other some years younger – it was hard for a Count to tell. They were very dirty and very thin.

"O, I bet you lads get up to some mischief," said Mitrovsky, grinning. "Why, I remember when my brother and I were your age – always carrying on with some scheme or another! I remember when I climbed the tallest tree on our estate and caught my britches on the top branch. My brother had to climb up then to get me – what fun! Do you ever do that lads? On your, ah, estate?"

"Uncle told us to look for water, sir. We'd better go."

"Aye," said Mitrovsky, placing the bees down and warming to his theme, "we had such japes! Spitting pomegranate pips at the gardeners. Baring our bottoms at the scullery maids. Looking for robin eggs and then bowling them down a hill. Ha ha ha! Oh, it does me good to think of it."

Despite the jollity in Mitrovsky's voice, his eyes looked dark and sad, but maybe that was just the way they were made – who knows?

"Aye, the years pass by like a dream. Or is that a line from 'The May-Fly's Dance'? Either way, it's true, right enough."

The boys dug their toes into the baked soil, the younger one still holding on to the bucket. Who was this ape anyway?"

Grinning, the Count searched in his pocket for a coin.

"There now – a shiny shilling! And it'll be yours if you can tell me the way to Hrůza. Now what do you say to that?"

"Hrůza, sir?"

"Hrůza, yes."

The older boy blinked. "'Tis just round that bend, sir. You can't see it now but it's right there – no more than an hour away."

"An hour? That far? Ah well. Many thanks, my lad. The Lord bless you and keep you in his care."

The Count passed over the coin and the boys looked at the shilling blankly. Then they nodded and ambled off in the direction Mitrovsky had just come from, the older one banging the boy's bucket with his stick.

Mitrovsky watched them go with a tender expression, his eyes the colour of pitch.

"Thank you lads! God speed! But tell me, tell me – what are your names? Um, in case I come across your Uncle, or such like?"

The two boys were no more than two little dabs now, their shapes silhouetted against the sun.

"Matej, sir," cried the older.

"What?"

"Matej."

The Count blinked, shielding his eyes with his hands.

"Matej? But … ah, and your brother, what's his name?"

But by now the two boys had already turned away from him, their bucket gleaming in the son.

"Your brother, my lad? Who be he?"

It was too late. The two little lads were gone.

"Oh well, no matter," said Count Mitrovsky to his bees. "There, look – blackberries growing on a hedge."

The bees buzzed, somewhat ironically.

"Not blackberries? Well, berries of some sort, and most delicious, I'll be bound!"

Alas, Hrůza was not around the next bend – nor the bend after that. Instead, the land seemed to stretch on forever, crisp and dry and even. After a while, the bees began to sound restless, their buzzing taking on a distinctly peevish tone.

"Hush, hush, there's no need for that," said the Count, gently. "I'm the one carrying you, after all."

The blue of the sky deepened and darkened, turning the colour of the river where the dye merchant had lost his load. Yellow rye, golden sun, purple sky: ah, 'twould all have been very beautiful, if only it hadn't been so hot!

The Count watched the sky change colour and mopped his brow. Had he really been tramping abroad for an entire day? Little wonder the bees were beginning to get so grouchy. Another field, another ditch, yet more rye, each crop even more golden than the last. But where was Hrůza? He could have walked to Vienna in this time. And then he saw it: the post road.

Mitrovsky shook his box in triumph. "Look lively lads, we're saved!"

He climbed over a low stone wall and stared at the road. The way was perfectly blank in either direction. So which way should he go? O, if only he could toss a coin to decide! And then he remembered: Master Bilek's coin was the same on both sides.

"Bear, it is," he said squinting at the sun and then turning a sharp left, the day turning to evening, as one changes one's jacket before dining.

16

At the police station, Special Investigator Honzl conferred with Constable Komárek, Constable Polovný being 'missing without reason', the devil take him. According to Komárek, The Little Pig was a well-known haunt of criminals and 'anti-social elements' – "A bad sort, sir, a very bad sort indeed!" Mr and Mrs Ančerl of Peníze were unknown to Komárek, but Karlüv Hora "fancy schmancy – if you take my meaning." Honzl did. But what might connect such disparate individuals? And what all did this have to do with murdered cabbies – or plagues of dreams for that matter? Like a spider, this conspiracy had many legs: Bilek's case, Mitrovsky's 'literature', the aggressive nun. Honzl ground his teeth. What had the wench meant, he'd welched upon the deal? Nonsense! He had specifically requested that Eliška be dispatched to the nunnery – unless that clown of a constable had somehow screwed up, yet again. But what did some local hoodlum want with a novice sister anyway? 'Twas all very fishy. The bag of coins weighed heavily in Honzl's pocket, but fortunately nobody else knew of the 'deal'. And if some might question his decision to release Eliška and her mother into some third party's care – well, he could always amend the figures, delete the names, correct some of the columns in the official record of events.

The fat turnkey blinked stupidly. Yes, the ladies had departed –

into a very la-di-da carriage, if you please. Had they left anything behind? Well, the gentleman was very welcome to inspect the premises – "'Tis all very clean."

Scowling venomously, Special Investigator Honzl clomped up the stairs and burst into the room, whereupon he discovered Mrs Jedličová *déshabillé* and eating a pancake.

"O my goodness!" cried the good lady, leaping up from the sofa and diving behind a screen. "Sir, you find me in a most unadvantageous position…"

"Madame, I had no idea…"

Honzl stared at the embroidered screen and pulled a face.

"I had heard report that you had been transported to convent at Žádost – along with your delightful daughter."

"Why yes, yes that's quite right."

"And yet," said the Investigator, glaring at the decorative sheep on the lady's screen, "here you are."

"Yes."

"Still in the Powder Gate."

"Why, yes."

"With no clothes on."

Mrs Jedličová paused. "Why, yes, yes, of course you're right, my dear sir. You see, I forgot something and…"

"Your clothes?"

"Ha ha, yes indeed. What a foolish thing to do! O, I would forget my head if it wasn't…"

"Silence!" yelled the Inspector, by now greatly displeased. "I'm writing this down, Mrs Jedličová, every word of it. And drawing a sketch too! Now come with me – we'll get to the bottom of this, you see if we don't."

A strange squeak came from behind the screen. "With you, sir? But why, I have nothing to wear, and a respectable widow cannot be seen…"

"Respectable? Respectable?" By now the Investigator was grinding his teeth. "Here, wrap this rag around your … wait a moment – are these Count Mitrovsky's things?"

Mrs Jedličová's wig-less head peeped around the corner. "Those? Oh no sir, I am sure they're just some old rags…"

Honzl's wet eyes seemed to glisten. "Yes, yes – I do declare they are! Well, Mrs Jedličová, how do you explain these?"

Mrs Jedličová stared at the Inspector with her beautiful green eyes. "They're just schmattes sir – no doubt been lying around the tower for years. What would a Count be doing leaving his clothes behind in a lady's chamber? It 'aint right, sir. I'm a respectable widow."

The Investigator stamped his foot and ordered the good widow to emerge – "Wrap yourself in those tatters, if you want". Then he called for the turnkey and ordered that the lady be transported swiftly to the police station, where she could give an official account of herself, and the deficiencies in her wardrobe.

"My angel!" said the turnkey, eying up the lady's ample charms. "What are you doing here, my beauty? I'm sure I saw you climbing in that carriage…"

"Enough!" yelled the Inspector, very hot. "Take this lady away for questioning. I only hope that you have a prettier song to sing when I return."

As the trembling Mrs Jedličová was led away, her seven beauties concealed 'neath the Count's ratty cloak, Honzl wiped his eyes and spat. O, was there no end to the strangeness of this case? At least he now knew – for a fact! – that the fake Count (what true Count has weevils in his wig?) was unquestionably part of the affair. Honzl pressed his book to his chest and set off for the Golden Tiger at a trot. This time the Chief Investigator wasn't going to let Mrs Koppitz stand in the way: not even landladies were permitted to impede the course of the law.

Mitrovsky was obviously hiding something in that stupid *armoire* of his – who carried around a piece of furniture anyway? Hidden away between all those ribbons and trinkets was something else – something incriminating, if Honzl's instincts were anything to go by. O, if only he had arrested him straight away – or when he found him with his pinkies on Bilek's box…

All at once, the Chief Investigator felt a prickling sensation on the back of his neck: was he being observed? He spun around, his skin tingling as if pricked by a pin.

"What? Who's this, the dog…?"

Aye, someone was following him, picking their way through Hrůza's back roads, their eyes like a dagger in his back.

Honzl quit Thursday Street and set off down the nearest alleyway, casting a furtive glance over his shoulder.

Behind him, some gloomy figure followed, a big fellow, heavy as the coalman's load. But who was it? Some pickpocket? Some assassin? Or was it Mitrovsky himself, dragging his shadow like a sack?

Honzl ducked down Friday Street, and then took off like a hare. Another square, another passing cart, another statue of St John of Neponuk, holding his head out like a loaf. By now the Investigator had lost his bearings, but no matter: one filthy alleyway was much the same as another. But it was no use. Whatever passageway he took, the man followed like an errant thread, the Inspector's boots stumbling betwixt the cobbles and the weeds.

After a while, the way led between a scribble of dilapidated hovels, the ruins slumped like pigs in the dried-up mud. How quiet it was here, the streets sombre and lifeless, the houses swollen with fatigue and age. A broken-down fence marked where someone had sought to grow spinach and radishes, though the plants now looked dry and yellow, the leaves coated with a sulphurous dust. Yes, an air of eternal neglect clung to everything, the air tired and motionless: no place for a Special Investigator to meet his end.

As Honzl rounded another corner, he violently collided with a figure coming the other way, the fellow's face taut and cruel, his mouth an angry slash.

"What? Mind yourself, you …"

Honzl looked at the fellow and the fellow looked at him. Under a shabby peasant jacket, the cur was dressed in surprisingly expensive britches and boots, the finest on offer in Vienna. But it was the fellow's hide which gave him away: skin as pale as parchment, veins the colour of ink. That and the fellow's horrible eyes, of course.

"Horáck?"

"Honzl?"

The two Special Investigators – one from the Ministry of Extraordinary Importance, the other from the Office of Forbidden Texts, the Ear and the Eye – gazed at each other distrustfully.

"You? What are *you* doing here? And in such a stupid disguise…"

"Yeah? Well, I might say the same of you, you chump…"

"Chump? Why…"

"Not that anything could hide those peepers of yours..."

The two inspectors glowered as if about to come to blows, the foul, yellow eyes of one staring into the sore, reddened eyes of the other.

"What are you doing, Honzl? Checking out the sanitation?"

"Don't take that tone with me. I might ask what the Department of Forbidden Texts is…"

Horáck spat. "I don't have to explain myself to any two shilling Investigator. You don't scare me, Honzl. We got the Pope supporting our department – two at a pinch."

"Two? Ha! Why you don't even…"

At that moment, a second figure emerged from a nearby ruin, his peasant garb likewise topping Imperial issue boots.

"S'alright, sir – I've locked her up, good and tight."

Honzl glowered. "Her?"

"Keep your flap shut, you clown!"

"Just what's going on here, Horáck?" said Honzl, looking the fellow up and down. "What does the Department of Forbidden Texts want with…?"

"You 'aint my boss, Honzl – I don't owe you nothing. Besides, what's a Special Investigator doing sniffing around in such a sleepy little town? Emperor lost a button?"

"How dare you! You swine! You dog! I'm writing that down, you see if…"

"Yeah? Make sure you spell my name right, you clod…"

Still sneering, the two investigators abruptly turned on their heels and headed off in different directions – only for Honzl to double back, and sneak around as soon as he reached the first corner, immediately bumping into Horáck once more.

"What are you doing, you dope?"

"What am *I* doing? What are…?"

"You following me?"

"Are you following *me*?"

"Why would I want to follow you? I've got grown up business, Honzl."

"You swine! I will have you know that I am here on important business – official business in the service of…"

"Yeah, yeah, yeah – we all throw grain for the cock. Stay out of my way, Honzl. I'm warning you…"

"No, no – I am warning you…"

"Yeah?"

"Yeah."

Grinding his teeth, Honzl followed a dismal road back between two rows of misshapen houses, the bowed passage no wider than a cart. No pedestrians, no beggars, not even a passing hen: the street was quiet as a closed book.

As soon as he could, the Special Investigator once again doubled back. Horáck and his ape were hiding something – some prisoner by the sound of things. But why would they stash the baggage away in some tumbledown shack? To keep the prisoner away from prying eyes, true – but was there another reason, something more underhand? Honzl wouldn't put anything past those dogs in the Department of Forbidden Texts – ink on their fingers and glue up their nose.

Honzl edged his way back toward the ruin – and ran smack into Horáck once again.

"I don't believe it!" yelled the swine, tripping over Honzl's feet.

"Stop following me!"

"I 'aint following you – you're following me."

"Nonsense."

"Get out of my face, Honzl."

"What? Why…"

"I'm telling you. You better watch your step…"

"Me? Listen, I…"

"Ah, tell it to the Judge…"

With this last rejoinder, the two men once again parted, heading in opposite directions along the sun-baked street.

Honzl licked his lips and ducked out of the sun. Such impudence! What scum! Besides, two special investigators in this dismal little burg? 'Twas more than coincidence – something strange was afoot. And what about the burly figure that had chased him down this rabbit hole in the first place? Was he too an agent of the Department of Forbidden Texts? Or were there other shadowy forces at work here? The Chief Investigator looked over his shoulder. Was the villain still out there? Had he observed his little spat with Horáck, listened carefully to all that was said? Honzl shivered. Curse this place and its seditious dreams! He would drown before he ever got to the bottom.

Suddenly a figure lurched out of the gloom, causing the Investigator to jump most comically.

"Sir! Sir!"

It was Polovný.

"Sir, sir, I have to speak with you."

"You idiot, you cur…"

"Sir, he's spoken to me. He came to my room, told me what to do…"

Honzl looked at the Constable and groaned. "Spoken? Who? You're not making any sense, you ape…"

"The Emperor, sir. The dreams sir – they're linked to the birds. The nightingales. He told me not to let 'em get away…"

Honzl looked at the constable closely. His eyes were wild, his wig askew and sticky.

"Constable, stop this nonsense, you're not making any sense …"

Somewhere a door banged shut and the two men jumped. Two birds flew up, squawking crossly – not nightingales though, but crows. The crows settled on a higher perch, silently re-arranging their feathers. Crows two, nightingales none – but wasn't that the world all over?

17

Eliška gingerly opened her eyes: same bed, same quilt, same petunias in a blue cracked jug. Aye, she was still in the gravedigger's bothy. For once her toes hadn't carried her off, down a crooked alley and away from the path, those restless feet of hers, dragging her away, like a leaf in a stream…

Outside the hut it was already dark, as if a barrel had been placed over the town. Had she slept the entire day? Well, why not? Was the waking world such a prize? In her dream the Emperor peered out of her mother's apron like a baby, his face red and angry, as if His Majesty had filled his pants. Mothers, mothers everywhere! Could they listen in on your dreams too? She imagined her mother with a glass pressed to the wall, her ear like a sponge, soaking up all the sounds of the world.

Eliška's stomach ached and her lips felt dry. She felt as if she were a hundred and two rather than seventeen: had she been asleep that long? Fortunately, there were no mirrors in the room, or mothers to fuss over you, cleaning your face with spit.

Scratch, scratch, scratch went the door. 'Twas the puppy, dirty as a cinder and only half the size. It sniffed at Eliška's pot and then jumped up on her bed, three black paws and one white, soft as a summer night. Eliška looked at it distrustfully. Stupid dog. What did it want with her anyway? It circled the bed and whined pitifully, getting on her nerves.

Cursing, the girl shoved the pup from her bed and walked over to the dusty little window. Despite the lateness of the hour, the yard seemed mysteriously busy, Saint Vojtěch ablaze with light. What was going on out there? Under the torches, she could see figures coming and going, footmen, servants, grooms, a carriage pulling up, its doors painted gold and black. An image of the glass coach and the little grey horse rose unbidden to her mind. O why couldn't her feet have taken her someplace else? Why take her from one trap to another?

The first time her feet had gone a'wandering, was when she turned thirteen. On Monday she was found in the linen cupboard, on Tuesday up a walnut tree, on Wednesday in the back of a hay wagon. Her parents were distraught, the priest baffled. Some said 'twas because a door had slammed at the moment of her first bleed; others that a rook had flown into her bedchamber at midnight. Doctors prescribed a tincture of sage, liquorice and the urine of a chaste youth, but nothing seemed to work. Once a month, the girl's feet would carry her thither, no matter how many doors were sealed, windows shut, or gates barred and locked.

"'Tis no illness but a sign," averred her father. "The girl is possessed, cursed by a witch…"

"Oh hush," said Mrs Jedličová, the real brain beneath the hat. "Here, have some more pierogi, you're wasting away, poor lamb…"

But what to do, what to do? Physicians came and went. Ointments were applied, wet bandages too. Her parents tried shackles, fetters, tying her to her bed as if strapping her into a corset. Next, they barricaded the doors, nailed up the shutters, and hid away the key. And yet, and yet … around the ninth of each month she would still be found wandering, drifting, perched at the edge of the well with her eyes tight shut and feet the colour of clay. And then one sweet spring night, Eliška was discovered in the bed of their neighbour's son, a gentle soul by the name of Ernö, a simple lad, nose like a water-spout, goose-down on his chin. Apparently Eliška had broken into his bedchamber, tip-toed to his blanket, and rubbed herself up against him in a manner most unbecoming to a young lady. Much disturbed, Young Ernö began to scream and yell, which is when Eliška woke up, finding herself unchaperoned in the bed of a young man, neither of them adequately dressed, or even wearing a hat.

Needless to say, Master Ernö's parents – a most respectable couple by the name of Ančerl – were much vexed by this turn of events.

After all, what could follow such a calamity but the inevitable stain of disgrace? In order to avert scandal it was agreed that the youngsters must marry forthwith. Unfortunately, however, the youngsters themselves were not so keen. Eliška found fault with Ernö's nose, while Young Ernö had no wish to wed the kind of girl who found herself in strange men's bedrooms. The families insisted, the couple refused, and poor Mr Jedličovsky expired, one Tuesday evening around six-ish, face-down in a plate of creamed kidneys, as any husband would wish.

After this, it was up to Eliška's uncle to step in and restore some sense of propriety. It was agreed that the girl should, without undue fuss or distraction, be sent to take her vows as a novice of the Sisters of the Holy Visitation in Žadost, where the walls were four cubits thick, solid enough to prevent any "nocturnal perambulation," as her uncle put it. The Ančerls protested – what, should their Ernö be ruined too? – demanding that the girl should be conjoined with their son 'by force, if necessary.' Eliška picked at her nails and rolled her eyes. Which was worse – a nun's wimple or Ernö's nose? 'But by then Eliška was sequestered in a carriage with her mother, the sun beating in through the window, dust covering everything, like regret, or time.

And now here she was in the gravedigger's hut, staring out at the gloomy spire of Saint Vojtěch, watching a procession of carriages arrive, the guests lining up as if for a funeral, or a wedding.

The crowd murmured, the puppy whined, an owl hooted: surely one of these three things was a sign? Eliška climbed to her feet and stretched. Outside the door, she could hear the gravedigger and his wife still talking in low voices – had they been there all day?

"We have to tell someone," said the woman. "What about her family, her parents? O, they'll be crying, poor dears, no one feels it like a mother…"

"Well…"

"Father Vobecký then…"

"No, no… "

"She can't say here, Franta. We'll get into trouble, right enough. What if she's a wanton child or something?"

"Hush, there 'aint…"

"Franta, either you go to the police or I will…"

All at once an image of the two dead cabbies paraded before Eliška's eyes: what, she should be returned to the Powder Gate? Back to her mother? No, no, anything was better than that!

"I'm telling you Franta, you better…"

"I tell you…"

"Did you see her toes? Black as the Devil's arse! 'Taint right, Franta, you mark my words…"

But by now Eliška's toes had gone: the girl had pulled herself out through the window and hopped down onto the cool grass. What a pair of dumplings the gravedigger and his wife were, thick as Grandma's soup! Aye, the world was full of morons and cretins; throw a stick and you'd be sure to hit a blockhead somewhere. Eliška hid behind a gravestone, watching the guests lining up by the church, an endless row of frockcoats and gowns, as if the stained-glass windows were mirrors instead. What a parade of imbeciles! Two by two, they passed through the doorway, a infinite procession of idiots, stretching on forever…

18

It was already dark by the time Mitrovsky made it to Hrůza, the sky the colour of strong Rhine wine. The Count was exhausted, the bees noisy. The smoke had worn off and the bees sounded distinctly cranky, buzzing in and out of the box as if plotting something, or composing a letter of complaint.

Černý's Hill was the place where the good people of Hrůza came to deposit their dregs, cartloads of refuse from the market, buckets and pails from houses, scraps and waste from everywhere else, the droppings heaped in a a great steaming mound of trash. The smell was extraordinary – worse than Mitrovsky's cologne. Foxes and dogs rummaged in packs, the rat population greater than Hrůza's human one: better teeth too.

Still supporting his tray of bees, Count Mitrovsky plodded along toward the dump, weeds poking between the stones like rag pickers' fingers. Pah, what a place! Wisps of litter and straw blew this way and that, chased by scraps of wrapping, handbills, all sorts of peelings and scrapings. In short, no *Schönbrun* palace. Great clouds of flies gathered everywhere, big fat bluebottles, bloated as aldermen. The bees buzzed indignantly. Didn't this clown know he was transporting royalty? How had things come to this? A passing mutt saw Mitrovsky and wagged her tail. A rat peeked under Mitrovsky's skirt, then ran away, squealing.

As the Count rounded the dump, a voice boomed out from the gloom.

"Bilek? Bilek, that you?"

Illuminated by the smoky light of a lantern, a cluster of figures moved among the murk, the number of legs uncertain. Mitrovsky squinted.

"Aye, aye, 'tis…"

Shapes appeared: two men and a nun.

"Okay, Bilek, you better have the honey…"

"Honey?"

"Your box."

"Ah…"

"Don't screw with me Bilek, I'm warning you…"

Yes, it was the two bandits who had ambushed them on the road – and there was young Master Halas, resplendent in habit and wimple. The lad looked cheerful and well looked after, albeit with a pistol pointed at his head.

Mitrovsky came a little closer, until the bandit gestured for him to stop.

"That's far enough, you dope. And you better be alone, Bilek – if you want the sister to stay healthy, that is."

In the smoky light of the lantern, the bandit looked paler than ever, his skin bleached and papery, like a book left out in the rain. But O, what a cover! Sharp nose, thin mouth, two red letters for eyes. The fellow stared at Mitrovsky maliciously.

"Still in that ridiculous get-up Bilek? Well, whatever floats your boat. Now hand over the box."

"The box?" Mitrovsky glanced to his side, as if noticing the coffer for the very first time. "Oh. Aha. But first you must unhand Master, ah, Sister, Halas."

The bandit scowled.

"No dice. Give me the box first. Any double-cross and the sister's history."

The Count glanced down at the box; inside the bees hummed

233

with frustration. One escapee had lodged itself inside Jedličova's wig and seemed to be building something in its wool.

"So you want this box…"

"The box, yeah…"

"The box I'm carrying…"

"Yeah, Bilek, the box. Now quit stalling and hand it over. We 'ain't got all night, you know."

Whistling 'My heart beats faster and faster/as I say to the girl by the door', Mitrovsky took another step forward.

"This box, which, ah…"

"You simple or something? Just give me the damn box."

The crate was heavy and awkward, the catches loose and the drawer awful sticky at one end. Mitrovsky handed it over and the villain grinned.

"Okay, okay – you're a smart boy. Now you stay there, while I check out the goods. Polách, keep your gun on the nun. You better not be pulling a fast one, Bilek…"

"What, me? No, I…"

Horáck threw open the lid and with a terrible noise, a great wave of bees fell upon him, surprising the fellow most rudely and knocking him to the ground. There were bees everywhere: in his eyes, his ears, his hat. It seemed as if the whole world was made of bees.

The other bandit looked on in horror. The sound was terrifying. The very air seemed to throb.

"Boss?"

In his surprise, Polách forgot to fire. Instead, he just stood there, open mouthed, as the storm broke above Horáck's head.

Quick as a flash – for everyone knows that Counts can move surprisingly quickly when they need to – Mitrovsky gave Polách a shove, retrieving Halas from his grasp. The lantern fell to the ground and went out. Horáck slipped sideways into a ditch.

In a flash, Mitrovsky grabbed hold of Halas by the shoulders and plunged into the gloom. A pistol shot resounded behind them, though whether aimed at the bees or the Count, 'twas hard to tell. Bees, bees, bees everywhere! The swarm dived into the ditch, covering Horáck like a cheap suit.

Running as fast as they could, the Count and Halas sought refuge in a darkened yard, Mitrovsky lathered in dirt and honey, Halas blinking like a frog.

"Master Halas! O you young pup, are you alright?"

Halas stared at Mitrovsky's face and smiled. The lad made a very convincing nun, cheeks like Saint Zenobia – ah, what a doll he'd make!

"O Master Halas, 'tis good to see you! I thought I'd never hear your sweet voice again…"

Footsteps echoed on the lane: someone was coming. Putting one hand over Halas' mouth, Mitrovsky peeped outside. There was the bandit with the pistol, the cur glancing this way and that, like a hunter looking for rabbits.

"Shhh," whispered the Count. "Keep *schtum*!"

Fortunately, the fellow – and his very nice Viennese boots – walked on past, pistol hidden 'neath his jerkin.

The Count mopped his brow with Mrs Jedličová's hanky. "We've got to get out of here, my dear Halas. Those fellows are very cross, though heaven knows why – that was a pretty bit of honeycomb, thirty groschens worth, at least…"

Halas offered a tentative smile. How innocent the lad looked! As if the milk were still wet on his lips…

"Let us withdraw to the Golden Tiger," said Mitrovsky. "Perhaps Master Bilek was right and 'tis time to quit this town."

Halas nodded.

From the yard, the two 'ladies' – one bursting out of Mrs Jedličová's *ensemble*, the other hidden 'neath a sister's dugs and toggery – followed a circuitous route along the backstreets of Hrůza, avoiding squares, jug-houses, and other places where a passing nun might easily be molested. Fortuitously, the town was quiet and still, the air smelling of beer and roses, the stars twinkling with a kindly glow.

O, the sweet, sweet scent of summer! Keeping one eye out for their pursuers and the other on their hems, Mitrovsky and Halas stuck close to the alleyways, the shop-signs hanging above them like a poor man's gallery.

"Nearly there," said the Count, winking broadly, "I do believe that the Golden Tiger is…"

But then he saw the villains over by the Lunatic's Bridge, searching hither and thither, the bandit's mug puffed up like a bullfrog.

"The poor lad," whispered the Count, innocently. "Whatever could have happened?"

Halas tugged on the Count's sleeve and the pair took off down a nearby passageway, emerging onto a quiet street lined with sombre-looking trees.

"Shhh," hissed Mitrovsky to the sweet-faced Halas. "Not a word!"

With that, the Count and nun tip-toed stealthily toward the deserted lane, their footsteps dainty as milkmaids. The pair thence pitter-pattered past a warehouse and a charcoal-burner, before arriving in front of a gloomy church with a tall central spire, the graveyard separated from the road by a row of dark, serrated trees. Several expensive-looking carriages were lined up outside, accompanied by smart, liveried footmen, the foppish fellows lounging about, hand on hips, discussing the price of rye. Although late – later than an owl's supper, as they say – the church blazed with light, clusters of figures moving this way and that, like silhouettes in a puppet show.

Out of the corner of his eye, the Count glimpsed the two bandits running back and forth erratically, the one with the inflamed face seeming most vexed, his mug puffed up like a dumpling in the pot.

"Halas," whispered the Count. "Not a word!"

Heads down, the pair mingled with the crowd in front of the gates, a most respectable gathering of citizens, at least for a dump like Hrůza. The ladies wore skirts wide as gateposts, the gentlemen long peacock feathers, Mitrovsky admiring their stockings most appreciatively.

"'S'okay," he whispered, "we'll be safe in this crowd, you mark my words."

Halas stared at the Count's beard and nodded. Alas, Mitrovsky's was not the best disguise in the world, his wig flattened, bodice torn, hairy chest poking through most rudely. A noble woman? Ho, even a mole could sniff out the truth.

As Mitrovsky and Halas slipped inside, a footman in long burgundy jacket and pristine white ruff approached from the side, peepers screwed up and nose in the air.

"Bride or groom?" he asked, taking in the ladder in Mitrovsky's tights and the whiskers on his chin.

"What?"

"Bride or groom, ah, Miss."

"Miss? Yes, Miss, ha ha ha." The cogs in Mitrovsky's head turned, but no cuckoo came out. Bride or groom? Which one was he?

The Count giggled and pointed at Halas a little hysterically. "Bride, bride, he's the bride!"

The fellow froze.

"What?"

"Ah, I mean, she! She's the bride!"

The footman's eyebrows arched, an unreadable expression

237

racing across his face.

"The bride, you say?" The footman clapped his hands. "Ježek! Štěpán!"

The Count looked round, clapping his hands too.

"Um…"

At this the footman leaned in confidentially. "I'm terribly sorry, sir. I didn't realise you were in disguise…"

The Count moved his lips, but no sound came out. Out of nowhere, two burly servants appeared at his side, both wearing marvellous stockings, one a delicate pink, the other the colour of a robin's egg.

"Ježek, Štěpán: Miss Jedličová has arrived. Take her to the vestry and be quick about it. And tell Mr and Mrs Ančerl that the bride has arrived."

The two flunkeys nodded, whisking Master Halas away before the Count could do anything much about it. Poor Master Halas! Inside the wimple his eyes were wide and unblinking, like a calf sniffing the butcher's apron.

The footman nodded, slapping the Count on his back. "Thank you for escorting her, sir – Mr Ančerl is most grateful."

"What? Oh, yes…"

"You will be well paid for your service."

"What? Yes, yes, a cheque will be fine…"

Just what was the fellow going on about? Taking a step back, Mitrovsky paused and looked around the church. 'Twas quite a spot – cherubs gambolling about the high, blue ceiling, bearded statues in pointy hats, and a line of candles illuminating a series of gloomy tableaux: Saint Vojtěch founding the monastery in Břevnov, Saint Vojtěch baptising Géza of Hungary, Saint Vojtěch murdered by pagans. The church smelt of beer, beeswax and incense, Vojtěch looking extremely grumpy, as if afflicted by gout.

Bowing, the footman withdrew and whispered something to a

wealthy looking couple – Mr and Mrs Ančerl? – who were standing to one side and staring at Mitrovsky rather strangely. What was all this about a wedding? Well, any port in a storm. Glancing around, the Count heard a strange buzzing above one ear – a stowaway bee, perhaps.

Next to Mr and Mrs Ančerl stood a bright young fellow, clean of face, and innocent of cheek – the groom, perhaps? Well, a long life and much happiness to him! Mr Ančerl exchanged a few words with the footman, and the footman nodded. And with that the priest was produced, a tiny fellow with a beard like a fishing net.

The church organ started, the guests rose, and then, as if response to an audible gasp, the bride arrived arm in arm with a footman, the maiden dressed in a chaste brocade gown, silk petticoat, silk covered shoes, silk everything. And such lovely ribbons too! Enough to bring tears to one's eyes.

'O Master Halas,' whispered the Count. 'My lad, you've never looked lovelier.'

The footman, bride, and sweet-looking flower-girl processed solemnly along the aisle, the flower-girl beaming, the bride's face hidden 'neath an innocent veil. Halas' feet were a little big for his slippers but otherwise he carried off the *ensemble* with aplomb, gown well fitted and modest, the bodice virginal and maidenly as befitting any respectable bride. In his gloved hands, Halas carried a fresh posy of hyacinth and lavender: a lovely touch, thought the Count, dabbing his eyes with a cloth.

Heads bowed, the bride and groom stepped forward, the priest climbing up on a box.

"This her?" the Father said, eying up the bride. "You sure?"

The groom looked at his parents and then nodded.

"Okay, okay, let's get it over with. No Pops? Okay, okay, let's cut to the chase." The priest coughed and removed a noodle from his beard. "We are gathered here tonight, blah blah blah – what? Nobody else needs to sleep?"

Mr and Mrs Ančerl exchanged dignified glances. Heaven knows where the priest had been dug up from – in the summer it was hard to get a booking.

"Okay toots, repeat after me, I Eliška Darja Jedličová, take thee, Ernö Bedrich Ančerl to be my lawful wedded husband…"

The Father paused: nothing doing. Was the dame even listening? Young people today: hopeless, just hopeless.

"You okay? I said, I Eliška Darja Jedličová…"

Before the venerable father could get out another word, the church doors flew open and Honzl and Polovný stumbled in, banging and clattering as the Constable tumbled over a chair. Everyone turned to look at them, the priest glaring as if they'd dripped soup on his alter-boy.

Honzl scowled. "I told you to put your ear to the door, not …"

"'Tis the Emperor, sir…"

"What?"

"There, sir – in the painting! That's him dressed as a hermit, setting fire to the laurel leaves of the pagans…"

"Quiet you dolt…"

The Special Investigator ground his teeth in irritation; Povolný hadn't stopped squawking about the Emperor all night. What had got into him? It was as if the Constable were befuddled or bewitched, prattling away like a Holy Fool, his eyes as big as dinner plates.

As the Priest went back to his papers, Honzl looked around the church and scowled. What had that foul-mouthed nun said – Saint Vojtěch's at midnight? But who knew the place would be packed like Fibich's offal shop? The Special Investigator squinted at the choir and ground his teeth. They sure didn't look like choirboys – the guy at the front had no teeth for a start.

The priest pulled a face. "Okay, anybody else coming – another cart load, maybe?"

Then, smoothing down his cassock, he turned back to the happy couple. "Okay, where were we? I Eliška Darja Jedličová …"

At the rear of the church, the Count peeped at the newcomers from behind a pillar. The fellow with the eyes: what was *he* doing here? And accompanied by the police, to boot…

Instinctively Mitrovsky took two steps backwards, failing to notice that Mrs Jedličová's wig was now dangerously close to one of the high church candles, the good lady's hairpiece smoking most alarmingly.

The Father coughed. "I said, I Eliška Darja Jedličová…"

The bride looked like she'd been daubed there by a painter.

"C'mon kid, what is it? We've all got things to do. Hey, what's the matter? Cat got your tongue?"

The bride stayed *schtum*, the groom wrung his hands, the in-laws looked on awkwardly. Mitrovsky felt a little awkward too; what was that funny smell? Suddenly – and with a gentle 'poof' – Mrs Jedličová's rug lit up like a torch, horse-glue proving most flammable. Smoke billowed from the summit, Mitrovsky's head smelling like a pan of burnt milk.

Meanwhile, back in front of the altar, the priest looked at the bride suspiciously.

"Eliška? Hey kid, are you in there?"

The priest screwed up his eyes.

"C'mon – do you take this clown or don't you?"

Mr and Mrs Ančerl looked at each other rather uncertainly: they were paying good money for this? Over in the alcove the Count's head resembled a flaming brand.

"Mummy, Daddy, I don't think she wants to marry me,"

mewed Ernö.

"Ernö, hush…"

"But Daddy…"

"There, she said 'yes'," said Mr Ančerl, testily. "Yes, yes, yes. Now let's move on…"

Mitrovsky sniffed: what was that smell? Like wool mixed with turpentine. Was something burning? A wet dog perhaps?

"C'mon kid, we all gotta sleep. The guy's no pearl, but…"

All of a sudden, the top of Mitrovsky's head felt very, very hot. How hot? Hotter than the ovens of Hell.

The Count galloped unsteadily across the nave, his wig a flaming comet, his head a burning stump. With a great cry, Mitrovsky ran from his hiding place and gratefully plunged his head in the baptistry. When he came back up, the eyes of the entire church were upon him.

"Good, good, carry on," Mitrovsky mumbled, fishing out his wig like a drowned cat. "'Tis all extinguished now, don't worry"

The priest looked at Mitrovsky's dripping beard and shook his head: what kind of party was this? Still, if they were paying to light the candles…

Honzl squinted at the Count and began to scribble in his book.

Polovný whispered "'Tis the Emperor" and Honzl shushed him angrily.

"Okay, okay, pipe down at the back." The priest shook his head and sighed. "What a crowd. Now where was I? Oh yeah. C'mon toots, do you…"

All at once the church doors burst open and the two bandits – nay, Investigators – appeared, brandishing their flintlocks and grimacing most terribly.

"Oh, for Pete's sake…" groaned the priest.

The fellows looked most wild and agitated, especially Horáck, whose face resembled a trampled strawberry.

Spotting Mitrovsky squatting in a small puddle, Horáck pointed his pistol at his head

"Mrrwr mw foo," he snapped. "Mrrrruyth mrrw wooomrw ..."

Alas the swelling was such that the fellow could no longer form words, his lips resembling a foul and inedible patty.

"Mrrw www mumwruu…"

The other bandit stepped smartly forward.

"Sir, do you want me to…"

"Mrrww mmmwrr…"

Apropos of nothing, Polovný shouted "The Emperor!" and the guests sprang to their feet as if slapped.

A shot went off, just missing Saint Vojtěch.

"Hey!" yelled the Priest. "What do you jokers think you're…"

"Stop!" shouted the second bandit, throwing back his cloak. "Stop in the name of the law!"

"It's the *fizl*!" yelled one of the alter-boys, her pretty earrings shining. From underneath her cassock she pulled out a flintlock, eying up the crowd. But who should she shoot first?

"Master Halas!" cried Mitrovsky, "Master Halas, follow me!"

The priest mis-heard this as 'marry me' and stared at Mitrovsky, agog.

"Hey buddy, you can't…"

Ernö threw up his arms and Mitrovsky upended him with a well-placed shove. Immediately, Mister and Mrs Ančerl leapt up to protect their son.

"How dare you! He's a delicate boy…"

"He has asthma, you brute…"

"Mama, I've twisted my ankle…"

The Ančerls glared at Mitrovsky most angrily.

"I'm sorry my lad," said the Count, beard still dripping from the baptistry, "but the truth is, he can never be yours…"

All at once a second shot rang out, followed by yells, screams and cries. Who was shooting? Honzl, Polovný, somebody else? The choir boys began pulling various weapons – sticks, cudgels and the like – from their cassocks, setting upon the crowd in a violent manner.

Honzl too, leapt to his feet.

"I'm writing this down!" he yelled. "Right here in my book …"

Bewildered, Mr and Mrs Ančerl turned their fury on the Count.

"You swine! Our boy is most sensitive and emotional. Just look at him! Look at that delicate bloom!"

Windows were broken, statues overturned. Mitrovsky bowed like a courtier. "My Lord and Lady, it has been a wonderful ceremony, but 'tis time for us to go…"

Ah me, what a scene! So many people were in disguise, it was hard to work out who was who – servants, masters, altar boys. Saint Vojtěch looked up from composing 'Lord Have Mercy Upon Us', and silently shook his head.

"Farewell and adieu," said the Count, bowing. "It's been lovely, but we must be on our way…"

With that, Mitrovsky and Halas exited stage right. At the rear of the church was a little door, and behind the door, a cosy nook – the priest's dressing room, perhaps. Whatever it was, Mitrovsky locked the door and lifted up the veil, Master Halas blinked back most innocently. Ah, how fresh and happy he looked – as any bride should be on his wedding day.

"O lad – let us get out of here," said the Count. "I've lost count of the number of people who want to harm us…"

The lad nodded, but before they could escape, a feminine figure appeared in a second doorway, leading to the church yard.

"Did you see him?"

The men turned: Eliška!

"That stupid boy they want me to marry. In those stupid green stockings..."

Mitrovsky blinked,

"Eliška, my dove, is it you? But what are you doing here? How did you..."

"Like, did you see his nose?"

"Um..."

"Who could marry a nose like that?"

"Well," said the Count, "his parents seem very nice..."

A sound of heavy blows came from the locked door: the patrons of The Little Pig were starting to hack their way inside.

"I think they want to break your heads," said Eliška indifferently.

Mitrovsky nodded and the three ran helter-skelter 'cross the church yard, Halas in his wedding dress, Eliška in her night things, Mitrovsky in Mrs Jedličová's gown. The night was warm, gentle, perfumed as a rose. At the front of the church a tangle of shadowy shapes spilled out. Thugs, choir boys, the *fizl*? 'Twas very hard to say. The thugs mingled with the footmen and the butlers, everyone running every direction all at once.

"Stop them!" cried someone or other. "They're getting away!"

In the general confusion, Count, Bride and Somnambulist slipped over the church wall, their beautiful gowns ballooning over the other side. They then bolted along the little lane, ignoring the great commotion behind them. But how to make their escape? Should they go back to the Tiger, down by the river, or along the dusty lane? Before anyone could make up their mind, a handsome carriage hove into view from the other side of the square, a fine copper-yellow coach, driven by four piebald horses. Mitrovsky reached out his arm, the horses reared, and the carriage came to an abrupt halt. O, thank the stars! Mitrovsky's face floated in the dust while the two cabbies looked down upon the assembled personages most doubtfully.

"Good souls!" yelled the Count, "you find us in a moment of great peril. Please kind sirs, look into your hearts, and come to the rescue of these fine ladies…"

A figure leaned forward and Mitrovsky paused. Wait a minute, wait a minute … inside the carriage was a gentleman in a tall, chimney-pot hat, accompanied by two figures in black, the figures long, thin and extremely narrow, like spider legs, or the cracks on a cup.

Moosendorf!

"Um, that is to say…"

Moosendorf looked at the Count and his companions and smiled. "Of course, sweet ladies, get in…"

The Count looked at Moosendorf and then at the two skinny fellows somewhat uncertainly.

"I mean, we wouldn't want to intrude…"

"Nonsense, my fellow," said Moosendorf, his voice surprisingly high. "Leap onboard, there, that's it, in you go…"

Eliška pulled at Mitrovsky's sleeve and shook her head, her feet pulling her in the opposite direction.

"Climb in, climb in, there's always room for the mayor!"

On the lane behind came the sound of yells and gunfire: the two bandits – or Investigators or whatever they were – had spotted them and were advancing menacingly.

"Come, come! What are you waiting for?"

With his assailants so close at hand, the Count had little choice. He bundled Eliška up the ladder, followed by Halas in his wedding gown.

The door slammed shut and the cabbies whipped the horses just as a shot ricocheted nearby. With a great crash, the carriage then took off.

"A close one, eh my prince?" said Moosendorf, with a wink. "O, worry not, my fellow! We've all had to escape our creditors in a dress. Let me introduce myself – my name is Leopold Moosendorf, Brno's chief theatrical impresario. And these are my companions – Gunter and Emil – say hello boys!"

The two fellows – skinny heads, long bodies, delicate, elongated limbs – smiled and held out their hands.

"Halloo!"

"Guten Abend!"

Mitrovsky looked at the fellows and nodded.

"Ah – and they are…"

Still smiling, Moosendorf leaned over and whispered in Mitrovsky's ear. "The theatrical sensation of the age, my dear fellow! Tush, tush, 'tis true! These lads are going to be the talk of P – you see if they're not!"

Eliška, Halas and Mitrovsky all stared at them, taking in their long fingers, fine hands, and strangely elongated joints. How skinny they were! Like two long streaks of paint.

"Really?" said the Count, staring as if hypnotised. "But what …?"

"Expressive dance!" boomed Moosendorf with satisfaction, at which point the two lads assumed a most artistic pose, a posture both dramatic and artistically challenging, especially within the cramped confines of a carriage.

"Ah yes," said the Count, "but of course."

"Trust me, my friend – the good people of P will go crazy! It's the sensation of the age…"

"Well, I can plainly see that…"

Mitrovsky looked out of the window and saw the streets pleasantly racing past. Saint Vojtěch was receding far behind them, the trees and the spire, and then Hrůza also vanished, taking with it its Favours, Emperors and strange dreams. Before them lay P – and who knows? – perhaps other letters too.

The horses whinnied, the wheels clattered, and the cabbies

yelled. Outside, another day was dawning, the last stars of night vanishing like History. Mitrovsky looked at where Eliška was squeezed in next to Master Halas, Halas' eyes sparkling, Eliška staring moodily out of the window. But where was her mother? Well, mothers were like weevils: they always turned up in the flour. Mitrovsky smacked his lips and began to hum, 'A sparrow brings the bread/the tit-bird brings the salt...' Ah, what a fine Count he made! Cheeks powdered with arsenic, eyes as black as rabbit holes...

ACT IV

1

Curiously, Count Mitrovsky had no recollection of the ride to P at all. Had it taken one day, two? Nor could he recall any details of their approach to the city itself. No golden spires, no magnificent castle; nu, not even that famous bridge, you know, the one with the funny-looking statues, spanning the, um, something or other, down below.

Instead, Moosendorf's carriage pulled into the lot at the back of the 'Little Theatre' in the evening's gloomy half-light, the yard filled with bits of discarded stage sets, a poplar tree hanging around by the stage door, waiting for an autograph.

"Say, what is this dump?" asked Eliška, looking out at the rotting door frames and fireplaces, a rat hopping up half a staircase. A soft, yellow dust covered everything, fluff blowing across the yard like old men's hair.

Moosendorf looked at the girl askance.

"Dump? Ha, my dear, I should say not! Why, this is the famous Little Theatre of P!"

Mitrovsky nodded. "Little Theatre? Yes, yes, I believe I've …"

"Not to be confused with the so-called Big Theatre, though, of course, the Little Theatre is much larger…"

"Larger?"

"Yes, yes … a strange historical quirk. Why, every fool knows that the Big Theatre could fit inside the Little Theatre's lobby."

"Ha, I know that!"

The *impresario* shrugged modestly. "'Tis more of a pet name, really, a diminutive…"

The travellers looked about at the broken furniture, barrels of rags, and lumps of blackened wood; no one, not even a mother, could love this. A fake Roman column rested against half a portico, a golden throne upturned by a large wooden goose, the bird's paint flaking mournfully.

"Now then," said Moosendorf, "how about a sup and something to eat before you're on your way, eh? Your belly must think your throat has been cut."

"O my prince," said the Count, "you must have read my mind." Mitrovsky embraced the *impresario* manfully. "God reward you sir."

"Not at all, not at all. There – that's decided then." Moosendorf stalked across the yard and rang a bell. "Svanda, Svanda, my lad, where are you? Out playing 'Fool' with the Devil?"

With that, a stagehand appeared, a broad-shouldered fellow with a square shaped head and narrow, lively eyes.

"Alright, alright – who's there, gadding about like a chicken?"

"It is I, Moosendorf," said Moosendorf, pushing out his chest. "Heralding the theatrical event of the season…"

Svanda looked at the crowd and screwed up his eyes: what tut was the old fool selling now?

"May I introduce Gunter and Emil – *les mouvement mystérieux*. Say hello boys!"

"Hallo."

"Gutten Abend."

The two fellows climbed out of the carriage as a spider climbs out of a crack; nimbly, spryly, and a little too fast for comfort.

Svanda scowled and turned to the Count. "And who's this – the clown act?"

Moosendorf chuckled. "What? No, no, why this is the famous

Count Mitrovsky, disguised, for some reason, as a dame."

"Delighted to make your acquaintance," said the Count, executing a courtly bow and tearing his bustle in the process.

Svanda shook his head: Moosendorf's acts got worse with every year.

"And the nun?"

Halas blinked and produced a rather creased card from his wimple. 'My Name is Janos Halas. My throat is enflamed. Can you please direct me to Doctor Pustrpolk, 5 Temný Street, P? I do not know the way.'

The stagehand scratched his head and nodded. "Temný Street, Temný Street … nu, I know it. 'Tis only a few streets away – behind The Broken Pitcher. But…"

"What ho!" boomed Mitrovsky. "You hear that lad? We'll have you singing again in no time! What's that saying – I'd like to eat honey with your lips! Ha ha ha! He'll make a fine catch, eh Eliška? Look at the marvellous way he fills out that habit. O, I bet the good ladies of P will be head over heels!"

Halas looked across at Eliška and coloured. Eliška wrinkled her nose. "Yeah, it's a winning look…"

"This way ladies and gentlemen," announced Moosendorf, leading the way. "Svanda, fetch us a jug and a bite to eat."

"If I can find anything in my traps…"

"Such a jolly fellow! Well, this way my friends, this way…"

The party followed Svanda's lantern down a low, wooden passageway, the corridor reeking of paint and glue, as if decorators had knocked the place up in a week. Passages led first one way and then the other, the doors painted shut with not even the smallest window to let in a chink of light. Stairs led up, then straight back down again, the corridors whimsically twisting and turning, filled with all sorts of boxes and crates; indeed, the whole place was a vast labyrinth of junk, every last nook crammed with oddments and nick-nacks, from mirror frames to bedheads to boxes of stuffed birds. 'S'true – there was crap, everywhere! Old teapots, rusted armour, ancient tools; shelves buckled with rotting crates and boxes of straw, the junk arranged without rhyme or reason, as if filed away by mice.

"What a marvellous place," said the Count, wide eyed, "Why, 'tis like climbing in a magic box. And yet this is The Little Theatre, you say…"

"Why, the largest theatre in all of P!" said Moosendorf, pulling a face. "The so-called Big Theatre – pff! Barely enough room to stuff a goose…"

The Count nodded, then caught sight of his stockings; tush, such a state! As a result of his many adventures, Mrs Jedličová's *ensemble* was no longer *comme il faut*, the garter undone and ribbons bedraggled, not to mention the damage done to his gusset. Alas, this was no outfit befitting a gentleman: gentlewoman, either.

Coughing discreetly, The Count beckoned Moosendorf closer. "My dear fellow, my wardrobe might also benefit from some refreshment. Do you think…?"

Moosendorf's eyes sparkled impishly. "But of course, my dear fellow! Svanda! Svanda, could you help?"

The servant poked his thumb in the direction of a small, yellow door. "He can root round in the prop room if he likes. There's sure to be some kind of rag in there."

The Count removed his wig and bowed before Moosendorf like a courtier. "You're a pearl, my darling, an absolute saint."

Moosendorf grinned broadly. "Think nothing of it, my dear Count – 'tis the least we can do." With that the *impresario* gestured toward all four corners. "As you can see, The Little Theatre has many chambers – I'm sure you'll make yourself at home."

"O," said Mitrovsky, beaming, "'tis like I've lived here my

whole life…"

Alone in the dressing-room, the Count closed the door and scampered about like a child. Alongside one wall was a rack of costumes, on the other, a dirty chair, table and mirror. The walls were papered with old handbills and sheet music, the pages yellow and peeling, pretty girls and moustachioed devils, donkeys pasted on top of shepherds on top of gambolling children. In short: rather busy.

Breathing hard, Mitrovsky closed the door and rifled through the rack. Wide trousers, black velvet tailcoats, waistcoats the colour of ripe lemons: what an embarrassment of riches! He picked out white pantaloons, a vest with a row of pearl buttons, and a bright red jacket with lily of the valley lining, embossed in purple – a fine jacket, a beautiful jacket, a jacket one could live in forever. The Count then turned his back to check his stockings down to his ankles, bending one leg: yes, yes, delightful. And such pretty bows too!

The sight of these wonderous trifles made him think of his own armoire, last seen in The Golden Tiger: O, my drawers, he reflected, wither do you wander now? The Count had lined each one with all sorts of trinkets and curios, from French handkerchiefs to Hungarian ruffles to a ball of Moravian cheese, the latter encased in a thick crust of orange wax. Aye, thought Mitrovsky, where again would he find such magnificent ribbon, such rare silk, all kinds of ladies' mischief? True, some kind of beetle had made its home there, but even so…

Seating himself before the mirror, the Count applied powder to his cheeks and kohl to his eyes, rouging his lips for good measure. His beard, he combed and pomaded, spraying himself with rose water and topping the assemblage with an impressive wig, the approximate size and shape of a bird cage. Mitrovsky looked at himself in the glass and winked. Yes, yes: every inch the Count! True, the hairpiece smelt of terrier, and the pearl buttons were made of glass, but still … if only Mařenka could see him now! He pictured her beautiful eyes, her beautiful frills, her beautiful wig – but then, when he looked in the mirror, he saw an angry, round woman attacking him with a broom.

"Pig, dog, scoundrel! Out!"

"What?"

"Out! Out I say, damn your cap…"

"My darling, I was only trying…"

"Imposter! Crook! Thief of a good name! I turna my back, and looka what I see – a rat in my basket!"

The woman was small, dark and deliciously angry, her brows two zigzag lines, her eyes a pair of small black wasps.

"Darling, darling, please…"

The woman – some kind of dresser or makeup *artiste* if the number of rings on her fingers were anything to go by – made a swing for Mitrovsky's wig, knocking over a low shelf of bottles and brushes in the process. O, what a magnificent forearm she had! Pinned to a scrap of paper, a swine herd and shepherdess looked on indifferently.

"Swindler! Cheat! Fake! I see righta through you, you pane of glass!"

Alerted by the falling bottles, Moosendorf and Svanda appeared in the doorway, throwing themselves on the good lady's broom.

"Abriana, my angel! Abriana, please, leave our guest alone!"

"Guest? Phoo! Is fraud! Is hoax! He usa my paint stick – and my best brush too."

Her bosom heaving, Abriana stared at the Count as if he were the source of all her unhappiness – maybe the world's too.

"A curse on his ancestors! A family of villains … may his hair stuff my shirt…"

Moosendorf grabbed hold of one end of the broom, Svanda the other. "Abriana, Abriana, Abriana … You mustn't beat the audience…"

"She's off her nut," said Svanda.

Mitrovsky bowed.

"My angel, if in any way I have offended you…"

"Pah! You I no hear. Hear, why hear? He flicka his tongue like a cow flicka 'is tail."

Abriana glared at the Count as if he were two dirty boot-prints on her bedspread.

"Now Abriana, he's a count…"

"Ha! That much is true…"

"No, no, a real count…"

"Him?"

"Abriana, please! Come and join us for a jug and a slice of rye. My dove, I beg you, put down your brush…"

Reluctantly, the dresser laid down her weapon and stood there panting.

"Abriana – meet Count Mitrovsky, a travelling, ah, Count. My dear Count, meet Abriana, our dresser and makeup *artiste*."

Abriana cursed under her breath – something low and Italian, to do with mothers and pigs – but allowed Mitrovsky to climb out from beneath her broom. The Count re-arranged his wig and kissed the woman's hand, gazing up at her with his old dog eyes.

"My darling, let's not be cross. Look, this fellow has found a plate, mayhap a hunk of cheese…"

"I sow grass on your mother's grave," she hissed, one palm flat, the other in the shape of a horn. "In your eyes, I spilla the salt…"

2

On a stained blue cloth, Svanda summoned up a jug of beer, a crust of bread, a plate of leftover cutlets, and what looked to be the remains of a Sunday *Bábovka*, albeit somewhat nibbled by rats. A second stagehand – some old guy with a round, pockmarked head – as well as a seamstress, two cleaners, and a carpenter, had joined the party, Eliška now dressed in daywear, Halas clad in britches. Moosendorf entered with his contortionist act, along with the stage manager, Wranitzky, a pasty fellow with a moustache like a scrubbing brush. Abriana stared at the Count as she might a stranger's hair in her wash tub. "I spita your soup," she whispered.

Yet for all that, they were a merry company and tremendously knowledgeable when it came to the theatrical goings on of P.

"You hear about The Gossip? Burned down last night."

"The Gossip? No…"

"S'true. A candle from the temple scene. Set fire to Heller's bird costume."

"That cooks his goose!"

"Was he in it?"

"Who, Heller? Not a chance. Spends more time in Roskošova's tights from what I've heard."

"Yeah, yeah, her husband's taking up duck-hunting…"

"So, it's burnt down? Nothing left?"

"Just the stage door and the picture of Weigl in a toga. Not even the flames would touch that."

"Hey, what was that rattrap that burnt down last week, you know, the one by Pipkov's bottle shop?"

"What The Pearl? Mm – they say it was Pintcher and his pipe. He was building the Forest of Arden and hit his head on a branch."

"On a bottle, you mean."

"The place went up like a tinderbox. And when the fire-wagon turned up, they couldn't unfurl their hose."

"You know all about that, Pavel…"

"What?"

"As Mrs Bortošova said by the fireplace…"

"Dirty son of a Moravian cow! You want a smack in the mouth? Nothing wrong with my pump."

"I'm joking, I'm joking – hush, have some *Bábovka*…"

"So, what happened to The Pearl?"

"The fire crew had got the hose tied up in a knot – not even the captain could untangle it. Instead, he put down a blanket and the cast sang 'Farewell My Sweet Homeland Air' as the place burned to the ground."

"You hear about The Golden Palm?"

"Let me guess – burned down too?"

"Nope. Neighbours heard screaming and someone ran the fire bell. But when the wagon turned up it was just Liduška Venclová singing…"

"Who was screaming, the audience?"

"Screaming for a refund. The fire crew stayed for 'Morning is Wiser Than Evening', and then burnt the place down themselves."

Mitrovsky, enjoying himself very much, helped himself to another cutlet.

"The theatres in this town sound very, ah, combustible…"

Moosendorf nodded, "'Tis a hazard of the profession. A combination of wooden props, candelabras and high drama…"

"When The Tulip burned down, they say you could see the flames from M."

"M, N, O, P … all the letters in between."

"Didn't they rebuild it?"

"They started to, but then somebody knocked over a bucket of tar and the whole place caught fire again."

"It was a dump anyway. The fire-crew was the biggest audience they ever had."

"What, The Tulip? Listen, I saw Myslivěk there and…"

"All that was left was a single staircase, and a door opening out into space."

"If Liduška was singing, I'd take that step…"

"Hey, leave her alone, she's an angel…"

"Myslivěk was singing 'Let the Worthy Guests Assemble'."

"At The Tulip? He'd be lucky…"

Wranitzky gazed at the empty jug rather mournfully. "Did you hear about The Starry Path?"

"The Path? Let me guess – cinders."

"The police had it closed down – orders of the Emperor. Arrested Zeller and Musil. Said they were putting on a seditious show."

"What 'A Pocketful of Fleas'?"

"Yeah."

"Well, crimes against music, maybe…"

"The Department of Forbidden Texts put the *libretto* on the list. It denigrates standards of cleanliness in his Majesty's realm, apparently."

"What? That's the dressing room…"

"Of course, everyone knows that the pocket is really the Emperor's britches…"

"It is?"

"What did you think that song was about – 'O Happy Cock A Crowing?"

"I thought it was about a chicken…"

"You're the chicken, you dope…"

"Anyhow, Zeller and Musil are in the slammer. Two hundred gulden to spring them…"

"Yeah? How much to keep them there?"

The cleaner scratched her nose. "So 'A Pocketful of Fleas' is set in the Emperor's pants? I don't get it. What are the fleas?"

"You don't want to know."

Svanda spat. "The Department of Forbidden Texts sees filth everywhere. What are they going to ban next? 'Why are you neighing, my Valiant Steed'?"

"As the Empress said to the bishop…"

"Hey, keep it down – you want to get us shut down too?"

"What – you think The Department of Forbidden Texts is listening in?"

"Who knows? I heard they send spies who go 'round in disguise…"

"What?"

"S'true. They turn up unannounced, snoop around and then write everything down in a book…"

"Oh, come on! What kind of jerks…?"

At this the manager stopped talking and the whole crowd stared intently at Mitrovsky, the Count absent-mindedly licking his bone and humming a country air. Nothing could be heard but the sound of the Count's jaws and the ticking of a clock. "*Diablo*," whispered the dresser.

"Ha ha ha, this is all very amusing," said the Count, his mouth full of pork. "O what a merry life you thespians lead, with your fires and your censor and your fleas." He paused to wipe his mouth on his sleeve. "Say, has anyone here ever heard of a fellow named Bilek? Apparently, he's Brno's leading theatrical *impresario*…"

At the mention of Bilek's name, Moosendorf went stiff as a board. The colour drained from his face, his eyes bulged, and his lips twitched as if a piece of *Bábovka* had gone down the wrong way.

"Bilek, you say?"

"A champion fellow! He accompanied us part of the way to P, but alas we were separated after an unfortunate murder…"

Moosendorf clutched at his knife and fork. "Bilek? He's here?"

Wranitzky nodded and put his hand on Moosendorf's shoulder. "He arrived but a day or so before you. He's staying at The Jade Eye. You know, that joint on Podvodník Street."

"Bilek, here?"

The assembled diners exchanged anxious glances.

"Ah, excuse me, please," said Emil, one of the two contortionists, "what is this Bilek, please?"

Moosendorf blinked very rapidly. "He's Mister Nobody from Nowhere – second most successful theatrical manager in all of Brno…"

Svanda coughed. "Second, well…"

Wranitzky kicked him sharply under the table.

"And, ah, Master Bilek, ah, is he…?"

"Yeah. Putting on a show."

"A show? Bilek? Ha ha ha," said Moosendorf, without laughing.

"Mm – at The Big Theatre."

"Big?"

"Though everyone knows that The Little Theatre is much larger…"

"Of course!"

"And this … this, ah, show. What kind of…"

Wranitzky shrugged. "It's some big secret. Bilek is keeping it under his hat."

The two dramatic dancers looked at each other confused. "Under hat? *Unter* what hat please?"

"I cut his beard," muttered the dresser, holding up a knife. "I cleana his chin…"

"Listen, it's nothing to worry about," said Wranitzky, taking hold of Moosendorf by the shoulder. "Who cares what clinker Bilek has dragged here in his sack? Your act will be all that anyone is talking about. Eh, lads? What do we say?"

The two spidery fellows grinned. "Yes, yes. *Sehr gut*. Bilek and his hat, ha ha ha."

"Good pork," said Mitrovsky, wiping the grease from his chin.

At that moment, a bell rang someplace off in the depths of The Little Theatre and everyone jumped to their feet, the prop-hands brushing the crumbs from their stockings and dutifully returning to their tasks, or the avoidance thereof.

"Um, Count Mitrovsky – might I have a word?" said Moosendorf, manoeuvring the Count carefully away from the others.

"A word? Well…"

"Ah, in private, I mean."

Moosendorf and Mitrovsky stepped into a secluded alcove, the space occupied by a fake pot plant, a baptismal font and a plaster of Paris angel, the angel looking very snooty indeed.

"My dear fellow," said Moosendorf, picking the crackling from Mitrovsky's chin, "you are obviously a man of great learning and wisdom, a true prince among men."

Mitrovsky nodded and wiped his fingers on his cuff.

"Now whether or not you are employed by The Department of Forbidden Texts is of no concern of mine…"

"Or mine…" said Mitrovsky with a wink.

"But I think you will concur that this Bilek is a doubtful character, of uncertain morals and dubious nature…"

"Bilek?"

"And if I were employed by the Department of Forbidden Texts, then I would investigate this ah, pageant of his, forthwith."

"Yes, yes, so would I!"

Moosedorf stared at Mitrovsky's guileless chops intently. He resembled some kind of large, hairy dog who might recognise his own name, but for whom all other words are foreign entirely.

"After all, who knows what that villain might have hidden in his sack?"

Mitrovsky pictured the *impresario's* case and nodded. "Mm, yes, the fellow was awfully attached to his luggage, like a babe to her mama's paps."

Moosendorf nodded. "I imagine the Department of Forbidden texts would be most interested in such a parcel, I mean, to get their mits thereon."

The Count solemnly blinked his assent; aye, there was something about that case, some sort of dark enchantment. Moosendorf smiled slyly and shepherded the Count a little further into the darkness.

"And I too would be most interested in its contents – ah, from a purely professional standpoint, you understand."

"Professional? Well,…"

"If I could perhaps scrutinize this box – take a gander at what sort of nonsense pleases the, ah, less discerning palate…"

"Ha, ha, palate…"

Moosendorf looked at the Count foxily. "Perhaps this might help cover any, um, unforeseen expenses." And from within the folds of his cloak, the *impresario* produced a small sack of coins, the bag tied with a very fetching piece of turquoise ribbon.

Mitrovsky looked at the bag and made a funny shape with his mouth. "What a beautiful trim!"

Moosendorf smirked shrewdly.

"If we understand each other…"

Mitrovsky looked at the bag and then mournfully shook his head.

"O my stout fellow! I would love to help but I am already burdened with a multitude of tasks. First, Master Halas requires transportation to this physician behind The Broken Pitcher; second, Young Eliška must be returned to the gentle ministrations of her mother, the poor lady beside herself with worry, as is any mother's wont; third, I must forthwith procure a reputable purveyor of ribbons and frills, my own stock having run awful low; and fourth, I need to nail myself a couple of nightingales, 'cause you know, Mařenka's carriage won't hang around forever and I'm already two weeks in the hole. Look, look, can you see? The horses are grown restless, the groom idly scratching his nose…"

Mossendorf looked at the Count frostily; yes, these damned censors were tricky devils, right enough.

"But of course, my dear man," the *impresario* purred. "But perhaps this might help…" And so saying, he produced another small bag from beneath his cloth.

Mitrovsky looked at the stitching much as a cat might look at a bobbin. But again he shook his head.

"That is a pretty bit of stitching, right enough, but my quest is a just and sacred one, and besides, for these nightingales, I am on commission. This Mařenka, she intends to depart, and I intend to depart with her, in the very same compartment, if you get my drift…"

Moosendorf's sugary smile faltered: curse these book-burning clerks and their bottomless pockets!

"Yes, yes, yes," Moosendorf muttered, hastily. "Well, perhaps this might sweeten the pot." And so saying, he somehow produced a third bag, juggling them adroitly, as befitting a member of the show-business fraternity.

"O my prince," said the Count, sadly. "You must really want that gravy…"

"So – do we have an agreement?"

The Count looked at the ribbon and then nodded. "For you, my treasure – anything! Besides, I too have more than a passing fancy in the insides of Bilek's drawers…"

"Of course, of course – the Department of Forbidden Texts never sleeps! But you bring it to me first, *kapeesh*? Then you can burn it to cinders for all I care."

Mitrovsky nodded and hid the three bags somewhere in the pockets of his magnificent jacket, making his shape seem to bulge all the more.

"Now then," he said, patting the lump most tenderly. "I believe that fellow spoke of The Brass Ball…"

"The Jade Eye. It's on Podvodník Street – and by lucky chance, a passage leads right from The Little Theatre virtually to the front step."

"Really? 'Tis lucky indeed…"

"Would you care to follow me? No time like the present! After all, who knows what weeds Bilek plans to sow?"

Moosendorf took the Count by the arm and began to steer him away down yet another low, wooden corridor. Nevertheless, like Lot's wife, Mitrovsky lingered to take one look back.

"Master Moosendorf, would you be able to bestow on me a great favour? 'Tis Master Halas and the fair Eliška; these two youngsters are in my care, and…"

"O, worry not, good sir. They are most welcome to tarry a while here at the theatre – why, I'll even throw in half price tickets for my own modest show."

"*Mouvement mystérieux?*"

"Is there any other kind?"

"What an angel you are!"

Moosendorf shoved the Count further into the darkness, Mitrovsky stumbling over a stuffed marmoset, an ancient tea-service, and the frame of a spinning jenny, all of them smelling like the contents of an old shoe box.

"What a rabbit warren this place is," said the Count, squeezing his gut past a series of door frames which seemed almost to form a corridor of their own. "Why, for the Little Theatre it seems…"

"Enormous? I admit, its dimensions must seem most perplexing to those inexperienced in theatrical matters."

"And this is merely the back-stage area? Why the auditorium must be…"

"Huge! Magnificent! Bigger than that of The Big Theatre, anyway."

Mitrovsky admired the tea-pots, jam-jars and wig-stands, and whistled. "O, my good fellow, what a delightful life you must lead – what with your dancers and your clowns and your tall spindly fellows dressed all in black."

Moosendorf's shoulders bobbed up and down. "Yes, yes – *la vie artistique!* When the boobs in the front row throw pennies, 'tis most gratifying…"

And with that he threw open a door onto a dismal alley, a large rat taking fright like a curse. In the lane beyond, scraps of handbills flew up like cinders from a bonfire, spinning and spiralling in the breeze. Moosendorf looked up and down the street and then grabbed Mitrovsky by the shoulders.

"The Jade Eye is just down the street. Look for the sign of a horseshoe, then a fork, then a needle and thread."

"Horseshoe, comb, saddle."

"Horseshoe, fork, needle and thread."

"Right."

"Just meet back at The Little Theatre. With the package, understand? One peek and then we'll throw it on the midden."

"But of course. Farewell, sweet prince. The hours we are apart feel more like days…"

"The box, Mitrovsky."

"But of course."

Waving farewell, the Count passed under the sign of a flour sack, a fishbone, and a comb, the moon splashing the closed stores with a bluish light, illuminating the square and the gallows. A few bars were located down here – The Little Boy, The Lost Coin, Under the Frog –ruffians swaying this way and that, singing 'She played the Queen of Spades' with gruff, manly voices. Nearby, a wooden sign hung off-centre above a mangy and discoloured curtain: a Jade Eye. Did the eye wink mischievously? Hm, who knows? In the labyrinth of the world, anything seemed possible. It was late, still hot. A night watchman strolled past, silently watching the night.

3

Inside the Jade Eye, beer made its way from jug to throat as if bubbling up from a happy spring, the place filthy with drunks, among them Bilek and his hat. The impresario hung onto the bar as a drowning man hangs onto a branch, already three sheets to the wind – unlaundered too by the look of 'em.

"Lishen," he slurred into the ear of the landlady, Mrs Šeborova, "s'gonna be a shensation… a senshashion … the talk of the town! You boobs in P – you've never seen anything like it…"

"That right?" said Mrs Šeborova, wiping out a jug. "Listen, Bilek, I heard this tune before. What was that last act of yours, the Musical Milkers of Most?"

"Thosh dames went over big!"

"I heard the front row were trampled…"

"S'my fault some jerk made a sudden noise?"

"Well, it sure wasn't applause." The drunk sitting next to him gave a snort. "Face it Bilek, you haven't had a hit in years…"

"What? What about Pilss … Pilsudski – the Pole with the musical carp?"

"Harp?"

"Carp. The fish rang a little bell with his mouth. The kids, they loved it."

Mrs Šeborova shook her head and poured another drink. "The kids in Brno, maybe but this is P … you're not some burg like Q or R. The people here, they're sophisticated, cultivated … hey,

Rozkošny, get your boots out of that spittoon! You think I clean this dump for fun?"

"Listen lady," said Bilek, resting his cheek on the counter, "thish show – s'most amazing thing you ever heard. S'artistic, poetic: like an angel pouring honey in your ear. Don't blame me when you're selling your mother for a ticket…"

The drunk snorted again. "Your mother is the only one who'll buy one…"

"Pfff – jerks like you know nothing…"

Watching from a stool in the corner, Count Mitrovsky slowly drank it all in: Bilek's hat, his stockings, the fashionable little bows by his calves. But where had he stowed his box? Stealthily, the Count slid from his stool and rolled across the floor, settling behind Bilek like a cloak. With his enormously long and slender fingers – for Counts have tremendously long fingers, as everybody knows – he carefully extracted from the *impresario's* pocket a large brass door-key as well as the one to his strong box, the keys jangling like a cherub's fart.

Innocent of this chicanery, Bilek's jaw was still clacking.

"This show, it'sh gonna go down in history."

"Yeah, like the Battle of White Mountain…"

"I'll give you a thirty-year war you jerk. S'classy, you know, artistic. When you get to hear these birds…"

His fellow drinker belched. "Birds? Ah c'mon Bilek, – not that canary act again. You know what happened last time…"

"How was I to know that Madame Semenova had allergies?"

"Allergic to be shat on…"

"Why you boob, you wouldn't know Art if it was covered in feathers…"

"What, you got Mozart in that case? Or a leg of pickled pork?"

"I'm gonna pickle your pork, you boob…"

Meanwhile the Count had carefully procured the keys and

slipped away. From the taproom, he stole away to a back room, and thence to the public stairs. The steps were steep and narrow, smelling of smoke and goose-fat and something indefinable. Shadows dripped down the walls like a stain.

The Count looked at the fob. Room five, five, five…Yes, this was the place!

As quietly as possible, Mitrovsky unlocked Bilek's door and slipped inside. The bed, chair and table were short and squat, like members of the same hard-working family, the room clean, neat and smelling of carbolic. And there was the strong box, tucked into the sheets like a baby. Mitrovsky stole over, inserted the key and turned, the latch snapping open with a pop.

Inside, cushioned by soft, off-white lining (a very nice bit of cloth, truth be told) was a most peculiar collection of objects which the Count carefully extracted one by one: a seemingly empty glass stopper, a tiny table and chairs, each no larger than a nut, a miniature trampoline, two matchsticks with a line of string hung between them, a minute ball, a toy cart, a scaled down carriage, and a diminutive ladder with a thimble of water at the base. Mitrovsky unscrewed the stopper and shook: tiny specks immediately scattered and ran, many of them seeming to make tiny little jumps of triumph.

"How peculiar," whispered the Count, rubbing his hand through his beard. "Why, if I didn't know better…"

Was this really Bilek's act – a minikin circus? Perhaps Moosendorf was right, the Big Theatre really was no bigger than a snuff box…

The Count flicked the little ladder somewhat sceptically. *This* was the secret of Bilek's box? Bugs? But who would pay to see bugs?

Confused, the Count sat back on Bilek's bed and scratched his tights. Bilek was going to conquer P with *lice*? Who would even see them from the stalls?

All of a sudden, the Count felt something nibble at his knee joint. What was it, a flea? He scratched lustily. Yes, something had bitten him, the rogue. Cursing, he rubbed his leg, abrading himself with great vigour. Bloody bed bugs: pick another corpse to feast on! But the bugs kept on biting and his tights kept on itching. Nu, nu, such pain! And with that the Count's leg flew up in a violent spasm, booting the strong box clean across the room.

"Whoopsies," said the Count.

Still rubbing his knee, Mitrovsky wandered over to where the case lay upturned on the rug, the carriage smashed, the tiny tight rope snapped. The Count picked up the shards with his fingers: pish posh, what a catastrophe! Even the teensy bucket had been upended.

Stuffing the midget furniture back inside the case, Mitrovsky saw that the box's lining had also come unglued, a gap opening up like a pocket. Slipping his hand inside, he found a sheath of papers within, the parchment covered with strange, indecipherable signs – musical notes, it seemed. How strange! But what was the point of them? Perhaps such hieroglyphics might mean something to a tuba-player or the like, but to a Count – well, they might as well be written by a Russian. And then he saw it: written at the top of the page in a clear hand were the words 'At Dawn, Two Nightingales'. The Count's heart seemed to stop. Was that Nosek's poem inscribed between the lines? But no, curse it – just more of those damned squiggles, as if a beetle had crawled out of an ink well. The Count stared at the parchment stupidly, as a pig might look at an almanac: the signs obviously meant *something* but what this might be was beyond his powers of comprehension.

Then: footsteps on the staircase, heavy breathing, consternation.

"Mitrovsky? What the hell are you doing here?"

Bilek stared at the Count through bleary eyes, the *impresario* swaying from side to side in the doorframe.

"Why Master Bilek!" exclaimed the Count, the sheath of papers crumpled in his mitts. "Ho, how I've missed you! And just look at you – that smile's so sweet I won't need sugar…"

Bilek looked down at the score scrunched in Mitrovsky's paws.

"You clown, what do you think you're…"

Mitrovsky grinned, then threw the glass stopper at Bilek's head. "The fleas! They've escaped!"

As Bilek dived to the floor, the Count pushed his way past him, taking with him the score as well as several of the performing bugs, travelling in his britches.

"Stop! Stop! Thief!" yelled the impresario, struggling to get back to his feet.

At the bottom of the stairs, the assembled drunks stared at Mitrovsky somewhat suspiciously. The Count fluttered his handkerchief.

"Thief? He means beef. I hear the room service here is…"

The crowd made not altogether encouraging noises. Mitrovsky smiled beseechingly and placed the handkerchief to his nose.

"My darlings, I feel there has been a terrible misunderstanding…"

With this classic Count's gambit, the scene suddenly became very confused indeed. Punches were thrown, tables upended, violins broken. Nevertheless, the Count somehow managed to crawl free from the wreckage, his wig rudely manhandled, but otherwise more or less in one piece.

Out on the street the night was all over him like a pickpocket, the air warm and close, scented with juniper and booze. Mitrovsky barely had time to straighten his ruffle before Bilek appeared in the doorway, his expression most unsympathetic.

271

"Mitrovsky, you bastard, I'll get you, you jerk…"

And with that the Count took to his heels, disappearing into the night as if falling through a trap door.

4

Mitrovsky hastily retraced his steps, jogging past The Little Boy and The Lost Frog in a great hurry, his shoes clip-clopping noisily on the cobbles. "Horseshoe, comb, saddle," he whispered, "horseshoe, comb, saddle." Specks of ash blew in on the air, crunching in his teeth like bugs. Horseshoe, comb, saddle. Or was it fork, needle, horse? Either way, the Count felt terribly hot and sweaty, his embroidered jacket sticking to his hairy back like a curse.

Still, the passage had to be around here somewhere, and with it the door to the Little Theatre. The Count ran his hands along the walls like a blind man buying a mule. The passage was dark, dreary, but if you squinted carefully, you could almost make out a rough outline, like the dusty space behind a purloined painting. As for the door itself – poof, gone, disappeared back into the wall. But how? Behind him, the Count could hear footsteps, yells, heavy breathing, while before him a painting of a broken pitcher hung haphazardly in the gloom, the drop of milk eerily realistic, as if fresh from the udder. The Broken Pitcher, The Broken Pitcher – now where had he heard that name before? Glancing over his shoulder, the Count sprinted across the road and up a dark, narrow stairwell, squeezing himself into the darkness as a beetle in a hole.

At the top of the stairwell, a narrow beam of moonlight illuminated a crooked sign – Doctor Pustrpolk, Physician and

Doctor of Medicine (Veterinarian, Monday & Thursday), the letters written in an untidy hand, 'Thursday' barely fitting on the sign.

Hearing movement down below, the Count pushed urgently against the doorway, a little bell ringing as he stumbled into a narrow, wood-panelled lobby, the room redolent of Turkish tobacco, medicinal herbs, and hooch.

Panting like a dog, the Count closed the door and placed his ear to the wood: nothing. Had he lost them? Straightening his wig, he carefully unballed Bilek's score and placed it in a pocket: the nightingales would have to wait. Now where had he heard of this Pustrpolk? And then it struck him – Halas' enflamed throat, the card, Temný Street in P. Yes, yes, Dr Pustrpolk, prince of the physician's art!

With that a night-shirt arrived containing a skinny old man with an enormous moustache, the rest of his features resting atop it, like birds sitting on a branch. The fellow carried a lamp, a poker, and a sceptical expression.

The Count bowed and smiled amicably.

"Doctor Pustrpolk?"

The fellow looked the Count up and down. "That depends. You the bailiff?"

"Why…"

"The police? Mrs Pustrpolk?"

"No, no, I…"

"In that case I'm Dr Pustrpolk. Here, you look terrible. Step inside my office and I'll see what I can do."

The Count mopped his sweaty neck and smiled. "No, no, you see I am here for a friend…"

"Yeah? That's what they all say. And what happened to this friend of yours? Soreness, itching, pain when you piss?"

"Oh no, nothing like that…"

"O, come on, we're both men of the world! Now climb up on this couch and pop your beard on the table. Though I should warn you, I charge extra for night-work, as the actress said to the bishop…"

Pustrpolk loped obliquely, as if into a strong wind, but what was Mitrovsky supposed to do? Obediently the Count followed Pustrpolk into his office – in reality, an old kitchen table, covered in a filthy cloth.

"There you go, you hop up. Sorry about the stains, but my last patient was an Alsatian."

The Count paused on the threshold and sniffed the air suspiciously. "Um, I think I might be looking for a different Dr Pustrpolk…"

"That quack? I wouldn't give him the time of day. Trust me – his patients only check out in a winding sheet. Why would you want to go to him? Pustrpolk – I wouldn't trust him to cut my nails. Now, that's it, up you go, take the weight off your cloak. Okay, tell me all about it – what's the problem? Boils, sores, spots? If it's the horseman's complaint, I've got two tubs of ointment at five groschen a pop."

The Count climbed up onto the table and lay there like an enormous slice of ham, his eyes dark and sad, lined with big black rings.

"No, no, my good fellow, I'm…"

"Tired? Fatigued? Unable to provide masculine satisfaction? Listen, you can be straight with me, it's the Enlightenment. You just lie there, I'll go and get my medicinal mallet."

Mitrovsky fluttered a handkerchief. "O my angel, I fear you are mistaken – my name is Count Mitrovsky and…"

"Count? What makes you think you're a Count?" Pustrpolk tapped on Mitrovsky's head and peered suspiciously in his ears. "A count? That sounds like crazy talk. Next thing you know, you're the King of France or the Pope's mother. Listen, if you were a Count, what would you be doing in a dump like this? I mean, just look at this table – would you find a Count on a table like this? I wouldn't put my poodle on such a thing. Well, I rest my case." Pustrpolk winked, patting down his night-shirt as if looking for a cigar. "Okay, I think we're done here. My assistant will issue the bill on the way out."

"No, no, I…"

Pustrpolk sighed and tapped the Count on the head.

"What, more? Okay, Mitrovsky, you're a tough nut to crack. Now take off your tights and I'll take a look – I've got I've a needle and thread out back."

Stretching out his arms and legs, the Count settled down and made himself at home.

"You see doctor, this friend of mine…"

"Friend?"

"Master Halas. You see, the lad, he, ah … he lost his voice." Mitrovsky pointed toward his own throat, as if at a visual aid. "Who knows what happened? Perhaps he went out with wet hair, or put on a damp scarf, or mayhap was frightened by a goose."

Nodding, Pustrpolk pulled out a large book. "Go on, go on …"

"Well, whatever it was, now the lad can't speak at all..."

Pustrpolk nodded and scribbled in his pad. "Yes, yes. Goose, you say?"

"And has a card – Dr Pustrpolk, 5 Temný Street, the celebrated throat specialist. Eh, my lad, is that you?"

Pustrpolk jumped like a scalded cat and marched up and down the room.

"Listen, before I answer that question, let me ask you something – do you know anything about medicine?"

"Not a thing."

"In that case, I most certainly am. Okay, you can put your tights back on now, your knees are making me sick."

Pustrpolk wandered over to an empty bottle, weighing it in his hands with a melancholy air.

"Okay, okay. You sit there and I'll mix up a cocktail. I'm sure I've got some liverwort round here somewhere."

"O, you wise medical fellows," said the Count, smiling broadly, "'tis as if you have a cure for everything! Why, I met this peasant and…"

"Peasant?" Pustrpolk looked outraged. "Listen, I'm a scientist, a qualified physician. What, you think I won my certificate in a game of pinochle? Okay, forget I said that. If the police turn up, we don't know nothing and the horse ain't mine."

While the doctor went off to check his larder, Mitrovsky lay back on the couch and scratched his behind. O, these tiny bit-players – would they ever let up? But at least one of his quests was at a close. How thrilled Master Halas would be to speak again! Mitrovsky imagined his voice to be that of a young blackbird or the murmuring of a brook in spate, gentle and lively at the same time.

Pustrpolk returned carrying a tray like a waiter.

"Okay Mitrovsky, listen up. In the morning, I recommend a tea made of cinnabar, musk and a syrup of cloves, with a booze chaser. It won't do any good, but it's one hell of a pick-me-up. Then this pal of yours, give him a dose of this – it's one-part red wine vinegar, two parts prunella, and three parts nightshade water. Or is it one-part nightshade, two parts prunella, and just a dash of lemon juice? Either way, you can also use it on pancakes, or to remove mould. If that doesn't work, brush his tongue with lead plaster – that'll teach him."

Mitrovsky bowed. "O my good fellow – Science marches on! Why, just yesterday we were taking the powdered leg of a deer and a hair from a strong young man…"

Pustrpolk clapped Mitrovsky on the back. "Hey, don't knock powdered deer till you've tried it. And if you ever need hair, my brother farms it on his back."

It was warm, late, the sky the colour of Viennese ink, like Pustrpolk's bottle. Lost in thought, the Count stared at the elixir and then scratched aggressively at his leg. "Tell me Doctor, do you know anything of music?"

"Music? What, this friend of yours wants to sing now? Listen, one step at a time. You want my advice, start with whispering then build up."

Mitrovsky reached inside his pocket and brandished the sheet music with a flourish. "You see, by pure chance, this musical score has fallen into my hands…"

"Pure chance eh?"

"And, knowing but little of such matters…"

Pustrpolk scowled, then looked the scroll up and down. "Musical appreciation? Well, you've come to the right place. Bettelheim the peddler sold me a harpsichord just last week."

The doctor strode over to a low table and pulled back a sheet. Beneath was what appeared to be a tiny organ, complete with wooden pinblock, soundboard, hitchpins, and jack. Like a peasant, the keyboard seemed to be missing a few teeth, the lid held up by a stick.

"It's a beauty, eh? Comes with a lute stop, just like my cousin, Minnie."

"And do you play?"

"Music runs in our family, like diabetes. Now pass me that score and I'll see what I can rustle up." Pustrpolk planted his behind on a small stool, cracking his knuckles theatrically. "Two nightingales, you say? That seems like at least one nightingale too many, but I'll do my best."

Pustrpolk ran his fingers up and down the keyboard, squinting at the score myopically. But, O what a sound! The tune was sweet, sad, and full of poignant longing. When the performance was over, both men were in tears, Mitrovsky dreaming of Mařenka, Pustrpolk because of a splinter.

"Why, that's beautiful," said the Count. "But isn't that the tune to 'Waltz me Round the World, Willy?"

Pustrpolk slammed down the lid.

"Well, hail and farewell Count. It's been lovely chatting, but us doctors have to get our sleep – it's you patients who get to lollygag around in bed all day. Now, tell your friend to take the potion once before meals and twice during the hundred year's war."

"O, my lad, however can I thank you?"

"For us doctors, this purse of coins is thanks enough."

Mitrovsky handed over Moosendorf's purse, bowing low. Pustrpolk nodded and slapped him on the chops.

"Well, so long Count. If you ever need anything to get rid of those fleas, just let me know. In the meantime, if you spill the elixir on a tablecloth, try vinegar and white wine. And if that doesn't work, I'd buy another tablecloth."

And with that the good doctor unlocked the door and shoved the Count outside.

"And the way back to the Little Theatre?"

"Horseshoe, comb, saddle – you can't miss it. Hail and farewell Mitrovsky. Remember, if anyone asks, you're a Count and I'm a Doctor and don't let anybody tell you otherwise…"

And with that the door slammed shut, the sign hanging crooked on its nail.

5

Whistling softly, the Count wandered up and down the maze of cobbled streets, each block bleaker and gloomier than the last. 'Twas the hour before dawn, the 'hour of orphans', lonely as an insomniac's thoughts. No cats, no dogs, no mice: even the street signs seemed blank, the houses flat and empty as a curtain, their doors a black coat of paint.

Aye, 'twas a strange place, right enough. The closer one got, the more it seemed to break up into blobs and patterns, like a bib, or a painter's smock. Only from far away did P resemble a city; up close, you could see that the curtain's hem was tattered and frayed, the fabric stained beyond recognition. Yes, a curious place, like a painted backdrop, you had to be standing in just the right place for the illusion to work at all.

And so hot – stifling, even! The streets smelled of sweat, scorched feathers and tar, yellow dust grating against the Count's teeth, the air heavy and still. Something made a rasping noise nearby, dry as a beetle's wing; otherwise the only sound was the hum of night-hawk moths, the creatures circling round the Count's hairpiece, turning to dust when cornered.

Still chasing moths, the Count turned a corner and ran straight into a policeman, the fizl's uniform speckled with powder like a cake.

"Stop right there!"

The constable paused and inspected the Count's wig intently.

"Now then my lad – what are you doing up and about at this time of night?"

Mitrovsky froze, his fingers dancing up and down as if playing the flute.

"Who, me?"

"Yes, you."

The Count fluttered his handkerchief. "Why, my name is Count Mitrovsky, returning from a nocturnal adventure, as us Counts are wont to do…"

Immediately the constable broke out into a broad, lascivious grin. "Ah, a Count, eh? Oh, you Counts with your midnight escapades … a beauty was she, sir?"

"What? Um, a beauty, yes…"

"How does that song go? By night she makes the daylight stray…"

"Ha ha, that's her."

"Moonbeams settle in her hair…"

"Moonbeams, yes, yes, the very thing…"

The two men breathed deeply, the last few stars beginning to vanish, replaced by the pale wash of day. Then the constable squinted and scrunched up his red, berry-like face.

"Did she have dainty feet, sir?"

"Feet? Um…"

"Shapely little feet, with tiny rounded toes?"

"Ah, I…"

"And her instep? Was it elegant? Charming?"

"A delight!"

"The arch of her foot?"

"Divine!"

The constable nodded, looking down at Mitrovsky's shoes, perhaps imagining ten tiny toes in their place. All of a sudden he begun to sing, 'Ah happy, little feet/How you crush the buds of spring'. His voice was rich and resonant, and when he was finished, both men had tears in their eyes. "Well, off you go, sir. You'll be needing your rest. After your exertions, I mean…"

"Aye, farewell, sweet prince, it's been a joy…"

"Good night sir."

"Good night."

Mitrovsky bowed and elegantly retreated, one eye on the alleyway, the other on the fellow and his stick. Fortunately, the cop stayed where he was, pollen collecting like dust on his uniform. Somewhere a cock crowed: dawn.

Unsure where to go, the Count followed a hazy, zigzag route past a row of vacant-looking houses, the moon withdrawing discreetly as the sun rose to take its place. Wasn't there some famous astronomical clock which illustrated this? Pish, wasn't that why visitors came to P in the first place? But it was hard to imagine many travellers gathering in this spot, the houses old and empty, cobbles worn, roofs sagging – even the light seemed tired. A misty sun rose in the sky, but half the street remained at midnight, the houses filled with darkness as a scuttle is filled with coal. There was no dew – only dust, great yellow clouds of the stuff, collecting in the street like gnats.

Mitrovsky turned a corner and immediately collided with a tall, lumpy fellow with a nose like a mushroom, the fellow running in the opposite direction and holding a case to his chest.

"Stop!" somebody shouted. "Stop thief!"

The miscreant bounced off the Count's stomach, yelling some obscenity in a coarse Moravian voice. While the Count struggled to get to his feet, the villain took to his heels and ran off down a darkened alleyway, leaving both Count and strongbox behind.

Rubbing his knees, Mitrovsky spotted an elderly gent limping painfully along the street, one leg shorter than the other, as if his tailor had mixed up the measurements. The fellow extended one delicately gloved hand and helped the Count to his feet. "I am forever in your debt, sir. If it hadn't been for your quick thinking … well, I shudder to think what would have happened."

The old gentleman had just emerged from a carriage, the *fiaker* parked outside an inn, two girls peering out from the window.

"Why, think nothing of it," said the Count, picking himself up. "I am glad to be of service…"

"What?"

"Service!"

"Servant?"

"Service!"

The old fellow shook his head. "I'm so sorry, my hearing is not so good these days. My eyes too, truth be told. My good man, won't you join us for a bite to eat in The Golden Spike? We have been travelling all night and my daughters and I are famished. Please say yes! It can be my way of thanking you for saving all our worldly goods."

Mitrovsky shook the man's hand with great vigour. "O my dear man! Well, 'tis dawn after all…"

The old duffer was dressed in a military *justacorps*, with black tails and white stockings, what remained of his hair cut short in the military style, and greying at the edges. Something about him seemed familiar, though the Count couldn't quite put his finger on it. Had he once bought ribbons from him? Rented a wagon and horse? The fellow's face was stamped with age and anxiety, his eyes cloudy as a Moravian summer.

"Marvellous!" The old fella glanced back toward his carriage. "Girls, girls, come meet our champion. My daughters, sir…"

The carriage door opened, and two young ladies disembarked in a snowdrift of fabric and tassels. Although of similar age, his two daughters could hardly have been more different, one plump and ruddy, the other pale and thin, her melancholy face hidden by a delicate, crotched, veil.

"Lida, Lena, come meet our most honourable defender! Why, if were not for him, then … I shudder, sir, I really do! That's it, girls, say hello! And your name is…?"

The Count bowed. "Mitrovsky, sir."

"Mussorgsky?"

"Mitrovsky."

"Muzachelli?"

"Mitrovsky, sir. Count Mitrovsky."

"Count? Ha ha ha! Well, yes, indeed! And I am the Baron Gluck … but call me Anton, please. Now, shall we break bread within? Kapper, ensure that our luggage is brought inside and see to Nanny."

"Nanny?"

"The girls' nurse. Although she too is advanced in years, as you can plainly see…"

Inside the cab an ancient, mummified figure peered out nervously, her round grey eyes practically popping out of her head. Mitrovsky bowed.

"Honoured to make your acquaintance."

"Good grief!" whispered the desiccated governess, her pale lips pursed. "What is that thing, a bear?"

"Ha ha, no, my name is Count Mitrovsky and I am no bear at all…"

"Good gracious, I've never heard of such a thing. Mitrovsky? I don't believe a word."

Gluck smiled, patting the Count on the arm. "Please don't vex yourself, my good man. Nanny has been in the family for years, but in recent times her mind has become somewhat… wandered. But what is one to do, leave her out in the snow?"

"Ha ha, a trick question, I presume?"

"She's really quite the darling. And besides, she loves the girls very much…"

"Those angels?" said the Count. "How could she not? O, what a happy family, like a painting hanging on a wall!"

"Yes, yes – a happy family is a gift from God. But please – let us retire to the Golden Spike. 'Tis nearly six and you must be starving."

"The pail is hard to fill…"

"But of course…"

With that Gluck drew the Count gently toward the inn, Kapper following on behind, a mountain of luggage on his back.

Whilst a litter was sought to convey Nanny from carriage to chamber, Gluck and his two daughters accompanied Mitrovsky to the dining room of the Golden Spike, a surly-looking waiter yawning into the crook of his arm. Soon a plate of fresh *tvorog* arrived at their table, accompanied by the cheek and dried spine of a sturgeon.

"Delightful, delicious!" said the Count, smacking his chops loudly. "O, if only every day could start this way – I mean, in the company of such charming and agreeable friends. Hm – are you finished with that *tvorog*, sweet prince?"

Gluck smiled. "Please, please – help yourself. When you reach my age, you no longer have such an appetite for life."

"Oh come, you're not as old as all that. Why…"

"You're awfully kind dear fellow, but I live only for my daughters now, the poor darlings…"

Mitrovsky glanced at the two young ladies and nodded. The pale one dabbed at her red nose with a napkin, while the other loudly chewed on the sturgeon cheek.

"Alas my darling Lena has – ah, suffered a misfortune, a disappointment, shall we say…"

The Baron patted his daughter's hand, lovingly.

"A disappointment?"

"My daughter, dear heart, is a gentle soul, a spotless, unsullied vessel. And as such, this, ah, disadvantage hit her particularly hard. A most cruel blow sir, most cruel..."

Lena stared at her plate with an expression of absolute concentration.

"And this, ah, tribulation has upset our family most earnestly – and our fortunes, truth be told. There is a devil, sir. A devil by the name of Lame Patočka. And, alas, we are in debt to this devil for a considerable amount. Indeed, if I may be entirely frank with you, for the entire value of our family estate."

"O my darling!"

"And unless we can secure suitable funds, our home will fall into this Patočka's mitts, and we will be in the poor house, or else living in the fields, like some kind of mouse or a weevil."

"O sweetheart, what a terrible story! Why, I feel my heart breaking too..."

Mitrovsky stared at the family with his dark, lugubrious eyes. Losing one's estate was like losing one's name, like being scratched out from the very Book of Life... The Count chewed on his cake and swallowed. A fellow without a home, was just a rag, a scrap of a man, neither an inhabitant of this earth nor a phantom from the dead, neither one thing nor the other.

The Baron grasped his daughters' hands and smiled sadly.

"But we have a plan, have we not my dears? With our last remaining funds, we have secured board and lodgings here in P, as well as tickets for a new opera at The Big Theatre. And this opera will be the means of our salvation my angels, will it not? For there my beautiful daughter Lida will charm the good bachelors of P, and by such artistry, secure a husband of means, which is to say, a saviour, a fine gentleman, able to pluck Lame Patočka from our back."

Lida pulled out a fish bone and nodded. "I've got a new frock," she said, flatly.

"Why this sounds like a most ingenious plan," said the Count, admiring the girl's fleshy wrists and sparkling green eyes. "A beautiful fruit like this … oh, the men of P will be all a'quiver!"

Lida shrugged. "You think?"

"O Princess! Your charm and beauty shall entrance the male sex – and no need for nightingales or magical books or other such nonsense! O, my sweet! You are an angel, an eyeful, a rose among goose-weed – um, no offence to your sister, of course…"

"You are very kind, dear Count," said the Baron, "and obviously a man of great feeling and refinement. Tell me – do you perhaps know any such eligible families in P? A suitable introduction would be most advantageous, especially as we only have funds for a week."

The Count fluttered his handkerchief in mock modesty. "Oh, I know many important people in P – Pustrpolk the throat surgeon, the theatrical *impresario* Moosendorf, Master Bilek, also a theatrical impresario, a passing policeman, the doorman at The Jade Eye…"

Gluck beamed.

"My dear friend! Ah, 'tis good fortune to come across such a gregarious soul – and so well connected to boot! Hm, Count, dear Count Mariinsky … would you condescend to join us at The Big Theatre tonight? Poor Lena is feeling most unwell, and is unable to accompany us – the misfortune, you understand…"

Mitrovsky looked at the ill-starred young lady and nodded sympathetically. "The misfortune? Um…"

"We have a spare ticket and a seat in the finest box. Please say yes, dear Count. And then, perhaps afterward, you might introduce us to some of your friends…"

"I would be honoured, dear sir. Tell me, do you think refreshments will be served at this theatre? I am particularly fond of salty snacks."

"Well, that's settled then. Tonight at eight. The Big Theatre – you can't miss it. We'll arrive early to check out the crowd. Then, Lida gets into position, and you drag in the big fish in your net … hm, my friend, eh, what do you say?"

"Ho, I would say the money's good as in Patočka's purse! Eight o'clock then. I will brush my best jacket and blow the dust from my wig. Farewell, my darlings – until that enchanted hour …"

And with that the Count bowed deeply, his wig slipping to one side and dipping in the billy-jam. Lena took one look at his hairpiece and immediately burst into tears.

"Hush, hush, my darling … O, if only your mother could be here! She'd know what to say, rather than the words of a foolish old man. O, oh my angels!"

And with that the Baron broke down himself.

"Your mother … she … she…"

Lida scowled. "Dad, please…"

"She…"

"Dad, people are starting to stare…"

"O my angel."

Watching her father sob, Lida took Mitrovsky by the beard and swiftly steered him away.

"Mm, your mother," said Mitrovsky, thoughtfully, "Ah, whatever…"

"Shh, shh, not here."

"What?"

"People are looking, C'mon, over here, to this nook."

And with that, Lida led the Count toward a secluded corner and then looked him square in the eye.

"So, this opera tonight…"

"Tonight, um, yes…"

"And these big shots…"

"Well, I wouldn't say…"

Lida's eyes flashed. "Listen, Mitrovsky, no deadbeats, you understand? And no creepy old guys. Or anyone with a beard like a rhododendron. Some guy who's cute looking, you know? Who'll be kind to me … not like that dog was to Lena…"

"Hm? well yes, but of course." Mitrovsky stared at the girl's remarkable green eyes, the colour of a forest at midnight. She seemed to remind him of someone, though he couldn't say who.

"Are you listening to me, Count? No time-wasters. And no seminarians, either…"

"My darling, you can count on me. Ah, you will be the belle of the ball, the brightest star in the sky…"

"Just find someone with their own teeth."

"I'll do my best…"

Mitrovsky fluttered his handkerchief, bowed, and withdrew. Outside, another hot summer's day was served up, brown and burnt, as if baked in the Devil's very oven.

6

Peeling plaster, crumbling walls – feh, no wonder there was so much dust in this place. Passers-by blinked sleepily at the sun, wishing they were in O or Q or some other burg, where the sun was kind, the weather your friend, and every day a holiday. Meanwhile Mitrovsky inspected the Glucks' ticket and pulled on his beard: The Big Theatre, eight pm. The Big Theatre, yes. But how on earth would he find it? He hadn't even found his way back to the Little, and he'd been there once before…

Suddenly the remaining hairs on Mitrovsky's head stood on end; observing the Count from across the street was a thin panhandler of a most low and humble station, his rags resembling the nest of a mouse fallen upon very hard times indeed. The fellow watched the Count playing with his handkerchief and then marched toward him, peering at his hairpiece most intently.

"Karel! Karel, is that you?"

The Count turned to face him, narrowing his eyes in the sun.

"I'm sorry my good fellow, do I know you?"

The panhandler grinned a toothless grin. "'Tis me, Karel – Vojtěch! What – you don't recognise me, now? But I recognize you, you old tart, even decked out in all that finery."

"This? Well…"

"Trying out for a part in Mispickel's opera, are you? And what role might that be – the fat Count?"

"Count," said the Count, "Count, well, indeed."

The two men peered at each other as if inspecting a pot for cracks.

"Um, I'm terribly sorry, but have I had the good fortune to make your acquaintance? I'm afraid I…"

"Know me? Know me? It's me, Vojtěch! What, I've lost weight?"

"I do beg your pardon, but…"

"Vojtěch! We went tramping together in Brno – O, we saw some dives, you and I! And had a few scrapes in 'em too! So why that face? You forgot all about your buddy?"

"Ah…"

The tramp scowled.

"Listen Pal, there's no need to play the Count with me, dressed up like a side of beef at Christmas…"

"Um…"

"Where did you get the monkey suit? Off the peg at the *singspiel*?"

Mitrovsky bowed deeply. "I'm awfully sorry my darling, but I fear you're confusing me with someone else. Here, take this shiny coin and…"

The tramp's eyes flashed. "What?"

"A shiny coin – here, look, it…"

"Feh, don't you take that tone with me. Who do you think you are? No stinking Count, I'll wager…"

"Ah, well…" And with that the Count began to smartly back away. "Well, this is all very interesting, but I have important business at The Little Theatre and …"

"Business? Business? You son of a bitch! I know you – don't you go putting on airs and graces with me…"

Reaching into Moosendorf's purse, the Count threw a coin at the beggar and then took to his heels. The fellow – Vojtěch – shook his fist angrily.

"Good day, my darling!"

"I know you!" yelled the tramp.

"Adieu!"

"I know the games you play!"

The beggar shook his fist angrily, but by the time he'd picked up the coin, both the Count and his wig were gone.

7

According to Babinsky, for the connoisseur of administrative tasks, censorship is by far the most gratifying and pleasurable of bureaucratic duties. Ah, he would say, is there anything more agreeable than sitting by a warm fire, flicking through the pages of some lofty tone, consigning whatever one disagrees with to the flames? Let the rain fall, the wind howl, the door rattle; the censor sits snug as a mouse in its nest, nibbling away at the pages, scratching and snuffling, lifting a finger only to erase the most indelicate and objectionable of passages. Yes, yes, yes – better than stamping documents or drawing up lists of prisoners, that's for sure. After all, censoring is mainly indoors work, requiring little in the way of heavy lifting: you don't even have to wear an apron! Scrape, scrape, scrape, goes your quill; otherwise, you can spend the rest of your day reading and daydreaming, picking your nose and gazing out of the window with pale and dreamy eyes.

But in the summertime, the regional office of The Department of Forbidden Texts tends to become somewhat hot and stuffy, the ink gumming up the inkwells and the pages sticking together somewhat disobligingly. On such days, censors, like foxes, are forced to stir themselves and hunt for prey elsewhere – in theatres and opera-houses in the centre of town, ten minutes away by carriage, but worth the exertion, none the less. After all, the theatre-owners treat the censor as a kind of prodigal son, waiting on him hand and foot: honey cakes, strudel, *Makový koláček*, maybe a glass of strong Rhine wine. You might think theatrical types would be cross or sore about a censor's amendments – but no, no, not a bit! Rather they seemed to appreciate a censor's wise expunctions, congratulating him on his sensitivity and clear thinking. True, once in a while a few works had to be banned, and occasionally a librettist dragged away in a covered wagon, but for the most part these trips were like a holiday excursion. Smiling faces! Open hands! Master Babinsky – how wonderful to see you! Here, try a slice of *Marlenka* cake – Fedora just baked a fresh batch.

Today though, the staff and players at The Big Theatre seemed somewhat skittish, even – what's the word? – offhand. No pastries, no honey cake, not so much as a sniff of blackcurrant jam: just what was going on here? Instead of serving him, stagehands shuffled this way and that, lugging Greek busts and bouquets of fake flowers from set to set, sweat dripping from their brows.

"Herr Ullmann," snapped Babinsky, "is no plum cake to be found?"

The stage manager bowed and scraped, simpering like a courtier. "I'm terribly sorry, Master Babinsky. Mispickel's opera opens tonight and there's still so much to do…"

Ullmann was pale, balding, short as a note from the gallows.

"Really, Herr Ullmann? Why, I approved that opera weeks ago. You haven't been making changes have you, you naughty man?"

"Changes, my lord? No, no, no. Well, only minor ones. Alterations of an artistic nature."

"Nothing for me to be concerned about?"

"Not at all, my dear Babinsky – here, let me see if we can rustle up some nutty cake and a jug of sour cream…"

"Nutty cake, you say?"

"Fedora! Fedora! Some cake for our guest!"

The cake was delicious, the cream agreeably cool. Yes, yes, thought Babinsky, nothing to see here! Ten minutes later and the official censor was already striding back to his carriage, brushing the crumbs from his jacket with a perfumed hand. He was just about to climb the steps when a voice hailed him from the stage door.

"Master Babinsky? My good sir, I wonder if I might have a word?"

The censor turned and gave a jump; he was faced with a stranger with the most awful yellow eyes, greasy and large, like two poached eggs swimming in a pan.

"Ah, and you are...?"

"Inspector Honzl, an Investigator of the Ministry of Cases of Extraordinary Importance."

"Babinsky – Evžan Babinsky, Official Censor, Department of Forbidden Texts."

Honzl's foul eyes blinked in the sun.

"Yes, yes. I was told that I would find you here. I wonder if I might speak with you. 'Tis on a matter of the utmost gravity."

Still paralysed by the fellow's yolks, the censor rashly agreed.

"The Leather Boot?"

"I'm sorry?"

"The Leather Boot. It serves chicken soup with nettles, as well as the most marvellous duck, dressed in a rich raspberry sauce ..."

"Yes, yes, whatever..."

For some reason this Honzl fellow seemed disinterested in the Leather Boot's long and capacious menu; rather he seemed somewhat more interested the matter of a long, complicated case involving sedition, stolen property, murder, and the impersonation of a nobleman.

To be honest, Babinsky struggled to make head or tail of any of it.

Had he heard of a certain 'Count Mitrovsky?' No, the censor had not. Had he heard tell of any strange dreams, or peculiar visions? Babinsky did not believe he had. Had he ever sampled the local delicacy of Hrůza, sometimes called an Emperor's Favour? Alas, the censor had not – though they sounded most delightful!

"Delightful? Delightful? 'Tis treason sir, the work of revolutionaries!"

Babinsky looked on, mildly. "Oh come now…"

"I tell you, Master Babinsky, such pastries are inflammatory and ruinous, intended to undermine the authority of the crown. I'm writing it down, Babinsky! Writing it down in my book…"

Babinsky smiled wanly, patting the Inspector on the arm. "Well, if you say so, my dear chap, if you say so…"

Although lunch was excellent and the duck most flavoursome, the Special Investigator remained on edge, scowling and grinding his teeth throughout.

"So tell me Babinsky, that establishment you were frequenting…"

"The Big Theatre?"

"Big Theatre, yes. What was the nature of your investigation there, if I may be so bold?"

Babinsky picked at the duck with gusto. "Oh, nothing special. Mispickel's new opera opens tonight, and…"

"An opera, you say? And what is the nature of this … opera? A revolutionary hero? An oppressive king?"

"What? Oh no, nothing like that – a trifle, really, pure frivolity. I've read the libretto and it's all the usual nonsense – lovers, peasants, some bit with a bear. Quite innocent, I assure you."

"Innocent? Nobody is innocent in this world, Babinsky – I would have thought a censor, of all people, would know that."

Babinsky smiled and presented his palms. "Oh, you're being too harsh, my dear chap. 'Tis no more than a soap bubble, a bagatelle. And besides, Mispickel's tunes are always most delightful. He's only a child – did you know that? Nine or ten, or so I've heard. And already the most talented composer in all of Bohemia."

"Mispickel, eh?" said Honzl, writing the name down in his big book. "M, I, S…"

"Of course, Jessel, the librettist, is a scoundrel and a rogue – quite the debauch, or so I've heard – but that matters not. Mm, with tunes like Mispickel's, whoever listens to the words? Half the time they're in Italian anyway."

"Jessel," said the Inspector, turning to a fresh page. "And his character is licentious, you say?"

Babinsky helped himself to a dumpling and blushed. "Well, he is one for the ladies…"

"Hm. And his politics?"

"Politics? Oh, I don't think we have any cause for concern on that account. All the fellow thinks about is pleasure – a most dissipated and profligate individual, as librettists often are."

"Hm. And you have read this … filth?"

"Foo, it's quite sweet really…"

"And there is nothing that might be construed as demeaning to the Emperor?"

Babinsky chuckled. "Oh no, not a thing. It's a love story, with a funny bit where a squirrel steals a fellow's wig … ha, ha, really quite amusing…"

Honzl stared at the censor with his horrible yellow eyes, like two candles lit for the dead.

"I see. Well, thank you Mr Babinsky. I have written all this information down – right here in my book."

All at once a new thought seemed to occur to the Special

Investigator, his nose sniffing like a dog.

"Just one last question, my good man. Have you heard of an *impresario*, a rascal who goes by the name of Bilek?"

Babinsky chewed on his duck and thought. "Bilek, Bilek … hmm. Yes, I believe he's some small-time agent – novelty acts and the like. But why ever do you ask?"

"A small matter of a stolen case … but 'tis of no importance. No, Mr Babinsky, I am investigating a matter of sedition and mass poisoning, a trail that leads from Hrůza to P –perhaps to the steps of the Big Theatre itself."

Babinsky smiled tipsily. "Sir – The Department of Forbidden Texts stands ready to assist."

"The Department has no jurisdiction in this case," snapped Honzl, bumping the table with his knees. "This is my case, mine!"

"Well, yes, but of course…"

The Special Investigator scowled. "If you need me, I am staying at The Silken Ladder," he said, reaching for his hat. "If you hear anything about this opera – anything at all – I insist that you inform me right away. This is a serious matter, Mr Babinsky. not some frivolous game."

Babinsky burped. "Yes, yes – if I hear anything, you'll be the first to know."

"See that I am."

Leaving Babinsky to settle up, Honzl departed stage right, still clutching his book to his chest.

'What a disagreeable fellow,' reflected the censor, watching him go. And such horribly unpleasant eyes! One wouldn't look at a goat with eyes like those. But what on earth was he doing here? And why did he care about this opera? After all, whatever may or may not be smuggled between Jessel's lines was a matter for the Department of Forbidden Texts, not The Ministry of Cases of Extraordinary Importance. No, something was up here, something that yellow-eyed swine wasn't letting on.

"Honzl, eh?" he whispered to himself, "hmm, Honzl. H.. O... N..." And with that he wrote down the letters in a large, black book.

8

One bloodshot eye opened, then the other. Was the banging coming from the door on his left or from the inside of his head? Bilek rubbed his temples and winced: definitely the door. He staggered from his bed and opened it, Ullmann and some jerk in a velvet cap waiting on the other side.

"Bilek! What the hell happened? You look terrible…"

"Yeah? Well, you 'aint no beauty either."

The *impresario* had a bruise on one cheek, a cut on the other, and his collar torn as if in mourning. He'd also been sucking on a bottle, his breath capable of stripping wallpaper from five paces.

Ullmann and the other guy exchanged glances: none of this augured well.

"Bilek, what's happened?"

"S'okay – a little trouble is all. Nothing I couldn't handle…"

"Trouble? What kind of…"

"Okay, okay, not so loud."

Ullmann looked at Bilek and screwed up his eyes. "Just tell me you've still got your case."

"Sure, sure, of course I got it…" Bilek scratched the crook of his arm aggressively. "What, you think I'm the kind of bozo who would let some mug run away with my bag?"

"Um…"

"Listen, I got the score, so put a lid on your soup."

"Marvellous! Wonderful!" Ullmann paused. "So where is it?"

"You think I keep a thing like that at The Jade Eye? What am I, a moron? It's safe, okay? I'll get it. You 'aint got nothing to worry about. You'll have it by the end of the day."

Ullmann's buddy shook his head and the stage manager frowned. "End of the day? Listen, Bilek, the show opens tonight, and the singers haven't so much as…"

Bilek scowled and patted down what remained of his hair. "Okay, okay, I hear you. What do you want me to say? I'll go get it, drop it off right away…"

Again, Ullmann's mute pal shook his head.

"Perhaps it's best if we accompany you," said Ullmann, extending a hand. "Make sure no harm comes to you, or to your, um, precious case."

Bilek pushed his face up against Ullmann's.

"Listen pal, I don't need no babysitter. What, you don't trust me?"

Bilek's breath was as foul as the back of a tannery.

"No, no, nothing of the sort…"

"Give me a moment to scrub up and then I'll go get it. I'll see you bozos back at The Big Theatre. And listen – this thing, people 'aint heard nothing like it, you take it from me…"

Ullmann and his friend said nothing,

"That's settled then. I'll see you clowns at the Big Theatre. Now gimme a moment for my ablutions. A gentleman's gotta look the part, you know."

And with that the two men reluctantly departed, Ullmann's buddy most downcast, whispering despondently in the stage-manager's ear.

Bilek waited for them to go, and then reached for another bottle of booze. What a mess! He never should have trusted that damn Count – what kind of Count patches his coat with cat anyway? No Count worthy of the name, that's for sure.

But then, there had been something screwy about all of this from the start, one damn thing after another. If he hadn't been down on his luck – if those lousy Musical Milkers of Most hadn't lost control of their cow – then he'd never have ended up in this mess. But what could he do? No dough, no acts, no prospects: and then he heard some whispers that Mispickel's new opera was a wash out, missing a big number. Ullmann was pulling out his hair. The Big Theatre was willing to pay out for a knock-out aria – something to, you know, really 'shake the rafters', make the swells in the boxes rattle their jewellery. But what could Bilek do? He only had his flea act, and Ferdie, his big star, had an injury to his knee. What a waste! What an opportunity! With only a week till the opening night, Ullmann was ready to sell his mother if only he could get his hands on a tune.

A day or so later, Bilek had been stepping out of The Chicken's Foot when he bumped into some guy coming in – a rake of a guy, stick-thin, his dentures clattering up and down like a rattle.

"Tell me," the fella said to him, voice like silk, "have you ever heard of the poem, 'At Dawn, Two Nightingales'?"

"A poem? Whattya take me for, a moron?"

"'Tis the most beautiful, most tender, most enchanting poem in all the world," said the stranger, his shadow nodding its head, "why to hear it is to have one's heart broken, feel one's soul start to ache…"

"Yeah, yeah, yeah," said Bilek, halfway out the door.

"And when set to music, to a sympathetic or suitable score, why the effect is quite mesmerising."

"Wait, what?"

"A heavenly aria, the words of the poem combined with the most divine of chords, a tune capable of transporting one to the seventh heavens…"

"Yeah?"

"And it just so happens that I have such a score – Nosek's poem set to music, a sweetness unmatched by wine, or even the most ardent of…"

"That right? And this jingle is for sale, you say?"

"It's kept in a strongbox in my carriage. If you come with me then I'll…"

"No way, brother. I know jerks like you – I get in your carriage and there's some bruiser waiting with a blackjack." Bilek winced. "Listen – you bring it here, and then I'll take a peek. But no funny business, *capeesh*? I know the kind of ape who hangs around The Chicken's Foot."

Bowing, the salesman withdrew and disappeared into the darkness, reappearing moments later with a scroll of paper in his hand, the score encircled by a jet black ribbon.

"At Dawn, Two Nightingales," he said.

"A couple of birds, sure, I hear."

Bilek took the score and swiftly scanned the notes, humming the tune in his head. Hmm, not half bad. In fact, it was quite the ditty – da de da de dum.

"Okay," he said, "I guess this'll do in a pinch. How much do you want?"

"Whatever you have on you," said the stickman. "Whatever you possess of value."

"Whattdya mean?"

"Just what I say. Whatever you possess of value."

"Yeah?"

Bilek stumped up his purse, his ring, his cufflinks, even his gold tooth.

"This better be worth it," he said, his breath whistling through the gap.

"My dear fellow, you have heard the music," said the salesman. "'Tis possessed of an infinite dreaminess, an ethereal quality that touches everything…"

"Yeah, well, it better."

"But remember to keep it safe, to protect it from prying eyes and busy hands, for weak-minded souls will be drawn to the score like moths."

"Moths? Okay, okay – I'll hide it in the box with Ferdie and my performing fleas. That way, nobody will know any better."

"Most wise," said the stickman, eyes closed, "most wise."

And with that the two men bowed and wished each other a pleasant evening, heading off in opposite directions – Bilek back to his room, the stickman to a dilapidated carriage lined up outside.

"What a weirdo," muttered Bilek, under his breath. "But that melody – you know, it's really got something…"

Indeed, the more the *impresario* played the tune in his head, the more pleasing and beguiling it became.

'Those suckers in P,' he thought to himself, 'they 'aint heard anything like it…"

He sang along in his imagination. 'This tune … why, it's gonna blow the roof off, make a million. What a ditty! When Ullmann gets a load of this, the jerk will cream his pants…"

Now, standing drinking moonshine straight from the bottle and nursing his swollen head, his case and those damn nightingales seemed awful far away.

"I gotta find that damn Count," muttered Bilek, pacing up and down his chamber, "the sneaky little bastard. And when I do…"

Bilek threw his bottle at the wall.

9

While all this was going on, the Count himself was busy tramping up and down the dusty lanes of P, his greasepaint cracking, the resin coming unstuck on his wig. A mustard-coloured haze lay on the city, the bricks radiating an oppressive and discomforting heat. What a rabbit warren this place was! How the Count was supposed to come across any theatre, whether large or small, was a mystery. Rather he felt that with every step he took, he was drifting further and further through time, the city knee-deep in dust, like Pompeii or some other such ancient burg.

Coughing into his handkerchief, the Count passed a cemetery, a synagogue, and a stall selling blighted apples, the peasant fish-eyed with a hair-lip, her fruit all yellow and wormy.

'Mm,' thought the Count. 'Maybe not.'

From there, Mitrovsky passed a dog-catcher's hut, a tanner's booth, and an old peasant carrying a bundle of sticks. No, this was not the most salubrious of neighbourhoods. The hovels were cracked and uneven, the blackened chimneys bestowing a mournful sense of timeless neglect. Was this really the city of P, home of a hundred spires? Between old wooden houses, warped by both heat and damp, blind alleyways grew like goose-weed, dark as mine-shafts and filled with all sorts of oddments and rubbish.

Turning left by a yard filled with wood shavings, Mitrovsky passed the opening to a carpenter's workshop and peered inside.

In the shade, an old man was silently at work, methodically shaving the edge of a coffin; above him, Gambrius, the king of beer, watched from a street sign, one hand holding a toasting fork, the other a foaming mug. 'O,' thought the Count, 'how wonderful to be in a jug-house, a stein in one hand, a sausage and mustard pot in the other '– why, his belly rumbled just thinking about it! But first he had to find his way there, out of this maze of crumbling yards and closed doors, the wood as black as graveyard earth.

Thankfully, when the Count turned a corner, he found himself on the edge of a broad, shady square, the trees covered with an odd milky fluff like the inside of a rich man's mattress. Ah, this looked a more pleasant spot! By The House of Five Small Bells, a middle-aged couple strolled together arm in arm, their heads bobbing together most affectionately. Mitrovsky paused and scrunched up his eyes: something about the lady seemed oddly familiar. Was it Mrs Jedlicǒvá? Yes, yes – the Count did believe it was! As soon as she spotted the Count, Mrs Jedlicǒvá gave a little squeal and hopped excitedly from foot to foot.

"Karel, Count Mitrovsky, is that you? O my angel, whatever are you doing here? And you've lost so much weight too…"

"Mrs Jedlicǒvá?"

The good lady was dressed in a smart orange and yellow frock, a tall, yolk-coloured hat sitting atop her wig like a plant pot.

"Fee, how thin you look! Just look at you – I could see through you on a sunny day!"

"O, my princess!" said the Count, bowing deeply. "Is it you? Or has an angel climbed down from Heaven?"

"My darling Count," said Mrs Jedlicǒvá, delighted and offering her hand. "What a sweet, foolish man, you are! But look at you – an empty belly and dark rings around your eyes…"

Mitrovsky smiled and slapped his belly. "Oh, fee – I'm right enough. But you, Mrs Jedlicǒvá, whatever…"

"I have great news," said the good lady, beaming. "Here, let me introduce you to my fiancé, Mr Wendling. Josef, say hello!"

Wendling grinned, winked, and thumped the Count on the arm. "Oh, but we've met, eh old fellow, eh, what do you say?"

"Um…"

"What? You don't remember?"

At this, Mrs Jedlicǒváva burst out laughing. "Why Josef was my gaoler in the Powder Tower in Hrůza, if you recall."

Mitrovsky clapped his hands like a child. "Why, the turnkey!"

"That's right," said the good-natured gaoler, chuckling. "I helped this lady out when she lost her clothes, one thing led to another and, well, here we are! These days we've spent together – why it's been the happiest time of my life!"

And with that the two lovers gazed at each other with a look of great affection. Then the good lady pulled herself away from her fiancé, pressing herself upon the Count most urgently.

"Karel, Karel, might I have a word?"

"A word? Um…"

"Please my darling man, please tell me – my angel, Eliška … whatever became of her?"

"Eliška? Well…"

"I spoke with the sisters of the holy visitation in Žádost, but she never arrived. O, my good Count, have you any news? Please, my darling, I beg you…"

Mitrovsky beamed. "Why – she's here! At The Big Theatre. I saw her but a few scant hours ago…"

"My Eliška? Here? O my good man, can it be true?" Mrs Jedlicǒvá looked close to tears, her chin trembling with tender emotion.

"Weep not, dear lady," said the Count, fluttering his handkerchief. "Eliška is safe and sound, accompanied by Young

Master Halas, the lad no longer in a dress."

Mrs Jedlicǒvá composed herself and kissed the Count on both cheeks.

"O, you prince, you treasure! I cannot tell you how happy you have made me! Josef, my sweet – let us return home and I'll cook up a batch of *palačinky*, you know, the ones made with almonds, the kind Eliška adores. The poor darling – she'll be famished, dear heart, just skin and bone! And then we'll surprise her, surprise her with a basket of sweet treats, all sprinkled in sugar and cocoa."

"But of course, wait for me out front. I'll bring her to you, lead her back to the path."

"O, you angel!"

"Tish, Madam, 'tis the least I can do…"

Overcome with emotion, Mrs Jedlicǒvá kissed the Count twice more and then returned to her jolly turnkey, her face as red as a pickled winter salad. The gaoler patted his wife's arm and gazed into her eyes adoringly.

"O, 'tis grand news, my angel. But what d'you think she'll make of our engagement? When last I saw your daughter, I was your turnkey and you my captive. D'you think…?"

"O, she'll love you just as much as I," said the good lady, wiping away the tears, "And then we'll be a happy family again with no more wandering or roaming from the path…"

"My dumpling!"

"My pet!"

Count Mitrovsky watched the two lovebirds depart with some degree of satisfaction: how wonderful to make someone so happy! But then he thought: no, hold on, Eliška was at the Little, not the Big. Oh well – all would come out in the wash! When he looked back at the square the couple were gone, the square as deserted as a stage.

10

"Ullmann, Ullmann, Ullmann," whispered Babinsky softly. "Whatever have you done?"

From his network of theatrical informers, the censor had learned of all the various misfortunes to have befallen Mispickel's ill-starred opera – vicissitudes Herr Ullmann had been most anxious to conceal.

Fibich – cast in the role of the lovelorn suitor – had lost first his pantaloons, then his dignity, and then his voice, all after a lively night out at The Seven Bells. Now Fibich could do no more than whisper and croak – a problem for any leading man.

At the same time, Berta Lauterova, the ingénue, had disappeared along with the third violin, Rezniček; malicious tongues whispered they'd checked into Karlovy Vara as Mr and Mrs Mendel, the young lady wearing most inappropriate hosiery, the gentleman without a hat. Berta's role was small but important, like a pin. How were they supposed to do the garden scene without her?

Even Masha the bear, crucial to the plot and secured at some considerable cost from a Ukrainian circus, had taken fright and run amok, mauling the manor-house set and savaging two members of the woodwind section: only the swift actions of the first bassoon had served to subdue him.

Aye, the production seemed accursed, ill-starred from the start. But the worst thing, the unbelievable thing, the thing that had to be mouthed *sotto voce*, was that Mispickel's score was just no good. But how could that be? Mispickel? No good? This was the musical prodigy who had composed his first plainsong at four, an opera at six, a symphony in short pants. Why, everybody knew it – Mispickel was a miracle, a phenomenon, a wonder of the natural world– and such cute curls, to boot! And yet for all that, 'those in the know' complained that his latest score was 'tame and conventional', lacking in sublimity, the divine spirit, a really big number, the kind even the butcher can whistle. Yes, what it needed was a great aria, a gorgeous refrain, a chorus caressed by greatness: instead it had 'Lo, My Socks Are Missing', a tune so dreary you forgot it the moment it was performed.

Babinsky leaned back in his chair and sighed: why was he always the last to hear about this stuff? And how was he to blame? Hey, if someone said a piece was Mispickel's, he assumed it was gold – why not? Jessel's damn stories never made any sense anyway – usually something about a marriage broker and a music teacher and some young girl who'd lost her broach in the woods. Listen, if it was sung by a pretty girl, who cared? It was a long time since Babinsky had mooched around Hušek's field, dreaming about poetry – now he had more practical things to worry about: lunch at The Golden Pear, dinner at The Blue Duckling, burning copies of *New Czech Songs for the Beautiful Female Sex* in the Department stove.

I mean, how was any of this *his* problem anyway? Nu, if Ullmann's show was a flop, who cared? He was a government censor, not a sponsor. The only thing that mattered was whether anybody slandered his majesty in verse, and on this score at least the opera seemed off the hook. Babinsky rested his mitts on his ample gut contentedly. Yes, yes, all was right with the world. So what if this Honzl was sniffing around? A stolen strong box was of no concern for The Ministry of Forbidden Texts – try lost property instead.

At that moment there was a knock on the door: Babinsky's servant.

"Someone to see you, sir. From His Majesty's Imperial household."

"From the what?"

"It's in Vienna."

"Yes, yes, well, what are you waiting for…?"

With that, a most elegant functionary was ushered in, the fellow wearing wide cream trousers, a pea-green tailcoat, fringed buttons, and a gilt tiepin in the shape of a bird. What a marvellous figure he cut! Beneath his magnificently proportioned trousers could be glimpsed snow-white stockings, and a splendid pair of Viennese boots, polished like the mirror room in the Klementinum.

The two worthy gentlemen bowed, their noses almost touching.

"Chief Censor Babinsky? My name is Gassmann, designated envoy of his Imperial Majesty's Household Staff. Sir, I bring you great tidings of joy! His Imperial Majesty, the Divine Sovereign, Holy Roman Emperor, and sole ruler of the Habsburg lands, is to grace this miserable backwater with his presence, and, moreover and *apropos*, is at a loose end tonight, the French ambassador having blown him out."

"He is?"

"I mean, Saturday's looking fine – meetings with the governor in the Sternberg Palace, a trade delegation from Antwerp, followed by canasta with the Dušeks. But tonight, nada."

"Hm, I see."

"But the word is, you have a new opera opening – by the child genius Mispickel, I believe. I've heard that Mispickel dreams in music, writes the notes straight on a chalk board…"

"Um…"

"Yes, my dear fellow?" Gassmann's eyes narrowed. "Is there a problem here?"

"Problem? Ha ha, I should say not!" said the censor, fingering his collar.

"Listen," said the envoy. "We need to be sure there's nothing in this bauble that might provoke or vex our Majesty, his munificence being kinda ticklish in this respect. Have you heard of the pamphlet, 'Why is the Emperor Not Loved by His People?' It didn't go down well, I tell you."

"But, but … everyone loves the Emperor!" barked the censor. "I love the Emperor!"

"You love him, I love him, Anežka the cleaning woman loves him. But ever since that hoo-ha about the war tax … well let's just say, the people have become more opinionated..."

"Outrageous! Disgraceful!"

"But you see my point, Master Babinsky. You see how important it is that nothing in this opera upsets him or foments displeasure in any way? Between you and me Babinsky, His Majesty has a most delicate nature, and is prone to rash acts when irked – rash and violent acts, if you get my drift…"

"O, you have no worries on those grounds, dear sir. 'Tis a love story, an *amuse bouche*."

"And the music?"

"Beautiful, dear sir, inspired – like a cherub pouring *becherovka* in your ear."

At this Gassmann seemed to relax. "Okay, book the Royal Box for eight. His Majesty looks forward to the *théâtre d'occasion* with great relish. Make sure the champagne is on ice and the royal box has been valeted. The full service, not just a duster."

"We are deeply honoured, sir."

"You bet you are. Oh, and Babinsky? If anything arouses His Imperial Majesty, it's your neck on the block."

Babinsky wobbled his enormous chins.

"Neck, block, ha ha ha."

Gassmann withdrew.

"*Adieu* my good fellow. His Emperor will be precisely seventeen minutes late – make sure you hold the curtain."

Babinsky watched the perfumed flunkey with a sinking heart, the rouge draining from his cheek. What a disaster! Not only was the music hopeless, but something else was amiss here too; foo, why else was that dog from The Ministry of Exceptional Cases sniffing around, sticking his muzzle in the pail? Something stank here, and not just the wig box. Still, Chief Censor Babinsky wasn't about to let his head get separated from his shoulders. And with that thought in mind, he ordered his carriage to be readied for The Big Theatre without delay.

11

"Please, sweet prince – just a ditty, a few bars…"

Nothing doing: the door remained closed.

"C'mon son – for your poor old Pa! Just a few notes – you know, a bit of a tune, a jingle…"

"G'way!

"Rudy, Rudolf my prince – don't be like that. C'mon – for your dear old Dad. A chorus, a theme, eh, what do you say? For Daddy?"

"I said go away!"

"Why, you ungrateful little brat! You open that door, you little monkey, or…"

All at once the music teacher threw himself against his son's door, pounding at it with his soft gloves.

"Mother, Mother! Rudolf won't open his door! Thankless tyke! Ingrate! You open that door and get back to your harpsichord, you rogue…"

Pressing his ear to the door, the music teacher could hear the soft clunk of billiard ball on felt.

"He's playing billiards, the little punk! Hey! Get on with your composing, you layabout!"

Dressed in shawl and cap, Mrs Mispickel appeared on the staircase. "Hush! Let me talk to him now. Son? Rudolf? Rudy, my boy, how 'bout a duet, eh? Something, you know, catchy, pleasing to the ear…"

Nada. The door stayed shut.

"Eh Rudy? There's a good boy. For your Momma, eh? A sweet sounding air. Something we can sell the sheet music for."

"M'busy."

Mr Mispickel threw up his hands. "Busy? Busy doing what? Knocking balls around, that's what! Listen, you deadbeat, you put down that cue and…"

At that moment, a bell rang down below and minutes later, the Mispickel's daughter, Emma, climbed the stairs, accompanied by a sallow looking fellow cursed with the most disagreeable eyes imaginable.

"Momma, Poppa," said the girl, "this is Inspector Honzl, from The Ministry."

The Mispickels desisted in their activities, regarding the newcomer with some degree of trepidation.

"Ministry?"

"Of Cases of Extraordinary Importance."

"Extraordinary, you say? Well, inspector," said Mispickel Senior, pulling up his dressing gown, "whatever can we do for you?"

The fellow's yellow eyes took in the scene without blinking.

"You are Mr Mispickel, the Music Teacher?"

Mispickel bowed.

"And this is my dear wife, Emily, and our daughter, Emma. Emma, fetch the Special Investigator a cup of something and…"

"No need to trouble yourself" said the Inspector, his poisonous eyes flashing. "And your son is Rudolf Mispickel, the composer?"

"Yes, indeed," said the music teacher, glancing anxiously toward the door. "The Bohemian virtuoso, the wonder of the age … a prodigy, sir, a rare and wonderful phenomenon! Would you be interested in commissioning a new work sir? A melodic piece? Something for a show?"

The fellow's eyes examined the teacher most balefully.

"I wish to talk to your son about his work for The Big Theatre – an opera, I am led to understand…"

The music teacher pulled on his cuffs.

"Mm, opera, well, yes, but of course. Our Rudy writes operas like a hen lays eggs – it's really quite remarkable. As if God is humming a tune right into his ear."

"If I might speak with him…"

Mr Mispickel swallowed. "Yes, yes, but of course! Rudy – there's a gentleman here from the Ministry – he wants to talk with you, my lad."

There was a pause.

"M'busy."

"Rudy, my angel, he's an officer, he needs to…"

"Tell 'im to get lost."

"Rudy, I…"

"He can bugger off!"

"Listen, you little…" All at once the music teacher remembered himself, turning around with an air of regret. "I'm sorry sir, when his blood runs hot, there's nothing we can do."

The Inspector looked on with an expression of unguarded disgust.

"I fear you misunderstand me, sir. I wish to speak with your son on a matter of great importance. Kindly instruct him to open this door."

"Mm, yes, yes, but of course. Rudy? Open up! The police want to have a word with you…"

"So what?"

"Um…"

"Tell 'im to clear off!"

"Ha ha ha, clear off!" The music teacher shrugged as if to say, you see, my dear fellow, there's nothing I can do.

Mrs Mispickel swiftly curtseyed and placed herself between them.

"Begging your pardon, Inspector, but our Rudy well, he's a little highly strung – you know, being a genius and all. Not that he was always like this – oh no, sir. As a lad he was the most amiable of souls, sweet of temper and mild in nature. But when he turned twelve – ooo, sir, we can't do nothing with him. S'like a curse, sir! As soon as the first spot appeared on his cheek – bang!"

"Bang?"

"S'like he became another person. Now all he wants to do is play billiards all day – balls, balls, balls, that's all he cares about. We can't get 'im away from that table."

"Hmm,"

"As for composing – well, that's gone out of the window. We can't even get him to whistle a tune."

All at once the Mispickel's daughter, Emma, piped up, her voice clear and bright.

"Maybe I could write something…"

"Why, Emma, whatever...?"

"I've been working on a melody and…"

Mrs Mispickel chuckled and clucked her tongue. "Foo, Emmy, the very thought! Now you run along and fetch us the tea things, there's a good girl."

"But mother, I've been…"

"Run along, I say. This gentleman hasn't got the time to be listening to such nonsense…"

"But…"

"And fetch a jug of cream – the poor Inspector's in need of refreshment, the poor man."

The girl picked up the hem of her skirt and walked downstairs.

"O, young folk today!" said Mrs Mispickel, currying favour with a wink. "They grow up so fast! Before the sower takes a step, the reaper's already there. But what can you do, sir? Time scurries away like a mouse. Now, won't you join us for a cup of something in the parlour? We would be honoured to…"

Honzl's eyes resembled two large holes with something horrible on the other side.

"I wish to speak with your son."

The Mispickels exchanged worried glances.

"Rudy, well, yes…"

"On a matter of great importance."

"Mm…"

"Therefore, kindly request that he opens his door."

The music teacher tapped timidly upon the wood.

"Rudy?"

"Leave me alone!"

"Rudy, my prince?"

"I said leave me alone…"

"Rudy, the gentleman…"

"Tell the old git to clear off!"

The music teacher hammered on the door with great vigour, while the Inspector ground his jaw like a pestle and mortar.

"You swine, you cur, you ungrateful brat! Open this door this moment, or I'll tan your hide, you little pup!"

"I am staying at The Silken Ladder," said Honzl, very slowly. "When your progeny is feeling more communicable, I humbly request that you bring him there to see me. I wish to speak to him on matters of great importance – matters relating to the holy personage of the Emperor himself. In the meantime, you can rest assured that I will be writing all this down, sir, right here, in my book…"

Realising that he wasn't actually carrying his book, Inspector Honzl turned on his heels and departed. Downstairs, Emma was humming a most beautiful melody, though the Inspector failed to notice. Such insolence! Such disrespect! But the Mispiskels would be called upon to explain themselves, oh yes they would…

From the music teacher's two storey house, the Special Investigator retraced his steps back toward The Silken Ladder, passing the butcher's booths and the Aunties selling wool outside the Jew's Gate. O, what a mess! Like a broken way-sign, the case pointed in all directions. Nevertheless, he was certain that this opera was somehow at the heart of it, although in what fashion he knew not. Well, this time the Count would not escape his grasp: this time he would throttle Mitrovsky like a rabbit.

When the Inspector returned to his room, he found the landlady wringing her hands in a pose of great agitation.

"O, Master Honzl, sir! Oh dear, oh dear, I simply don't know what has happened…"

Honzl narrowed his nasty eyes. "Happened, Mrs Destinová?"

"Your friend, sir – the lad you told me to keep an eye on…"

"Constable Povolný, yes."

"He's gone, sir! Slipped out when the maid was changing his sheets. Ran off down the road shouting something about the Emperor – raving, he was sir, off his nut…"

"I told you Mrs Destinová, I told you to lock the door…"

"I'm sorry sir – 'twas the maid, she left the door open and he slipped out like a cat."

"Very disappointing, Mrs Destinová – very disappointing indeed! I'm writing all this down, writing it down in my…"

"Please sir, I beg of you…"

"You should have thought of that earlier, Mrs Destinová, oh yes indeed…"

Sweeping the woman aside, Honzl strode into his room, his boots squeaking on the walnut floor. Where had the constable wandered off to now? But then the lad hadn't been right since Hrůza, nibbling on those Favours and raving about the Emperor

– nutty as a five-pound fruit cake, as any fool could see.

And yet, and yet… the clod seemed to know things, almost as if the Devil were whispering in his hat. What things? Things about the opera, Bilek's case, a plot against the Emperor. Aye, somehow that fool of a town constable had stumbled upon some great secret – and now he was gone, run off like a cow when the gate's left ajar. What a fool he'd been! Your elbow is close, but you still can't bite it. Shaking his head, Honzl stalked over to his writing desk and retrieved his book. Somewhere in here was a clue, an inkling… He scribbled away obsessively for a while and then slammed it shut, the cover heavy as a coffin lid.

12

In the constable's dream, Bilek's case was buried beneath an old, dead larch, the box filled with black earth and old newspapers, next to a milk tooth, a long, curled fingernail, and a willow-teeth rake, its handle whittled to resemble His Majesty. When he spoke, the sharp wooden teeth clacked up and down like a rattle.

"The nightingales are in P. They fly south, toward their nest. Catch them before they lay."

Povolný nodded, the buttons undone on his jacket. Somewhere a jackdaw croaked – kaf ka, kaf ka, kaf ka.

"The bird catcher's cage is empty. Follow the trail of crumbs. The truth lies behind the curtain."

As the puppet's jaw fell still, Povolný's eyes popped open. Yes, yes, the curtain – nu, there was no time to lose! And with that the constable made a run for it, dashing down the stairs and out of The Silken Ladder, still in his police uniform but with bare toes, the soles of his feet black as a coal man's rag.

Nightingales, crumbs, curtains: these were not idle nocturnal fancies, but rather a form of unearthly divination, a way to the very centre of things. Povolný had no need of fortune tellers or cards; these clues came to him whenever he nibbled on one of Fleischmann's Favours, as if a lantern lit up in his skull. But how to find one's way? P was very different to Hrůza, as wide as the day was long.

Still, at least one thing had changed – the constable no longer saw His Majesty's ugly mug in every passer-by. The Auntie selling crayfish looked like an Auntie selling crayfish, the butcher like a butcher, the angel on the apothecary sign free from the sovereign's moustache – or 'the Imperial plumage', as t'was known in the capital.

Whistling 'O how eagerly she loves', the bare-footed policeman followed the crowds passing along Manekýn to the Old Town Square, merchants, shoppers and pickpockets all mingling together, giddy as children on a windy day. Many of the stallholders had closed up early, and the peasants wheeled their wares down toward the river along The Royal Way, their carts squeaking cheerfully. Caught up in a great surge of hoop skirts, black capes and crepe caps, Povolný followed the throng past the Old Town Hall and on toward Loutka, and the river. On Chrlič Street, wealthy horse-traders jostled with lowly tinkers, ladies in shawls of Flemish lace mixing with gypsies in bright headscarves and embroidered skirts, all of them pushing past The Church of St Nicholas and the Maisel Synagogue, a ceaseless stream of humanity, moving as if possessed by a single thought: but where were they going and why?

And then, on the broad road leading alongside the river, he suddenly saw it: a train of splendid carriages, all painted in gold and black and all bearing the Imperial seal, pulled by a team of magnificent white horses, each one wearing an embroidered tabard and blinkers, daintily stepping along. Mouth open, the constable pushed his way a little closer. The noble carriages conveyed a most remarkable retinue of staff: pages, cooks, ladies-in-waiting, along with valets, tailors, wigmakers, footmen, musicians, secretaries, general servants, councillors – even one for the *heiduck*, whatever the hell that was. As each carriage passed, the people pressed their faces as close to the window as possible. Was that a diamond hair clip, there a silk fan? Even the flunkies looked haughty as noblemen, decked out with heavy silver buttons and tailcoats of midnight blue. As for the ladies – well, they were simply divine, their expensive satin dresses deeply *décolleté*, trimmed with lace and fastened with the most fascinating of jewels.

The constable rubbed his eyes and elbowed his way to the front. 'Twas a caravan of swells, right enough, wearing enough brocade to sink the royal barge. But whence were all these worthies going? And how did they keep their wigs so stiff in this awful heat?

All of a sudden a tremor passed through the crowd.

"Is that 'im?"

"It's him, it's him!"

"The Emperor! I can see his conk!"

The Emperor? Frozen by the side of the road, it was as if somebody had stepped on Povolný's grave, or rather as if his dream had somehow passed through the veil of sleep and invaded the waking life.

"Where, where, I can't see!"

"There!"

"S'him!"

"Look son – the Emperor, riding with his nose!"

The Imperial Carriage was by now but a few feet from the constable, Povolný within spitting distance of the subject of his dreams. Was this why he had been brought here? Was this the meaning of his vision? Before he had time to think, Povolný had pushed free from the crowd and threw himself against the carriage door.

"Your Majesty, my lord, I'm here!"

The lead two horses reared up, and the Imperial buggy came to a sudden halt.

"Your Majesty – the nightingales, where are they?"

As footmen and Imperial guards hastened to the coach, a face suddenly appeared at the window, his nose familiar from bank notes, coins and seals.

"What on earth…?"

Povolný saluted.

"The nightingales, your majesty. Where do they fly, and how do I catch them?"

"Nightingales? What the devil are you…?"

"It's the crumbs, sir … they lead me here." Povolný pointed at the carriage. "To the curtain."

His Majesty fingered the fabric suspiciously. "My curtain? You mean, the drapes? What in the blazes do you want with…?"

But before Povolný could answer, two guards wearing nice Viennese boots appeared from nowhere.

"Sir, sir!" cried Povolný, "please, we must speak!"

But it was no use: the escorts advanced in a most unfriendly manner, seizing hold of his person and roughing him up right soundly. Then, just as they began to march him away, the constable suddenly broke free, making off down the street, still yelling about nightingales and curses and the like.

The guards shrugged and then withdrew.

"Unbelievable," said His Majesty, shaking his head.

"Joe, who was that poor unfortunate fellow?" asked a feminine voice inside the Emperor's carriage.

"That jerk? Who knows?"

Thoughtfully, the Emperor rubbed the carriage drapes between his fingers. What was it he'd said? Nightingales, crumbs, curtains? All nonsense, right enough. Scowling, the Emperor pulled the curtains tight shut.

13

His expression as vacant as a hen's, Mitrovsky gave a great and comical leap. Strutting along the road was some kind of sergeant major, coat two sizes too large, cap slipping down over his eyes, banging away on his drum as if attempting to wake the dead.

"Lads, lads!" he hollered. "Come join His Majesty's Imperial Army! Recruiting now! All welcome! His Majesty's Imperial Army awaits you! A plate of salted beans and cup of ale for all new cadets!"

The Count fluttered his handkerchief flirtatiously.

"Salted beans, you say?"

The recruiting-sergeant – a short, stocky fellow with a 'tache like a chimney-sweep's broom – broke into a wide, beaming smile.

"What ho, stout fellow! Interested in a career in the army, are we?"

"Why, I've always dreamed of such a thing! And a plate of salted beans, you say?"

"Yes, yes! A life of adventure and discovery."

"And the beans?"

"Ha ha! I can see that you're a character, with those frilly cuffs and that wig. Well, come with me, good sir – we'll get you your beans and then get you signed up."

Mitrovsky bowed deeply, his eyes two mouse-holes in his face.

"I thank you most kindly. Why, I imagine 'tis a most romantic life in the army?"

"Yes, yes, 'tis a fine life. Marching, drilling, drumming – fee, just look at this uniform!"

"'Tis a fine piece of cloth…"

"Beautiful stitching – thread as fine as human hair…"

"How wonderful!"

"Yes, the Army knows how to look after its own. Stout boots, smart jackets, buttons like stars in a well. And as for military stockings – why, fine as the down on a baby mink. You just need to touch it – a treat for the fingers! Now, jump in my sack and we'll get you signed up. Why, I can picture you in a great coat with matching braid – worsted lining, pea green with a golden trim."

The sergeant had large grey eyes and soft, pink cheeks, his whole face radiating boundless welcome and warmth. Aye, a capital fellow! Only the fact that his apparel was far too large prevented him from cutting quite the dash.

Keeping time with his drum, the cheerful sergeant led the Count along a dusty lane of tumbledown houses to a small, wooden door, its dimensions the exact width of a coffin. On the other side was a long, baking hot yard, an old man sitting at a long table and blinking at the sergeant somewhat venomously.

"Right," said the sergeant, heading toward a crude, makeshift hut. "All we have to do is sign you up and then we can get you measured for your uniform, leather belt, the lot…"

"Marvellous, marvellous!" said the Count, admiring the stitching on the fellow's tights. "And I believe you mentioned beans?"

"Um…"

"Salted beans, I believe … and perhaps a sup to drink?"

"Fear not, His Majesty's Army is always true to its word. You wait here and I'll go fetch you a plate … why everyone knows that military beans are the saltiest beans of all!"

With that, the recruiting-sergeant headed off in the direction of his hut, stumbling a little in his over-sized shoes.

Mitrovsky watched him go and then stole over to the old geezer sitting by the table, the fellow dressed in beggar's rags, gazing at the Count with a look of exquisite bitterness.

"Well, the recruiting officer seems a nice chap," said the Count, seating himself with great ceremony and proffering a gloved hand. "Karel – Karel Mitrovsky. And you are…?"

The beggar stared at him with an expression that could sour milk.

"Hmm," said the Count, rubbing his hairy chin. "And are you here to sign up too? Why, marching, dress uniforms, singing in the military baths – sounds like a dream, does it not?"

The old man's lips curled back in a sneer, but no sound came out – well, a kind of hiss, perhaps.

Mitrovsky moved his chair a little further back.

"Mm, yes, perhaps we'll bunk together…"

The fellow scowled while the Count turned his face to the sun and blinked his great black eyes. It really was tremendously hot, strong yellow light collecting in pools beside the fence. But where were all the other recruits? Well, perhaps today was a slow day. Tish tosh, who would choose to march up and down in this heat? The air seemed almost supernaturally transparent, as if made out of glass.

Still contemplating the drill-yard, Mitrovsky watched as a bear slowly padded out from behind the hut, sniffing the air and shuffling its way toward him, as if its paws were very sore indeed.

"Well, hello my darling," said the Count, stretching out his arms. "You're a great beauty, aren't you?"

In response, the old black bear lolloped over and laid on her back so the Count could tickle her ears.

"And what a sweetheart you are! As pretty as a picture-book."

In truth, her teeth were brown and rotted, her claws dirty, and a meaty stench radiated from her maw. Nevertheless, the Count cheerfully scratched her dry skin, murmuring endearments while the bear made little affectionate grunts.

"Lala!" yelled the sergeant, returning from the hut with Mitrovsky's beans. "Lala, you tart, what are you doing on your back like that?"

Mitrovsky grinned.

"O, hush, she's such a dear! Like a big hairy angel…"

The Count's gloves were now brown and fetid, but he didn't seem to worry. The sergeant grinned.

"Lala's the regimental mascot, sir – been with us for years. 'Course, military life has rather gone to her belly, but what can one do? Here's your beans, my good man. I've taken the liberty of bringing the sign-up papers and a quill."

Mitrovsky took the sergeant's beans, sharing half with Lala's tongue.

"What a magnificent creature! Wherever did you find her?"

"Oh, I forget the details, sir. Liberated her from a band of Russian gypsies – all dressed up she was, wearing a hat with bells…"

"Ha ha, quite the sight. Lala, my darling, please stop…"

The bear tried to lick Mitrovsky's beard, her tongue tremendously long and black, whilst the old man stared at the two of them venomously, spiteful as a pantomime devil.

The recruiting agent waved his papers in the air.

"Aye, we're all very fond of her – one of the regiment, she is, right enough. Now, where's that quill?"

"Yes, you soldiers live such a wonderful life. Do you know, my brother Matej also ran off to join the army? S'true, every last word of it! He disappeared somewhere fighting the Turks, but I'm sure he'll be back one day, you know?"

The sergeant looked at him rather curiously.

"Your brother? Well, yes indeed. Now here's the ..."

"Father was awful sad when he went away – his noble heart was broken. 'Course he couldn't see so well by then, and his mind was kind of wandered... Aye, who knows what might have happened to him if I hadn't come along. 'Matej, Matej, is that you?' Tell me my darling, what else could I do?"

The sergeant looked at him a little suspiciously while Mitrovsky cheerfully fondled the bear's chops, wiping off the drool on his cuffs.

"But then, one son is as good as another, what do you say? But the years went by and still Matej didn't return, just like that song – 'The Maid Went to Fetch the Water', Eventually we had to sell the orchard and Old Zofie turned green and Ondrej ran off with the bull, and before you knew it, the whole estate was filled with nettles and dog-berries..."

When he looked back up, the sergeant was poking a quill and sheet of paper under the old beggar's nose, making funny little noises as if trying to coax a stray cat.

"And what about you, Brouček? Ready to sign now?"

"Beer!" barked the old man.

"Beer, ha ha! Well, you've already had two jugs, I think that's ..."

"Beer!"

"Well, yes, but just one more, you rascal..."

"Beer!"

"Tis a hot day," said the Count. "Perhaps I might partake of a little refreshment too."

"What? Oh yes, yes ... we don't skimp in His Majesty's Army!"

A few minutes later, the sergeant returned with two enormous steins while still clutching the sheaf of papers.

"Now, let's get your cross, shall we?"

While the old man scowled, Mitrovsky idly picked up the

recruiting sergeant's papers, lazily allowing his eyes to skip across the text. Ten years minimum service, wages of such and such, no return home for six months, report to the fortress at R at o-six hundred... The Count nodded wisely, fending off the bear at the same time.

"This is all tremendously interesting," he said slowly. "But do you perchance have any sauerkraut to go with these beans? I find that they wake up the beans in a tremendously convivial manner."

The sergeant blinked. "Sauerkraut?"

"Aye, just a little pot. Oh, and perhaps a little mustard too."

"Yes," said the sergeant, brightly. "Plenty of sauerkraut in His Majesty's army."

"That's the spirit!"

"Sauerkraut, well, yes indeed…"

Mitrovsky watched the sergeant retreat to his hut, and then gobbled down his beans, necked his beer, and daintily wiped his chops.

"Yes, yes, a wonderful life in the army – but perhaps one more suited to my brother than to me. Well, so long dear fellow –you'll find your way, God willing. And farewell you, dear Lala! O, what a sweetheart you are…"

The old bear nuzzled up against him, but Mitrovsky swiftly gathered together his things; the recruiting sergeant was already emerging from his hut, brandishing pots of sauerkraut and mustard, as well as another plate of salted beans. Mitrovsky glanced at him and then waved farewell to the bear.

"Well, farewell my darling. I'll remember those eyes of yours forever."

As the sergeant approached, carefully balancing all the vitals in the crook of his arm, the Count leapt to his feet and took off out of the gate.

"Hey!" yelled the sergeant.

"Rwarr!" yelled the bear.

The beggar said nothing.

The Count playfully scampered from the drill yard and back out onto the streets, whistling 'I hate a dreary life' as he skipped in front of the knife sharpener's cart and past St Julian's, its spires sharp as a carpenter's nails.

Still licking the brine from his chops, the Count was already thinking about Mařenka, the nightingales, Bilek's score; indeed, he was so caught up in his dreams that he didn't even realise that Lala had staggered to her feet and followed him, her huge black nose sniffing the fragrant air.

"Lala, Lala, where d'you think you're going?" yelled the sergeant.

But the great brown beast was gone.

14

In pursuit of the librettist Jessel, Honzl called first at The Red Lobster, then The Queen's Slipper, and thence at The Old Grey Wolf, out on Stork Street, famous for its succulent pork knuckles cooked in fat. The landlord at The Red Lobster – a bald Thuringian with a double chin, soft little hands and an enormous paunch – muttered something about serving Jessel a few nights ago, though he couldn't be sure. The guy at The Slipper – a scrawny guy with a brush of hair like a squirrel's tail – remembered Jessel supping with some 'dusky beauty' but couldn't remember when: a Tuesday, maybe? The landlady at The Old Grey Wolf hadn't even heard of him. "Librettists? We don't serve that kind here…"

From there, the Special Investigator followed a green thicket of nut trees down to the river, moving from The Pigs' Feet to The Golden Cockrel to The Cunning Little Vixen over by Cow Island. There, Oskar the pot-man, recalled Jessel drinking in the company of a tall, skinny fellow, dressed all in black and with sharp, wooden teeth – a most peculiar gentleman, thin as a rake.

Honzl's pen quivered feverishly, scratching away in his large, black book.

"What? Wooden teeth? Go on, go on."

Unfortunately, there was little else to tell. Afterward, Jessel had climbed into an old-fashioned tarantass, harnessed to an ancient grey nag. 'Twas midnight. The bell rang, the hooves clip-clopped, and then the librettist was gone: whither, the pot-man wouldn't like to say.

Honzl nodded, his eyes the colour of sulphur. So, the librettist had skipped town? Well, let him go to the Devil. The pieces were starting to fall into place, oh yes indeed…

"In town to see the Emperor, sir?" asked the pot-man, wiping down the counter with a sorry-looking rag.

Honzl looked up from his book.

"The Emperor is here?"

"Why, yes sir."

"In P?"

"Yes, P…"

"But what on earth is he…"

"Attending Mispickel's new opera, sir, at least that's what I hear."

The Special Investigator ground his teeth until his gums began to bleed. Was this a coincidence? No, no, no. Somehow Nosek's nightingales were caught up in this – a clear case of sedition, whatever that fool of a censor might say. His thoughts immediately turned to that fake-Count, the fraud who called himself Mitrovsky. Just who was the swine, anyway? The instigator of some conspiracy? An assassin plotting to harm his Majesty? A revolutionary insurgent or anarchist? One thing was certain: wherever the plot led, there too was Mitrovsky, the fat spider at the centre of the web…

Out of nowhere, some clumsy oaf stumbled down the steps, hat crumpled and frock coat shiny with dust. Honzl blinked. Hadn't he seen that hat before? Bilek! Bilek the *impresario*.

The dog stumbled from drunk to drunk, grabbing them by the collar and breathing fumes in their faces, all the time muttering like a madman.

"You seen him? Jerk with a moth-eaten wig and kohl around his eyes. Calls himself Count Mitrovsky – hides beef patties in his cuffs…"

Drinkers scowled and shook their heads, manoeuvring their pints away from his path.

"C'mon, c'mon, you must have seen 'im! Tall clown with a beard – talks kinda fancy, but you can count the moth-holes in his jacket." Bilek's eyes were wild, his jacket buttoned in all the wrong holes. "Listen, you gotta talk to me. Big guy with a gut – carrying a strong box, a most precious box, if you get my drift… C'mon! Talk to me! One of you slobs musta seen it…"

With that the *impresario* seized hold of the Special Investigator's collar and then paused.

"Hey, hey, wait a minute … s'you…"

Honzl's horrible yellow eyes sizzled like eggs in a pan. "Unhand me!" he yelled. "Unhand me, you dog!"

Honzl looked at the swine with distaste. Bilek's eyes were wild, his cloak dishevelled, his belt undone. Aye, he looked even worse than when he'd emerged from the privy back on the road.

"What on earth are you doing here you dog? You were ordered to remain in Hrůza, and…"

Bilek belched, loudly.

"Yeah? Well, what's it to you, ya dope?"

"What? Why…"

"Yeah, yeah, yeah – you'll write it all down. Big deal! Listen, I don't see no constable, so…"

"Constable? I need no constable, you swine…"

"Swine. is it?"

"You tell me…"

Honzl paused, pointing at Bilek with his pen.

"Listen Bilek, all this is wasting time. You seek Mitrovsky, am I right? He has something of yours?"

Bilek shook his fist in the Investigator's mug. "Thieving rat ran off with my box. You seen 'im, huh? Big jerk – when I catch him,

334

I'm gonna…"

"Yes, yes, your precious box, I've heard that tune before. But tell me, Master Bilek – what exactly is in this case of yours? I mean, you've been…"

"My box?"

"Yes, yes, your box."

"You wanna know what's in my box?"

"Listen Bilek…"

"Shh, shhh, over here." And with that the *impresario* stumbled drunkenly into a gloomy corner, speaking directly into the Special Investigator's face.

"S' the missing number for Mispickel's show – you know, the big tune near the end? The show-stopper?"

"What?"

"The number, you know, da tune. The score's hidden in the lining."

Honzl contemplated the fool dispassionately: was that it? All this trouble for a song?

"But Mispickel's opera opens tonight…"

"Damn right."

"With the Emperor in attendance…"

"The Emperor? Ha! Ullmann will pay big, the dumb ape…"

"And this, ah, song…"

"S'a beauty! Sweetest thing you ever heard! Like your Momma whisperin' sweet nothins above your crib…"

"Hmm – and nothing, ah, subversive, insulting to the dignity of his Majesty?"

"What? No, no, no. 'S a love song, a ditty…"

"Hmm."

Honzl's pen scraped away at the page. Whatever was going on here, all paths led to the Big Theatre. Had the cabbies been murdered by someone seeking out the score? Was this what that bastard Horáck had been looking for in Hrůza? But if it was just a love song, why should The Department of Forbidden Texts even care?

"And Mitrovsky is in P too?"

"You bet he is. Little shit stole my case from The Jade Eye. I'm gonna pluck that jerk's beard from his chin, dig out his eyes with a spoon…"

"Listen Bilek, I'm staying at The Silken Ladder. If you hear anything of the Count's whereabouts, you must inform me immediately. Immediately, do you hear me? This is a matter of extraordinary importance, relating to the very safety and wellbeing of his Imperial Majesty Himself…"

Bilek looked sceptical.

"Yeah? Well, I'm staying at The Jade Eye. If you catch hair or hide of that creep, you let me know. I'll make it worth your while – I mean, if The Big Conk's in town, then Ullmann will pay double…"

"The Jade Eye, yes, I'm writing it down…"

"I bet you are."

The two men stared at each other with obvious distaste. Well, one hand washes the other: perhaps they might be able to help one another after all. With a slight nod, each fellow then departed, Bilek's hat and Honzl's eyes heading off in different directions, the scent of pork knuckles heavy in the air.

15

In The Tin Bucket, Count Mitrovsky filled his plate with crumb-stuffed carp, served with a sliced egg, bitter herbs and a nip of *slivovitz – lahodny*! The Count smacked his lips with satisfaction: 'twas a most agreeable lunch, the fish falling from its bones as if removing its coat. Who could begrudge a gentleman his noble repast? And ten pfennigs a plate to boot...

The Count was about to order a second helping when a fellow in a blue tailcoat plonked himself down beside him, the fellow's wig neatly powdered and curled, as if just returned from the *friseur*.

"Excuse me, old chap – that bear outside, is she yours?"

"Bear?"

"The one scrabbling at the door with her claws..."

"Oh, you mean Lala! She's awful fond of me, you know."

"I'm sure!"

"Follows me everywhere, like a duckling chasing after her Mama. Pay no attention to her! She's a most charming thing – an angel, a darling. Been with me all the way through the streets of P – caused quite a stir, let me tell you!"

The fellow nodded as if weighing up the situation shrewdly. "Yes, yes. But tell me, my good man – this bear, is it for sale?"

"Sale? Well..."

"The fact is, the Big Theatre is in need of a bear for its show tonight – Mispickel's opera, you may have heard of it? Our current bear is inconvenienced, and by happy chance we happen to be auditioning for another."

Mitrovsky fluttered his handkerchief. "Auditioning, you say?"

The fellow's curls bobbed up and down. "We seek a wild and savage animal for the scene in the forest, and I have a hunch, a feeling, that your bear would be just right."

Mitrovsky glanced out of the window at where Lala was chewing on a hitching post.

"Ah, my lad, I'm not sure Lala has much experience of the stage…"

"Pff, your beastie will be perfect – eh, good sir, what do you say?"

Still smiling, the fellow winked and produced a small bag of coins, jingling it in front of Mitrovsky.

"Tis a most dramatic role, the opportunity of a lifetime…"

"Yes, yes, I'm sure, but Lala, well, she…"

The fellow then produced a second bag, this one even heavier.

"She'll be well cared for, sir – her own dressing room and everything."

"Really? Um, I'm not sure that…"

"A life of fame and fortune!"

"Um…"

Still smiling, the fellow finally produced a third bag of coins, tied up with a cherry-red ribbon, in a bow.

"Come, my fellow, come – 'tis a pretty life on the stage."

Mitrovsky stared at the ribbon and rubbed his chin; it was a nice bit of stuff, right enough. But what should he do? He could hear Lala grunting outside, rubbing herself up against a rag-man's cart. Well, the poor beast couldn't accompany him everywhere: he had an appointment with the Glucks, for a start.

And with that the Count broke into a wide smile and shook the fellow by the hand. "Fee," said the Count, "I like the curls of your wig, and 'tis a most charming and dainty purse. Let us shake on it and the bear is yours!"

"Marvellous!"

"O Lala! What marvellous dreams await!"

Unfortunately, when the pair tried explaining this to Lala, the beast seemed most resistant, moaning mournfully and cleaving to the good Count's side.

"Lala, please my darling, it's for the best, you'll see. You'll be happy there – it's a romantic life on the stage, what with all that dressing up and make up and curtains. Please Lala, desist! I can't carry you there in my lap…"

The theatrical fellow watched the bear carry on, swaying from side to side and trying to lick Mitrovsky's cloak.

"Sir, if you will…"

"Lala, my angel, stop that."

"Sir, the show starts at eight."

"Lala, sweetheart, please…"

The fellow in the curly wig checked his pocket-watch and sighed; this act would run and run.

"Sir, perhaps if you accompanied your bear, it might help? Then, when we reach the Big Theatre, we can…"

"The Big Theatre! Why didn't you say so? Nu, I have tickets for there, for this very evening, truth be told."

"Perfect! If you could but escort your bear, then we'll be there in time for the rehearsal."

"Of course, of course – lead the way my good lad!"

At this Lala grunted and scratched her ears, an urchin boy pointing at her with a stick.

"To the Big Theatre! Come now Lala, leave those boys alone …"

Chaperoning the bear, the two gentlemen made their way along the streets, the air heavy with the scent of honeysuckle and juniper, the sun burning a hole in the sky.

Yes, it was a hot day, right enough. Flower-sellers, pickpockets and peddlers mixed with the festive crowd, whispering about the visit of The Emperor.

"You heard the news? He's 'ere."

"In P? No!"

"One in the eye for those jerks in O!"

"Yeah? What about Mispickel's opera?"

"Tonight at the Big. Something about a magic poem."

"Kid's a genius – and still in diapers!"

"What – no, he must be in britches by now."

"Either way, he's a, whatchamacallit, a prodigy,"

"And such curls!"

Seeking to avoid the crowds, Mitrovsky, Lala and the guy from the Big elected to take a quieter path, passing an ancient well in a three-cornered square, and thence under signs for cobbler, cooper, furrier and weaver, like pictures on a deck of cards. Peasants passed by carrying barrels of herring and cages full of hens, ladies with parasols out buying crayfish, placing their wares in linen-covered baskets. Lala sniffed the air and moaned.

"Ah, the theatre, is it far?" asked Mitrovsky, wiping away the slobber.

The other fellow grinned.

"No, no, not far. Here, we'll take the back way. No bears front of house."

Mitrovsky and Lala followed the agent past a long line of timber-framed houses, the one at the end sagging like an old man taking a bow. These were working people's homes, with a workshop on the ground floor and a common yard out back. A woman opened a window, saw Lala, and screamed.

"So, this show of yours," said Mitrovsky, patting Lala on the chin. "'Tis full of songs, is that right?"

"A most prodigious quantity of notes. As if Mispickel has written down the chirruping of a nightingale!"

"A nightingale?"

"Figuratively speaking."

Whistling 'Sleep, little one sleep/your garden's growing pale', the trio cut down a gloomy alley and then headed down a little lane, wild strawberries and tall nettles bestowing 'pon the route a rural air.

"Are you sure this is the way? We seem to be…"

"O, 'tis better to be discreet. Don't want to scare the horses!"

"Horses? Um, well no…"

From there the lane snaked between the rear of various ramshackle buildings, lime-wash curling away, the broken crust revealing the dirty brick below. Dust, chalk and plaster blew everywhere, collecting in odd little clumps and balls. Lala sneezed, a string of yellow snot adorning her muzzle.

Mitrovsky looked around and sniffed. "Um, and this is…?"

"Right here!"

Still grinning, the curly haired agent opened a wooden door and led both bear and Count into a long, hot yard, the place unexpectedly a-buzz with activity and conversation. Cap-wearing carpenters and burly propmen carried newly painted panels and backdrops from yard to door, while over by the far wall, a line of fat, bearded noblemen lined up noisily, decked out in a comical variety of fancy cloaks and ridiculous-looking wigs.

Both bear and Count looked around in some confusion. The yard was filled with all sorts of oddments from discarded stage sets, fluff blowing across the yard like old men's hair.

"Števa!" yelled the agent. "Števa, you dog, where are you?"

All at once, a broad-shouldered fellow with narrow eyes and black, shiny hair appeared from one of the doorways.

"Števa," said the agent. "Good news! I have secured the services of this fine and noble bear. Do you have a spot of lung soup to lure her inside? She's a sensitive soul and inordinately fond of her master."

"That thing?"

"Yes, yes, why…"

"Kinda long in the tooth, don't you think?"

"Oh, nonsense, why..,"

"Well, if you say so." The fellow grimaced and examined the old bear's pelt. "Come on Auntie, let's find you a pot to lick."

"Capital! Now, my good sir, it seems as if … sir? Sir?"

But Mitrovsky had already wandered off to the long line of barons and counts, playing with his handkerchief and eying up their ruffles most covetously.

A fella with a wispy beard and a tatty scroll wandered over.

"You here for the audition?"

"M'sorry?"

"The fat Count. You here to audition?"

Mitrovsky looked at the long parade of counts and blinked.

"Um…"

"Here." The fellow handed him a small piece of paper, which Mitrovsky read slowly, moving his lips. "There's just one line – 'Softly, Sweet Prince, take me to my carriage.' Think you can manage that?"

"I…"

"S'okay buddy, you'll do fine. Okay, next!"

And with that, the next-in-line passed through a darkened doorway, the nobility walking in one-by-one, as if shuffling off unto Eternity.

Mitrovsky looked down at the slip of paper. Softly, Sweet Prince, take me to my carriage. Yes, yes, all seemed clear enough. Still whispering the words, he took one last look at the yard and then assumed his place in line.

"What's a man? A rat with a tail between his legs. I a-spit on their britches."

Eliška closed her eyes, allowing the dresser to dust her face with a box of powder.

"Issa true. Only a man with no tongue never lies. The rest – dog, pig, snakes. You letta some stray in your 'ouse? Men – no good, no good…"

Eliška stared at the yellowing handbills without comment. Smiling lovers, shepherdesses, lovelorn poets; they all stared back at her brainlessly, the paper yellow and torn, coming unstuck at the edges.

"Men? They coat their tongues in sugar – You so sweet, so beautiful, kiss, kiss – then, in the morning – *ciao bello*, the pots are in the sink. Foo! Better a prick outta your eye then look atta a man. You listen to Abriana – no go near 'em, no listen to their lies. What – their words like velvet? They slink in like a cat, you chase 'em out with a broom…"

Abriana brushed rouge onto Eliška's cheeks as if painting a house. What did Eliška know of men? Her Father plucking his nose, Ernö and his stockings, Uncle Jaroslav and his downy chin. As for the clowns she'd met on her travels – the hairy Count, Halas with his puppy-dog eyes – maybe she was better off with the nuns after all.

"A man, he rhyme one word with another, make itta sound like music, then boom – his paws are down your shirt. You think he means those fancy words? Ees all a trick. Ees snake in the grass – bastardo! There!" She paused. "All finished! Look at you, my angel – you drive all the men crazy, pretty girl."

The girl looked at the mirror and nodded. Was this the same girl who had boarded a carriage in M? She hardly recognised herself. It was as if she'd been made anew, like a figure on a stage.

"Here – you needa pretty silks too. Those rags of yours – poof, no good! What, you gonna live in a nunnery?"

Eliška shrugged. "Momma wants me to go to the sisters of the visitation."

"Nuns? Those dried-up little bitches? Ha! They could no get a man if they tried. You seen their get-up? You wanna dress like a corpse? Listen: either eat the soup or jump ouuta da window. Nuns? What man wanna kiss a nun? Like-a kissing ice. Feh, you no getta-a man dressed like that."

Scowling, the dresser handed the girl a low-cut, parrot-blue dress, lavishly finished with lace at the neck and sleeves. Eliška looked at the gown uncertainly.

"But…"

"Try, try! The men – they take one looka you and howl at da moon. But when they come – you beat them, my girl, beatta them with a big stick…"

Eliška didn't understand: did she want to turn heads or no? But then, there was so much she didn't understand. Why she had to marry Ernö, why she had to go to the nunnery, who had murdered the cabbies…

Yes, the world was full of jerks. Sometimes she thought that there was some printing press somewhere, churning out one idiot after another, bossy mothers, stupid uncles, useless boys – O, if only she could turn the page! Or at least find a place to nap, somewhere to rest her aching head. "Don't sleep!" her mother scolded. "I know those toes! They'll take you off, far from the beaten path." But wherever they took her, she was always surrounded by pinheads and morons, an endless parade of idiots. Listen, if her toes were so smart why couldn't they carry her someplace the people had brains – like, Vienna, maybe?

All of a sudden there was a knock on the door and Abriana's brow furrowed.

"What? Whatta you wan' now? We working in 'ere. You wanna stick of make-up, come back another time."

The dresser pulled open the door and there was Master Halas, his hair neatly combed and his peepers blinking like a frog.

"Whata you want, you pup? I knowa your kind – sniffing round, looking for a treat. What, you make-a your big eyes sparkle? I go fetch my broom, chase the dirt away…"

Halas stared at the dresser's bangles and opened and closed his mouth.

"What? Whattaya want? *Faccia di culo*. Hey, what is it with you? Out with it! You got poisoned teeth? Crazy boy. You no-a understand shit."

Master Halas stared at Eliška, his mouth wide open like a door.

"Hey!" growled Abriana, angrily stamping her feet. "You catcha flies with those lips? What, you never seen a girl before? Yeah yeah – I pull the other one. C'mon, c'mon, we all grow old. Hey, hey you! You gotta hair on your tongue?"

Halas swallowed, blinked twice more, then handed Abriana a card, something scribbled on the back.

"Ha, whatta trick is…?"

He gestured with his chin toward Eliška.

"Oh, her is it? I should have known. You dirty dog! I know boys like you…"

Abriana handed Ěliška the card, Eliška picking it up with the tips of her fingers: Janos Halas, enflamed throat, Doctor Pustrpolk,

Temný Street, blah blah blah. Eliška looked at him blankly.

"What...?"

Alas, any further discussion was curtailed by the arrival of Moosendorf and Wranitzky, the stage manager.

"Abriana, what are you doing here? You think Gunter and Emil can dress themselves?"

Abriana scowled and muttered angrily beneath her breath. "Stupido men. Can't even put on their tights..."

As she made a move to leave, Eliška saw Halas grimacing and pointing at the card: what did the dumb cluck want now?

"M'tired," she said in a sulky voice. "I need to lie down..."

Moosendorf smiled under his wide-brimmed hat. "Of course, my dear, of course! Best to rest up while Gunter and Emil practice – 'tis a most remarkable bit of business, a truly astonishing act."

Wranitzky wagged his finger. "It better be, Moosendorf – what with Mispickel's opera on at the Big."

Moosendorf wrinkled his nose. "The Big? Why..."

"Yes, yes, we know! All I'm saying is that these boys better be good, Moosendorf. I'm counting on you..."

Meanwhile Halas continued to stare at Eliška, trying to get her attention. The other side! The other side of the card! But the girl wasn't biting.

"M'sleepy," she repeated. "Can I go and lie down?"

Moosendorf nodded and took her by the hand. "Of course, my dear, of course. There's a room backstage where you can rest, unmolested. Abriana, you attend to the two boys. I'll escort young Eliška to her room."

Halas made one last attempt to point to the card but to no avail, Eliška leaving it abandoned on the dressing table.

"This way my dear, this way. You'll need to be wide awake for *les mouvement mystérieux*..."

"Just wanna sleep..."

"Of course, of course, it's been a long trip…"

Holding a candle aloft, the impresario led Eliška along yet another narrow and cluttered corridor, each shelf piled high with all sorts of dusty junk: samovars, empty perfume bottles, christening jugs, a stuffed marmoset, a comb made of horn. The place seemed less like the rear of a theatre and more like some ancient, disordered museum, random exhibits piled up without any sense of order or progression. Boxes of cufflinks, dirty cloaks, fans, screens, wig-stands: who needed such trash? And all the time a strange yellow dust covered everything, like a sulphurous pollen, or a sprinkle of powdered bone.

"This way, my dear. O, the Little Theatre seems to go on forever! Of course, it's much larger than the Big…"

Eliška watched Moosendorf's candle flicker softly in the gloom, her steps heavier and heavier, her eyes beginning to close.

"Aye, these corridors are a real maze. What's that book, *The Labyrinth of the World*? Ha ha! 'Tis a riddle right enough."

Together they passed a box of coat-collars, a fake plum pudding, a great-coat with a charred hem. Yellow clouds of dust hung in the air whilst invisible mice scuttled about on sharp little claws.

"M'tired…"

"Of course, my dear, of course, but we're nearly there…"

"S'far…"

"Patience, my dear, patience."

Moosendorf opened a low door and ushered Eliška into a plain little bedroom, a dirty curtain hung up as if the bed were on a stage.

"There, my dear, you don't look at all well…"

"Smells funny…"

"Well, all theatres are prone to the odd patch of mould but still – 'tis pleasant enough. Now you just have a nice lie down…"

Moosendorf withdrew with a bow. Eliška sniffed and wrinkled up her nose: the sheets felt fusty and terribly cold. Would she wake up here, or would her feet carry her someplace else, someplace far from the path? Well, it was too late to worry about that now. Life was just a dream anyway. What did it matter where she ended up, in this world or the next?

"M'sleepy," she whispered. Then she fell asleep, as if plunging over a precipice into the darkness beyond.

17

What was it again? Softly, Sweet Prince, take me to my carriage
Yes, yes, all seemed clear enough: carriages, princes, etcetera –
why, even a child could say it.

Mitrovsky nodded sagely and placed the paper back in his
pocket. It was only when he looked back up that he saw that
somehow the long caravan of noblemen had vanished, leaving the
Count all on his own, the top of his wig brushing the cobwebs
from the ceiling.

Fortunately, backstage at the Big wasn't all that dissimilar to the
Small, no, not so different at all. Here too the shelves were lined
with all sorts of oddments and whatnots: clay birds, milking
stools, a rusted butcher's hook. Ho, what a treasure trove!

Whistling 'Extinguish not/ my tender spark', the Count
squeezed his way from one passage to another, the maze of
shelves stretching before him like a forest, a strange and singular
place, where all straight ways were lost. But would it kill the
owners to hire a cleaning woman from time to time? Threads of
dust and dirt hung from the shelves like tendrils, while patches
of mould bloomed in odd mushroom-like growths, the path as
crooked as a country lane and every bit as dusty.

The Count coughed. "My carriage, quick, my carriage," he
whispered.

Eventually the Count made his way to a slightly wider area,
like a clearing in the woods. To one side Mitrovsky could make

out a rectangular rack of canvas scenery, the edges ragged and torn, the fabric smelling faintly of horse.

One back-cloth portrayed a dusty lane, nettles and dog-weed growing at the side of the road, the sky thick with pollen and insects. Another showed a dense, blue forest, a wine-yellow moon illuminating violet leaves and branches. A third – more abstract – suggested a street scene, the blobs and marks slowly revealing themselves to be passers-by and shop-signs, the streets suggested by blocks of grey and brown, a weather cock daubed on in the form of a big black cross. A fourth suggested a burned-down village, a fifth a pleasant road-side inn, a sixth a ghostly cemetery at midnight, some kind of carriage parked out back.

Mitrovsky moved from scene to scene as if flicking through the pages of a book. Yes, yes, most piquant! Then he abruptly held his breath. The last scene showed a beautiful green and golden garden, the gentle light filtered through a soft, verdant canopy, dabs of white suggesting doves, or rabbits, or perhaps flowers in bloom.

Entranced, the Count breathed in deeply, his heart seeming to swell inside his breast. Ah, in such a place like this he had spent his happiest hours – frolicking with Betka on the lawn, playing *boules* with Lida and Lena, chatting with Anton and eating little sugary balls. O, enchanted world! And at the heart of it, her hands encircled by golden thread, sat Mařenka – big eyes, tiny lips, her delicate pin gleaming like the first star of evening.

Aye, thought Mitrovsky, 'tis true: the hours spent in these grounds had been the most contented of his life. O, if only he could have stayed there forever! To sit by the table, stretch out one's legs under the nut trees, maybe with a drop of *slivovitz* in a glass; ho, was there anything more blissful, anything closer to happiness this side of the veil?

The Count's brow furrowed.

Why had he ever left there? Why pursue these birds? Weren't such tiny moments of joy enough?

But then, hadn't Mařenka asked something of him, eliciting a promise, some oath? Well, perhaps. Though of course Count Mitrovsky had made an awful lot of promises in his life…

Sighing deeply, the Count turned away from the canvases and plunged back into the maze of props. On one side were stacks of old pots and pans, on the other locks without keys, a broken mousetrap, a clock without a face. Lost in thought, Mitrovsky wandered into a side passage humming 'O you faraway world' and flicking his handkerchief at the dust.

All at once, the Count moved from the shelves to a somewhat wider area, the space sprinkled with sawdust and filled with ropes, boxes and barrels, looking as if it might have been occupied just the moment before. Was there somebody there? Some stagehand? Above him machines moved, a wheel span, and a hidden pully system abruptly came to life, manoeuvring a new piece of painted backdrop into place.

Looking skyward, the Count stumbled out of the wings and onto a large wooden platform, the stage sloping down toward the seats, tapering at the back. The seats were empty, the auditorium deserted.

"Hello?" hollered the Count. "Anybody there, my lad?"

Nothing doing: stalls, circle and boxes silent as the grave.

"Hullo? I seem to have lost my bear…"

Lamps flickered and the floorboards creaked. From the stage, the seating seemed awful steep, as if gazing up at a mountain pass. And at the top: The Imperial Box, cruel and remote as an eyrie.

Wandering onto the centre of the stage, Mitrovsky hit his mark, then stopped. The stage was set up as a lady's *boudoir*: dressing table, writing desk, canopied bed. On the table was a mirror, comb, trinket-box, and jar of fat, red insects, their tips glowing like tapers

351

at dusk. Mitrovsky was just giving them a shake when a woman entered stage right, heavy make-up, black eyes, wearing a loose-fitting Adrienne gown, dainty shoes, and a big wig with butterfly pin glittering near the summit. She fanned her bosom and Mitrovsky jumped.

"Karel?"

The Count blinked. Was the gal Mařenka? But how on earth...

"Karel, what are you doing here? Don't you know the time? It's late, Karel, too late for anything."

Mitrovsky opened his mouth, but no sound came out. Then he swallowed, licked his lips, and strode out onto the stage.

"Late? Why, 'tis not yet seven. That's a lovely gown you're wearing by the way – that fabric, is it silk?"

Mařenka – or the woman playing Mařenka – walked over to the dressing-table and paused.

"You promised me, Karel."

"Promised?"

"You know what I mean. You made a vow, a solemn oath."

"A vow? But of course! I mean, us Counts are tremendously good at making vows."

"Are you even listening? You promised me, Karel! Promised to watch over them. Do you remember? Just one thing I asked of you. To watch over Anton and the girls, to save them from sorrow. And you swore ... swore on your honour..."

"Well..."

"Pledged to protect them, keep them from all harm. Defend the family name! But instead, instead you jumped onto the nearest cart and..."

"Well..."

"Tramping for nightingales and such things..."

"Nightingales?"

"How could you, Karel? You said that you cared for me – for

all of us. You said you'd protect them, console them, after ... after I left. You promised! Promised to watch over them. And now, look – Anton stooped and broken, the Estate lost, Lida struck down by misfortune…"

"I think that was Lena..."

"Where were you Karel? Where were you when misfortune came knocking at the door?"

"Ah…"

"Not to mention poor Betka pining away. That dog loved you, you know."

"'Tis my supply of meat."

"O Karel!"

Mitrovsky gazed at the back of Mařenka's neck. The powder had been applied rather badly, heavy clumps collecting round her neckline, and the sight made him strangely sad.

"My darling…"

"Hush! I don't want to hear another word."

"But…"

"Not another word, Karel. I can't bear it…"

And with that Mařenka – or rather the actress playing her – suddenly burst into tears, sobbing loudly into the crook of her arm. Mitrovsky hovered by her side, uncertainly.

"My angel, if in some way I have displeased you…"

Mařenka's shoulders shook convulsively, her head bobbing up and down.

"My darling, I promise you, I would never…"

Mařenka continued to sob.

"That is to say, I would never do anything to displease…"

At that, Mařenka looked up with an expression of pure hatred. "Ha! Swindler! Cheat! Fake! I see right through you, you pane of glass!"

"Sweetheart?"

Brandishing her hairbrush like a dagger, Mařenka leapt to her feet, glaring at the Count through narrowed eyes.

"I know you! I know what you are!"

Mařenka looked deliciously angry, her brows two zigzag lines, her eyes small black wasps.

"Why, I am Count Mitrovsky of …"

"Liar, swine! Lies and poison. Men say it, but they don't mean a thing."

"Darling?"

"You no gentleman. You no gentleman at all."

Mitrovsky took two steps back and fluttered his handkerchief as if wounded.

"Darling, please …" He glanced anxiously at the fireflies. "I brought bugs."

But t'was no good. With that the actress playing Mařenka collapsed onto her dressing table, folding up like a marionette whose strings had all been snipped.

"Mařenka?"

No answer.

"Mařenka, my darling?"

Nothing. Instead, the fireflies went out, the lights were cut, and in the darkness the Count heard a curtain being lowered, scenery swiftly wheeled from the stage.

When the lights came back on, Mařenka, the dressing table, even the canopied bed – they were all gone. On an empty stage, Count Mitrovsky stood alone.

18

Who was it who said that the theatre is a great classroom? Pastorius? Trediakovsky? The dresser at Madame Blatsky's? Either way, Young Halas had already learned a great deal, just from sitting backstage at the Little Theatre. To wit: that Maturova couldn't carry a tune, Smaha's singing wasn't worth the table leg, and that Menzel was a talentless bum – no offence to his relatives.

"As for Šubert … you ever hear him sing 'Have Pity, Moon?"

"Have pity, alright…"

"Like a cat being strangled."

"Yeah, a sick one. When he sings, deaf people close their eyes."

"Ha! They're the lucky ones."

"Šubert? You couldn't put him in a cage and charge seven schilling for admission."

"So why does Škroupova keep him on the rota? To pickle him for the winter?"

"They 'aint got a barrel big enough. When he played the hermit Beneš, even the claqueurs booed."

"I heard it's for his trouser roles…"

"That's one way of putting it."

Young Halas nodded sagely without the slightest idea what anybody was talking about. Still, why should he? His mind was occupied with thoughts of Eliška, thoughts of a most tender and sentimental nature, truth be told. O Eliška, he sung inside his head, only one girl's face has ever moved me…

Then, almost as if he had willed the scene into being, the girl herself floated across the stage before him, her skin pale as moonlight on a frozen lake. Halas blinked. Eliška? Yes, Eliška right enough, but there was something different about her, something somehow stopped. The girl's face was blank and strange, her movements stiff. Halas stared at her open mouthed. Had he somehow summoned her, lifted her up out of his thoughts as a pail is pulled from a well?

But before the lovelorn swain had a chance to do anything, the girl left the stage and slipped out of the theatre by the back door, leaving behind nothing so much as a footprint.

The stagehands continued gossiping, but Halas was no longer paying attention. Had that really been Eliška or had he merely imagined her? No, no, it was the real girl, right enough.

Bidding a silent farewell to the theatre staff, Young Halas grabbed his hat and followed, the opening leading first to a yard, thence to an alley, and then out to the main street, crowds of townsfolk strolling this way and that as if summoned for the specific reason of impeding his progress.

Yes, it was a busy evening right enough: peasants, drovers, tradespeople hurrying home. Panic clawed at the lad's insides. Eliška! Had he lost her? He anxiously looked up and down the street, disquiet breaking over him like a wave. No, no, there she was, standing stock still outside Putt the moneylender. But what did she want there? What did she have to exchange? Without looking, the girl then suddenly marched straight across the road to Endler's rug shop, her face as frozen as a canvas.

By now Young Master Halas was merely a few steps behind, following Eliška's unshod feet through the crowd. Hat in hand, the lad pursued her through market squares, long colonnades, and beneath lines of little wooden signs, the lower windows of the shops grilled and barred, the upper storeys sagging like a landlord's belly. On White Sparrow Street, he seemed to lose her for a moment. One moment she was standing behind a furrier's cart, the next she appeared framed in a doorway between The Three Ostriches and Bendl's Butchery, her expression wooden and spirit-less, her eyes barred and shuttered like a gate.

Eliška, Eliška! Halas flapped his arms and clapped his hands, but the girl didn't even notice, wandering this way and that as if on some fanciful whim.

Aye, there she was, drifting in front of a tinker's wagon, insensible to the fellow's curses! And there she was again, turning up outside the Church of Saint Nicholas, lips pursed and eyes closed, as if looking at some other mysterious world.

But then, just as Halas pushed his way through the crowd, Eliška entered the wide and spacious square housing the Big Theatre only to disappear entirely, fading away among the crowd as a single raindrop might be swallowed up by the ocean.

Halas stopped and mopped his brow. Had she somehow entered the building? Wandered into the yard around the back? Red faced and out of breath, the lad ran up and down the square, his eyes as wide as saucers.

Gazing up at The Big, the young lover felt more and more certain that the girl must have somehow opened a hatch and slipped in, like a pigeon, or a cat. But how to follow? The lad started to march up the steps, then stopped. A long queue had already formed, and there he was *sans billet*, bereft of even a coin. O, it was hopeless, hopeless! Behind the Theatre, the yard-gate was locked, sour-looking flunkies hanging around out back. Halas marched round and round the theatre but to no avail. Eliška had gone. The way to The Big was shut. His tights were sticky and hot.

Dejected, the lad wandered down a gloomy side-street, where the dust collected in clumps like plaster. Eliška, he thought, O light of the world! Would he ever see her tights once more?

But then, as he passed a particularly sad and doleful alleyway, a most peculiar feeling came upon him, a kind of tingling between his ears, and when he looked up, he saw a crooked shadow approaching him, followed by a long skinny fellow in a cloak.

"My dear fellow," said the stranger – a skeletal fellow with a mouthful of sharp, wooden teeth – "do you by chance lack tickets for tonight's performance? Yes? No? Well, I can't say that I am surprised – Mispickel's operas are most popular, are they not? And with the Emperor himself in attendance – why, such tokens are rarer than a hen's teeth!"

Halas looked at the skinny fellow and blinked.

"Fortunately," the emaciated stranger went on, "I happen to have a ticket here in my possession. A ticket for this very evening! And I hear that this opera contains the most beautiful, most tender, most enchanting music in all the world…"

Halas stared at the slip of paper wide-eyed.

"But what will you give me for this docket, eh young sir? What would you pay for such a thing?"

Wide-eyed, Halas reached in his pocket for a coin.

"Nu, no need, no need! Here, young man, take it freely. Gratis, my young friend – on the house, as they say. Please, please! I am certain that you will find the spectacle most edifying. A once in a lifetime performance…"

With these words the gaunt figure retired to the darkness of the alley, leaving Master Halas standing there with a ticket in his hand, his fingers all a-tremble. The young fellow blinked, skipped, and raced back toward the theatre. Eliška, Eliška! Somehow, he felt certain he would find her inside its hallowed walls. And what would he do when he did? Why declare his love, of course, what else? Yes, yes, there was still time! Halas silently mouthed the words to 'If my purse were only full', his eyes tremendously round and bright.

19

Chief Regional Censor Babinsky arrived at the Big Theatre good and early, nosing around the drapes, demanding plum doughnuts with a little jug of sauce, and generally getting in everybody's way. When he saw Ullmann, he pounced.

"Ullmann, Ullmann, wait up! Listen – you're sure there's no last-minute amendments?"

"What? Here, have some pancakes."

"No changes to the plot, the script? Nothing that might offend or aggrieve His Majesty?"

Ullmann smiled thinly, his silent buddy likewise.

"Master Babinsky, please. What kind of establishment do you think this is? Here – help yourself to some coffee and sit. We're awful busy as you can clearly see."

"Yes, yes, I can clearly see that." Babinsky squinted at the feverish activity. "Listen, you're absolutely certain that there's nothing in this opera that might be misconstrued…"

"Nothing, nothing! Please, my good man, take a seat. The doors are already open…"

Babinsky scowled. "Ah, good, good! Well, just one plate of pancakes then. And perhaps some raspberry jam."

Still unconvinced, Chief Censor took up his refreshment and withdrew to a quiet corner, observing the goings-on from a few inches above his plate. Why was Ullmann so agitated? Of course, a visit from the Emperor would do that to anyone, but still –

something else was going on here, 'thickening the soup' as they say. Babinsky clucked like a hen, narrowed his eyes, and spilled a spoonful of jam down his shirt. If Ullmann was lying to him, he was building his own gallows…

Meanwhile backstage, Inspector Honzl of the Ministry of Cases of Extraordinary Importance also followed events with great interest, blinking his horrible yellow eyes and scribbling incessantly in his large, black book.

The Inspector ground his teeth like a pestle and mortar; despite extensive enquiries, he had been unable to locate any information in regard to Bilek's box, his missing constable, or that ersatz Count, curse his eyes. Still: all paths led to the Big Theatre. The Emperor was due at eight. All he had to do was wait. The scraps would leap onto his plate themselves.

Still engrossed in his book, the Special Investigator took a wrong turn and stumbled through a prop door into the yard below. As he bounced down the steps, he upended a short, stout gentleman, wearing a tall chimney pot for a hat.

"Hey! Whattya doing, you bozo?"

Honzl glared at the *impresario* with undisguised contempt.

"Bilek! What on earth…"

"Shh, shh!" Bilek placed a hand on the Special Investigator's lips. "Pipe down, willya? If Ullmann gets wind, I'm up shit alley."

Honzl brushed himself down and retrieved his book from the yard.

"You have failed to locate your strong box, I presume…"

"My case? Nothing doing. That creep Mitrovsky, he's gone to ground like a rat."

Honzl nodded. "Yes, yes, but he's close – I know it. The conspiracy is…"

"What, you been taking laudanum? S'no conspiracy – it's a

tune. Sheesh," Bilek spat and rubbed down his hat. "I don't know Honzl, sometimes I think you're as nutty as the rest…"

Honzl glared at the *impresario* but decided to bite his tongue. He would write this down later though, oh yes, on a fresh page of his precious book.

"Nevertheless, I am certain that Mitrovsky aims to pass over the contents of your case to some party within. You must disguise yourself and wait in the wings. You hear me Bilek? If you see our friend the Count, alert me as soon as possible."

"Alert? Alert nothing. If I see that jerk, I'll stick him right there and then."

Honzl smiled a thin smile.

"Well, yes, that's also a plan."

Front of house, the Glucks – Anton and Lida, Nanny having stayed behind to nurse Lena through her misfortune – also arrived early, promenading up and down the square, showing off Lida's parasol and quietly sizing up the swells. Out front, this was one impressive joint; Haffenecker columns, soft sandstone, elegant stucco and pretty pink plaster. The Glucks clucked their tongues appreciatively. Why, with the Emperor in attendance, all the great and good of P would be there, like flies on a ham. Surely Lida could make the acquaintance of some gentleman with a full purse? To this end, the girl was dolled up to the nines: plunging neckline, ballooning hoop-skirt, the remains of the Gluck family jewels around her neck. And her wig: exquisite! Like a cloud fallen out of heaven.

"When do the crummy doors open? I've got to get myself a good spot."

"Patience, my angel, patience. O, what a dream you look! A true vision of loveliness…"

"Dad, don't…"

The tender Baron's jaw began to tremble, his gentle eyes filling with tears.

"O, if only your mother could be here to see you. Your mother, she…"

"Dad, Dad, hold it together."

"It's just – oh, how she would have loved to see you here tonight, your cheeks all a-glow, dressed in all your finery."

"Sheesh, people are looking."

The Baron dabbed at his eyes. "I'm an old fool, I know…"

"Don't screw this up."

"No, no, of course."

Lida blew the curls from her face and scanned the gathering crowd somewhat anxiously. "Now where's that clown Mitrovsky?"

At the sound of his name, a jolly female voice piped up behind them.

"Mitrovsky? Count Mitrovsky? Why what a coincidence! We're here to meet the dear man too!"

By happy chance, Mrs Jedličóvá and her fiancé were standing just behind them, as well-dressed as their purse and status allowed, Mrs Jedličóvá in a mustard-coloured gown with a waistline that came up all the way to her ample bust, her hair frizzed and adorned with feathers, the turnkey modestly attired in a dun-coloured jacket and cap.

Baron Gluck bowed graciously and smiled. "You know the good Count?"

"Karel? But of course! A darling man, a saint!"

"And are you here to attend tonight's performance?" inquired the Baron, examining the prison master's cap.

"O good gracious no, sir!" said the old turnkey, turning red. "All those notes, sir – it's not a thing for the likes of such as I."

"Notes?"

"Notes 'aint for the common folk, sir, begging your pardon. They stick in a working man's ears, an awful devil to shift."

"Oh, come now," said the Baron solicitously. "Why, you fine people…"

"We're here to meet my daughter, sir, Eliška," said Mrs Jedlicǒvá. "And is this your own darling daughter, my lord? O, what an angel!"

Lida curtseyed and the Baron began to well up with emotion. "Yes, yes, the apple of my eye! My other girl, Lena, she, alas, can't be with us tonight, a misfortune…"

"Dad…"

"Oh, if only my darling wife could be here! She would be so, so…"

"Dad, please…"

"O my good man!" exclaimed Mrs Jedlicǒvá. "Please don't distress yourself. Look, here I have some *Koláče*, topped with cheese and poppy seed – I've got some here, right in my basket."

"My wife, she…"

"O sir – just look at you, wasting away. That's what grief will do to you, sir, strip the flesh from your bones! I mean, just look at me…"

"Um."

"My Eliška, sir – she wandered from the path. Her naughty toes carried her off and took her away from me. But that kind Count Mitrovsky – he's found her sir, my treasure, my little apricot. And he's to bring her to me, sir, right here tonight."

"Dad?" said Lida, watching the crowd. "Dad, we need to get in line."

"What? Oh, marvellous! Well *adieu* my good lady, sir – please pass on my best wishes to your darling girl. When we see the Count, we'll tell him that you await him outside."

"C'mon Dad, let's go…"

"You go, sir," said the prison-guard, smiling. "You enjoy your notes."

"Here," said his wife, rooting in her ample basket, "I've got a bag of raisin and almond rolls hidden away…"

"Worry not, my good lady," said the Baron, taking his daughter's arm as she pulled him through the door. "I have little appetite these days – yes, yes, I'm an old man! Give my love to your daughter. I'll tell the Count you await him on the steps."

"You're a darling," said Mrs Jedlicŏvá with feeling, "a wonderful man…"

"Adieu my good people."

"God bless you, sir."

"*Adieu.*"

Further down the line, Moosendorf and his German contortionists mingled unobtrusively with the crowd, the *impresario* disguised with a prop nose and stage wart, his companions affecting a theatrical limp. Gunter and Emil gazed up at the front of The Big and whistled.

"Phew, vot a beaut!"

"Much bigger than the Small."

"You bet!"

Moosendorf looked over his shoulder and scowled. "Nonsense – 'tis an optical illusion, is all. The builders threw up this grand façade to make it look bigger. But round the back – tiny."

"Tiny?"

"Teeny weeny. Feh, you could fit the entire dress circle in The Small's cloak-room and still fit in an Auntie." Moosendorf pulled his hat down and re-arranged his nose. "Remember: don't draw attention to yourself. We're here to see what that dog Bilek has got planned – some shoddy spectacle, no doubt."

"Shod? Vot is shod?"

Under his disguise, Moosendorf scowled.

"I mean, why the Big would want to secure the services of such a second-rate agent is itself quite the mystery. What would somebody like Mispickel want with somebody like Bilek? But perhaps Master Bilek has already mislaid his case – I mean, who knows? He can't fit the Musical Milkers of Most in there can he? Ha ha ha!"

Les mouvement mystérieux looked at each other uncertainly. Mossendorf wasn't laughing, he was saying 'ha ha ha.'

"Milky? Why Milky, plizz?"

And with that the heavily disguised trio headed inside.

By just before eight the audience had all been admitted and found their seats, a line of staff awaiting the arrival of His Majesty's carriage.

Instead, however, a more modest droshky arrived, depositing the young composer, along with his doting parents and sister, Master Mispickel emerging most reluctantly, fingering the collar of his shirt while pulling on the tails.

"What are you doing?" hissed his father. "Stand up straight, will you? Look, the court artists are sketching…"

"Don't wanna wear this stupid jacket…"

"What? Do you know how much that thing cost? Don't pull on it so, you'll stretch the fabric."

"S'stupid…"

"I'll give you stupid, you little…"

Mrs Mispickel tenderly intervened. "Oh hush, don't vex the child. Eh, Rudy? 'Tis a special night, right enough. I mean, what with the Emperor and all…"

"He can bugger off as well"

"Rudy, please! It's a great opportunity! Why if the Emperor likes your work – foo, we'll be in clover for the rest of our lifelong days…"

The composer blew out his cheeks.

"Who cares?"

"You little pup!" muttered Mispickel Senior, "ungrateful little brat…"

As soon as the Mispickels began to ascend the steps, Ullmann appeared from inside, accompanied by his assistant, like a cloak.

"Marvellous! Wonderful!" beamed Ullmann, nervously. "And, ah, has our maestro composed a new ending? Um, something for the final act?"

Mispickel shrugged, his parents more than a little embarrassed.

"Our Rudy, ah, he's been awful busy," said Mrs Mispickel, pulling at the fingers of her gloves. "Um, what with his schooling and his mathematics and all."

Ullmann's face immediately fell. "Nothing?"

"You must understand," said Mrs Mispickel, taking the theatre manager by the arm, "our Rudy is a very sensitive soul, as all geniuses are prone to be. But don't you worry, our lad'll knock you up a new tune soon, you know, a real belter…"

Ullmann looked as pale as milk.

"But the Emperor is here tonight!"

Mrs Mispickel smiled sympathetically. "Yes, yes, and this opera – ooo, I'm sure he'll love it."

Ullmann nodded sadly, accompanying the Mispickels inside. Emma, the Mispickel's daughter, gazed up at the beauteous lobby in rapture.

"Mother, Father – what a beautiful place. Do you think that one day I too might have my music performed in a place like this?"

Mrs Mispickel immediately creased up laughing. "You? Ha, I should say not! Now run and get me some of those corn-flavoured snacks. Your brother's operas are ever so long…"

Minutes later, the Emperor's own Imperial carriage finally arrived at the Theatre, a splendid state coach pulled by eight huge Holsteins, one of them releasing a magnificent pile of dung, right outside.

The royal nose appeared at the curtain and sniffed. O, these provincial bergs! Why did he ever agree to come here? Grit in the bread and bugs in the sheets. What was the saying? Better to stay in Vienna and eat cream with a spoon.

Nevertheless, he accepted the cringing bows and tributes proffered by the staff and headed inside. Mispickel the genius? He better be. Still, at least it wasn't canasta with the Dušeks – what a bunch of stiffs they were.

"Your Imperial Majesty," said Ullmann bowing low, his buddy doing likewise. "How gracious of you to bless us with your Regal Presence."

"You bet it is. Listen, how long is this thing? It was four hours by carriage and my heinie is killing me."

"O, your grace! Why, 'tis, um, just the right length to, ah, enchant and transport."

"Listen – is there a water gnome in it? I can't stand gnomes."

"No, no gnomes…"

"And nothing with witches and goblins? I hate that spooky stuff."

"No, no, 'tis a love story, my Lord, a most tender and romantic…"

"Romantic?" The Emperor glared at Ullman as if about to strike him dead. "Listen: no stout-hearted peasants or clever servants, okay? None of that revolutionary crap. You know what I mean – the ploughmen are all saints and the landowners all crooks. What was that opera? The King and The Kitchen Boy? I can't stand that shit. It makes me so mad…"

Ullmann bowed lower and lower.

"Your Majesty, please! I can assure you that there is nothing unseemly or seditious in tonight's performance. Why, 'twould not bring a blush to the most innocent of cheeks…"

"Yeah? Well, it better not. And there better be a big number at the end – you know, a real zinger – that way my stewards know when to get the carriage ready…"

Ullmann's eyes bulged. "I am certain that your Majesty will not be disappointed."

"Yeah? How certain?"

"Pretty certain?"

"I guess that will have to do. Okay – get me to my box. And make sure that the seats are padded…"

Ullmann and his buddy bowed low.

"But of course, your highness, but of course…"

As the last of the Emperor's retinue entered the theatre, the square outside the Big emptied and fell silent. Only one ragged figure, his uniform as greased as a kitchen pot, still clung to the shadows: Povolný.

Slowly he fished in his pocket: one last Favour remained.

Taking it in his lips like a holy wafer, the constable closed his eyes and breathed in. The Favour would show him where to go … a trail of crumbs, an unfinished sentence, a musical score … yes, yes, he could hear an orchestra tuning up somewhere, the overture beginning to swell into life…

20

The curtain rises 'pon a reception hall in some provincial manor house: you know, rough-hewn chairs, parquet floor, waxcloth hung on hooks, that kind of stuff.

In the foreground stand two shadowy figures, poignantly silhouetted. One is an old greybeard with a pickled face and rheumy eyes, the other a callow young pup, dressed in the garb of a soldier, though to be honest, his cloak is too long and his boots far too big – where did he get 'em, the dressing up box?

Out of the blue, the old fella starts to singing and pretty soon it's clear what's going on, the young guy taking leave of his father before heading off to war, though the father doesn't look too happy about it. Let my manly tears flow, he sings: why should I be ashamed? Tears cannot hurt anyone … With that, the son begins to sing a tender song of parting, serenading his father, explaining that he has given his oath, signed up, rented a horse etcetera. Besides – the estate is kinda fusty this time of year, his tights are itchy, and who wants to be holed up in this dusty old burg forever?

Well, things go back and forth for a few more verses, but finally the old guy relents, his voice breaking a little as he sings.

"Farewell my son, Godspeed on your journey! You'll find your way, God willing, Look! The moon is shining, and the night is clear. Drink from this cup and then let us part."

The two sup from the jug and embrace and, you have to admit, it's quite a number, not a dry eye in the house. Then the son exits stage right, tripping over his sword on the way out, which gets a laugh from the cheap seats and a scowl from the Emperor.

Alone now, the old man turns sadly from the window and takes to his large, unmade bed, his song plaintive and melancholy, based upon the old folk song, 'But I am finished with ploughing.'

When he's done, the old guy pulls the covers up to his chin and falls silent, the light behind the window turning from yellow to red to blue, denoting the passage of time. Every once in a while, a serving woman comes in with a leg of lamb and walks out with a chamber pot, while the orchestra goes about its business, particularly the violins, as if on commission.

Eventually though, the strings too, fall quiet, and silence reigns once more. Gradually, the light turns a peculiar shade of violet and dust blows across the stage. In the orchestra pit – not a peep.

In the pause between numbers, Count Mitrovsky crawled out from behind the bed and lumbered across the stage on all fours, his jacket unbuttoned and wig skew-whiff.

Had he nodded off for a mo? The last thing he remembered was talking with Mařenka, who seemed awful sore about something, as women are wont to do. But what was is it that had made her so unhappy? His jacket, his wig, his cologne?

Someone coughed in the audience and Mitrovsky gave a comical little leap. Just where was he? Peering out into the gloom, he saw – as if in a nightmare – that he was on the stage, the auditorium packed with people, the seating terribly steep and vertiginous. The Count blinked: what was he doing here? Everywhere he looked, unknown eyes seemed to be staring back at him, from the *parterre noble* down to the stalls, the auditorium in the shape of a horseshoe, the fresco on the upper level showing two masks, one happy, one sad, while at the very top, in the depths of the Imperial Box, His Majesty's nose poked out obscenely.

The Count froze. The Emperor? What was he doing here? From the corner of his eye, he caught sight of a square-faced man looking at him from a box – a prompter? The guy seemed to be mouthing something, though for some reason Mitrovsky struggled to make out the words. Mmw ffwmp fuff?

In desperation, the Count began searching through his pockets for his lines, unearthing only a shell, some nut peelings and a handkerchief reeking of *Lillas de Perse*. Mouth open, he danced from foot to foot as if in urgent need of the privy, simultaneously fluttering his handkerchief and bowing.

"Ah," he said uncertainly, slowly licking his chops. "Yes, well, indeed…"

At this the old man suddenly started singing. "Matej? Matej, is that you?"

The Count nodded and took his hand.

"Yes, it's me, Father."

At this the old man almost jumped out of the bed. "What? Who the hell are you?"

Mitrovsky looked out at the audience, embarrassed. "Ha ha, 'tis me, your son. What, have I changed so much? Well, soldiering will do that to a man, what with the Turks and cannonballs and all"

The old man – who, on closer inspection, didn't seem all that old, his face touched up with beetroot juice and his hair painted white – glanced first off-stage and then back at the Count.

"You aren't Matej …"

"Um."

"What the devil are you doing here? You shouldn't be here at all…"

Mitrovsky gave a jolly wink, pinched the old man's cheeks, and scampered to the other side of the bed.

"Soft, sweet prince," he boomed, "take me to…"

Before he could finish the line, two burly prop men emerged

from the wings, each carrying a large net and a stick. Dodging to one side, Mitrovsky playfully upended a large armoire, skipped behind a curtain, and then fled, stage right, pursued by an angry ape with a club.

In the Royal Box, The Emperor looked down in disgust.

"What the hell is this? It this one of those, whatjamacall it, modern things? Who is that clown?"

The beauty fanning herself next to him shrugged her powdered shoulders. "I dunno, sweetie…"

"Better not be some kind of experimental thing. I hate that crap…"

"Shhh…"

"Why are those slobs chasing the fat guy? It makes no sense."

"Shh, look, the next scene's coming…"

With that a curtain came down, the backdrop illustrating some kind of field after a battle – burnt down trees, churned up land, that sort of thing. A big old oak tree was wheeled out on casters, followed by a ragged line of soldiers, some of them still putting on their tights. In the centre, the young guy from earlier also turned up, his arm in a sling and a blooded rag around his throat; helpfully, he pantomimed that he was wounded, his voice-box pierced by an errant spear or arrow or some-such pointy thing. Fortunately, the soldiers sang loudly to make up for it, lamenting his fate by singing into his beard, while maidens in peasant-dress skipped among them, dancing the *rezanka* – Heaven alone knew why.

In the wings, the Count had other worries. Still trying to ditch the propmen, his pursuers sought refuge in the whimsical galleries of props, crouching behind the *papier-mâché* head of a devil and panting loudly.

Had he lost them? He peered out from between a Hussite chalice and a barrel of herring, searching the darkness for assailants. Yes, yes, he seemed to have given them the slip; well, Counts were well known for their evasive manoeuvres and running away and hiding and the like. Suddenly, he felt a heavy hand on his collar – Bilek.

"Bilek!" said the Count, jumping like a cat. "O my angel, how marvellous to see you! I've been looking for you absolutely everywhere…"

"Yeah? Tell it to the hangman, you louse…"

"Darling, please – there's no need for unpleasantries."

"What? You stick it to me good and wanna be pals?"

"Well, I wouldn't say stick…"

"Yeah – what would you say? You make off with my stuff and think that's okay?"

"Sweetheart, you have my word that…"

"Shove it, Mitrovsky. I got better things to do than dance with you. You just better have it."

"I, ah…"

"The score, you dope."

"Score?"

"What was in the case, I mean."

"Case?"

"Don't play dumb with me, Mitrovsky– you know what I mean. The strong box, the crate."

Mitrovsky gave a funny little flourish and held his handkerchief to his nose.

"Your box? But of course, my dear– I've kept it safe, right next to my bosom, or whatever bosom I could find…"

Still smiling, the Count fished in his tights and held out a gloved mitt.

"Here look!"

"Huh?"

"Can you see?"

"See? See what?"

"There!"

"What?"

Mitrovsky unfurled his glove to reveal a tiny black speck sheltered in the palm of his hand.

"Wait a minute, s'that...?"

"See? I've kept the fellow safe and sound, fed the little imp myself..."

"Ferdie?"

"Aye, 'tis him, the little scamp."

Bilek bent closer. "Ferdie? S'you?"

Bilek brought his face all the way down to the Count's palm and Mitrovsky swiftly clapped his hands, catching Bilek's nose in his paws.

Howling with rage, the *impresario's* eyes began to water.

"Why you little..."

In a flash, Mitrovsky dived back down a cluttered passageway, Bilek yelling and gesturing in his wake.

"Mitrovsky, you bum, wait till I get my paws on you!"

Were they still singing on stage? Well, no matter. The Count nimbly danced behind the curtain, his shadow appearing on stage like a demon, or a ghost.

Bored, the Emperor turned to his mistress and whispered in her delicately powdered ear.

"What act are we in?"

"Shhh!"

"What, you like this stuff?"

"Shhh! What's wrong with you? S'a great song. Good and loud."

Down in the stalls, Moosendorf turned to his companions and sniffed.

"A monstrous quantity of notes, eh lads?

The two contortionists glanced at each other uncertainly.

"Boring, boring, boring! No, there's nothing new here – though I did like the bit with the fat Count. Rather like our own dear Count Mitrovsky, don't you think?"

"Ha ha, a fat man!"

"*Großer Darm!*"

"But I don't know – maybe they've still got something planned for Act Two. Listen – this number's going on forever. You two slip backstage and see if you can see anything funny…"

"Funny?"

"You know – peculiar, strange. And if you can screw up Bilek's plans then so much the better."

"Screwing?"

"*Wo ist die schraube?*"

Moosendorf clapped the fellows on their shoulders. "That's it boys, off you go…"

As *les mouvement mystérieux* slipped furtively out of their seats, up in the balcony Chief Censor Babinksy folded back a new page of his copybook and tutted, loudly. Just what was going on here? He couldn't recall any fat guy in a wig in the first act, never mind a chase across the stage. And what did that ghost have to do with anything? Still, for now at least, the scripted business seemed back on track.

Up front, the soldiers had finally quit their bellyaching about the war while the young guy dramatically collapsed, falling on his behind like a sack of beans. Looking very much alarmed, the peasant girls rushed to his side, gathering him in like the summer harvest; unperturbed, the soldiers tramped off stage, their hats and helmets slipping down over their eyes. Curtain.

Scene Three. A quaint peasant's hut, the joint decked with flowers, rustic looking nick-nacks, scythes and the like. Two figures: the injured young soldier and a gal.

The young guy's looking a lot more perky but still can't sing, as symbolised by the red scarf around his throat. Instead, a beautiful young peasant girl sings a charming melody while the other peasants call by inbetween chopping wood or trips to the well or whatever peasants do all day when the opera's closed.

After a twirl about the hut, the guy mimes that he wants to go hunting, but the girl shakes her head; a huge and terrible bear stalks the woods about the village, said bear demonstrating a marked taste for soldiers, peasant girls, hunters and such like. More dancing ensues and then the guy goes back to bed, the peasant girl lying down and chastely napping on the floor. Off stage a loud howl is heard – though, to be honest it sounds more like some fat guy blowing into a horn – and somebody rolls the moon up against the door.

Fortuitously, Mitrovsky had slipped away backstage, searching for the way out amidst a long line of doors: ho, what a maze this place was!

Keeping one eye out for propmen, and the other for irate impresarios, the Count stealthily made his way past a line of dressing rooms, stepping as daintily as a Polish princess. Suddenly a door flew open: Halas!

"O my angel," bellowed the Count, hugging the lad to his chest most manfully. "How good to see you again! And in such wonderful britches too."

Halas grinned, nodded, and began searching his pockets for a card, but before he could produce one, the Count drew him urgently to one side.

"The most marvellous news, my lad – I have it!"

Halas blinked.

"The cure! From Doctor Pustrpolk! A true medical marvel, a wonder of the scientific world."

Halas stared at the Count somewhat blankly.

"Look! The bottle's right here, secreted within my jacket. Eh my lad, what do you say? A neat trick, don't you think? O Sweet Prince! We'll have you singing 'Your Guelder Rose is Blooming' in no time…"

Pausing only to glance up and down the corridor, the Count shoved his patient inside a dressing room, carefully resting the bottle on a shelf.

"Yes, yes, yes … that Doctor Pustrpolk was quite the fellow…"

Halas started to mouth the word 'Eliška', when an alarming howl echoed down the passage, causing the two men to leap in the air.

As the howl reverberated around The Big Theatre, Halas and the Count looked at each other, one skinny and one fat, as if in a circus mirror.

"O, take no notice," said Mitrovsky, confidently. "That's just Lala … a real sweetheart…"

Halas blinked.

"I met her during my time in the army – O lad, the stories I could tell!"

Turning back to the cupboard Mitrovsky did a sudden double take. He'd placed the bottle on a low shelf next to other bottles – hair tonic, perfume, various cleaning materials– and momentarily couldn't recall which was which.

With a casual shrug, Mitrovsky unstopped a bottle and handed it to the lad.

"Now my dear heart, what did the good doctor say? Was it once after meals or twice in the morning? Well, no matter – drink up, my prince, drink up!"

Halas nodded, drunk deeply, and began to turn red and choke. Mitrovsky looked at the label uncertainly.

"Or was it that one?"

Halas was still gasping and gagging as Mitrovsky uncorked a second bottle.

"Yes, yes, I recall it now … a somewhat greenish colour…"

Halas coughed and wept, violently fighting for breath. Mitrovsky handed him the second bottle, whereupon the lad bent over and wordlessly began to gag.

"Or was it puce?"

As Master Halas flopped onto the dressing room floor, the door flew open: Honzl, accompanied by his horrible yellow eyes.

"Yes, yes," he chuckled, "the very pair…"

Honzl had spotted Master Halas upon his arrival, following the lad as he slipped away from the lobby and headed backstage. He now regarded the Count and Master Halas in a most sinister fashion, rather like a villain in a cheap play.

"So – you have made your way from Hrůza to P, have you? All the way to the very nose of His Majesty…"

Mitrovsky looked shifty. "Us?"

"Perhaps you thought you had evaded me, escaped? But no, no, I would say not – no one evades the Department of Exceptional Cases! I've written your names down, you swine. Written them right here in my…"

On cue, Mitrovsky threw his bottle, showering the fellow in amber liquid. The Investigator screamed.

"My eyes, my eyes!"

Grabbing hold of Master Halas, the Count swiftly dragged him into the next room along, moving a heavy chest to try and block the way. The room was filled with rack after rack of theatrical costumes, from guardsmen to tinkers to fools.

Outside: banging, shouting, consternation. Special Investigator Honzl had summoned assistance and a mob were beating on the door.

Inside, from the rack of clothes, two eccentric figures emerged,

Halas dressed as a flugel-player, Mitrovsky some kind of mangy beast. And with that they fled through a rear exit and out into a passageway, the Count's little stubby tail following on behind.

In a private box, Lida looked around the Big in disgust. Old guys in wigs, husbands in mauve pantaloons, flunkies in white linen gloves; what use was this to her? She looked at the wrinkly chops and stooped shoulders and sighed. Where was she going to find a husband here?

"What a con," she whispered. "And this song is going on forever…"

The Baron patted her arm. "Shh, my darling, hush. Why…"

"Oh, it's hopeless! And where's that ass Mitrovsky? He said he'd meet us in the lobby…"

"Shh, darling, please. People are beginning to stare…"

"So what? Don't we want 'em to stare? Isn't that why I bought this stupid fan?"

"Darling…"

"I can't stand it! You stay here, I'll go look for that jerk in the lobby. You ask me, he was just some kind of bum. A guy in a jacket like that, he doesn't know any swells at all…"

Before her father could stop her, Lida flounced from the box and descended a narrow, precipitous staircase between the galleries, bumping into Ullmann, his silent assistant, and a propman.

Ullmann bowed deeply, then turned back to the prop guy.

"He isn't here – where the hell is he?"

The stagehand bent over to catch his breath. "The Devil knows. Who is this boob anyway?"

"I don't know, but he's ruining the show."

"You think The Little Theatre hired him? Sounds like one of their dirty tricks…"

"Who knows? We just gotta get hold of him before the Emperor gets wind. Now you go check upstairs and I'll go back down. I'm sorry Miss."

Bowing once more, the two guys allowed Lida to pass. Her face masked by her fan, the young lady subtly inclined her head and then descended the stairs. Ullmann turned back to his assistant.

"Listen, we still got two more acts to get him. But watch out – he's got accomplices. Must be some sort of gang…"

The assistant nodded. From the orchestra pit the music became more ominous, someone sawing away dramatically, like claws scraping their way through a door.

Act One, Scene Four: The Forest at dusk. Can you believe it? That fool of a soldier has ignored the peasant gal and gone off hunting, dressed in some sort of Tyrolian get up: where did he get the tights, at Škroups?

Bow in hand, the fellow pads between the trees, although since the whole copse has to fit on the stage, the woods aren't so very thick; no kidding, you could hop from one side to the other in just a couple of strides.

A red bandana still around his neck, the guy mimes that he's some big shot huntsman, crouching and hiding, sniffing trees and bushes and the like. Down in the orchestra pit, a flautist makes the sound of a blackbird, the percussion makes like a woodpecker, and the cornet mimics the hoot of an owl. Yeah, yeah, yeah – it's a regular aviary. Suddenly there's a grunt and a growl and the young guy freezes: the bear!

For a moment, the monster seems to be accompanied by a flugel-horn player – the Devil knows why. The bear also seems to be going in the wrong direction, but then it hits a tree with its head and stops.

The young guy starts to thread an arrow, but: too late! Right away the fella slips and twists his ankle. This 'aint looking good. But wait, wait … the bear seems old and friendly and has hardly any teeth at all.

Relieved, the young fellow rubs its belly while the bear rolls about obligingly. Ho, this beast is nothing to be afraid of. Why such a scary legend?

Anyhow, the guy is just about to head on back, when out of nowhere, he spots on the other side of the forest, between one old dark tree and another, the gates of a manor house, and inside a beautiful garden, with roses and paths and a fountain in the middle, you know, one of those fancy ones, with some kind of nymph in the middle.

And strolling around out there, taking in the evening air and sighing and cooing, is some dame – a beauty in a hoop skirt and high wig. Ah me, what a gal! She languidly picks a flower and sings some ditty about how God's little bird knows neither labour nor unrest. Entranced, the soldier hides behind a fake tree, breathing heavily. But when he tries to join in with the honeyed aria, he abruptly remembers his wound: mm, the fellow can't sing a note! Downcast, the young lover steps back into the shadows, his tender heart rendered in twain. How's a fella supposed to signal the depths of his great love when he can't even whistle? No, no, it's useless – and with that, the soldier heads mournfully back to the village, full of confused thoughts. Was this why the peasant girl told him such fearsome stories – just to keep him away? But why would she do that? The guy exits stage left, still fingering his muffler.

As he departs, he leaves behind him the old mangy bear, the brute standing upright on two legs gazing at the garden in a pose that is almost human. What? Is he in love with the dame too? Or has he just seen an old scratching post? Alas, we cannot know.

The Emperor closed his eyes and tried to sleep: even canasta with the Dušeks was better than this.

"Baby, can you get me some of those snacks?" asked his companion, fanning herself furiously. "You know, those salty twists?"

"What? Can't you wait for the intermission?"

"C'mon baby, m'hungry…"

The Emperor clacked his teeth. "Fine, fine." Clapping his hands, he summoned a liveried servant, who bowed stiffly. "Get me a bag of pretzels will ya? And make sure they got plenty of salt…"

The flunkey nodded and hurried away from the box, the Emperor's squeeze cuddling in closer. "Thanks, Baby…"

The Emperor picked his enormous nose and squinted at the stage. "You following this thing?"

"Shh, it's good! I like the fat bear, he's cute…"

"Yeah, if you say so…"

"C'mon, look, the next bit is starting…"

The guy sneaks back to the hut, looking kinda sad and dreamy. In the morning the peasant girl asks him if he's been to the forest and the guy pantomimes 'what me, no way!' pulling on an innocent face. Delighted, the girl throws herself around his neck and kisses him with wild abandon, whereupon the young soldier looks back at her, very much surprised. It turns out that the gal is crazy in love with him and wants to marry him and decorate their hut with hearts and garlands and paper dolls and the like – who knew?

Well, with this news the young guy looks at her kind of funny. I mean, she's awful pretty and all, but she hasn't got any shoes and her hut is terribly draughty. Besides – his dad is a Count and lives in a big old house, and there's the dame in the garden to think about too…

Peasant girls being very sensitive to this kind of thing, the girl then tells him that if he agrees to marry her then she'll collect all kinds of herbs and berries from the forest, whip up a potion, and this will return his voice to him, allowing him to talk and laugh and sing.

Sing? His eyes a little crafty, the young fella hastily agrees. Yes, yes, he pantomimes – it's a deal!

In celebration, the girl does a little dance, and then sings a tremendously long song about married bliss, not noticing that during the last verse the guy has already got back into bed and gone to sleep.

Anyhow, the next bit goes on forever. The girl skips around the forest collecting all sorts of weeds and shrubs, and it seems that each one has got a different song about it, which to be honest, feels like padding.

In their box, Mispickel Senior turned to his son and slapped him.

"What – this the best you can do?"

"Gerrof…"

"A song about rag-wort?"

"Shurrup…"

"What kind of tune is this? You think the Emperor wants to hear about goosefoot?"

"Mum!"

"Hush Vojtěch, let the boy be."

"If you spent as much time composing as you do playing billiards…"

"What's it to you? You sold it didn't you?"

"Ungrateful Little Pup…"

Below the Mispickels in the stalls, Moosendorf chuckled softly. What a disaster! Mispickel's golden touch had surely failed him. What was the girl trilling about now? Rosehips and cow parsley? *Les mouvement mystérieux* would clean up at the box office – honestly, you wouldn't believe the shapes those boys could twist themselves into! And to think he had paid that slob Mitrovsky to find out Bilek's secrets – what a waste of dough. If this was Bilek's big secret, he might as well go back to The Musical Milkers of Most…

Yet for all that, Gunter and Emil had been gone an awful long time. Moosendorf straightened his hat; he couldn't afford for 'em to fall into the mitts of The Big – who knew what those jealous fatheads might do?

A little uneasy now, Moosendorf apologised to the people sitting next to him and went off to take a look. Listen, acts like *les mouvement mystérieux* didn't come along every day. What those

Germans could do in their tights would bring tears to your eyes…

While Mitrovsky (in bear costume) was busy being patted by the young soldier, Halas drifted off into the wings, whereupon he was set upon by a stagehand with a Hungarian moustache.

"Hey! Hey you!"

Halas pointed to himself with an expression of mute innocence.

"Yeah you. What are you doing there? You want the audience to see you?"

The young man blinked: he was still feeling a little nauseous after Mitrovsky's cocktail, truth be told.

"You betta get back to the orchestra pit. Hey – not that way, you dunce! Here, down these steps…"

Halas nodded, obediently padding his way into the pit, hanging around at the back, before somebody pointed to a seat.

"Where the hell you been? Paleček has been doing his nut."

In the gloom, Halas slowly blinked.

"Pissed again, huh? You gotta stay out of The Lost Sheep. That dump will be the death of you…"

Halas enthusiastically nodded.

"Sit down quick. Your flugel-horn's over there. Your big solo is coming up. Don't screw up, pal – not with the Emperor's conk in the house…"

Halas looked at the Emperor's Box and then down at the flugel-horn with big, innocent eyes.

"Lucky you got here before Act Two…"

Halas picked up his instrument and nodded. Fortunately, the conductor was looking the other way – a scowling, hunched fellow with mean little eyes. Halas examined his instrument uncertainty; how was he supposed to find Eliška now?

On stage, the gal has finally finished with her weeding and not before time too. Gathering them up in her basket, she takes the herbs back to her hut, depositing the whole lot in a cauldron with four brass feet. More dancing and skipping ensues. Out of nowhere, the sky darkens – all credit to the lighting department – as if a storm is brewing. Soldier-boy gets out of his bed and inspects the brew. Yet more dancing, followed by some song about the herbalist's art. Don't ask: it's nothing to get the critics in The Lame Horse excited. Finally, the girl finishes her dance and produces a cup. Dipping it ceremoniously in the cauldron, she then hands it to the soldier, who quaffs it pronto. Lightning flashes. Is that some jerk dressed as a bear hidden in the corner of the hut? No – must be a trick of the light. The soldier throws his head back and begins to sing a ditty of celebration – hurray, hurray, he can finally wag his tongue once more! The boy and the girl then dance about the hut, and he promises that he will marry her in the morning, when her mum and dad can get there, and the village priest and the guy who sells baked goods. The girl claps her hands, and the guy kisses her and then he goes back to bed. Curtain.

Up in the Royal Box, the Emperor opened one tired eye. Was it over? Another song about duck weed and he would've had to use his socks to block up his ears.

The door to the box opened, and the flunkey entered, bearing pretzels. But wait a minute, this wasn't the same guy! What the devil…

"Your Majesty," said Povolný, brandishing a salty twirl. "You are in great and terrible danger…"

"Who the blazes…"

"A plot, your Majesty, a plot against your very person…"

The Emperor's girlfriend looked across the box and wrinkled her nose. "Sweetie, are those my pretzels?"

"Your Majesty, I…"

The Emperor scowled. "What's going on here? Where the hell is Otto?"

"Your highness, the crumbs they led me here … a secret dream only the Favours can know…"

"You some kind of loon? Guards! Guards!"

"A conspiracy, sir – treachery!"

"Yeah? Guards! Guards! Get this joker outta here!"

"Beware the Nightingales, Your Majesty, beware their song!"

Before Povolný could get out another word, two guys in leather tunics appeared and removed the constable by force. The Emperor glowered and smoothed out the wrinkles in his jacket: sheesh, what a flake! Even while he was being dragged away, the jerk was still shouting about birds and biscuits, paths and crumbs.

"Well, that was odd," said the Emperor, fingering the end of his conk.

"Hey, what about my pretzels?"

"Pipe down willya? Can't you see I just had a lunatic in my box?"

"All I asked for was a snack…"

"Oh, for crying out loud…"

News of the intruder was swiftly communicated to the Theatre Manager: an assassin was at large, a hitman, some kind of terrorist.

Ullmann turned to his assistant. "The fat guy?"

His assistant shrugged.

"Well, we better not take any chances. Redouble the search. If in doubt, knock heads."

Prop men were dispatched left and right while Povolný was frog-marched backstage and pummelled with sticks.

Honzl pushed himself forward. "What the hell are you doing? Get your hands off my constable!"

The propmen stopped.

"Constable?"

"He may look like a maniac, but he is in fact a member of the

Hrůza constabulary… Povolný, Povolný, can you hear me?"

The constable groaned and Special Investigator Honzl fumed and ground his teeth.

"This isn't the right man. The assassin calls himself Mitrovsky – Count Mitrovsky. I've got it all written down, right here in my …"

"Mitrovsky, huh?" Ullmann nodded. "M-I-T, okay, okay. Um, no reason to bother His Majesty, right?"

Honzl's eyes were two blisters of yellow paint. "His Majesty?"

"I mean, don't want to spoil the show…"

Honzl stared at the Manager with absolute contempt. "I'm writing it down," he spat, "writing down every last word…"

Act 1, Scene 6. Late. A painted moon has been hung from the rafters, the hut dipped in darkest night.

While the peasant girl sleeps, the young soldier slips from his bed and sneaks out the front door. This time he's not dressed as a hunter, but adorned in soldiering garb: cloak, tunic, regimental tights. With one last look at the girl, he slips outside, softly whistling 'How soon my youth flashed by'.

The forest is silent, dark. No bears, owls or twittering of any kind. The fella makes his way to the manor house and immediately spots the dame, still dressed in her hoop skirt and wig and wandering about the garden. Hasn't she been to bed? It's like she's been painted onto the scenery with a brush.

Anyhow, right away the guy starts to singing about some tender spark, sweet longings, that kind of stuff. It's then that he notices the dame looks kinda jittery, "A soldier," she cries, "please sir, I am in dire need of assistance!"

Straight away, the guy puffs up his chest and marches on over, trying to look as military as possible.

"My husband!" sings the lady. "My husband has been kidnapped by

the bandit, Patočka. Please, my Angel, will you help me? He has been ransomed for five hundred zlatnik and I only have ten shilling in my purse…"

The soldier looks at her askance. Husband?

Yes, yes – her darling husband, Anton, has been captured. Will the soldier help her? The bandit's camp is in a clearing in the forest – two blocks past the dead elm, turn left.

Still playing the role of the soldier – and clearly enjoying the sound of his own voice – the guy gives his solemn word. He will rescue this unfortunate Anton – on this he pledges his most sacred vow.

The dame is thrilled and sings a little song to say so.

Bowing deeply, the soldier then takes leave of the enchanted grove. However, he only goes a couple of feet when he stops to think things over. A husband eh? The soldier scratches his nose. And this Patočka fella sounds like a bruiser, bandits often being folk of general ill will and violence. Bandits and Brigands? Best stay out of their way.

Deep in thought, the fella wanders off through the undergrowth, his scabbard clanking away by his side. How was he supposed to know the dame was married? And what's this Anton guy to him?

The soldier is still mulling things over when from out of the gloom a messenger appears in a three-cornered hat.

Bowing deeply, he approaches the lad.

"Is he Matej something-or-other?"

Yes, yes, indeed he is.

"Wounded at the battle of Žižka's oak?"

"The very one!"

"Injured by a sharp, pointy thing to the neck?"

Yes, yes, yes. But how did the fellow find him?

The messenger shakes his head. There is no time to explain. The old Count is very ill and will croak it any day. The lad must return forthwith and claim his inheritance – his relatives are already there and over the estate like weevils.

"Aunt Inka and Uncle Ignaz?"

You better believe it.

The soldier pauses, thinking things through. On the one hand he promised to marry the peasant girl; but on the other hand, he also promised to help this dame reclaim her husband too. What's a guy to do?

"Do you, by any chance, have a carriage?" he asks.

And with that he goes off with the messenger, whistling 'An infant, merry as a bell', his boots too big, his hat falling down over his eyes.

Watching the action from his seat, Chief Censor Babinsky felt a sudden prickle of fear.

What had once seemed like a harmless bauble, some sort of sentimental curio, now seemed in retrospect – at least when looked upon in the Emperor's presence – a very different prospect indeed.

Aye, the Count's son was plainly a swine! First he tricked the peasant girl and then reneged on his sacred promise to the dame in the wig. What a creep! Was this some kind of democratic propaganda? Revolutionary sentiment? Underneath all the harmless stuff about pondweed and camomile, was there some kind of seditious message or code? Foo, just look at the way the young soldier wore his hat – plainly intended to make His Majesty's Army look absurd.

The Chief Censor nervously fingered his collar. What the hell had he been thinking? This was no trifle, no *amuse bouche*. Beneath the thin coating of sugar there was a bear-trap, a bomb! And it wasn't as if he hadn't been warned; the guy from Vienna had told him about his Majesty's prickly sensitivity, his hair-trigger temper.

Babinsky snapped shut his book: he had to talk to Ullmann, right away. And the swine had better have some answers…

The Theatre Manager though, had other things on his mind. Two

German guys had been apprehended, sneaking around out back. And, he had to admit, they did indeed look pretty sinister: thin as a fakir and monstrously tall and brittle, their skin pulled tight o'er their bones.

"Okay you swine – what are you doing snooping around the Big?"

"Snoop? Vot is snoop?"

"No snoop! We move…"

"Move?"

"Ja, move mysteriously…"

Ullmann and his assistant looked at the pair incredulously. Dressed all in black, and adorned head-to-toe in a kind of skin-tight stocking, they resembled some kind of horrible insect, osseous and long.

Angrily, Special Investigator Honzl pushed himself forward.

"Don't give me that! You are part of a group, a cell, working with the criminal Mitrovsky."

"Ja ja, the fat count!"

"We know him! Very jolly!"

"Ha ha, a jester, funny clown…"

Honzl's eyes bulged horribly: who were these cur?

"So – you admit that you know the man?"

Emil and Gunter looked at one another.

"Ja…"

"And work alongside him…"

Again, the contortionists exchanged glances.

"Work? Nein, nein. Ha ha, the Count, too fat."

"What?"

"He get stuck in a barrel, ha ha!"

Ullmann tapped the Special Investigator on his shoulder. "Inspector, I think these fellows are…"

"*Les mouvement mystérieux*," said the fellows, springing into poses of an artistic and physically challenging nature.

"What the blazes?"

Honzl lifted up his book as if about to squash the dancers flat but was stopped by the sound of angry steps approaching.

"I demand that you let these artistes free!"

All eyes shifted: marching in from a corridor was Moosendorf, his hat bobbing up and down on his head.

"Moosendorf?" snapped Ullmann, eying up the impresario coldly, "what the hell are you doing here?"

"Looking after my assets – now unhand those boys. *Les mouvement mystérieux* are booked to play at The Little– a sold-out performance, I should note…"

Ullmann and his assistant snorted. "These guys? You giving away tickets now?"

"I'll have you know that these fellows are the talk of Europe, their aesthetically pleasing forms discussed in artistic soirees the length and breadth of…"

"Sure, sure – a big hit at the circus…"

"How dare you?"

"Just after the Bearded Lady and before the bear with his hoop…"

"Why you dirty…"

"Listen Moosendorf, such novelty acts might pack 'em in at the Little – I mean, how many seats have you got there, twelve? – but the Big is the home of quality entertainment."

Moosendorf sneered. "What – like this damp squib of a show?"

"Listen, Mispickel is the greatest genius that…"

"One song about pondweed and another about socks? Anyone can see that the Emperor is bored out of his mind…"

"Yeah? What do you know about The Emperor? I don't see him squeezing his conk in the Little."

"Foo, everyone knows that the word 'little' is a term of

endearment and that the Little is actually much larger than…"

"Bullshit!"

All eyes turned once more. Another figure had emerged backstage, a diminutive fellow in an enormously tall and slender hat: Bilek.

"The Little 'aint got room for a mouse's fart…"

Moosendorf bristled. "So – Master Bilek? Brno's second most successful theatrical *impresario*…"

"Second? I haven't heard of any other dope stepping up to the mark…"

"What are you doing here Bilek? Another milking act? Or have you dusted down your fleas?"

"Hey, you leave Ferdy out of this. Those lice, they're a damn good show…"

"If you're eight years old…"

"Yeah?"

"Yeah."

Was it Moosendorf or Bilek who threw the first punch? In the melee it was very hard to tell. They were still on top of each other when another stagehand came running up to Ullmann.

"Boss? We gotta problem. The bear won't come out…"

"Huh? What d'you mean, the bear won't come out?"

The stagehand shrugged. "She's pining or something. Won't budge. Just sits on a stool and moults."

"But, but … the bear's been on stage. Act one, scene four – the forest at dusk. You know, when Matej sneaks off to go hunting with his bow."

"That wasn't our bear. She's backstage sniffing her tail…"

Ullmann and his assistant looked at one another blankly. "Then, who the hell…"

Honzl stamped his foot and ground his fangs. "Mitrovsky … Mitrovsky disguised as a bear…"

Bilek and Moosendorf paused in their fight.

"Mitrovsky? He's here?"

"Dressed as a bear?"

Ullmann turned back to the stagehands. "Okay – you need to tell everyone to be on the look out for a fat count disguised as a bear. Answers to the name Mitrovsky. And don't let him get anywhere near the Emperor, you understand? If the Royal Proboscis gets a sniff, it's our necks on the line…"

"A problem, Herr Ullmann?"

All eyes turned as Chief Censor Babinsky emerged from out of the gloom.

"Nothing we can't handle," said the Manager picking up a plate of pastries. "Here – try a *trdelník*. They're terrifically sweet…"

Act Two. Several years have passed and the young guy now wears a fancy beard on his chin – he's put on a few pounds too.

He's a Count now, and dressed in countly gear: fancy britches, ribbons on his frock coat, gold buckles, that sort of thing. His face though seems furrowed and sober, as if weighed down by regret and remorse – or maybe just too many knedlíky, who knows? Hat in hand, he bids farewell to his retinue and walks down to Žižka's oak, the field much changed from that battle many years ago: cornflowers grow where soldiers once fell, and someone has planted clover and rye.

Well, the fella is just hanging around, cooling his heels and chatting with the birds, when an old peasant with a greenish beard strolls past, pushing a wheelbarrow full of junk.

"What ho," sings the peasant, "a fine day for rambling."

In song, he then tries to sell him some worms, a bag of pigeon dung, and a horn allegedly belonging to one of Přemysl's oxen, along with his hazel rod, mint condition.

The Count though, ain't buying; instead, asks the old timer if he knows of a peasant girl who once lived in yonder hut, a tender young thing with pretty green eyes and hair the colour of gold.

"Yonder?"

The peasant nods and sucks on the tip of his beard. Yes, he knows the girl of whom the Count sings – once celebrated as a great beauty, though – alas! – much has changed since then.

For some swine had promised to marry her and then skipped town, despite all his assurances and honeyed words, the whole village learning of the young gentleman and the nature of the girl's misfortune.

A little while later the girl married Hurník the Butcher, known for his foul temper and unpleasant air, though he could do you a good deal on chops. She had borne him three children in four years, though the cost had been great, her youth swept away with the blossom. She now lives in the village of Hromada, in a clearing by Benka's ditch, if the gentleman cared to visit?

"No," sings the Count sadly. "I do not think I shall."

Placing his handkerchief to his lips, he then asks if the old man might know of a lady who lived in a big old house in the forest, a stately manor, blessed with a beautiful garden, almost like paradise itself.

"Ho," sings the old peasant; "that story is even more tragic."

A cruel bandit by the name of Lame Patočka kidnapped the lady's husband, intending to offer his soul for ransom, five hundred zlatnik, not a penny less, interest too. With no ready cash, the lady promised him the only treasure she had to hand: namely a night of love in order to secure her young man's release.

This dame being quite the looker, Lame Patočka readily agreed, picking her up in his carriage and then dragging her off to his foul and rancid bed.

That night though, while the bandit lay snoring, she took the cutlass from his side and chopped off his head. Then, overcome by guilt and shame, she plunged the blade into her own heart, so that her virtue would be avenged, and her saintly husband would not reproach her for what she'd done.

The old man pulls on his beard.

Some say her ghost still haunts the forest; others say that her garden is guarded by a great shaggy bear. Who knows what the truth of things is? One cannot know what one doesn't. Her husband, Anton, moved to the city of P many miles from here: the young gentleman could visit him if he so desired.

"No, no," sings the Count: "You are very kind, but I do not think I shall."

And with this, he thanks the peasant most kindly and walks off alone into the woods. Wait a minute, is that a bear watching him from behind a tree with his big, sad eyes?

It is, it is, a bear!

"That's him, there!"

"Where?"

"Third tree along."

"Mitrovsky?"

"Yeah – you see his gut?"

"S'him, alright."

"In the bear suit?"

"Yeah."

"Okay, okay – Plicka, go get him."

"Me? What about the audience? The Emperor?"

"Cut the lights and tell the orchestra to play."

"Play, play what?"

"Who cares? Something long and loud. You distract the Emperor, we'll nab the Count."

"Paleček won't like it…"

"Who cares? One tune is just as good as another. Now go get a mallet and a net. This time that bozo 'aint getting away…"

Down in the orchestra pit, the news quickly spread. There was some kind of lunatic on the loose, dressed, for some reason, as a bear: they all had to play until someone managed to grab him.

Halas took all this in and blinked.

All of a sudden, the stage went dark and various shadows crept from tree to tree. Cued up by the conductor, the orchestra started playing 'The Farmer He Wears a Tulip/On his Long Fur Coat', while propmen roamed the stage.

Promptly, Halas went into action. Every time he saw a figure approach the tree masking the Count, he blew his flugel-horn as loud as he could; thus forewarned, the Count swiftly dived behind another trunk, propmen stumbling this way and that, falling over one another in the dark.

The rest of the horn section stared at Halas rather threateningly; what was the dumb lug doing? Nevertheless, he continued to parp his notes of warning, the Count skipping nimbly from tree to tree.

By now, of course, the audience were growing steadily more restless. There were sporadic whistles, catcalls, hisses. Someone started slow clapping near the back, the clamour growing slowly louder.

In the Imperial Box, His Holy and Eternal Majesty was beginning to lose his rag.

"What's going on? Why are they playing The Farmer He Wears a Tulip again?"

His mistress rubbed his sleeve beseechingly. "C'mon honey – have a pretzel."

"What are those clowns doing? I swear I heard that twice twice already…"

"They're good and salty…"

"Listen, if that doll starts singing about liverwort again, I'm outta here."

"Just relax, willya? Can't a girl enjoy a night out?"

Meanwhile Lida, the Baron's daughter, had bored of tarrying in the lobby and made her way quietly backstage.

Once there, her ears pricked up upon hearing Mitrovsky's name.

"Mitrovsky? Count Mitrovsky?"

Ullmann turned to look at her. "You know him?"

"Said he'd meet me in the lobby – introduce me to some loaded guys…"

"Did he now? Well, m'sorry Miss, but this Mitrovsky, he's some kind of assassin…"

"Assassin? This doesn't sound like my Mitrovsky."

"I don't know what he said to you, but…"

"He told my dad, promised…"

"Listen Missy, what do you want me to do? A Count didn't keep his word? Big surprise. Meanwhile, we got bigger fish to fry."

"Big lug gave his oath."

"Yeah? Well, there's a lot of it about…"

On stage, the propmen seemed to be getting closer and closer, despite Halas' urgent tooting and the Count's nimble feet.

One propman tried to grab his bear costume, while another went after him with a net. Then, just as it seemed the stagehands were about to nab him, Mitrovsky toppled backwards into the orchestra pit, upending conductor Paleček and scattering the sheet music like autumn leaves. Paleček stared at the Count, open mouthed.

"What the hell…"

"I'm most terribly sorry," said the Count, brushing himself down. "I seem to have disturbed your Farmer and his Tulip…"

"It's the lunatic!" shouted Paleček. "Get him!"

At the conductor's order, the timpani section approached menacingly, wrestling Mitrovsky to the ground. In the scrum, the bear costume was ripped, and the pocket of his frock coat torn:

Bilek's score fell from it, joining its compatriots on the ground.

"Please, please," yelled the Count, "I am a simple and innocent bear!"

But 'twas no use – a xylophone player pinned his arms and a flautist grabbed hold of his beard.

"I assure you," said the Count, "there's a perfectly innocent explanation for all of this."

It was to no avail: the beast was in the net.

In the stalls, the audience didn't know whether to applaud or boo. Jeers echoed from near the rear, but there was also some appreciative laughter in the Gods.

Dragged off-stage, the Count was frog-marched toward Babinsky, Honzl, Ullmann and his assistant.

"So – the famous Count Mitrovsky," hissed Honzl, glaring at him with his liquid, yellow eyes. "We meet once more. But this time there shall be no second act!"

Ullmann looked at the fat Count rather doubtfully. "What – this is the hatchet guy? The assassin?"

"Don't let him fool you," said the Special Investigator, tapping his ledger, "he's not as stupid as he looks."

"Well, I wouldn't say that," said the Count, winking playfully.

"You're certain it's him?" said Babinsky. "The revolutionary?"

"Oh yes," said Honzl, sneering. "'Tis the fake Count whose every gesture seeks to mock our nobility and class."

Pushing himself away from Moosendorf, Bilek landed on the Count.

"Okay you bum, where is it?"

"Um…"

"The score, ya creep. If you lost it, I swear I'm gonna…"

Precipitously, a couple of propmen leapt out of the wings and pulled the impresario back.

"Mitrovsky is in our custody now, Master Bilek," said Honzl, "care of The Ministry of Cases of Extraordinary Importance."

Babinsky bustled forward.

"Yes, yes, but let us not forget that the Department of Forbidden Texts is also involved."

"Involved? Involved how?"

"Um, well, this opera it, ah…"

As the two investigators squabbled, Lida stepped forward and looked the Count directly in the eye.

"You promised me, Mitrovsky… promised to introduce me to the richest cats in town…"

Although restrained by the propmen, Mitrovsky gamely attempted to bow.

"O my dear…"

"You men are all the same – just like Lena and her misfortune …"

"My darling, I…"

"Say one thing and do another – so much for your sweet words…"

"Well," said Honzl, staring at the remains of the Count's bear costume with his horrible yellow eyes, "do you have anything to say for yourself, you dog?"

Mitrovsky paused and tried to raise his arms. "Soft, sweet prince, take me to…"

But before he could finish, the sound of angry hissing and jeering rose up again from the stalls.

Ullmann stook his head out through the curtain. "Uh oh," he said.

All at once, a harsh voice cried out from the Imperial Box. "Hey, you slobs, get on with it! You jerks think I've got all day?"

A feminine hand appeared alongside the Emperor's snout.

"Baby, please…"

"What a dump! I told you we shoulddda gone to Q…"

As if scalded, Ullmann and his assistant leapt up and began frantically signalling to strike up the band.

Flustered, the conductor gazed down at the nest of papers around his feet: what the hell were they supposed to play next?

Meanwhile, Ullmann shoved the guy playing Matej back on stage.

"Get out there, quick!"

"What? But what…"

"Act Two, Scene Two – the garden at night. Now take this lantern and sing."

And with a mighty shove, Ullmann propelled the young soldier back on stage. The garden backdrop was unfurled, just the other side of the forest. Blue trees, rosebushes, the fountain with the naked chick.

While the conductor was still looking for his score, His Majesty's nostrils quivered furiously.

"Come on, come on – what a crock of…"

Finally, Young Mispickel could take no more.

"Blow it out your butt, old man!"

"What?"

"Shut your trap, you big-nosed bastard…"

Horrified, his parents tried to hush him.

"Rudy, please…"

"Sit down you little pup, you want to send us to the gallows?"

"Stupid jerk…"

The Emperor's nose shook with rage.

"What did you say?"

"You deaf as well as stupid? You wouldn't know a good tune if it inched its way outta your behind…"

"You little punk…"

"Rudy, sit down…"

"That's it, we're going home right now…"

"Big dope..."

The Emperor turned to his mistress. "Who is that kid? I want him in chains, right now. Hell, what a dump! I could have gone to M or N you know ... anywhere's better than a hole like this..."

At this, disgruntled murmuring could be heard from the crowd. The Emperor looked down at the audience in disgust.

"What a cess-pit! These clowns in P really are the scum of the earth."

Loud booing burst, this time directed in the Emperor's specific direction.

"Boo me, will ya? You boobs need to show some respect."

Cat calls, whistles, a steadily growing growl. The Emperor's nose resembled the tip of an axe.

"What they say in O is right – this really is the arm-pit of the Empire..."

Something was thrown at the Imperial box, but missed: a stone, maybe. It hit a candelabra and caused a candle to topple over; fortunately, a flunkey appeared to extinguish the flame.

Ullmann's face was a sickly shade of grey.

"What the hell's going on – what do they think they're doing? One spark and this place will go up like a firework. Get hold of Mispickel and order the pup to quit. And tell that boob to sing."

The soldier looked about the stage somewhat fearfully: he was bound to get it in the neck, one way or the other. Should he start to sing the next number or wait for the conductor to give his cue? His pantaloons felt damp, the dye starting to run in his beard.

Then, just as it seemed things couldn't get any worse, a terrifying apparition appeared before him, a spectral figure, pale and awful, materialising before his very eyes. Ah me, what a sight! Was it a vision, a phantom? The girl's sombre aspect was frozen, her feet untouched by shoes.

Scared out of his wits, the soldier fainted dead away, his lantern crashing to the floor and setting fire to a nearby tree.

"Hey, this isn't in the script," complained Babinsky.

Blind to the flames, the ashen figure advanced stiffly forward, her features impassive, her garment most flammable: Eliška?

"Fire! Fire!" yelled Ullmann, hitting his assistant on the head. "If that tree goes up, the Big is done for!"

"But who's the …"

"Who cares? Fetch a bucket!"

But before anybody else could act, Young Halas flew up from the orchestra pit, sweeping poor Eliška up into his arms and plucking her out of the terrible conflagration. O Eliška! Halas looked down at her frail and combustible body. Thank the Lord – the girl was unharmed. In the blink of an eye, he then beat out the flames with his horn-player's jacket, smoke rising dramatically above the stage.

"El … Eliška?" he croaked.

Yes, the boy could speak, though whether Pustrpolk's elixir, a bottle of hair tonic, or the excitement of the moment was responsible for this vocal transformation was impossible to say.

Eliška opened her eyes.

"Oh," she said softly. "S'you."

"Eliška, I…"

"Uh, you better turn round,"

Blinking, Halas reluctantly turned away from Eliška and gazed about the Big. The eyes of all the audience – and the Emperor – were upon him.

"Get on with it, ya clown!" yelled a voice from the Imperial Box.

In a blind panic, the conductor picked up the first score he could get hold of: Bilek's, of course. Marshalling his players, the orchestra frantically began to play.

Halas swallowed hard: what, they expected him to squawk? In a square cut into the stage, he could see the prompter's box, some shadowy figure holding up a card. Had he seen this fellow before? Well, he had other things to worry about now. Reading the cards and breathing deeply, Halas slowly began to sing.

Afterward, few of the survivors of the Big could agree on what exactly they'd heard that night.

Some spoke of a tender love song, a sweet, soft ache in the soul; others recalled a melancholy lament of regret, a bitter accounting of all the misfortunes of life, laced with sorrow and loss. And still others claimed that the words held a secret revolutionary meaning, instigating a kind of insurrection or call to arms: hey, what d'you think burnt that fleapit down, a candle-stub? But all agreed that it was the most beautiful music in the world.

Listen: it's the middle of the night and a nightingale is singing. What's that, what's he singing? Who knows – do I look like a guy who can speak nightingale? All I know is, it's dark, it's late, he's lonely. Maybe he's singing to see if he can find a mate. Or maybe he's just singing to chase away the blues – a forest at night can be a pretty gloomy place. Okay, okay, there's a moon, maybe even a few stars. And let's say that some of these stars are twinkling prettily and the night is soft and warm – does that make him any less lonesome? If anything it makes the ache even worse.

And so he sings and sings until his tiny voice is broken. He sings 'cause he's a nightingale and he sings 'cause otherwise it feels as if the darkness of the forest will swallow him up entirely. Tra-la-la, Tra-la-lee – hey, you know nightingales, flowery stuff. And this bird, he sings the whole night long, the same funny, little tune, the only thing the fella seems to know, and it seems as if it's the only thing you can hear in the whole wide forest, in the whole world, maybe.

But then, just when you think this night will go on forever, dawn finally breaks and softly, softly, very far away, he hears another voice singing – a second nightingale. At first our guy thinks he's hearing things, that it's just an echo or some other random bird – a blackbird, maybe. But no, it's another nightingale, singing its little guts out – tra-la-lee, tra-la-la – and our nightingale has never heard anything so beautiful, so that pretty soon they're singing to one another, a tender duet, trilling in perfect harmony, and this tune, you know, it's enough to break your heart.

And then, before you know it, it's morning, the sun rolls in like a bad penny, and before you've got a chance to take it in, the two little nightingales have gone.

Silence. Curtain.

In the vast auditorium, the only voice that could be heard was the Emperor's.

"Those birds done yet? It's nearly the end of the Eighteenth Century."

"Baby, hush…"

"I could've gone to the dog-baiting instead, you know…"

An angry hiss rose up from the audience. "Shhh!"

"What? You can't shush me, I'm the Emperor!"

More boos, hisses, yells.

"Why you bums…"

As the audience's grousing continued to rise, a second, louder growl could be heard, angry and ursine: Lala the bear.

Sniffing out the Count's distinctive perfume with her powerful nose – *Lillas de Perse*, applied liberally from head to toe – the bear burst free from her dressing room and raced to find him, a pair of distressed stagehands in tow.

She then gave a mighty bellow and passionately threw herself against the remains of the Count's bear-costume, scattering his chaperoens like pins.

"Lala, my darling," Mitrovsky exclaimed, "how wonderful to see you! Have you done something to your fur? Your nails?"

Lala licked at the Count deliriously, slobber hanging from her maw in strings.

"Ho, Lala, my angel, please…"

The bear moaned and shook her head.

"Lala, my darling, desist…"

As the staff of the Big tried to gather themselves, the stagehand in charge of the bear approached, gun in hand.

"I don't know what happened – she just went crazy…"

"Do something, do something!"

"What?"

"Anything! If that bear eats the Emperor, we'll lose our licence."

As Lala and the Count gambolled across the stage, the stagehand's hand unexpectedly jerked, a shot going off at random.

"What the hell you doing?" yelled Ullmann.

"The bear, the bear!"

The second shot clipped a chandelier, causing it to crash to the ground, fire swiftly spreading.

Ullmann blanched. "We're doomed!"

"Stop screwing around," yelled Bilek. "Clip 'im!"

The third shot missed the bear and entered the stage-hand's foot.

"O, for crying out loud!" yelled Honzl. Bilek shook his fist. Emil and Gunter held onto each other. Eliška looked down at her feet.

"Look, give it here, willya?" snapped Lida, blowing a strand of hair away from her face. "You guys couldn't hit a privy wall…"

So saying, she took hold of the rifle and carefully narrowed her eyes.

The Count was still capering merrily with Lala – the dumb beast.

"Lala, my darling, stop!"

The bear's expression looked blissfully happy – Mitrovsky too.

"Fire! Fire!" yelled Ullmann.

Lida paused, took aim, and shot, felling both Count and beast with a single bullet. Like a hand removed from a glove, the figures crumpled and fell to the ground, lying among the sawdust in a heap of fur and ribbons.

"No, I mean the theatre's on fire," said Ullmann, shaking his head.

He was right: flames from the chandelier were swiftly spreading, the Big as ignitable as a tinderbox. The ropes supporting the drop-scenes seemed to serve as wicks, the fire leaping from the backcloths to the curtains to the stalls. Columns of thick black smoke rose ominously. Wood crackled and popped, and the smell of scorched sawdust filled the air.

"Uh oh," said Babinsky.

Sparks leapt from the inferno, dancing across the planks like malicious sprites. In the blink of an eye both the floor and the supporting structures of the tiers were ablaze. Screams and cried filled the air.

"We gotta get out of here!" yelled Bilek.

Babinsky looked about him wildly. "Where? The fire is blocking the way."

"This way!" yelled Ullmann. "We can get out through the back way."

"But the floor…"

"Come on…"

By now the panicked audience were pushing and shoving each other as they flocked toward the exits. Wigs and hoop-skirts were on fire. The screaming was shrill and energetic. As the Imperial Box filled up with smoke, the stage collapsed in a roar of flames and exploding wood, showering soot and embers up into the air. Onlookers gazed at the charred remains of the garden and wood in horror. A strong smell of tar and sawdust assailed the senses, and thick, black fumes filled the void. Beams cracked and shattered, the few remaining shapes buckling into strange, twisted forms.

"We're doomed!" wailed Ullmann.

Honzl ground his teeth. "What?"

"There's no way across…"

Moosendorf grinned. "What? Nonsense! Emil! Gunter! *Allez!*"

Springing into action, *les mouvement mystérieux* unfurled themselves out like a rope bridge, their long, acrobatic bodies spanning the terrible crater.

"Hold on boys!"

"*Ja! Gut!*"

"*Der Grosse Arch.*"

Screams filling their ears, stagehands, censors, young ladies, constables, and Special Investigators gingerly made their way across.

"I don't believe it," said Ullmann. "Just like what happened at The Talking Dog…"

"And The Russian Court…"

"I heard somebody dropped a match in the peppermint schnapps…"

"That stuff made you breathe fire anyway…"

"Like the rum at The Broken Wheel."

"Something was rum there…"

Meanwhile, burning chunks of timber plummeted all around, snapping and popping as they fell.

"I'm writing this down," said Babinsky.

Honzl glowered. "… right here in my book."

And with that, an enormous flaming joist fell from the sky, engulfing Special Investigator, Chief Censor, ledger and all.

By now, the blaze seemed to illuminate all of P, the Big belching great clouds of smoke and embers over the huddled streets beyond. The sky was red and terrible. Soot fell from the heavens like black snow.

"I don't believe it," said Ullmann. "And on the night of Mispickel's opera too."

The survivors scurried to safer ground, trying to outrun the flames.

"Well, at least the Little is still standing," said Moosendorf. "Though now that it's P's largest theatre, they'll have to rename it the Big."

"Hey, I thought you said..."

"The Big! Ha ha, yes it has quite a ring to it."

The air smelt of scorched feathers and charred timber. Dense oily smoke rose up from a pile of barrels. The heat was incredible. Singed theatre-goers and fire-damaged propmen surveyed the devastation through red-rimmed eyes.

This time, Halas' voice seemed strong and loud.

"Eliška, where are you?"

Around him, the walls crackled, and the air seemed to bend and distort.

"Eliška, Eliška, Eliška!"

But it was no use. It seemed Eliška was destined neither for The Nuns of The Order of The Visitation nor Master Halas, nor her mother and her beloved gaoler. Instead, her feet had carried her far away, from P to Q to O, wandering ever further from the beaten path...

Halas stared at the burning pyre.

"Mitrovsky?"

And with that, the roof of the Big collapsed in a massive explosion, sending vast flames up into the night sky.

Ah me, what a sight! From a distance, the theatre looked just like a jar of fireflies, the sparks dancing and frolicking in the dark.

EPILOGUE

Mitrovsky awoke with his grizzled head resting 'pon the most wonderfully abundant and expansive pillow: soft goose feathers, fresh Dutch cotton, sweet little ribbons sewn with gold thread – 'simply divine! And next to him, only inches away, an exquisite little bump, rising up from the bedclothes like some gentle and welcoming island... Mařenka?

Yes, yes, 'twas she, her breathing subtle and composed, her lips delicately parted, her hair – her real hair this time, not some object of the *friseur's* art – spilling out like honey. The Count gazed upon her with an expression of infinite tenderness: how long he had waited, how long!

Did he feel passion? No, not really. For Mitrovsky, the idea of dressing a woman was much more exciting than the notion of undressing one: nu, all those fasteners and catches and hooks!

Besides, the bed felt so perfectly, indescribably wonderful – as supple and luxuriant as a hayloft. Why would anyone wish to move? Why would anyone wish to wake?

And yet, and yet...

How pale Mařenka seemed, how frail and delicate! Those deep black shadows around her eyes were neither blackcurrant juice nor kohl nor any other trick of the costumier's trade; rather they suggested a terrible indisposition, as if she were some kind of spectre just visiting this world, a vision or an apparition, one toe already in the next.

"Shhh," he whispered, "sleep, sleep. Foo, why wake? Dreams are sweeter than memories – or is it the other way around? Well, no matter. 'Tis like asking which comes first, the milk or the cow, ha ha! Tis all a mystery and that's the truth. What's that saying – a beard does not make a philosopher? Trust me, Mařenka, for I have a few grey hairs 'pon my chin…"

And then, from very far away, he heard it: the unmistakable chime of a harness bell, the cart rolling closer and closer, the tolling of the bell at once infinitely gentle and infinitely sad.

Mitrovsky leapt out of bed and stalked to the window. Was it dusk or was it dawn? The light had a strange, ambiguous quality, and though stars still flickered in the sky, a curious luminescence hung over the estate, as if it were sunrise and sunset, all at the same hour. The Count blinked: yes, yes, it was a queer brilliance, right enough. Parts of the garden lay in deep shadow, while others seemed as clear as glass, ablaze with fierce light. But really, thought the Count, rubbing his big, round eyes – what did it matter? The lime trees still smelt of lime and the grass sparkled with a heavenly dew. Tish tosh, why count the chimes? Tomorrow would arrive soon enough.

At that moment, Mařenka sleepily stirred. What was that she whispered in her sleep? Some name – Anton?

The Count bent down and placed one hairy ear by her lips.

"Anton!"

Mitrovsky paused and played with his beard. Why the Baron, but of course! A capital fellow and a true gentleman – ho, anyone could see why she loved him so! All at once an expression of great sympathy and sadness passed across his grizzled chops. Yes, yes, Anton – who else?

Taking care not to wake her, the Count slipped out of bed in his nightshirt and gently padded over to the door. From there, he disappeared down the hall, his steps both light and playful – for, as everyone knows, a Count leaves a lady's boudoir as discretely as a cat takes leave of its business.

From there, Mitrovsky stalked across the hallway and opened a door into a small, cramped bedroom, the niche almost entirely filled by a single, narrow bed. In it, an old lady in sleeping bonnet and gown stared up at him as if she'd never seen him before in her life.

The Count bowed deeply. "Nanny?"

"What on earth? Why I've never…"

"Ha, I'm awfully sorry to disturb you, my angel, but I fear 'tis the wrong door…"

"A beard? In a lady's bed chamber?"

"An honest mistake, I assure you,"

"Scoundrel! Rapscallion! In all my days I have never…"

"Ha ha, yes indeed."

Closing Nanny Friedrich's door, Mitrovsky crossed the hallway and backed into the door directly opposite, stepping into a large and spacious nursery, where two girls – Lida and Lena – lay contentedly in their cots.

"Oh, oh, sweet angels!" he exclaimed, "what a vision of loveliness thou art!"

Taking care not to wake them, the Count watched the girls breathe peacefully, their innocent cheeks as yet unblemished by any of the misfortunes of life.

"Sleep, sleep," he whispered, "pish posh, why wish the chariot of time to fly any swifter? Yes, yes, each day is just the right length, like the distance from your chin to the ground. O my darlings, dream sweet dreams! And pat the bed-bugs once for me…"

So saying, the Count gently closed the nursery door and proceeded down the hallway, his feet dirty and blistered, a clump of random hairs poking up from his head.

At the top of the stairs lay Betka's bed, the old dog snoring soundly.

The Count extended a hand and tenderly ruffled the animal's fur.

"Sleep Betka, sleep," he cooed. "In the morn we will rise early and chase rabbits, you know those little grey ones that live in the briars by Sima's farm, the ones you love so much…"

In her sleep, Betka's paws started to twitch and run.

"Hush my darling, no need to stir! Rest, rest. A dog dreams of being a man and a man dreams of being a dog … ha ha, there's some truth in the old saying…"

Pausing only to smooth the old dog's ears, Mitrovsky quietly descended the stairs. At the bottom, he came across a coven of servants discussing matters in hushed tones, the servants dressed in long blue coats with high collars, smelling of tallow candles and leather.

Of the flunkies, Mitrovsky recognised only Žloudek, though he looked different somehow, his severe features softened by lack of sleep.

Unaware of the Count, he addressed the assembled servants in sombre tones, ordering them to make haste and look lively, for the carriage approached and everything must be made ready, right away … Tonight? Yes, tonight. Mitrovsky rubbed his beard. Some carriage was coming for Mařenka – but why? He could recall booking no cab, calling any servant. Why should any cart be coming at all?

And then, as if waking from a slumber, from out of nowhere he abruptly recalled Mařenka's sickly pallor and wan appearance, his angel almost within sight of Eternity, her hands as cold as ice.

"Yes, yes," he whispered, "Of course."

Now he knew. In his heart of hearts, hadn't he always known? It was just as she said – she had to leave this place, travel to a place where the living cannot follow. Wasn't this what she had always told him? Wasn't this why his black eyes looked so sad?

Without a second thought, the Count strode out of the shadows, addressing Žloudek in a deep and manly voice.

"Softly, sweet prince, take me to my carriage."

Mitrovsky's night-shirt was an inch too short and Žloudek looked at him askance.

"I said, um, 'Sweet, soft prince, ah...'"

Žloudek and the other servants exchanged glances: who was this guy?

"What ho my fellow, no need for that frightened countenance or scowl – I am no ghost or hobgoblin, far from it! No, no, fear not my good man, for all has been decided."

Žloudek reached for a candlestick: should be clobber the jerk now or later?

"Listen – I will take your mistress' place, sit in her seat in her soul's sweet stead. Foo, is one bodkin not as good as another? O my sweet lad – let the lady live unmolested with the Baron, let her children enjoy their mother, and give Betka a belly-rub from time to time, you know she likes it. What? Why the long face? Ho, who would quibble with such an exchange? Listen, listen … as long as the line in the ledger adds up, who's counting?"

The servants stared at the fat guy, open-mouthed. Just what was the jerk going on about?

Undeterred, the Count threw up his arms.

"Farewell, Farewell – I go now to a better, cheaper place. Think of me kindly and sew a button on my jacket if you get the chance."

Bowing deeply, the Count pushed his way past the servants and threw open the front door, a wave of warmth rushing up to meet him, the night soft, perfumed, close. Above the house, the moon seemed piercingly bright, the shadows sharp, almost terrifyingly precise. Was that the moon or some other heavenly orb? The Count shrugged his shoulders: what was he, an astronomer?

Hitching up his night shirt, the Count hopped down the steps and approached the tarantass parked opposite. There was no cabbie, no groom, only a small grey horse, her ribs poking out from her thin flanks, tail like a chimney sweep's broom.

"Hello, my angel," said the Count, patting the old girl on the neck. "How kind of you to call."

The carriage was old, neglected, badly in need of a lick of paint. Nevertheless, the door opened without a creak, and the Count popped inside with a single jump.

'Hm,' he thought, settling down into his seat. 'Was that straw poking out from the cushions?' Oh well, beggars can't be choosers. For a pauper, four legs are always better than two.

Peeping out from behind the curtain, the Count gazed out at the Estate for one last time. "Goodbye, goodbye," he whispered, "goodbye to all I loved."

In the half-light, the gardens and avenues seemed somehow both well-kept and manicured, and at the same time somehow abandoned, half vanished from the world. Aye, it was easy to imagine the barns dismantled and sold off for lumber, the outhouses mere rubble, the hedges and fences all gone. But had this already happened or was it somehow yet to come? The Count rubbed his eyes; it was as if there were two pictures of the world, one on top of the other, like an engraving that didn't quite match. In one, the estate was neat and well-maintained, while in the other things had gone to rack and ruin, wild nettles growing higher than the gates, the lime trees chopped down for firewood. Yes, it was a different world, right enough! In one world, the flower beds were managed and maintained, the hedges clipped and the bushes carefully shaped, while in the other, tall weeds masked the ruins, the fishpond covered with slime, the statue of the nymph lying mournfully on her side. But which of these worlds were true?

Mitrovsky shook his head. Between the trees, the paths seemed pale and bone-like, thistles, dandelions and dogrose taking root. From the arbour, he could hear the sleepy twittering of owls, the distant whistling of woodpeckers. Were they waking up or falling asleep? The Count could no longer tell. The air was heavy, perfumed, hot. The lime-trees smelled so sweet that the Count couldn't help but breathe deeper and deeper. 'Yes, yes,' he thought, 'it's hard to say *adieu*.'

Even if he had only been a visitor – a trespasser, or a ghost – in these pages, the estate had made for the most pleasant hours of Mitrovsky's life – chasing sticks with Betka, playing with the girls, luncheon with the Drtikols. The Count looked at the vanishing lawns and trees and felt a powerful wave of emotion – should it all pass by so quickly? Was there no way to slow down the carriage, no way to arrest its motion? All of a sudden, he did not wish to leave. True, the few hairs on his head were grey, and his paunch spilled out like a cushion, but he was young, young! Why, it hadn't been so long ago that he'd been a little babe running around bare-arsed and rosy of cheek; how had that little boy passed from that place to here? Matej, Matej … but maybe that was someone else.

After a while the little track departed the estate, rounded the gates, and joined the old post road. A pale veil of mist hung over the lane like a curtain, the cart's wheels summoning up great clouds of dust and grit. Mitrovsky looked out at the view with his big, black eyes; look, he thought, here was the tree, there the ditch, there the forest beyond. The ditch was low and sandy, situated at a tight bend in the road. Had he glimpsed this scene before? Why yes, he did believe he had! Or had he seen in it some play, or heard it in a song? Maybe it was even some line from a poem … some days it was awful hard to remember.

Fibres finer than gold thread floated in the air, the film made up of dust, ash and the crushed bodies of moths. Then the yellow clouds of dust seemed to grow thicker and thicker until, after a while, the carriage started to disappear too, the horse and cart growing smaller with each passing minute, every passing year, turning from history into the mere memory of a song, until finally only the sweet, sad tolling of the harness bell remained.

Acknowledgments

Thanks to Carole, Carolyn, Julian, Philip & Jane at NB Design, Andy, Mererid and Ashley at the Books Council of Wales, and my colleagues at Swansea University, too many to mention. Dedicated, with all my love, to Pamela.

Also published by Watermark Press

Carole Hailey
The Book of Jem

In the aftermath of catastrophic religious wars, God has been banned.

As snow begins to fall, a young woman – Jem – arrives in Underhill.
The isolated community offers her shelter, unwittingly unleashing events that
threaten their very existence.

Jem announces that she has been sent to Underhill by God to prepare the
villagers to fulfil a devastating purpose. Some believe she is a prophet and defy
the law to join her God's Threads religion. Others are certain she is lying.

With their fragile community beginning to fracture, Eileen, the first and most
devoted of the believers, decides to record the birth of this new religion in her
own Book of Jem.

As God's Threads gather for the apocalypse, the words Eileen has written will
determine the fate of Underhill and, ultimately, of Jem herself. But can Eileen be
trusted to tell the truth? And how can anyone know what to believe?

**'Bold storytelling, with the satirical force of Naomi Alderman's
The Power but its own claustrophobic sense of place.'**
FRANCIS SPUFFORD, author of *Golden Hill*

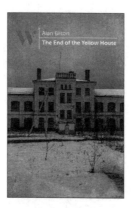

Alan Bilton
The End of the Yellow House

Central Russia, the black earth forest, near Voronezh, 1919. As the civil war rages, White forces, accompanied by feared Cossack divisions, advance ever closer to Moscow. In the chaos, the Yellow House, a sanatorium at Bezumiye, becomes cut off, the superintendent found murdered, a strange black box atop his head.

As the distinction between doctors and 'guests' frays, the murder sets in motion a nightmarish series of events involving mysterious experiments, the secret police, the Tsar's double, prophetic dreams, giant corpses, possessed cats, sorcery, and the overwhelming madness of war. Into this dangerously combustible mix, a ragged and eccentric police officer arrives, calling himself Inspector Tutyshkin and claiming he has travelled to the house to investigate the superintendent's suspicious demise.

But in this strange game of madness, doubles and disguises, are any of the players truly who they seem?

'A bold and confident novel that throws us into the deep end of post-revolutionary Russian life with fervour and wit. There are knowing nods to Gogol and Bulgakov but the voice is entirely original, with a gem of a phrase on every page.'
Mark Blayney

'A brutal, but often witty and tender tale, *The End of the Yellow House* is a twistedly brilliant emotional rollercoaster.'
David Towsey

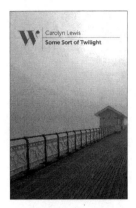

Carolyn Lewis
Some Sort of Twilight

These twelve stories are of people unsure of their place in the world – Cassie who discovers she can fly and has no-one to tell, Christine who's been in her friend's shadow for a long time, Bernard who loses his job through no fault of his own and Hannah who knows her father is waiting for her to sort his life out.

These stories combine pathos, humour and wisdom to explore how the ordinary can be strange, heartbreaking or comic, illuminating the inner lives of people who feel in some way they're on the edge of their own lives.

Carolyn's stories are a joy to read. Her characters are so perfectly formed that we feel we have always known them. Of course people collect coat hangers! Who doesn't one day find they can fly? Her empathy for them all shines through and we feel in very safe hands
SALLY BRAMLEY, WINNER 2021 CALEDONIA NOVEL PRIZE.

Edward Matthews
Border Memories

Why live one life, when you could live a thousand?

Sol works for a start-up that traffics in the underground memory trade –
harvesting memories from donors in Mexico and implanting them in Americans.

Sol's newest client is Mr. Bray – old, rich, well-connected, blind. Mr. Bray hears
rumours of a graveyard where miracles occur and has tracked down a young
librarian, Nora, who remembers it.

Sol's task is simple – find Nora, extract her memory.

But when Sol befriends Nora, he begins to understand who Mr. Bray is and what
he is capable of doing…

'As genuine art should, *Border Memories* explores important and ongoing
problems and confidently reimagines them for a new audience.'
MARGARITA PINTADO, AUTHOR OF *UNA MUCHACHA QUE SE PARECE A MÍ*

'*Border Memories* sires a dusk-fallen near future of abandoned lots and
rusted chain-link. Written with elegant restraint and a raptor's eye for the
small details, Matthews is less interested in whether memories make us
who we are, than who we become once memories are ours to give away.'
GLEN JAMES BROWN, AUTHOR OF *IRONOPOLIS*